The Vampire of the Resistance

Ruth Lewarne

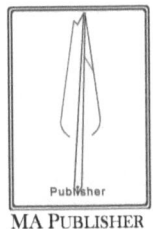

Publisher
MA PUBLISHER

Copyright © Ruth Lewarne 2020
2nd Edition revision September 2020

Produced by Writers' Champion (CW)
Published by MA Publishing (Penzance)
Published September 2020

ISBN-13: 978-1-910499-57-3

mapublisher@yahoo.com for further information and submission guidelines.

Cover designed by Mayar Akash
Typeset in Times New Roman
Title Typeset in Baskerville Old face

Paper printed on is FSC Certified, lead free, acid free, buffered paper made from wood-based pulp. Our paper meets the ISO 9706 standard for permanent paper. As such, paper will last several hundred years when stored.

CONTENT

Chapter One

Born but to die, and reasoning but to err

(Pope)

TIME: 1943 PLACE: OCCUPIED FRANCE

Incredible, Simone mused. I would never have dreamed that it would matter – and how much it would matter. After all the prejudice, fuelled by jealousy and fear, she was sure that she'd overcome – so much of it that she was always braced, ready to meet it, ready to prove once again that she was at least the equal of any man – it was a shock to discover that cosmetics mattered at all, let alone so much.

Yet here she sat, in a small boat on a choppy dark sea, the moonless night wrapped around her so that she could almost have been in space, floating on nothing, her sole companion a taciturn French fisherman steering her to shore without even a distant light to guide him. In the larger of her bags she carried medical supplies along with other, less innocuous items: In the smaller were her personal things, but when she was packing she hadn't considered all her likely needs and now all she could think was: Makeup. Lipstick. Powder. Mascara. She had none, and she was going to France – La Belle, birthplace of couture, home of the most fashionable and elegant women in the world. Well, stop brooding, gel. Roll your sleeves up, there's a job to do, you can't lead this life and still be immaculately turned out. She could practically hear her form teacher's voice, brisk, impatient with self-indulgence, and probably busy even now, training girls to be practical. And pushed deep down were any regrets the teacher may have had – about anything, including all the hopes swept away by the Great War. And Miss Johnson was not the only spinster from that era keeping her chin up.

For Simone had her troubles too. And it wasn't only the lack of cosmetics, or even the fear of being caught and executed as a spy. It was also the shadow of her father, stretching long across her life; many times she had been taunted and called a traitor's spawn, and it never stopped hurting.

Her father was quite famous, although sadly for her 'notorious' would be more accurate. He had been a noted scientist and a firm believer in eugenics, which once war was declared made him, in some people's eyes, like Hitler. But he was not an out and out traitor like Oswald Mosley. He simply shared a lot of Nazi ideas; so no one felt the need to imprison him. The hatred some people seemed to have for him was surely punishment enough, although he was the kindest person and a devoted father. The trouble was his opinions: he thought handicapped people should be put to sleep like old dogs, to improve the race. He thought trade unionists should be sentenced to lives of hard labour, and as for homosexuality... Well, he didn't talk much about that in the hearing of his wife and daughter, but Simone was sure he'd have devised a grisly fate for anyone who indulged in it. He ranked what he called the races into a sort of league table of intelligence, which in reality seemed to be based on shades of skin colour.

Lots of people thought like that, Simone had realised long ago. Her father claimed his prejudices were based on science, but Simone had never been convinced, basically because they boiled down to him being the very pinnacle of creation, and it was all too flattering to himself to be true, just as patriotism was often self-serving, convinced as patriots were that the bit of land they happened to be born in was the very best bit.

It wasn't because she wanted to rescue her father's reputation that she was here, about to disembark, with who knows what awaiting her. She was under no illusion that such a thing was possible. But the whispering she had to endure from her fellow students had finally got under her skin, and so when Deveraux had been trawling the universities for likely candidates for his training programme for spies, she decided to go for it. She knew perfectly well what her motivation was and so did he within minutes of meeting her: She wanted to prove that nobody in her family was a traitor, even if some of them held obnoxious views, because she at least was willing to make the ultimate sacrifice. Deveraux understood what her real feelings were about all that stuff. Nevertheless he picked her, for some reason of his own.

The trawler that had brought Simone to Brittany's coast was now out of sight, but then so was everything else. The lovely moon itself turned traitor when it shone on those who fought their country's occupiers, so operations like this had to be carried out on the dark nights of the month. She trusted that her guide knew his way along the treacherous coastline with, as the saying goes, his eyes shut. He'd exchanged a few words with his Cornish counterparts as they'd handed her over. Each had a small vocabulary in the other's language, although Simone had felt oddly embarrassed for her colleagues that they did not have their own tongue, which had died out, and they were, perforce, native speakers of English.

Notwithstanding, there was a connection between the Bretons and the Cornish, and they seemed like old friends, or business associates. Former smugglers, she guessed, but all she cared about was that they were good at it, used to night seas and clandestine meetings. All kinds of criminals come into their own in wartime. Their expertise was one reason for choosing this coast. The other was its nature, its length, its granite teeth, its sudden coves as well as its hidden dangers. It was very difficult for the Germans to police.

Suddenly they were touching sand, and two figures materialised from the darkness to drag the dinghy ashore. One held out a hand, which she could just see, and she took it, thinking he – or she – was helping her out, but the owner of the hand, clearly male once she had registered its size and hairiness, shook her off and said "No – bag," in accented English. So she hauled out the bigger of her bags and passed it to him, snatched her personal kit and scrambled after him unaided.

She heard the boat move behind her, but did not bother to turn and watch where it went: Her new guides were too businesslike. "This way," barked the talkative one, again in English, and before she could protest that she was a fluent French speaker and that therefore he did not need to speak in such brusque monosyllables, the pair moved off along the beach, carrying her bag, and she had to concentrate on keeping up. With such poor visibility, and such quiet companions, it would be easy to lose sight of them, and then what a fool she'd look, sought for by battle-hardened resistance fighters with much more vital things to do than play hide-and-seek with clumsy girls fresh out from Britain.

Now her guides stopped, and the larger of the men hoisted the bag of supplies on his shoulders, while his comrade turned to her and made an indistinct gesture as if to call on heaven. "We climb," he said. She wondered why he'd rather grunt along in English than speak fluent French.

No one asked if her night vision was good, though fortunately it was. They scrambled up into the darkness, but what Simone feared would be an unyielding cliff turned out to have a path snaking up it. Even so it was a difficult climb in the dark, and nobody bothered about slowing down for the stranger. At last she scrambled after them onto a road, behind which bulked what must be more hills, black against the stars. The low cloud had melted away, or perhaps they'd left it down at sea level. Visibility was better, but there was only as much as you'd need to find something you already knew was there. The deadly moon would not be shining brightly tonight.

Simone followed her guides for a very few steps, then a vehicle started up, and a car drew out from some hiding place just off the road. They climbed in, Simone still bringing up the rear. As she sat down, the driver turned around and said "Hello." The voice was a woman's.

"Hello. I'm…"

"No you're not," said the woman. "We'll tell you who you are, and who you were is something we don't need to know, and you should forget." Then, "For now," she added kindly, and the afterthought sounded unconvincing, as though she did not believe in any kind of future.

"My mother is French," Simone answered in that language, "I'm fluent so you don't need to speak English." She didn't add that during the latter part of her training they were not allowed to speak English at all, only French and German, with Deveraux being particularly hot on pronunciation. She understood that they wanted little in the way of information from her, and she knew why. The less they knew the less they could pass on if caught and tortured.

"We are not French. We are Breton," said one of the men, in French, and the strangeness of his accent was apparent now that he was speaking in what – she'd forgotten, she should have thought – was not his native tongue.

The winding coastal road made for a rather uncomfortable journey, but that was fine, since it kept Simone awake, and though she was desperately tired she wanted to see as much as she could; she had always needed to know where she was, even when skies were blue and danger didn't threaten. The car was being driven without lights; difficult for the driver but for passengers the night outside was more visible than it would have been in peacetime.

They stopped at last, apparently in the middle of nowhere. "The town's over there," said the driver. "Go."

Simone and the two men got out, and left the car with the driver. As they moved into the darkness Simone heard its engine start more quietly than she would have believed possible, and then slowly fade as the vehicle drove off. She must be a mechanic too, Simone thought. A good one, to make so little noise.

They came upon the town suddenly, concealed as it was in the night. No lights shone through the blackout, and nothing moved in the square into which they seemed to burst, straight from the middle of a field. Where, she wondered, were all the people? It was a very large square considering it abutted fields instead of thoroughfares.

One of the guides motioned her to follow, careless of whether she saw him in the dark. They crept around the edge of the square, hugging the shadows, in which at last she saw the outlines of shops and houses and bars shut up tight. She almost missed it when the man ahead ducked into a side street, but his comrade had elected to bring up the rear and was now behind her, and tugging on her coat as she went to walk past.

A dog barked, then changed it to a howl. The leader took another couple of turns, moving as quickly as though the bag he had on his shoulders weighed next to nothing. Simone could barely lift it at all.

At last they stopped at a gate; a back entrance, she guessed. The man behind her came up and opened it. A whispered challenge came from within what seemed to be a small garden. The man answered, and they stepped through, into a garden that seemed full of stone, and then through a door which was shut firmly before someone inside switched a light on.

So began Simone's second life, in which her name and nationality were different, and so was her profession. She had imagined herself a clandestine field surgeon, patching up the wounded with limited resources, saving lives by night in cramped and poorly lit rooms. It turned out that surgery on the living was indeed part of her work, but a small part. Her medical skills helped her adaptation to her new job of undertaker's assistant, and she spent more time on making the dead look pretty.

The funeral home was a good cover: Bodies were supposed to go in and out of such a place, and no one bothered to check the coffins, which was good as they also transported arms. Simone knew that her main usefulness was as a radio operator, the previous operative having moved on in some mysterious fashion that no one bothered to explain, but she knew that her time was limited. The codes had to be changed frequently: The Dutch Resistance had been set back a year when the Gestapo captured one of their radio operators and tortured the codes out of him. They used them to intercept communications and feed false information to the Allies.

Simone had no illusions about her ability to bear pain. She was certain she would be unable to resist torture, so she intended that she would never be caught. The job was supposed to last for a few weeks, until her replacement was parachuted in with his or her team. Then she would be free, for a short time, to search for her cousins, Maman's nephew and niece: That was the deal she'd done with a reluctant Deveraux.

Some of her new associates were people she'd not have met back home, and certainly among them there were those who would've been content if they'd never met her either. They were tough: Some of them had been in the first great war, but in any case they were tough by nature, with the dour outlook of people who wrestled with the land for a living. Their philosophy, by and large, was straightforward, and their patriotism was in truth a love of that which was theirs. But the virtue they had in abundance was courage. Marcel, for instance: It was well known he'd killed men in both wars, without the hesitation with which some people were afflicted. A few times they had been out to help unload armaments coming into harbour by night; climbing over cliffs, some with paths, others thick with bracken and bramble, had been difficult, and a little dangerous in itself. He was intolerant of any weakness, so Simone did not confide her terror of the great cliffs, but got round it by pretending they were smaller, and that she wasn't actually so far above the sea at all. By contrast, Marcel was like some cliff-bred creature, fearless.

But it was whispered to her, in tones of awe, that Marcel had once shot a German soldier, in the back, while the latter had left the safety of the truck he was travelling in to take a piss, and had evaded his victim's fellow soldiers when they searched for him. Marcel had then picked them off one by one as they searched.

That had been brave, though the woman who told the tale had hesitated a little, then added that the truck had been full of boys, really, under age, not even fully grown – but war was savage. Everyone had said that, even while congratulating him, but Marcel was utterly unmoved. And then the woman had added that some people were incredibly good at war and killing but turned out to be a liability in peacetime, a remark Simone ignored, having heard it many times before.

After two months Simone was still there, and it felt more dangerous every day. She knew she'd be shot as a spy if the Gestapo caught her. In training they'd all been told that if you wore uniform you'd be treated as a POW if captured. She was in civilian clothes, so there was no question of her captors bowing to the Geneva Convention. They could do what they liked to her.

She wasn't sure it mattered as much as she'd once thought. Since she'd landed she'd heard of uniformed radio operators being shot like spies – or dogs – out of hand. It was better than torture at least.

Then came the message from London: The team they were waiting for had landed miles from the goal and was holed up somewhere in the great forest that had once completely covered Brittany. Humankind had pushed the forest back to the edge of its towns and roads, but not as brutally or as conclusively as in England – it was still easy to get lost in.

Simone was sent out with Marcel to search as much of the likely landing area as two people on bicycles could. There were others searching, likewise in pairs, and carrying food and medical supplies. The radio equipment was too bulky, and besides, the operators were not making contact with base, which indicated damage.

Marcel was elderly and taciturn, but much more sprightly than he let on. His toothlessness made him look considerably older than he actually was, and was a useful disguise. He was not the first person you'd think of as looking like a determined saboteur, Simone had thought. Now that she was getting used to working with the old, she had begun to think differently. They could move around freely, being less visible to suspicious eyes.

Also, they were individuals. She'd had to visit her English grandma frequently in her rest home, when she was still alive, as well as encountering some of her contemporaries. Sometimes they were more individual than younger people, having got over the fear of being ostracised for not being exactly like everyone else, perhaps because 'everyone else' that mattered to them was dead. Or else they were rigid enforcers of conformity, thwarted witch-burners born too late who nevertheless were determined that the joyless lives endured by them should be imposed on any youth that dared to express exuberance. Sometimes their personalities seemed to collapse into an all-purpose fearfulness, so that a lunch served later than usual was a harbinger of apocalypse, and reassuring them was a time-consuming and finally futile necessity.

Marcel, though, was energetic, and although he looked gnarled and even bent, he moved as fast as a much younger man. Unfortunately he had only two expressions, one of which could be termed expressionlessness. The other was a sneer combined with a scowl, as if his nature was a well that had been poisoned. Some of the others whispered that he was evil, citing the young Germans he'd single-handedly massacred – but there was disagreement on this, of course.

He had been wounded in the Great War, so they said, though he himself was unforthcoming. He liked killing: She'd heard him say so. There'd been some after dinner boasting about successful sabotage missions, and the number of Germans who'd been killed, and naturally no one expressed regret about it. She had never been directly involved with that – she saved life, or tried to, and she operated the radio. But sometimes there was a mess-up, and there were wounded enemy soldiers, and there were times when it was OK to leave them, they'd seen nothing – and there were those who left them, and those who never knowingly left anyone alive. Marcel was one of the latter.

That could have been explained by citing carefulness, but everyone knew that in Marcel's case it was because he was evil. It wasn't any one thing, not really. It wasn't killing soldiers, it wasn't even about the sense of satisfaction that killing the enemy evoked in some people. It was because he enjoyed it too much.

Simone thought that it was probably just as well for Marcel that the Germans had occupied France, so that he could finally let it all out, and furthermore be hailed for it. He was a peasant, his parents were probably taciturn brutes like he was, he'd doubtless been beaten by them, he'd had no love, no education. He'd been sent to fight for a country that gave him nothing but contempt, and as a consequence was further brutalised, traumatised and wounded. She didn't know if he'd married and had children, but he apparently had no one now. He'd had nothing but hard labour to focus on, and his resentment. He didn't speak much, and he never looked her in the eye, but she could feel that he hated everyone and everything and as a consequence, had a monk's desirelessness, except for annihilation. His own could wait. Meantime his only pleasure was eradicating Germans as if they were a plague of insects.

They cycled across rough ground, along tracks which got so rocky they had to dismount frequently. Marcel was not delightful company, but he knew the terrain. She did not fear him, because he had his focus, and his rage was not directed at her, but she would not have dreamt of being alone with him in peacetime. He was old, and she was young, and big and strong for a girl, but the darkness in him had its own strength.

For an hour or so they searched, but with little conviction. Other operatives had been allotted their search areas, and it seemed to both of them that their quadrant was least likely to turn up anyone who might have got lost there, as it was both furthest from the landing place and nearest to the Chateau Joyeuse, as the locals called it, with gallows humour.

Simone was thinking, as she did every day, what it would be like to die, here and now; currently, there were gaps in the forest and long rays of lazy late sunshine lit up the world. The evening mist was still politely waiting its turn before it took over the landscape, and birds were gathering themselves together to roost. It was indescribably lovely, and a shudder passed through her along with the unbidden thought that perhaps she would never see another beautiful day – bad luck to dwell on such a possibility, she chided herself.

The light would begin to fade soon, she knew. She pointed at the sky and looked at Marcel, who nodded, and turned his bike around. Furthermore, just in front of them a turret was visible in a shaft of late afternoon light; beyond the massed trees, the rest of the Chateau lay, hidden for now. If they kept going this way, they would come upon it, which would not be good, since it was full of occupying forces, and according to rumour, these included Gestapo. The occupants might also include the operatives they were looking for, but if so their cause was lost. So they headed back the way they came.

They did not get far. There was no warning; just the sharp crack of a bullet, and Marcel went flying over his handlebars. Her bike collided with his as it tumbled. She fell and there was pain – and then nothing.

Chapter Two

Facilis Descensus Averno

(Virgil)

When Simone came round, she didn't know her own name at first. She felt aches, she felt sore, she was staring at big stones in a wall, and she was half sitting, half lying on something – a mattress, that was the word, and it was cold. Then memory returned, and with it fear. There was a word for where she was, too, and it wasn't hospital, though she knew she needed one, and it wasn't even prison – it was a dungeon, because there was light from a bulb above her, but there were no windows, and the stones looked old. She tried to move, and there was pain – in her ribs, it seemed – whiting everything out, and then receding a little. There was a noise, like a gurgle, a horrible noise that was the worst thing she'd ever heard.

"You're dying," said a voice, in German. Then a face seemed to swim into view and float above her, though that couldn't be right. Nor could the blood around the mouth, smeared as messily as chocolate might be on a small child. "Mmmm," it added, and disappeared again. Simone stared straight ahead, strangely incurious about what was happening to her, as the room and the pain began to fade. Then the face reappeared, at the periphery of her failing vision, its mouth wiped clean, and spoke in French. "You're delicious," it said, as if at a wine tasting, but Simone still didn't react. All she felt was gratitude that the pain was going away. Then it spoke in English, with a home counties accent. "You're dying," it repeated. It must have believed that Simone understood it, though she could not speak, for it continued in English: "I am making it easy for you to fade pleasantly away. Is that what you want? So young, so pretty, and an English spy – so not stupid, or they wouldn't have sent you. But stupid enough to throw your life away in this stupid war?"

At last the face of her tormentor came close to hers, and Simone looked up into arctic eyes, blue grey like glass but alight, chilly and feverish all at once. She felt the stirring of anger; 'traitor' formed on her lips. He read them.
"Ridiculous girl." He almost snorted. "A hundred years, fifty years from now, who will care? I have no country. I am an immortal and I offer you immortality. Consent."

Simone knew that she was bleeding from a wound in her side and that she would shortly die from the blood loss. Her mind was clear on that at least: Otherwise her sensations and perception were getting fuzzy, and that was a symptom; it also meant that the pain was fading and she would drift peacefully out of this life. Her soul would float out on the withdrawing tide of her ebbing blood. "I am Graves," said the traitor, showing excellent teeth. "Good joke, huh? I put many people in theirs – and I have pulled many others out."

"I am your saviour," he continued, "If you will accept me." Simone's dying body expressed its shock by a shudder, which surprised her more than anything else Graves was saying, partly because the rest of it was nonsense. It was a reflex, shock at a blasphemy that didn't really offend her. How could it? She'd been brought up a Catholic, but considered herself very lapsed. The medical training she had so far completed had accelerated the journey away from childhood belief. She was a scientist, taught by sceptical scientists, and being young, as enthusiastic about the potential of science to save as any devotee would be about their religion. Yet it seemed that her body remembered the doctrine of her past faith, that the teaching went deeper than she knew, into muscle, bones, blood. Her body recognised blasphemy of this magnitude, and recoiled. "No," said Graves, apparently reading her mind, "your body has no religion except survival, and after that, pleasure. And if it were a thinking vessel, and desired a religion, it would worship whatever opposed God, out of rage that it is born but to die. That trembling that you feel is fear of me. The animal in you knows what I am, though you deny it."

Simone lay bleeding to death, drifting away to the accompaniment of a madman's raving, and although her pain seemed to have faded along with her perception, the voice did not fade, but seemed louder. She would die, she thought in horror, to this; not the final rites of the Church, nor in the middle of a medical circus, with doctors trying to resuscitate her, certainly not surrounded by weeping grandchildren and great-grandchildren, but then she had accepted that her war work might mean the renunciation of any future family – any future life. She had contemplated bloody premature death, but she had not for a moment imagined this; this voice which would not let her die in peace, but spewed out a bitter distillation of every mortal's secret despair. The face that seemed to float above her had vanished from sight, but the voice seemed closer than ever.

"God gave almost everything to human beings except the one thing without which all else was a mockery, and *that* he withheld out of jealousy that we might one day rival our maker. He brings us to our knees and pretends we need a lesson in humility. As if the weakness of this body is not enough to humiliate the proudest spirit!" The voice became a kind of swollen whisper, a hiss that filled her diminishing awareness. "Though it is also the cup, the grail, that holds the vital elixir. Will you drink? This is the real holy communion. Will you partake?

This is the meaning of the water made wine. This is transubstantiation..." Each syllable of the word was rolled around an invisible, savouring tongue, and separately pronounced, like an oath, or a rite, or a great obscenity. Or like an official accusation, as a criminal charge might be read out in a court of law.

No shudder was evoked this time, though her parents would have been horrified at the piling of blasphemy upon blasphemy. There is nothing, Simone thought, but waste. This war – I don't care. I don't care who wins. I want to live. He's mad. What does it matter? There is no God. I only have this life, and now it's over. He can't save me. No one can. I want to live. This is nonsense anyway. What difference does it make? She tried to shrug, but she had no strength. But Graves must have spotted something. "You must consent. Don't you want to feel well again? I can help you!"

Afterwards, she would describe herself at that moment as variously and all at once confused, dislocated, weak, and of course, dying. All that was true. Whatever the reason, "Yes," answered Simone with the last of her breath, and in that moment, knew that there would not be another one; then the gentle Mother of all creatures, Her Holiness, withdrew from her lungs, her airways, her nostrils, and, softer than a butterfly, seemed to the beings that were present to hover in the air... waiting for the soul to follow... Immediately Graves moved to embrace Simone. He lifted her towards himself, and she felt the great wound in her side gape wider.

Night came down upon her eyes as he clamped his lower lip between his teeth and bit. As the blood welled he kissed her fiercely, returning the breath along with a trickle of his blood. The faculties of touch and taste returned, just as once, long ago, they'd been the first to arrive. Like a newborn too weak to suckle she felt her mouth fill with heat, and then it was coursing down her throat. Just in time, strength flowed into her, along with the strange nourishment, and suddenly she discovered herself sucking on Graves's lips with the vigour and determination of a healthy baby. Just as a mother will do to detach her baby from the breast, Graves slipped a finger into the corner of her mouth and Simone, startled, released his lips. She peered out through her eyes, her vision now also restored. Graves's face was inches away, his cold bright eyes staring at her, his lips swollen and bruised. "Enough. It's done. But you've lost much blood. I can't be milked any longer, but don't worry, you're in the right place."

He released her from his grip, and she swayed, but did not fall back. She put her hand to her side, and although it felt sticky, the flow seemed to have ceased. Gingerly her fingers explored the area. Something hard was there, newly formed, like a great scab. It couldn't be that, though, she'd lost too much skin, and there was damage beneath. And then she realised that the pain had returned along with the full use of her senses, and she moaned. Then a moment later, she knew it had lessened, already. Graves rose to his feet and smiled.

"Wait," he said. She looked around and the place seemed lighter, less gloomy, though there was no more light than before that she could see – still the low-watt bulb above her, but now for some reason she could see into the shadows beyond, though there was little there. Then she spotted a human form, and Graves moving towards it, and dragging it out into her small patch of light. It was Marcel, and he was alive. He too had a wound, in the upper leg, but the bullet must have missed the artery or he would have bled out by now. His hands were cuffed, and his face was bruised, his hands a mess. Clearly he had been beaten: One eye was swollen so much that it was effectively closed. He was looking at her, and he looked terrified. He must have seen what had happened between Simone and Graves.

Simone found herself embarrassed, and wondered at herself for experiencing such a... bourgeois emotion. For, hard upon the heels of this, her first reaction, was something altogether strange. Maybe it was not so strange, after all. Maybe what she felt had its analogue in nature. It was a kind of hunger, but a hunger of an intensity she could not remember having ever felt before. Unless it was indeed when she had been a baby, a bundle of instincts foremost of which was the urge to survive. Her whole being was suddenly focused on Marcel. She had been in love, or more probably lust – it was nothing like that. She wanted to devour Marcel, but not as she'd wanted to devour her lover. Then, it had been like wanting to possess his beauty forever, to merge with it, to make it hers. Marcel was no beauty, but she wanted him more than she'd ever wanted any man, more than she'd ever wanted food, more than she'd ever needed water, even.

She found herself crawling towards him, knew Graves was watching with pleasure – almost a paternal pleasure. She could sense his approval, like some carnivore watching its young with a newly slain corpse – and as she moved she watched herself, as if her will was not involved. And it did not seem to be: It was taking no part in this performance. A predator, an animal, was closing on its prey, and that was in accord with instinct, and the nature of things. Simone, she heard in her head, and it was the echo of her father's voice. All the memories of each time he'd said her name were borne on those two syllables. There had been times when he'd said them crossly, when he'd had cause, just or otherwise, to tell her off. He was a complex man, capable of tenderness towards her while espousing ideas that Hitler himself would have thought reasonable.

Mostly, he'd spoken her name lovingly, and sometimes the word had carried such a freight of love that now, as she heard it in her head, something warm and kind and good re-entered her heart, which she realised was no longer beating. So, not her heart, then – but something in the centre of her chest warmed, and swelled, and felt. She made herself stop moving. I'm in a dream, she thought. What's happening? Who am I? Am I dead? Who is she – who is Simone? Who was she?

She turned to look at Graves, who was frowning now. "What have you done?" she asked, and heard her own voice again at last. It sounded the same as ever, but the words came with difficulty, as if they were being mined from hard rock. Because I have no breath, she thought. Then she moved again, towards Marcel, and she understood that her desire to gorge herself on him was more comparable to her need to breathe in after breathing out than anything else, and therefore probably as necessary to her survival in this post-mortem state. It appeared that her instincts would propel her body towards him automatically, and that she could not allow her attention to wander for an instant if she did not want to become a murderer. She did not dare even speak again.

So there she was, on all fours, too weak to walk or even crawl away, like an animal with pretensions to self-control, between her victim and her puppet master, immobilised by the invisible civil war raging inside. Graves said nothing either; whatever else he was, he was patient. It was Marcel who finally spoke. Perhaps it was unwise of him to disturb the tension of the tableau, for it was likely to be his death that ended it: Perhaps he knew death was inevitable, and could no longer endure the torture of anticipation, though he had bravely endured the torture to which he had earlier been subjected, mere run-of-the-mill agony compared to this.

He deserved his moment, Simone saw. Her own condition was due to a different sort of pain, and soon she would lose her humanness completely, but for a few moments she felt attuned to this colleague whom she knew had kept his silence when, in another part of this grim place, they'd tried to make him tell them everything he knew.

His hands were bloody, the fingers twisted, some hanging useless. She knew what he had been through, from that, obviously, but there seemed to be a part of her that saw his mind, as if she could visit it, all of a sudden. His mind...

He too had been cruel, several times, and cruelty did not surprise or outrage him, even when visited upon himself. His bravery was partly a consequence of that acceptance, but mostly it was down to self-respect. He was a tough old peasant, a man of the earth, and unyielding as the cold earth under a winter frost, or the parched earth in a long-lasting drought. That was his identity. That was who he was. If he threw that idea of himself away, he would be nothing – dregs.

This nightmare was something he had never envisaged – no one could. He had witnessed the exchange between Simone and Graves and his disbelief had not lasted long. It was easier for him to accept the existence of such creatures than it would be for an educated person. He was not particularly superstitious because in his experience if Fate had it in for you then there was nothing you could do about it. No amount of running around visiting gypsies and having your cards read or wearing lucky this and thats would change what was written on your forehead.

Simone saw these thoughts form a kind of colourful rainbow around him, saw that he believed he had sinned, and so he did not expect to go to heaven. He would pay for what he'd done in Purgatory, probably for a long time. One day, when his time was done... but as for Simone, she had sold her soul to this devil here, because she was afraid to die.

Stupid, stupid, stupid. She doesn't believe that God is watching, doesn't believe in heaven, yet she believed enough in this devil to surrender to him? That's where atheism takes you, Marcel was thinking through his fear and pain, into the arms of the Devil, because you think all you've got to lose is life.

So when he said, "Please, don't kill me. Your soul..." Simone had heard it all by then, and before she could entertain any feeling for her fellow human it was too late for anything but prayers.

The woman in front of Marcel snarled like some mindless jungle cat. He could see her struggle, though. He was helpless; wounded, and handcuffed, but he had felt Graves's strength as he'd been pulled out of the shadows and he had heard about these creatures, though he hadn't expected to meet any. One thing he knew: They were stronger than mortals. He had no chance if she should break.

Simone thought: *My* soul! He has killed and tortured in the past – who does he think he is to speak of souls!

But this thought was her enemy, and she found herself inching forward again. Then she understood something more; that her new instinct of hunger for human blood was not isolated from the reasoning self that had accompanied her across the bridge between life and this undead state in which she found herself, and that instinct could co-opt her reason into their service, could force it to begin the task of justifying her actions, however terrible, until she was…

What? Like Graves? He seems…

But Graves had decided that enough was enough, so he bent quickly to snap Marcel's neck.

"He's dead, and he's fresh, and it was I that killed him. Now drink before it gets cold."

It doesn't make me a murderer, she thought. He won't get a decent funeral here anyway, and so it would be wasteful not to… But even as she justified her need, before she'd finished the thought, she found herself on the corpse, sucking at a wound in its leg.

"Use your teeth, look, higher, on the artery, it'll come quicker." Again, Graves was like a mother guiding her hungry baby's mouth so that it could feed in the most effective way. But whereas a baby may fuss, and work itself up, and delay the whole thing by crying and getting upset before it finds its way, Graves's pupil reacted to his reaching out to help her in a manner that recalled a hungry wolf rather than a human baby, though she'd never been a wolf.

At last she bit down, and would have been surprised to feel the lengthening of her canine teeth had she not been too engrossed to bother with surprise. Later she would hear it claimed that this lengthening effect was down to the gums shrinking back, and she would think that such an opinion could be held only by one who had never felt the sharpness of a vampire's bite. But for now, there was no thinking going on at all.

Chapter Three

Why, this is hell, nor am I out of it

(Marlowe)

"It is a vin-de-table, the wine from a dead man's veins, however fresh the kill," observed Graves. "For a real intoxicant, the divine spark must still be present, which is why the true connoisseur prefers to be the agent that severs the silver cord."

Simone returned to the splintered awareness common to all thinking beings and like all such homecomings, it was not pleasant. She touched her mouth and felt the rim of blood around it. Then she raised her head and regarded the creature who had witnessed her shame.

Graves was light-haired, but it was a dull shade, disciplined and polished into crisp waves, and with his blue eyes would have made for a charming combination if they had been a little less pale. Instead, their lightness shed an otherworldly glamour over what was a handsome, if rather too tall and thin a form. He was in mufti, but not the evening dress that Simone had seen worn by such beings in horror pictures. He would have been more suited to a romantic or comic picture, if one were judging him by his clothes alone.

He seemed amused, as if he fancied himself Cary Grant, verbally jousting with some witty career woman, for all the world like the final act of this drama would end with her submission to his charms. But everything was wrong, the wrong way round; this had begun with her submission, and all she had left to cling onto was the fact that her submission had not been total. She had not killed.

Her life was over. She was suspended between life and death, then – an unnatural monster. What would become of her she did not know. Perhaps Graves could tell her what this metamorphosis was, where it would lead, what its limits were. She did not want to ask. She did not want to look at him – it, an 'It' like she was now. She did not want to hear his voice, or be in a room with him, no matter what information he might be able to impart. Whatever she needed to know, she would discover, or else suffer from her ignorance; no matter, it was *her* ignorance, and so a thousand times better than his experience.

He was evil, and she was foolish, and if she wished to save herself, she must remain merely foolish. She had something left within her that she must protect: She could feel it. Perhaps it was her soul. She had to protect it from him.

She rose from her gruesome feast, and as she did her entire body sang with strength, as if she had changed sex, and become a man; not just any man, though, but an Olympic champion in the very peak of condition. She doubted her own sensations, and put her hand to her side. She felt the shredded jumper, the sticky bloodstains, and touched the giant scab that she'd felt earlier. It flaked off in bits as she did so, and her fingers brought her brain the news that now there was smooth flesh there.

She pushed past Graves, who said nothing. Ahead of her was a wide wooden door, shut. It looked old: The wood was dark, like iron. There was a heavy bolt across. She drew the bolt and it flew back. She pushed, then she pulled, then she pushed again with rage and impatience to be gone. The wood groaned and splintered. She stood back and kicked it, and somehow was not surprised when the door sprang open.

Outside the corridor was empty. She turned right, then heard voices and running feet. So she turned left instead. She came to some stone steps, and as she started to climb them voices behind her drew closer and she heard them shouting at her to stop, in German. She ignored the warning, and a bullet flew past her, embedding itself in the crumbling masonry. The next bullet struck her in the back, as did the next, and the next, and all the others after that. They stung, like bees, but she shrugged angrily and kept climbing. Her emotions were tumultuous, to say the least. She dared not examine how she felt: She feared she would go mad at once. Her mind, though, noted what was going on: I'm very, very strong, she thought, and these bullets don't hurt me. And this terrible wound has already healed.

As she climbed the steps became a spiral, as on her right a dark void opened up; part of the ground floor? She kept climbing as below she heard a shout that sounded like Graves issuing a command to cease firing. The first floor appeared, well lit by overhead lights, though still with stone flagged floor and granite walls stretching to her right, while further still wooden doors opposed each other in what must be a corridor. She climbed faster, and her feet seemed winged. She was not tired, nor out of breath. This is a dream, she thought.

She was climbing up stairs on the extreme right of the building, which she supposed must be the chateau. Now the rooms became smaller, and round, and there was one door, opposite the steps – this is a turret, she thought, and I must get out. She made for the door on her next climb, and when it seemed stuck, or else locked, she gave it an angry tug and it flew open.

She stepped out onto an open space, a battlement behind which the chateau sheltered, which formed a wide walkway with crenellated walls. It was dusk, and in the far distance the rim of the sea reflected pink and gold. She moved to the battlements and peered over. Directly beneath was the moat, which had long ago been dug next to the river, of which it was now a man-made tributary. Its tribute to the river was not, however, pure water from a spring, but foulness from the chateau, the foulest of all its detritus; the broken bodies that resulted from this Occupation.

Beyond that was the forest, the shapes within it now indistinguishable in the growing gloom. Behind her was the navy blue eastern sky, and far below it a village sheltering beneath the chateau's defensive wings of stone. The moon would soon rise from that direction, a mere sliver still but bright enough in the cloudless sky to make night operations too dangerous for all but the desperate.

She wondered what would happen to her if she jumped off. Then the door of the turret opened and Graves stepped out.

"Try it and see," he suggested. It seemed their condition did make them telepathic as well, although it could have been just that anyone who happened to observe her now could easily guess her thoughts, if they, like Graves, had also witnessed her degradation in the dungeon far beneath. She had fallen upon that poor corpse. She had avoided the kill, but she had been part of the fearfulness of Marcel's last moments, and then... she had fed the way scavengers do, on the leavings of a predator, like the most cowardly of animals.

So she jumped onto the western wall. "You made me worse than a beast," she spat, "but no beast would do this."

She fell forward, travelling downward for several feet. Then she felt a resistance in the air, slowing her down, and then it grew till it was like an updraft, buffeting her upward again. She pulled her shoulders back, and found the rest of her body followed. She was upright, in mid air. She sank a little, then moved her feet, as if she were walking, and rose slightly as she did so. It was like treading water.

She looked up, and saw Graves launch himself after her in a graceful dive. He changed it into an upward swoop when he reached her side, and hovered upright above her, laughing.

"Get away from me!" She snapped. "This is a nightmare!"

"Come on, old girl, don't go on so. This bit's all right, isn't it?"

She moved away, and found she was leaving him behind much faster than she'd reckoned to. She'd step, and the steps seemed to take her farther than the length of her legs. She was leaping, but slowly; gliding forward with each movement. It was impossible not to feel exhilarated, despite everything. She pushed down, to the ground, and the tip of her foot brushed the branch of a tree, which caused her to spring above the height of the receding battlements. She turned and stretched her leg, pointing her toes like a ballerina, and her next movement brought her back near Graves, who watched expressionlessly.

An idea was forming in her mind, and she hoped that Graves was not actually telepathic, while fearing that he was. Simone had read Marcel's thoughts, so Graves could too, although she did not perceive Graves's thoughts. Perhaps he knew how to hide them.

It was not relevant, since given what she'd been before the... change, it would not take much ingenuity to guess what she might now be thinking, especially since he had witnessed the struggle in the dungeon, proof that something of her conscience survived into her new existence. So she needed to throw him off her track, although it might be that such efforts were futile..

"I'm going home," she said, "I can cross the sea, can't I?" and turned west.

"Not easily," he answered, but she was already on her way.

"Be under cover by dawn!"

She heard that, and wondered, but kept on going. She found that she covered the most distance with her leaps if she pushed down to touch the ground, just for a second. The momentum would push her up and on for quite a way. It was not so much like flying, more as if she were wearing the seven league boots of fairytale, or if the air was a trampoline. She found she could remain upright in the air if she moved her feet. If she did not, she would sink a little and fall backwards, rather like being in water.

It took minutes to cross miles, and soon she was at the edge of the sea, which was by now just a darkness she knew to be there. It was pulling at her, even though she had no intention of crossing it, or ever returning to England as some kind of monster. Her parents wouldn't know what had happened to her. She would be killed on active service, as far as they were concerned, and that was sort of true, anyway. She wasn't exactly alive, like a normal person. So they would never know what she intended to do, and they would, sadly, not hear the story of how proud they were entitled to be. For this was a unique opportunity. She was bullet proof, it seemed, and so, unlike the many previous attempts on Hitler's life, an initiative by her might just succeed.

She felt a storm of restlessness sweep through her. Such possibility – but such potential for messing up. Worst of all would be if she became a demon like Graves, unable to prevent herself feasting upon humans, worse than any animal, who could not help but act according to its nature. What if the darkest of desires overwhelmed her will? She'd tasted Marcel's blood... The fear and restlessness were the memories of sin. They must be shaken off.

She sprang up and forward, and slowly descended several hundred yards out onto the sea. But there was no returning momentum, and to her surprise and dismay, she found herself sinking through the water, without even the buoyancy she'd once enjoyed; like a stone she plummeted several fathoms down into the darkness.

It was horrible, and she panicked. Which way was the shore? It was dark, and she noticed then that she could see a little, as a shape moved in the water, a few feet away. She must orient herself, or she could be down here at full fathom five forever. Was that a fish, or what?

She started to move in what must be the direction of the shore. England was out of the question. She hadn't planned to return, anyway, but maybe this resistance held a message for her, the message being that there was no going home – by any means. There would be regretting, but now, she wanted this to end.

It was like pushing through a wall of jelly. Whatever had happened to her body to make the air navigable and the water so – thick? It made terrible sense, because both elements were offering her body more resistance, one to pleasant and the other to very unpleasant effect.

She lost track of time as she pushed through the claustrophobic viscosity. At least she did not need to breathe, she thought, trying to still the fear that fluttered in her chest. Eventually she began to notice that she was growing cold, and realised that she should have felt absolutely frozen a long time ago. Clearly she could endure low temperatures without noticing, but hours of this immersion must be getting to her at last. It seemed that her body's heat regulating system had been quite altered in other ways too, because the considerable efforts she was making were not causing her to warm up at all. Now the cold was making her more sluggish. What if her strength failed her?

What if she were going the wrong way? She forced herself to think, to speculate on the new laws of physics that governed her now. She'd sunk like she had lead weights attached, plummeting down to the sea bed, yet now the same substance was resisting her, making her work hard to move through it. How could that be? I am a scientist, she told herself, and this is like a horror story. This is beyond what the scientific community could begin to incorporate in their worldview, but it is real, it is my empirical experience. There must be rules governing this new existence, and I will find out what they are before... it is over.

At last it seemed to her that the sea bed began to slope upwards, into what must be shallows. Still the ordeal went on, longer than she imagined it could, then, suddenly, her head was out of the water. It was wet, and she raised her hand through the jelly and touched her face, and felt the wet hair plastered there. It felt like thick bubbles of viscosity that got thinner almost like gel. But it seemed that the more it mixed with air the more it behaved like water. She had no idea why it behaved so differently when she was immersed. Maybe she should go back and ask Graves.

She staggered on to the beach and fell forward. So I can get tired, she thought, lying with her face in the sand. But it was a strange tiredness, and her body craved something that wasn't rest, or sleep.

It's blood, she thought. I need blood to warm me after that terrible cold. I need to be filled with life and courage. I feel... not really tired but dimmer, sadder. I could just let go and die here... die again. Perhaps if I lie till dawn.

The sun, in the movies, killed things like her. Didn't it? What else? Garlic. A wooden stake. Crosses. Holy water. Those last two items were odd, being made by man's beliefs. Unless God was real, in a specifically Catholic way. Perhaps none of it was true. She should have stayed, at least till she found out from Graves all she needed to know. Get under cover before dawn, he'd called after her, so that at least was probably accurate.

I can't stay here, she thought, and just die at dawn. Otherwise that's it: My life is over, and I've achieved nothing. If I survive a little longer, then perhaps I can do something astonishing with these abilities.

Without warning, a tidal wave of ravenous hunger rose from her stomach, more intense than she had ever felt, and she leapt to her feet. Dear God, she thought, what is this? I must feed! She sprang forward, and was up the cliff face in a couple of bounds, like some kind of great cat. Another wave of hunger rolled over her as if to obliterate every other thought, like the sea, when the earth beneath it quakes, and great waves roll across the land, destroying everything human.

I cannot control this, I cannot. What can I do? she thought, between spasms of ferocious need. This must be what childbirth is like. My will is helpless: My body's need sweeps everything before it. There must be animals here, there must.

She moved inland, looking by the light of the newly risen quarter moon. She remembered passing roads, parallel to them, alongside hedges, and she remembered a village or two between the sea and the chateau. She dared not go near inhabited places, not with this monstrous hunger overwhelming her, a thing with its own life... God, let me eat soon!

And then a smell familiar to country dwellers wafted from the ground, and her speeding feet landed in something even thicker than she'd found the sea to be, and she smiled as relief flooded her. A cowpat has saved me from mortal sin, God be praised, now where's the cow? She paused, and heard the lowing, then several others joined in. They've sensed a predator, she thought. Oh. It's me.

And then the hunger took her, so that she shot through the air as if aimed by a marksman, though without consciously choosing her direction. No matter, it seemed that instinct did not err when driven by so powerful a motor, and she found herself on the back of an animal; not yet a cow, a heifer perhaps, since it protested by running and throwing back its head, as well as making a lot of noise. Around it its fellows wasted little time in vocal expression of their terror, stampeding as far from Simone as they could.

Simone watched her other self – that was how it felt – as her teeth lengthened and grew sharp, and her nails did likewise, turning clawlike and allowing her to dig them into the shoulders of the animal, giving her purchase. It bucked beneath her as if at some Wild West rodeo, but her legs had gripped it at once, and they were strong again after the cold of the sea, and the moment of hopeless weakness that had followed.

She sank her teeth into the back of its neck, and the blood of life flowed into her, full of warmth and power. A tiny part of her wondered if she should try and exercise some control. What if each time she fed the beast inside her the human grew weaker? It was impossible to stop, though; easier to bid the incoming tide retreat. She had no choice, not at that moment.

The creature sank on to its knees, and keeled over, Simone still clinging on and drinking, sucking great spurts of blood from the ravaged artery. At last there was no more hunger, she let go, and what she had not yet been able to think of as her fangs retracted of their own accord. Replete, she allowed herself to fall off the animal's body.

She lay beside it as her human mind roared back to take possession of its fiefdom once more. Furious at its temporary exile, it unleashed all the self-loathing of which it was capable, which was a very great deal, especially now. First it bade her examine her stomach: she lifted her grubby shirt out of her waistband, and gazed down at her bloated midsection with shock. The distension was apparent; and it was not a normal meal that caused her belly to bulge like that; it was full of blood. She had dropped off the cow like a giant version of one of the bloodsucking ticks that normally preyed on it without doing too much damage. Sometimes they were transparent, and when one fastened on, the victim could sometimes see through it, see it full of his or her own blood.

She was having no difficulty, physically, digesting her meal. Mentally it was a different story. Her swollen stomach revolted her – the thought of what it contained caused her insides to heave. She turned on her side and threw up, and was even more revolted as a fountain of blood poured out of her mouth.

Ravaged by her heaving guts, she rose to her feet. Then a sense of physical well-being and strength filled her, and it almost felt like joy. She had not vomited up all of her meal, but she needed to get away from the horrible scene fast, or she would tear her own insides out, just to relieve the intensity of the conflict between her thoughts and her sensations. She headed east, away from the viscous sea, and she ran, and jumped, jumps that were longer and higher than any athlete could achieve, and with a fraction of the effort they must make.

Chapter Four

Whatever stirs this mortal frame

(Coleridge)

She considered returning to the chateau, and confronting Graves with the questions that were lining up in her mind and demanding answers. Something in her rejected this move: She did not want to go backwards on her journey. Or maybe she just couldn't bear the sight of her... what? Killer, or saviour? Or seducer? That was a more accurate description, since he hadn't sent her to oblivion, nor had he rescued her from suffering. And he hadn't quite forced her to this existence, either. He'd been very clear on that. Maybe if she avoided him she could avoid his mockery. He was the only one who knew she had a choice.

It wasn't much of one, she argued with herself. She got well past the chateau, keeping it a mile or so to her left but still in sight, as she didn't want to get lost...in a geographical sense. Her spirit grew lighter as she put the chateau behind her, and for a brief moment it soared as she leapt the width of a river – a smallish one, admittedly, and she'd probably need at least one boat in the middle to jump the Thames, for example, perhaps two boats where it was widest – but she gloried in her new ability, for the moment.

Then she saw the lightening of the sky, very faintly greying the horizon, like a wisp of smoke. She tried to remember some folklore – I thought I couldn't cross running water, but I can. Although if I get too close, so that it touches me, it stops running. So is that some other foul fiend? Not – the thing I am? Even her mind would not pronounce it... "The dawn thing" – what did he mean? Or was he just trying to make her afraid?

She found shelter by backtracking, just a little, to the river bank, and following it into where the forest grew thick alongside, where there was no room for a path. She pushed her way into undergrowth, beginning to feel afraid. What should she do? Dig? She kept moving through the tangle of brambles and branches, keeping alongside the river. It was going west towards the sea, so if she followed it back she would be heading east, more or less. The banks would be unstable, probably, and there might be temporary shelters, carved into the crumbling earth by the river. Perhaps she could just wait under water till sunset; but this was fresh, not salt. It might be different, it might not be deep enough. It might react unpredictably when the sun rose. She wished she could ask Graves, after all; but then, he might lie anyway.

At last she decided to push inland, though she hoped she wouldn't have to stray too far from the river, the only real landmark now the chateau was no longer in sight. There was nothing else here, and the darkness was fading to grey more quickly now. She had no time, and no patience. She moved fast, uprooting small trees if they were in her way, through the tangled brambles and creeper-like weeds that scratched her and impeded her progress almost as much as if she were an ordinary mortal.

There were also great stones, cropping out of the forest floor like massive fungi, some invisible to her in what was still the darkness, even with her night vision, which imparted a faint eerie glow to shapes, sometimes red-tinged, sometimes more purple. She ran hard into a huge chunk of granite, its outline made imperceptible by the moss that grew on it like camouflage. It hurt, and she cursed at the pain she had caused herself. Then she realised that here, in the lee of the sloping stone, she could find enough deep shade even when the sun stood high at noon.

Using the new strength that still astonished her, she pulled at some obstructive growing things at the side of the stone, and found another big slab of rock. Even better; even if there was no space where rock leaned against rock, even if it were too small, she could dig her way underneath.

But it was better than she'd hoped: There was a long wide-mouthed tunnel formed by the rocks which suited her purpose perfectly. One end was blocked by earth and undergrowth – the other end proved simple to excavate, and once the way was clear she flung herself into the tunnel, and just to be sure, pulled the debris she'd cleared across the entrance she'd created.

She lay and waited for the night to return. Outside it must be getting light. In here – was anything else in here, she suddenly wondered? Ancient bones, perhaps? Because beneath her was not earth, but a stone floor, like cobbles. This must be what they called a fougou, an underground chamber.

These constructions were probably contemporary with Stonehenge, she seemed to recall someone telling her. She remembered that they were common in Brittany, though she'd had more pressing concerns since she'd arrived here, and hadn't given ancient history a moment's thought till now.

A picture came into her mind; a visit to Stone Age village, back in Cornwall, when she was a child. It had a fougou, in the middle of it, so it wouldn't be a grave, would it? People didn't bury the dead in the midst of the living, because of decomposition and possibly also superstition – did they? And it wasn't superstition after all, was it? Probably for storage, though why give it a floor – to keep vermin out? Or was it a hiding place? No – if every village had one, invaders would know exactly where to look...

Her body felt neither cold nor the discomfort of lying on cobbles. It seemed to hover on a cushion of energy generated by her skin. It's not all bad, she told herself, although... insects suck blood, don't they? And they jump long distances, for their size. And... they have good night vision. Oh... and they are strong for their size, too. Is that what I am?

She gazed with her good night vision at her hands. They seemed normal, though very grubby, and her nails were broken and filthy beyond any definition of filth. Then she was asleep – without knowing it, of course, just like anyone else.

She dreamt of Graves, with a long tongue that furled back, unfurling it suggestively again and again. He had black fur on his arms, and when she looked down, so did she. Then he turned into a spider, and she was a fly in his web, and he was coming towards her, and she was wriggling, but she couldn't move. Then she was in a house, and she saw an ancient gilt mirror, and she ran and looked at herself in it, and somehow it turned into a cage, and she was in it.

It was difficult to tell the difference, but at last she was awake, and there still *was* a difference, though not as much as when she was... alive, or ordinary, or whatever she was... before.

How do I know if I can get out? Simone asked herself. If I'd only asked Graves, that would be more helpful, she complained. But no one was there to complain to, or about, except her. And she had no legacy of vampire wisdom to rely on, so she must work it all out the hard way. Why is it that the adjective 'bitter' so often precedes the noun 'experience'? As she framed the question, she was already moving to push the debris away from her little cave's entrance.

This is a birthing chamber, she thought, or a dying... It looks too cold and damp, though I'm not cold and damp – I think I'll never be cold and damp again. Or was it for storage? How practical. Or hiding from enemies... Oh, but they'd have to hide it better, not let half the structure stick up out of the ground – OK, as the Americans say, not that. Storage then, most probably. Though things would go mouldy so perhaps it was drier back then? For the walls dripped and moss grew on them – she shivered, reflexively – but she felt warm enough. Over her head a stone had gone missing and left a gap through which she could see light. I'd better wait for it to fade, she thought.

Archaeologists must be very religious, she decided, because when they don't know what something was for, they always hypothesise 'religious reasons'. Which could be right, of course, given life expectancy back in the deep past. Short lives and no painkillers – would make you either think of God a lot or... no. You'd think of God a lot, with anger, perhaps, but you would not invest everything in the world.

And then, just as she began to imagine ceremonies – about what, maybe being born again, like this was a womb, and you somehow made sure you'd get a new life, or maybe when you died they'd put you in here for your soul's sake, for some reason – her thoughts, skittish as anyone's thoughts, despite her strange condition, turned to the banal exigencies associated with occupying a body: I don't need to poo! Or pee! Doesn't seem so, anyway...

When she recalled her hunger of the night before, she felt afraid. It had not been like hunger, but like thirst; the sort of thirst, though, that you have when you wake as dry as bones and dust in the night, when you reach for water and drink it in gulps, more gulps than you thought you needed – but it was worse than that by far. She feared its return, even as she wondered where her meal had gone to, inside her body. She was no longer distended, but comfortable, just right, for the moment.

She did not dwell on that, because now she could see the light was fading, through her peephole, so with relief that she could now act, rather than just think, she crawled out of her hiding place and watched the last of the sunset from beneath a canopy of leaves, a tangle of hawthorn and oak, ivy and sycamore and others she couldn't name. As the sun slid out of sight and the night blue deepened she watched the world take on another kind of gleam, as if each object, rock or bush or tree, had its own inner light source, too dim to be visible by daylight, but bright enough to light her way.

And what would be her way? Where should she go? The world is not my home, she thought, and I no longer belong here; I should be dead – perhaps I AM dead, and no one can see me?

Well in that case... no. This isn't being normally dead, surely not.. well, in THAT case, I'll do the obvious thing, that anyone would do in my situation – it's inevitable that I kill Hitler. There. It's probably – fate. Only a vampire could succeed, if one thought about it.

And then she wondered – are there others? Like me? Vampires, maybe, but never traitors, determined to do their duty despite their nightmare change in circumstances? Perhaps – but why would the likes of Graves, if indeed there were anyone else like Graves, want to turn people into simulacra of himself? Surely they would be rivals for the precious blood. All right, there was a lot more of it easily available in wartime, but still… careless newborn vampires – that's what I am, say it, even silently, acknowledge it – such creatures new spawned, blundering about, would surely come to the attention of the authorities, and cause panic – even more panic than death from the sky, or enemy tanks with their cargo of foreign soldiers rolling down the streets of towns that did not, previously, belong to them.

Never mind whether there were others, or whether they were good or bad, Simone knew she must act to do at least one good and useful thing, whatever it cost her. She felt a thrill of determined anger like an electrical impulse in her veins. I will kill Hitler or die trying, by my humanity I will!

With this goal in mind, and no better mission having presented itself during the 12 hours or so she had determined on this one, she decided to look for a road, preferably one running east/west, because if she headed into the dark then she would be going, more or less, in the direction of Berlin. To her right she could now see lights – not many; a village or else a large building – why were they allowed to have lights on display like that? She wondered if the occupying Germans were so confident that Britain was weak – but no, the darkest days were over, the Yanks were in the war now, and the Allies were going to win.

And I'll help, really help. Why not? Perhaps it takes a monster to catch a monster, she thought. Perhaps all this… weirdness… was destiny, yet another word for fate. She was religious, after all, even if her religiosity had decayed somewhat, into superstition.

There *was* a road. She could see it now, not far off, but invisible till now, as no headlights pierced the dark. It was visible some of the time as she pushed through the scrub, and sometimes it was hidden as she moved. It looked to be beyond the river. Fortunately, she was able to see; probably like any nocturnal animal, she thought. But she was not quite an animal, not yet… Or maybe she was, and that was why she was able to enjoy the luminous dark, like full moonlight but not coming from one source; silvery yet with colours, tracing the shapes of all the living things. Everything had its life, invisible to ordinary human sight. On either side of the road, worlds of shimmering structures awaited her.

The road itself had almost no light intrinsic to it, as it was made from something almost lifeless, compared to what was around it. But there was enough brightness even in the most ancient rock to delineate its boundaries, so that it was like a paler, straighter river running through the night. Borrowed from God, she thought.

But she did not pursue that thought, fearful of where it might lead her.

Above her the high clouds were clearing and stars were peeping out. She looked up and then stopped, overwhelmed. Suddenly, it seemed, the sky was blanketed in stars, some pure diamond and silver, some scintillating with nuanced colours that shifted across the spectrum she knew and moved into something else. The beauty was astonishing, yet it did not seem more beautiful than it had been before her dark saviour saved her ebbing life. It was she who'd finally looked, she decided, because how could a night sky full of stars become *more* beautiful?

Something inside her dropped her to her knees and bowed her head, then it made her fall forward onto her hands – and a voice, her own, said, "not enough" and she went down onto the grass and weeds and patches of mud, her arms stretched in front of her and the rest of her body flat on the ground. I am worshipping, for the first time in my life, she wondered. The beauty of it...

When she rose and resumed her journey she was exhilarated and terribly afraid, all at once. She had been raised by lapsed Catholics. Clever students, which she had been, did not believe in God, and her parents' religion held nothing for her, not even for them. It belonged to history, or should do, along with other superstitions. Some great art had been produced, of course.

Beauty, though – why was everything so beautiful? And it had brought her to her knees. The world could have been made, and evolution taken place, without it being beautiful. But it was, and tonight the barriers between her and the universe had dropped, and instead of saying dutifully to herself, yes, that's beautiful, I must appreciate that, the veil had lifted and it had knocked her sideways.

That, she thought, is no accident, whatever the clever fellows at Cambridge say. Yet it doesn't have anything to do with any religion that I know of. There's no... judgement... in that sky.

Yet when she looked up again, it was almost with relief that she realised that, though it was no less beautiful than before, the intensity of her feelings had faded, somewhat, and her response was more cool appreciation than passionate awe. She could almost feel the thoughts, like clouds, obscuring the bright source of her initial, innocent joy. And it was somehow safe, this heading back to her habitual, wary mental patterns.

But I am a... vampire, she argued with herself. I'm not ever going to go back to a comfortable set of beliefs, surely? And I can't deny what I feel – felt. Or the implications. Which are... that there is a God. Because if that up there isn't holy, the word has no meaning. It's just that I haven't noticed it before. So the thing that stops us noticing is... the devil? What? Our own minds?

This was all fine and dandy, she reminded herself, but it was begging several questions, like, for example, how was it that she had to become a creature of darkness – a blood drinker, a *human blood* drinker – to see it? I must be more of a Catholic than I thought, Simone pondered, because that seems just wrong to me.

For the first time, or perhaps, the first time she could admit it to herself, she wished she could talk to Graves, and get some answers. Graves. What a stupid, obvious name, like some bodysnatcher hanging around cemeteries. With a pathetic sense of humour. Would he really have anything useful to say? Would he have experienced anything like this? She had seen him kill a man – Marcel, who carried his own darkness with him. Graves was Gestapo, the embodiment of evil, for heaven's sake!

For heaven's sake. Will I get to heaven, ever? What must I do for heaven's sake? What will become of me, no longer human?

It was the precision of that thought that helped distinguish the difference between sleeping and waking, but at last she was awake, and there still *was* a difference, though not as much as when she was... alive, or ordinary, or whatever she was once.

God, she was hungry, savage with it; no, she must not think like that.

She must not think of herself as savage, or hunger savaging her; any kind of dalliance with thoughts of that kind could be the finish of her as a human being. But as she stepped into the fading light she knew she must feed, soon. She pushed forward through the undergrowth towards the river. When she reached it, she decided to try and wade. It had to be quicker than pushing through a pathless forest with all kinds of trees and vegetation getting in the way.

But as she stood in the shallows she felt the same kind of resistance as she had from the unwilling sea. Now would be a good time to find a boat, but people didn't go boating in the dark – unless they were engaged in clandestine work.

Her night vision was good but there were strange things happening to her eyes. She was seeing a lot more than could possibly be there. Huge shadows, like mountains, seemed to be gathering like clouds around her small horizon, but when she tried to focus the shadows shifted shape. The river at her feet seemed to swell and spread and rear up, first to her chest, then past her head, except it wasn't: The viscosity wasn't enveloping her, and she wasn't getting wet. The forest seemed to be changing, the dark where the trees were, seemed to grow, expand, change shape, change species, become conifers suddenly and cast shadows of purple on a suddenly snowy forest floor. And beneath that wintry vision she saw – or sensed – it wasn't easy to distinguish which of her senses were operating, though – perhaps she had new ones – a featureless landscape, a wilderness of ice. And then she saw fire erupting from another direction; a volcano? Where am I? she asked herself. Have I died? I must have died. This isn't real. She fell to the ground again, but this time in fear rather than ecstasy, and shut her eyes.

This fear-filled disorientation wasn't the only imperative in her world, though. She had banished the visions but not the hunger. She was a predator and she had to feed. Simone got a grip on herself, stood up and opened her eyes. The world was shifting, titanic shadows danced in her peripheral vision, yet if she focused carefully on what was happening at the centre of her sight the shadowy chaos receded. It was as if she had one of those torches miners wear, strapped to their heads. As she moved forward, gingerly at first, the ground was there to greet her. The world remembered its manners, and politely became what she expected it to be.

She concentrated on dealing with the undergrowth, sometimes pushing through it, sometimes springing over rocks and trees, always keeping the river on her left. She tried to hunt, but the bird of prey she saw swooping from the sky onto its intended rodent meal was too swift for her pounce, and even the fortunate creature she had unwittingly saved proved too fast for her clutches. Look at what I am, she chided herself, a devourer of rats now, who cannot even catch them. At last she found her meal, a dog fox, perhaps slowed by age, that fell to her lunge. The taste was vile, worse than the cow. Perhaps herbivores were better.

Yet as she drained the beast, she felt a surge of strength, and with it, exhilaration. She hastened forwards. Hitler wasn't about to kill himself, now, was he? She laughed at her own joke. She disdained the sights that were there, still all around her, as distractions. She would eat again soon, she promised herself.

Then she heard it. Very, very quietly, oars were being plied upon the nearby river. It was not an animal. It was too rhythmic for that. She understood that her hearing was much sharper than it had been, and wondered how far away the boat was. It had become hard to tell, although once she was used to it, it would become easier again. Sounds accompanied her edge-of-vision landscape too, but they were echoey, as if they had travelled a long way, like the light from distant stars.

She crept as silently as she could to the river bank. She focused in the direction of the sounds, and was rewarded by the sight of a boat, several yards away, with what looked like two figures in it. And then she heard another sound; an outboard motor. Someone was coming down the river behind the boat.

The two oarsmen must have heard it too. Their boat began to come towards the bank Simone stood on, though there was no way they could have seen her. They shipped the oars as their boat slid against the bank, but there was little cover; the bank here was steep and featureless, nor did the trees overhang at this spot.

Their pursuers came round a bend in the river. They had been quiet but something must have told them that this tactic was no longer useful, for suddenly a great light was shining out and a voice started to speak in German.

"Surrender now and you will not be killed. Give up your arms, surrender."

Someone shot, into the air, and Simone saw the brief fire blaze. Then the light was shone in a sweep across the river and its banks, narrowly failing to pick out Simone herself, but mercilessly lighting up the poorly concealed boat carrying the two in front. As it stripped the darkness from them, they fired the revolvers they had, loaded and ready for the inevitable moment. She saw that they, too, had a motor, which was either broken or switched off so that it could make no noise.

The boat behind was bigger, and had a wind and water shield protecting the pilot. It must have been bulletproof, or maybe the fugitives' aim was bad, for there were no screams from the pursuers. It seemed all they had to do was duck.

A shot rang out from the bigger boat and there was an anguished yell from the smaller one. Simone decided it was time to intervene. Beware the water, she told herself.

She coiled and sprang, feeling the power of her lower body release her into the air. She did not yet have the measure of her strength and it seemed that she might overshoot her goal, but a small twist of her body was sufficient to make sure she landed right in the middle of the larger boat, almost knocking over at least two of its passengers. There was some shouting, which she ignored, and some shooting, which she couldn't ignore, as a bullet was making its way into her abdomen at very close range. The pain was indescribable, especially as the bullet came out of her back, surely carrying her insides with it. She dropped, and someone started to club her around the head while screaming. Someone else was kicking her really hard.

"It's a woman!" Then there was some more shouting, but at least the screaming had stopped. At last the clubbing and the kicking stopped too.

"She's dead," said one, incuriously. Another, keener on learning, knelt down to examine her.

"What a mess," he concluded.

The pain was diminishing fast. Deep in Simone's body, broken parts were seeking out their places in the shattered jigsaw of her guts. She could not help a groan when the healing itself turned a little painful.

"She's alive! Listen!" said the second speaker.

Suddenly, she felt herself fixed. So fast she was astonished, though nowhere near as amazed as her hosts. But they had little time to feel anything before she was furiously hurling them over the side into the river. She might be able to survive a high velocity bullet at point blank range, but she wasn't in any hurry to experience it again: It hurt.

"A mess, am I?" She had thrown three men into the river, and one remained. Her night vision was getting better; he seemed to be an officer, and he didn't seem to have a gun in his hand. Instead he seemed as if turned to stone by terror.

She hurled herself at his throat. She was so hungry. He went down with barely a whimper, and as she sank her teeth into his neck and tasted his blood it was the taste of heaven, bliss, better than champagne.

But as she drank she became aware of two things: First, that her bite must have anaesthetic properties, since he did not struggle, second, that the deep beat of his heart was slowing, then slowing some more.

With a huge effort she stopped feeding and sat back. His wound still dripped, still pulsed, in fact, and she found that she knew what to do: She drew the underside of her tongue carefully over the two punctures in his skin, and felt a sticky substance ooze from it, sealing up the holes, as she had somehow known it would.

Not bad, she thought, with no Mama bird to show me how to survive the outside world, and no nest either, for that.

"Lead me not into temptation," she whispered, and then thought, how odd. I'm an atheist.

But then, many things were different now, and not just since she'd become a – don't be afraid of the word, she chided herself – vampire. She had drunk Marcel's blood, but the life had just left him. This was different: The German was alive, and there was no comparison. As for cows, even alive, the dreary sludge they provided did not make her feel like this – like some immortal god, filled with strength and power, afraid of nothing, unconquerable.

Although she could still feel pain, unfortunately.

She was not the scared, depressed, *cursed* being she had been just, what... twenty minutes ago? Half an hour? Everything seemed different, and anything seemed possible.

She would play it cleverly, though. There were most definitely many, many more things in heaven and earth than she had dreamt of in her previous, ill considered philosophy. If vampires were real, then God might well be, not to mention heaven. And the other place.

She did not want to kill the man. She didn't want that following her, enemy soldier or not. Funny, when she had come here to help in the killing of enemy soldiers. Lucky, perhaps, that she had not directly killed anyone.

Most paradoxical of all, it was the taste of the blood of a living human being that, even while she was enjoying it, made her somehow know, more than any preaching could, how precious human lives are. She wondered if the men she'd thrown off the boat could swim. I gave them a chance, she told herself.

Not a god, after all. The gods of old did not care for human life, except sometimes those of their favourites – till they fell out of favour.

She leapt from the boat to the bank, leaving the man to chance and fate to deal with. There were enemy soldiers who were terribly wicked, as indeed, resistance fighters and British soldiers who were also bad to the bone, but through circumstance of birth found themselves on the 'right' side.

She proceeded by shoving through and jumping over the thick vegetation. It annoyed her to be impeded, but the mental inverted commas that her mind was putting around 'right' alarmed her, which was somehow a greater impediment. Never had she thought like that before. We were right, Hitler invaded other people's countries. He put all sorts of people that opposed him in work camps: Stories were emerging that he starved and tortured them...

And so had the British. It was a matter of historical record.

She was now furiously angry, solely with herself, and she wanted to get out of this damned devil's shrubbery. She leapt high, fuelled by rage and the blood of a living man. She could see the road clearly now, all silver and purple, lighting her route. She leapt from branch to branch, but not like a monkey, oh no – on the very tips of her toes, dancing through the air. And when she reached the deserted road she continued to leap along it, much faster than a man could run, grateful to have the way ahead laid out in front of her. For this road would lead her to Hitler, eventually, and he was bad, unequivocally bad, and his removal from existence would benefit millions.

Then she thought, well, perhaps I should have killed those Germans – after all, they would have executed that pair in the rowing boat. At least I stopped them – for a while. Meanwhile wispy cloud was blotting out patches of stars, just as her thoughts were beginning to blot out the fierce and feverish joy that came with the taste of living human blood... doubts; a self divided, anxious about whether it had done the right thing – ever, if she was in that kind of mood.

She wondered about those, like Graves, who feasted on humans without a care. She knew now that it was possible to limit oneself to animals and survive as this creature that she was. But he had been right about the intoxicating nectar that was human blood to one such as she. Graves did not need to kill people, he just liked their taste. Perhaps if she tasted one again, she would become like a drug addict, willing to do anything to anyone to just feel that high.

Yet she knew that she could not decide, not yet anyway, to abjure human blood. Having drunk of the German she could not promise herself that it would not happen again. She knew it would. But if she could only control it, there need be no lives on her conscience. If.

Her pace slowed, as she contemplated her bizarre fate, and the terrible risk of damnation.

She had considered herself a *lapsed* Catholic, an atheist, but given her situation, that position was no longer tenable. She had a soul, obviously, else what was it that survived her wounds to become this thing? And if she had a soul, didn't that mean it could be damned?

Chapter Five

Who shall change our vile body

(NT)

If her thoughts had been like wisps of cloud before, they were lowering dark cumulus now, bearing rain: She would have cried, but no tears came. But relief was at hand, for she was distracted by the grey and ochre shimmering shapes of a blacked-out town, upon her almost before she knew it.

It was as quiet as a vampire's heartbeat. The night was now quite old, but dawn was still nowhere near. Before the war it might have been lively; at least it would have been a little better lit. She could not tell how big it was, but it was large enough to have a town square, although it didn't take that long to get there. There was a statue of someone on a horse, outside a darkened town hall. Opposite, there was a hotel, also in total darkness, with no welcoming light. And there were some shops; a patisserie, charcuterie, tobacconist, even a clothes shop, all in darkness because the Allies might just decide to fly this way, even at the risk that they might drop their terrible cargo on their own supporters.

Simone didn't need food, or tobacco, but some feminine reflex sent her over to peer into the window of the clothes shop, where various items shimmered with the half- life light of cotton, silk and wool – mostly wool, of course, but the Germans had money – and mademoiselles on whom to spend it, she guessed.

Her focus shifted, and suddenly she saw herself. So, she thought, we do have a reflection. Oh, god, no… my hair! My clothes!

Was this the woman who'd wanted to bring make-up with her to Brittany? She looked like an old witch who lived in a hedge. Only worse; blood stains on her clothes, especially around her neck, her clothes in rags, and plain old dirt all over her, including her face: Anyone seeing her would think her a mad, dangerous savage… with sunken eyes like someone who'd just died… yes, she resembled a day-old corpse. Unsurprising, really, given that was exactly what she was.

Without further ado she drove her fist through the window and the glass shattered at her feet. It made quite a noise, which gave her pause: She looked around but no one came, and no one shouted. Yet someone must have woken – but this was a town of frightened people. If anyone had been roused from sleep, they had clearly decided that the better part of valour was to try and doze off again.

She walked into the shop and started helping herself to whatever was on the hangers. She didn't bother to check for size – she wasn't exactly browsing in Harvey Nichols. She tried to keep the clothes away from her filthy body. A bath was essential – but how and where? Would it even work, given how the water was when she'd stepped into the sea? Yet Graves had looked clean...

Simone walked out of the shop with an armful of clothes and looked about her. Still no signs of life. No, there was something; a brightness at one of the windows on the second floor of the hotel, peeping out from behind a curtain. It was brighter than the men in the boat had been, so it might be that her eyes were continuing to develop their new powers of perception...

Tucking the clothes under one arm, she leapt across the square and was at the window, holding herself aloft by lightly touching the rails on a Juliet balcony: If there had been nothing there, she would have drifted like a snowflake to the ground. I am several people in one, she thought, and smashed her fist through the window. There was a feminine scream, and a masculine shout, as she sprang into the room. Not enough noise, she calculated, to suggest to any listeners that the disturbance was something more than cries of passion.

A man crouched in the bed, about to jump out. He was pretty much naked, the bit of him that showed. A woman stood next to the window, wrapped in some kind of lacy, transparent thing. She had been the shape peering from the window. Simone leapt on the man, grabbed his arms – which looked quite beefy, but succumbed instantly to her strength – and sank her teeth into his carotid artery. Within seconds he was unconscious, anaesthetised by the venom in her little fangs. Reluctantly, she dragged them out of his neck and applied the coagulant beneath her tongue. Then she turned to the woman, who was silent, but only because terror had so overwhelmed her that she couldn't force a scream through her sobs of fear. Remarkably, there was no noise from within the rest of the building. A listener might conclude that the man had assaulted and perhaps murdered the woman. But if there were any listeners, they were careful to mind their own business.

Simone felt a surge of pity for the woman. It rose from her chest, as if her heart was in the middle, like a warm tide. She felt grateful beyond words for it. I am still human, she thought. Then she realised that the woman could see much less than she could in the darkness of the room – even the broken window did not help, for there was no moon, no streetlights or house lights, and the distant stars were invisible from where they were, and besides, their light came from so far away that it could not illuminate poor Earth.

The woman could not see her properly. What could she be imagining?

"Don't be afraid. I won't hurt you," Simone said, in French. "Do you have a candle?"

It must have been more than the woman could bear, to hear another woman's voice, from the shapeless creature of darkness that had leapt through the glass and killed (so she must be thinking) her man. She slid to the floor. But Simone needed her help, so she picked her up and shook her, gently.

"Don't faint. I want you awake. I promise I won't hurt you. We need light. Get me light!"

The trembling woman pointed to a bedside table. There was an oil lamp on it, and a large box of matches beside it. Simone drew the thick curtain across the window. Her leap had not torn it down: It had simply been pushed to one side.

Simone then lit the lamp. The woman gasped at the wild creature in front of her. Still, it must help, a little, that she was human shaped.

"He's just unconscious," Simone offered, gesturing at the bed. "But I could kill him and you in an instant if I wanted." Then she saw, on a chair, a German uniform. "So – are you French?" The woman nodded. "Then you're a collaborator?"

The woman fell to her knees and began gibbering in fast disjointed French.

"Slowly!" enjoined Simone, holding up a hand. "I don't really care!" And it was true, although when she was with the freedom fighters she had shared their often-aired disgust with such traitors. Now she found no room for blame in her heart, partly because she didn't want to spoil the lovely feeling that had so recently risen from that region, and partly because most people were caught up in this war – didn't cause it, didn't want it – and the culprits were far away from this room. The woman was just getting by: An alien army had invaded her land, for God's sake. Marcel, though, would have shot her. On the spot.

And besides, it was good to talk to somebody, other than monsters, or people trying to kill her, or people she was eating…

"Is there a bathroom here?"

Yes, there was, and what's more, it was ensuite. Unusual for a small town, but the man must be someone with both cash and clout. There was even a little hot water left. The woman, whose name was Martine, was eager to help and did not venture any questions. Simone watched as the bath filled, wondering how it would be to get in the water. Would it be jelly like? Did that matter?

She stripped off her clothes and climbed gingerly into the tub. The water was like oil on her skin, rather than jelly, but not greasy. It looked like water, but felt thick, like cream, or custard.

"I need shampoo," she said. "Your hair has not been washed in soap, I bet. Does he buy you good stuff?"

"From Paris, yes," Martine replied, her eyes politely downcast, either in fear or embarrassment at seeing another woman naked.

"Well, get me all your toiletries, then. Now!" Was Martine trying to hide her stuff? Ludicrous creature. I can do anything I want, thought Simone, to anyone I want. And was horrified that she'd thought it. I am several people in one, she reminded herself, and dear God, let the best person win, for the sake of my soul! If I have one…

Martine tipped out the contents of a white leather bag. "This is shampoo," she said, offering a bottle to Simone, who dipped her head underwater before adding some of the shampoo to her hair. It doubled to soap her body with too. She rinsed as best she could, let the water run out and then held her head under the cold tap to get the last of the lather out. What was really weird was that the water ran as fast as it always does until it touched her hair or body, when it seemed to thicken and slow down. It was strange to the point of being disorientating, especially as when it ran off her it seemed to speed up again on its way to the plug hole.

Martine found her towels, only slightly used, and began to chatter as she relaxed a little. She didn't sleep with the German because she liked him, oh no, she wouldn't do that. And not for presents, either, she wasn't that kind of girl. It was just that she had a sister and a brother, and a mother and a father, and work was ill-paid and unpredictable, and even if you did work you weren't paid much, and the German would sometimes give her cash, and sometimes goods, which would all go on her family.

She was very pretty, with that winning combination of thick black curls and blue eyes. She was petite, small-waisted, and small-boned. No wonder the German gave her presents. But Simone read a certain slyness there, and of course she was vain, and currently the girl is congratulating herself, Simone could tell, on having evaded death at her own hands; also on having convinced Simone, that she was only sleeping with the enemy to provide for her poor family, who would otherwise starve.

Well, thought Simone, God bless, for all that. Notwithstanding that, she demanded Martine's treasured Parisian toiletries, and all her cash, as well as her handbag, to carry it in. She went through the dozing German's clothes as well, and helped herself to all his money. After that, she chose some clothes from her heap, the ones that fit her, and stuffed the rest under the bed, partly to protect Martine from accusations of theft.

Of course, she'd forgotten about shoes. Her ruined clothes had been man's clothes, trousers and sweater and shirt (and a very grimy bra.) Her new outfit was a dress and a cardigan, and Martine's underpants and her too small bra, necessary because she had forgotten to steal underwear. But the shoes were virtually boots, and had received a terrible bashing, and looked it. And as for the socks... no, she would do without. Martine's dainty shoes came nowhere near her, of course.

Martine dared not protest as Simone purloined her various possessions, but she did pout a bit. At last, Simone concentrated on her and spoke to her as if she were a child, or a kitten.

"Now listen, I said I wouldn't hurt you, and I won't, but I'm going to put you to sleep now, all right? You'll wake in the morning, all will be well, and I'll be gone"

"No, no. Please. I'll be quiet, I won't tell anyone..." Martine clearly did not trust her.

Simone paused. Let's try a different approach, she decided.

"I've forgotten my hair, Martine! And my teeth! Do you have a toothbrush?"
Sulkily, the girl produced a toothbrush and some tooth powder, hitherto concealed in her overnight bag, in some pocket or other. Then, accepting the inevitable, she flourished a hairbrush, the last of her treasures, and handed it to Simone.

Simone cleaned her teeth, though the water was as gluey in texture as the tooth powder, which made the process lengthy, especially the rinsing.

"Will you brush my hair for me?" She gave Martine her best winning smile, though the girl still looked dubious.

Once her hair was brushed, Simone politely thanked Martine, then spun round and grabbed her head, pulling it down and sinking her teeth into the girl's neck. There was barely a whimper from Martine.

Gosh, I move so *fast,* she congratulated herself.

Then she thought, a pint won't hurt. That's what you give when you give blood. She's making a small donation to my cause.

In the end, she was nervous of taking too much, so it was probably less than a pint. Then she applied the coagulant. But it tasted so good – she moved to the German. I had virtually nothing from you, after all, she whispered aloud – then she was on him, wounding him with her teeth again – four little scars for him. She drank, more greedily this time, but still alert to the pulse, the beat, sensing instantly when it began to slow, and dragging herself off him before it was too late. She sealed his wound with her tongue and stood back.

No rest for the wicked, though: She turned the lamp off and tentatively drew the curtain. There it was; a lightening in the east.

Simone helped herself to the contents of the man's wallet, but did not trouble to steal from the girl till she was about to leave, then she thought it might cause the authorities – should the matter be reported – to think Martine had instigated something, maybe with an accomplice. So she fished in the girl's bag and took her purse.

She left the room by the door, and found the landing empty, and the other doors firmly shut. She couldn't recall if she'd made much noise, but if she had the fellow guests in this place must all be deaf – or very nervous.

At the end of the corridor was another door. Opening it, she found that it led onto stairs that went up as well as down. For some reason she couldn't explain to herself, she went up. Up one flight, and another door – peering out, there were fewer doors than on the floor beneath, and she was almost certain the rooms here were empty. It was wartime, after all. She carried on up the stairs, which had narrowed, and found a door so low she had to bend her head to open it. There was no corridor, just a room; furniture covered in sheets and a lot of dust, and beyond, another door, another room, all darkness and discarded junk, and no window. But it didn't matter, because she could see.

She was full of blood and fire, and perhaps she could have got out of there before dawn, but she was all cleaned up, and the idea of going out into the countryside and finding some den to sleep in, human or animal made, was unappealing. But she was sure she wouldn't sleep.

So she settled under a sheet over a chair and was very surprised when she heard a hue and cry below, in what seemed just minutes later, but was probably was much longer.

She felt a little scared at first, but then she remembered her confrontation on the boat. Bullets could not kill her, and human strength was pitiful against her. On the other hand, she did not want the whole of the Reich as her enemy. Armies have bombs, and prisons, and maybe they wouldn't know it at first, but if they simply kept her from getting to a safe dark place at sunrise, that'd do the trick.

Strength and invulnerability and the ability to see in the dark were not the only benefits her change had brought. She could hear much more sharply, which so far had meant little except an appreciation of how noisy everything was, even in the countryside, even in a quiet hotel, where birds squawked on the roof and rats careered around distant spaces somewhere in the walls, floors and corridors of the hotel. Now she concentrated, listening to the human sounds from below; two floors, but she could catch it...

A woman was crying and shouting, genuine hysteria in her voice. That'd be Martine. And a man was shouting in German. He was either accusing Martine of robbery or blaming another man, whose voice sounded conciliatory – the hotel manager? Then someone who sounded calmer than all of them intervened. He'd found – or his underlings, who must be responsible for the background noises which were probably sounds of searching, had – the 'stolen' goods under the bed. Then there was more noise from Martine, and Simone could make out her words, which were a stream of denial, and some yarn about a woman as strong as a strong man who'd forced her to do this and that...

Simone realised that she'd landed the girl in a real mess. Policemen, French or German, military or civilian, like neat answers. The man with the calm voice was not going to perturb and disappoint his superiors with lurid tales like Martine's. He was going to take the easy route out of this, by arresting Martine, obviously, and charging her with theft from the shop, and also from her companion. She would be thrown in gaol, and God knew what would happen to her, this being wartime, and normal rules being suspended. It might even be called treason, a French woman stealing from a German. She might die for it.

Simone started swearing to herself, like she'd never sworn. She'd heard some fruity language in her time, but had never used it herself till now. She had been a good girl... but that idea was at once both more and less relevant than it had ever been.

She still wanted to be a good girl, at some deep level, deeper than mummy pleasing, or daddy pleasing, or any desire to please anybody except herself. And the appearance of goodness was not enough in this new existence. It had to be real – or she would be lost forever.

She could move within the building, but she dared not risk daylight, even if, as seemed likely, the day was overcast. She could go downstairs and cause havoc, but she had never enjoyed unnecessary drama, and her interference would certainly be dramatic, and its consequences unpredictable. Instinct told her to bide her time, so she obeyed it, fretfully.

Simone heard sounds coming up to her eyrie which suggested that all parties in the scene below had decamped, probably to a court or a prison. She tried to sleep until dusk, but it was difficult. Her mind was a racetrack. Which solution would be the winner? None looked promising. They included killing everyone, killing everyone except Martine, killing Martine and sparing everyone else, and turning herself in, which was just silly.

Notwithstanding, when the day finally drew to a close she padded down to the floor below and exited a window, floating quite gracefully to the ground. There were no lights visible but for a few early stars, and a delicate quarter moon that would soon fill out with light as even the traces of sunset faded.

I hope this bit is easy, she thought. And it was. The gendarmerie was in the town square, exactly where it ought to be, next to the town hall, which, she supposed, also contained the courthouse. If Martine was being charged with anything, she had to be in one of those places. And they'd had all day to mess about in court, so Simone concluded that the police station would be her best bet.

Her vampire eyesight led her to the door, and she walked across the square with a certain swagger, much of which came from the unexpected pleasantness of wearing nice clothes and being clean. And a little, just a little, or so she told herself, came from the knowledge that she was a super strong being that very little could kill.

No need to draw attention to oneself, though.

She walked through the door and up to a frowning gentleman in uniform, sitting behind a desk.

"Good evening, monsieur. I am looking for a woman, a friend of mine, whom I believe to be in trouble…"

"Pierre!" the gendarme called at once. Another gendarme emerged from behind him.
"What's this?" the newcomer asked.
"She's friends with the pretty one," the other informed him. They both smirked. Simone gritted her teeth. "Can I see my friend?" she queried, without much hope.

"No. She's in a lot of trouble. Get a lawyer and come back tomorrow." More smirking.

"So she's here then?"

"Yes she is but you can't see her, it's too late." The pair of them just loved saying no. Simone had encountered the type and had often wished she could deal out some form of punishment. And now she could. But she was very restrained about it.

She was restrained because she was afraid. She was coming for Martine because she didn't want to leave a trail of chaos and misfortune for the innocent. That would be bad. And hurting the policemen would also be bad, although she could smell badness around them. It smelt horrible, like cologne made of very stagnant water, full of decaying matter.

She was even faster than she'd been before. She jumped onto the desk and grabbed the one that was sitting there, hauling him off the chair while reaching out for the other. They tried to fend her off but she'd buried her teeth in both of them so quickly it seemed almost simultaneous. The hit was stupendous, their blood like fire and sunshine down her throat, and she let them struggle a little, till, one at a time, she felt them sigh as the fight went out of them, and she gave them, not without regret, that final little under the tongue lick that released the chemical that put them asleep and left them alive.

Then she went behind the desk and through a door, and there were more doors, and stairs down, until she heard crying.

She went towards the door which concealed the source of the crying. "Martine," she called in a loud half-whisper, "it's me!"

The crying stopped, probably replaced by throat-closing fear. Better reassure the girl, she thought.

"I'm here to rescue you," she called, hoping that would help. "Where's the key?"

There was only silence in reply.

Simone felt a massive surge of impatience. It was a fault from her pre-vampire days. She would put up with a lot, but after a while she'd snap and stomp around, and was known to occasionally throw things.

The door of the cell was metal, solid. Can I? Simone wondered. I could look for the key…

But the coiled-up rage and anxiety of the day just gone was still with her. She was tired of waiting, tired of sneaking about: She felt her strength as if it were energy racing up and down her body, which was almost shaking with desire to act, to release some of that power.

There was a large metal bar across the door which was simply there to grab onto; there wasn't a proper handle that moved. Simone didn't wait to determine if the door opened inside or out. She just grabbed the handle and pulled, in an ecstasy of temper.

The door just buckled outward, which enraged her so much she pulled the thing right off its hinges and onto the floor, where it lay, mangled out of shape.

Beyond, in the cell, on a lumpy mattress on the floor, sat Martine, smears of mascara – or possibly, given the shortages, some substitute like shoe polish – streaking her face, which was dead white. That was a reaction, possibly, to Simone's arrival. The blotches of pink around the white were probably the consequence of a previous emotion. Her dress was ripped, and Simone smelt badness around her – but it wasn't hers.

She was staring at Simone as though she were the devil, which was entirely understandable.

"Have they hurt you?" If so, I'm responsible, thought Simone. And I'll kill them.

"They're going to take turns with me, they said. When it's dark. No one'll care about me, they said." The words were muttered, but Simone caught them all right.

"Come on, let's get you out of here before the locals find out there's been a gaol break."

The girl wobbled to her feet. There were bruises on her face and arms.

"Who did that?" asked the vampire.

"The examining magistrate. Leclerc. He was questioning me."

They walked out of the cell and up the stairs. Martine saw the two gendarmes, and had to grasp at Simone's arm to stay upright. Then she smiled.

They left the building. All was quiet, but Simone supposed that didn't necessarily mean that people had heard nothing from the gendarmerie, just that in this town it didn't pay to be nosy.

She wished she had a plan, but she'd never managed to plan more than two moves at the very most, on a good day, when she played chess, and life didn't seem to be turning out any differently.

"We're heading out of town. East," she said firmly. At least some of the tatters of her original scheme should be retained: They would go in the direction she had intended from the beginning. "I'm sorry, I'll have to carry you," she said.

Martine looked in no mood to argue. Simone picked her up like a big rag doll and slung her across her shoulder. It was awkward, having to hold her with one arm, but she weighed nothing: She felt no more substantial than a scarf.

Simone ran down the road, and then leapt, higher and further than ever before, till they were miles down the road. Then she slowed down, and set Martine gently on her feet.

"We'd better talk," she said.

Chapter Six

The god thou serv'st is thine own appetite

(Marlowe)

There were no signs of pursuit as yet, and Simone took time to wonder if there would be – after all, it was wartime, no one had died, the escapee was merely a suspected thief: On the other hand, someone might link the wounds on the guards and their strange episode of unconsciousness to what had happened earlier, on the river, and since the Occupiers were involved in both incidents, might decide there was something more serious going on. She had time to ponder this because Martine was clearly in a shocked state, and no wonder. She stood on the blameless road as if it were a boat tossed about in a storm and she was trying to find her sea legs. She was even gasping like a fish…

Actually she was hyperventilating, and Simone had seen this before. Suddenly Martine went down – Simone's reflexes saved the girl from smacking her head on the ground. Her breathing slowed to normal again, the wise body having taken over the organism once more while the conscious mind took a break from its troubles.

"Should've expected this", the vampire whispered to herself.

Finally the girl stood up, and Simone explained to her, carefully, what she was and what had happened to her. She left out the bit about killing Hitler. Also the part where she wasn't French, not entirely, and also the bit about what she was doing in France. She was too schooled in caution to blab to Martine, whom she didn't trust. Not at all.

After her exposition, Simone let Martine talk, and it was quite enlightening. Her new acquaintance had big eyes and a rather hard little mouth, and seemed to be all about survival, not surprisingly. She shrugged off her involvement with the German in the hotel, and expressed no particular shame about consorting with the enemy, and as for taking money from the same, well, that was money that had left a German pocket for a French one, so the whole sordid business was downright patriotic, when you come to think of it.

Behind the bravado there was a young woman from a family that knew poverty and understood life to be a struggle. And Martine was anxious to avoid any more of it, whatever it took. This wasn't stated, but the single mention of her parents conveyed it all.

"They told me I was lucky, and to make the most of what I've got, so that's what I'm doing." said the girl bleakly. "I used to send money when I could, then one day, I thought, 'Why should I?" and stopped. So they wrote and told me not to come home again."

Immediately Simone found a softness in her new acquaintance's face which she hadn't seen before. She had a tendency to do that, to look for the loveable. It should have been vanquished by the realities of wartime, let alone the brutal and scary days that had followed her decision to go into Intelligence.

But none of this was getting them any nearer an answer to the problem of what to do next. And she was aware of a growing hunger, a hunger that partook of the even more urgent nature of thirst, and more than that, too; a whisper of cold air blowing around her thoracic cavity, as though her heart and lungs had been wholly removed, leaving her to miss their presence at her centre.

"Aaaaah *God* it aches so!" The pain of absence suddenly expanded to include the world.

"What! What aches?" asked Martine.

"I have to leave you, I *have* to." The girl was food, she was water, she was life. To taste her again would be to come in from the cold.

Simone sped away, crashing through the undergrowth, in search of something that would keep the craving away. It wasn't too long before she came across a fox, and its proverbial cunning was not a match for her desperate speed. But it was host to parasites already feasting on its blood, which was in any case thin gruel indeed.

She needed more... more. She kept moving away from where Martine was, and was soon rewarded by the outline of a darker barn against a dark but starry sky. It turned out to house cattle, who set up a lowing that in turn switched on the barking of an invisible dog. But she could not wait to see if a farmer turned up, because she didn't want his life on her conscience.

She leapt onto the nearest cow, and felt her teeth lengthen as she tore into it. She did not hold back. One taste and she was a mad creature, vacuuming the blood from the beast's veins, so that it keeled over quickly. She was merciless, all her focus on draining the animal.

At last she fell back, bloated again on the feast, her stomach swollen, as disgusting as it had been before. This time she was grateful for the cow's unwilling sacrifice, since it had stopped her becoming a murderer. She didn't doubt it she would have drained Martine this time, and there would have been no dainty sipping, or indeed, self-control. She was not sure why it was different from before, but she knew that it was. Maybe she was hungry, maybe she was tired. Maybe there was a limit to her ability to control it. She needed to understand exactly how this business worked in order that... Very well, she didn't believe in all the mumbo-jumbo anymore, it was for children, or the uneducated. For want of a better language in which to describe it – no, more than that – for want of a better cosmology with which to explain it – she was desperate to avoid it – she was deathly afraid of falling into mortal sin.

Thankfully there was no sign of a farmer. Probably drunk, she thought. How wonderfully simple a way to dull the pain of life, even if you did feel grumpy the following day.

She rose from the corpse. The taste of its blood was metallic yet earthy, like beetroot and rust. Although, not really. Like brown ale? No, not quite, except if you thought of human blood as champagne. But it was a false comparison. There was nothing like the taste of human blood to an appreciative vampire. Cocaine? She knew people, former bright young things with the burnish fading, who claimed to be addicted to cocaine. But it was an inessential luxury, like champagne, whereas blood to a vampire was necessity itself.

There were no comparisons. Although a real drug addict would sell his mother when desperate, Simone, too full to wonder or be shocked, knew that when *she* was desperate, and there was no substitute available, she'd eat hers.

So when she finally returned to where she'd left Martine, and found the girl cowering in the bushes at the side of the road, she was again grateful to the cow that had satisfied the terrible, overwhelming craving, and she was horrified at what Martine wanted her to do next.

"Make you a dark thing like me?" Yes, replied the girl, she was sick of being weak, of having to cajole affluent men in order to live, foreigners to boot. Yet, she confided, she wasn't fond of Frenchmen either.

"Can't you make a living in another way?" No, it seemed there were no opportunities due to the war, but anyway, she didn't want to sew, or clean, or work in a factory. The money was terrible and she didn't want to live like a slave.

Simone tried to tell her that slavery was the condition of the majority of people most of the time, and went on to suggest that things would get better post-war, as working people all over Europe demanded their rights. But Martine was not interested in political analysis or obtaining control of the means of production, distribution and exchange. She was interested in her own destiny to the exclusion of others' fates. She wanted what was good for herself, and she didn't want to wait for some dubious utopia. So Simone carefully and conscientiously described as well as she could the nature and the strength of the hunger she had felt so recently, and then she told Martine about the cow, and its barn, and the smells, and the degradation of it all.

"Fine," said Martine, "But you didn't eat me, did you? Not the first time you could've, not the second time when you were hungry, so you controlled it all right."

Simone despaired. "I could do all sorts of things, but I control it. I control it just as long as I'm able. But maybe one day I won't be able any more, and then that's it, I'm a murderer. I don't want to be a murderer."

Martine just stared, as though the most unbelievable thing that had happened to her in the last twenty-four hours was Simone's unwillingness to kill people; much more unbelievable than the existence of vampires, which, if the premise was accepted, was logical enough. Finally, she let it out.

"There's a war on. Didn't you notice? And I'm not stupid, even if I haven't had an education like you. Your accent is a bit strange. Might fool a German, huh? You're with the Maquis, I bet. They using vampires now?

You don't want to be a murderer? What the hell are you then? You're no lover of Germans, you've come to help our boys kill them. And what have your choices to do with me? I'm not going to murder people, I'll eat cows like you do.

Ah, that's it, though, isn't it? You don't think I can control myself because I'm an ignorant peasant and you think you're special!"

Simone had had enough. Martine was partly right. Well, mostly right, to be fair. Simone didn't trust her to control the urge and some of that was because she was who she was, what she did for a living and where she came from. Martine did not strike her as the type to worry about right and wrong overmuch.

Simone's own position was strange and contradictory. She'd come to France to kill Germans, true, but the main goal was to drive them out of the country and contain them within their borders. Now she meant to try and kill the dictator responsible for all the death and destruction. But she had spared the Germans she'd encountered, sipped at their necks and left them their lives. If she'd come across the ones in the boat before Graves had turned her she'd have tried to kill them, although she had not directly killed any during her time with the Resistance.

She couldn't be doing with this girl. How could she explain what was only now becoming clearer? That since she had accepted Graves's offer, she had become more sensitive to the underpinnings of reality, or rather, the shared fantasy that passed for reality, and it seemed that the more she was in danger of losing her soul the more aware of it she became? Or maybe that was all nonsense, and there was no need to bring souls, and by implication, God into it.

It was simpler than that. Working with the Resistance for the sake of stopping Hitler was something she felt more than good about. Even if she lost her life, at least there was an equivalence of danger. In fact the odds of a German surviving the war while in France were better than the chances of someone like her. Given all that, she was able to like herself for what she'd volunteered to do, like a Spartan facing the Persians at Thermopylae. Almost – they knew they would all die, whereas she just faced grave danger. And as for dying, she'd already done it, once.

And that made her thoughts return to Graves, of course, and how he had saved her life. Should she have died? Was it better to die young and blameless, before you had a chance to stain your soul? Maybe it was a chance to go through a door having succeeded in life, or at least, not having failed. Grave was the danger in which Graves had put her, certainly if she had a soul, and there was an afterlife, but even if there weren't, the danger was that she would loathe herself, for killing to satisfy her gnawing appetite, for treating a person like dog food. And then what? She would never experience a moment's peace again. She would be yoked to her vampire cravings, day and night, through an immortal existence.

No, better to end her life than live like that. How though? Hollywood was not necessarily a guide, nor was Stoker's turgid fantasy, though there was a celluloid consensus around stakes through the heart, beheading, and sunlight.

As for Martine's wish, it was impossible, she was sure. Wouldn't she have to take Martine's life, for a start? That was not going to happen.

"There are many reasons I'm not turning you. I'd have to kill you for it to work, I think, and I don't even know if it would work. I don't know how to do it. And I've only been like this for a few days, I might get worse. All sorts of things could happen to me, and you... you might not like it, but you don't have to put up with it. I do."

"Very well. What am I going to do then?"

Simone was not convinced that Martine was reconciled to her decision, but she left it at that. She dearly wanted to give her the money taken from her client – which she probably hadn't had time to earn, a thought which pleased Simone – and just dump her there. But that would probably not work out well. So this time she gave Martine a piggy-back as she made her way east to the next town. The girl seemed lighter than before, or else Simone was stronger than before. Could be the meal she'd had. Could be something more; the vampire nature taking over more and more of her being.

As Martine's small hands wrapped around her chest, she set off, springing along the road like it was made of something bouncy.

The night did not confine its palate to black and navy blue, not for Simone's vampire vision. She could see all the colours of day, but they seemed to be more of an aura around whatever the object was, like the ghosts of colours, as if the object had moved on and left them behind. Things seemed to shimmer.

She had no idea, really, of how far they travelled before arriving at the next town; twenty miles? She saw its mediaeval castellated gateway, its ochre walls, but no actual gate, not any more.

She stopped by the gateway, and Martine slid off her back and turned to her with questions in her eyes. Wordlessly, Simone handed her the contents of the German's wallet, as well as Martine's own bag. It was something, but it wasn't that much: She could tell by Martine's expression as she inspected its contents.

"So that's it then?"

"Yes. Good luck," Simone said, and before there could be any further discussion, she took a leap from a standing start right onto the top of the gate, where there was a walkway between the battlements. It petered out quickly, one side of the wall having collapsed, possibly centuries ago, but Simone didn't need much beneath her feet: Just the slightest touch was enough for her to float and spring, and she ran along those battlements remaining with no trouble, until she came to a place where everything had collapsed, and the circle of the old protecting wall was broken. Here the town was extending outwards, and the fallen stone had been incorporated into the newer buildings.

I need decent shoes, she thought. Mine have had it, ever since I tried to walk to England.

She dimly remembered somebody telling her to use brown paper when smashing glass, but the details escaped her memory, so she just looked around the dark town until she found a shoe shop. She put her fist through the window. It hurt, and her hand bled, and she watched it for a moment as the blood clotted and the scab formed, only for it to almost immediately drop off, leaving unblemished skin, with just a few streaks of blood left. She licked them off, and almost fell over at the fizz in her mouth, as if she'd bitten through a live cable.

Cripes, if that's vampire blood, it could almost bring the dead to life – well, it does, she thought, it did me.

There was no hue and cry. Perhaps they were all asleep, or perhaps they were too scared of Jerry to so much as to peep from behind closed shutters. Simone grabbed a load of shoes, and then slowed down and inspected them for size. She took several to try on. Then she thought that, after all, it was theft she was committing. And then she thought, there's a war on.

There was no hue and cry, which was odd. Simone had been long enough in an occupied country, though, to work out that locals who found themselves in such a position were likely to be very cautious about venturing out at the sound of trouble, especially if it happened after curfew. There was bound to be a curfew; there had been back on the coast, in the town near which she'd landed.

Then she saw the bank. Probably with a vault full of money. It was midweek, so maybe that meant it had not been taken away somewhere. Could she?

Could she rob a bank? Bloody hell, why not?

She wanted to burst out laughing at herself. You haven't changed, she thought. You're still the person who will be cautious and controlled and plan ahead as much as you can, and then, suddenly, you'll grow sick of it all and decide that no one, absolutely no one gives a damn if you're cautious and virtuous, so why bother with it? Who are you trying to please with all your internalised rules and regulations? Life is far too short. And that's when you do something ridiculous and unwise, like coming to France undercover in the middle of a war: Though that had been planned carefully over a period of months, and she'd had training... But the initial decision had been in one of the wild moments. The rest, if truth were told, sprang from the desire not to go back on one's word, not to look foolish and cowardly.

So rashness and the sudden desire to do something really stupid had consequences when you found out you'd committed yourself to a dangerous course of action.

Yet all these life lessons learnt weighed as nothing against the fiery urge to run amok, and perhaps it was more than ever a necessity, after the self-control she had exercised around Martine. It had been an effort: The cow had saved her from becoming a murderess, but there had to be a different release, to let go of the grip she'd had on herself, more or less safely.

It must be safe if I don't kill anyone. Everything else is a big... so what?

So she kicked in the door of the bank, and waited for something to happen, but nothing did, not even an alarm.

There was a front office, a counter, and divisions along its length demarcating each clerk's position. She made her way behind this barrier, and there was a studded door, thick wood, locked against her.

Now, she thought, how strong am I? Shall I take a run at it?

For God's sake, idiot, stop thinking!

She didn't take a run at it. Filled with anger at her own inner Hamlet, the hero who wasn't because he overthought everything, she smashed her right fist into the door, no run-up, just her arm drawing back...

And she punched a hole right through that dark, seasoned wood, with no trouble at all. Then she did it again. And again. And then she stepped through the wreckage.

She was in an office. The far wall included another, smaller door, this time made of metal.

No thinking was happening now, or to be precise, it was thinking of a kind, but not what she was used to. Something seemed to tell her, in a kind of shorthand, borrowing her animal instinct for survival, that she'd need more than a fist. So she looked around for some implement to augment her natural powers. All she could see, on a desk in front of her, was a paper-knife.

Useless... but she picked it up, nonetheless. Perhaps she could unscrew the lock, or something... but she was never any good with *things*.

Too impatient; another trait which has survived your transformation, she observed to her new, instinct-led self.

Well, damn you, weakling, said the new Simone to herself, and then she took aim, and for all the world like a circus act, threw the knife at the lock of the metal door with every bit of strength she could muster. No calculation and nothing clever happened, but the brute force at her disposal did the trick: The lock shattered and the door flew open.

Behind it was a kind of small cupboard, in which there were locked metal boxes. Simone was getting really impatient now: She grabbed a box, ignored locks and keys and all that fiddly nonsense, and just twisted the top half in one direction, and the bottom in another. That seemed to do the trick. The thing crunched and then snapped apart, and a pile of German marks flew out and over the floor.

She didn't want to cart a lot of cash boxes around, so she repeated this procedure with the other metal boxes until she'd got quite a pile, both of marks and of francs, which were a kind of secondary currency under Jerry.

She stuffed them higgledy-piggledy into one of the boxes. That lot should last a while, she congratulated herself, and made to leave the building.

But not everybody had kept themselves to themselves that night. Outside there were a couple of cars which hadn't been there before.

And in front of each of them, pointing some heavy sub-machine gun type artillery at her, were two German soldiers, and behind *them*, in their cars but standing, their commanding officers, gesticulating and pointing at her.

Simone was quite intoxicated with her own strength, as well as her sense of daring, at that point. This, a little voice remonstrated, was just the kind of mood people would be in when they drove too fast, or did other, similarly reckless things, and then met with utterly predictable ends; a consequence of their previous feelings of invulnerability.

She decided to ignore the voice, recalling how much Socrates – her favourite figure from what she remembered of that part of her education which encompassed Classics – had relied upon his daemon, specifically when it advised him NOT to do things.

You, she thought, you, voice in my head, are no daemon, just as I, I, the vampire of the Resistance, am no Socrates.

And then she leapt.

The bullets ripped into her but did not have the power to alter her trajectory or hobble her leap. She felt some of them and it really, really hurt: The pain was almost enough to obliterate her, a searing fire that demanded almost all her attention, but her healing mechanisms were so powerful that she could almost see the forces of protection rushing through her body to each site where she was wounded. Then she understood that the bullets were being pushed out via the wounds they had created, and that was not an easy thing to endure, even if it was necessary.

But by then she was wrestling with one of the shooters. And shortly after, with both of them. She was aware of the officers in the cars, trying to take aim as well. Her impatience with the situation was growing. Suddenly she'd had enough, and she upended one of the cars and flipped it over. The German in front of her blanched, and threw his weapon from him, his face twisted in terror. His colleague, another lowly squaddie, followed suit, and ran off.

She, having nothing to stop her, grabbed the other car and turned it, with ease, onto its roof. Squawks came from within.

She was pleased that they were all still alive. And having no particular grudge against them – except of course that they were part of an invading army with no right to be here, and that they had free will, and could have refused to fight, but didn't... could have overthrown their evil masters, in fact, but didn't, and so were culpable, however they tried to plead that they were only taking orders – apart from THAT grudge, she didn't have anything against them; not enough to kill them anyway.

So she ran and then jumped onto a crumbling piece of mediaeval city wall, and then she was over it, and in open countryside, still clutching her box of money, before they could collect themselves. She kept close to the road going east, though. And as she travelled, she pondered the culpability or otherwise of those who followed orders, and leaders, they knew, or suspected, to be wrong, and immoral, and murderers.

Was a refusal to use your own brain a good excuse for participating in an unjust war? And what if you were convinced you were on the side that was just?

Simone had always known that she was too imaginative for this espionage thing. A coward dies a thousand deaths, the brave person only one. And then the coward is still alive to write about it.

The risks she took were based on a very strong feeling that something was watching out for her. It didn't preclude her imagining all sorts of terrible stuff but there was always that intuition that things would work out all right in the end. And look what had happened: She'd died, or nearly died, and she was still here. Not exactly what she'd expected, but still. *Had* she died? Or not?

Dawn could not be far away and she did not intend to sleep in some damp iron age construction again. Living as a fugitive was no fun. OK, there was fun to be had, but with the cash she could buy an identity, maybe, that would let her travel in comfort. It would have been a doddle before the war, but now money alone wasn't enough, you needed papers that satisfied the invaders.

She was on the road, making swift progress eastward. This is like a fairy tale, she thought. Being a vampire is like having seven-league boots, although her steps did not carry her seven leagues... whatever a league was. More like a couple of hundred feet, at the most, sometimes much less, twenty, thirty, and then she'd touch the ground, and push off again, like she was sailing. Although, really, it was nothing like sailing.

Sometimes she grew impatient. It was much faster than walking, or even running, but it was slower than driving. She tried running movements as she pushed forward but it didn't make her go faster. It was always going to be more of a sustained jump than anything else.

She barely noticed a long stretch of stone wall, capped by sloping slate, like an extended miniature roof, and an opening in it, on either side of which were rather large gate posts.

And then, as she passed it, she heard a male voice.

"You look like you're enjoying that," it said, in English.

She stopped, and turned around, astonished. "What did you say?" she replied, in French, though she felt her stomach lurch with fear, just as it would have done had she been alive. (*Was* she alive?)

"Any language you want, love, it's all fine by me," the voice responded.

Then its owner stepped from behind a gatepost. Dark as it was, Simone saw him quite clearly. He had dark curly hair and – her enhanced night vision revealed – a sallow complexion, as though nature meant him to have a suntan, but he foiled it by never seeing the sun. He looked like a native of the Mediterranean regions, but his English had an accent that originated on Britain's shores. He's Welsh, she thought, very faint, but definite. And he was like her. Wasn't he?

He bowed, without self-consciousness, swift and formal. Like a German officer, she thought. From the First War.

"Yes, I am like you. Older, though. A bit."

"And you can read my thoughts?"

He smirked, and she bridled. He was already off on the wrong foot, if he was going to patronise her like that.

"No, that was a deduction about what your thoughts might be. We can read minds; it's not hard. But people are very transparent, on the whole. And I respect your privacy."

"Yes, but why did you speak to me in English?" Simone asked, changing to that language. "How did you know?"

He sighed, a little theatrically. "I suppose I had better explain some things to you. But that's fine, someone needs to. But first, let us make ourselves comfortable. And safe."

He glanced along the road to where the sun would eventually come up. It did look a little less dark.

"Follow me," he invited, and pointed at the drive between the gate posts. Simone wondered what lay at the end of it. Would he hurt her? Would he be able to? But she didn't feel afraid. She supposed he was as strong as her, if not stronger, being male and being older, but she felt she could give a good account of herself if it came to it. And she didn't fear death, notwithstanding her doubts about whether she was dead or alive. She certainly should have, would have died back there in the chateau, so everything was extra. She thought that if death were finally to claim her, she'd accept her fate like a good sport.

They walked side by side, at normal human walking pace, for a bit; but it was a very long drive.

"Wait," he said, "I'm hungry. And I bet you are." He sprang forward. On the left of the drive was another paved track, which quickly deteriorated into squelchiness. They were in a farmyard, and she could smell the rank cattle smell, and hear the sudden lowing as the imprisoned animals caught the scent of the two hunters nearby.

"Now, this time don't kill, just take what you need. There are enough of them," her new acquaintance advised.

Without another word he moved, predator fast, and was dining on one of the beasts, which sank onto its front knees. It seemed like only seconds until he released it, and it wasn't dead, just a bit stunned, though it was hard to tell with the creatures. Then he moved on to another. Simone saw the pen that contained them, and it seemed they realised there was no way out, and no way to express their terror as he moved among them.

But they lived through it, and something like happiness awoke in her chest. Such was the relief that it brought her, this proof that she did not need to kill to live, that she wanted to laugh aloud, out of pure euphoria as well as at her own foolishness in not working this out for herself.

He turned to her. "Aren't you hungry?"

"Just a little peckish," she smiled, as her heart danced like a slave whose chains had just been struck off. "I had a big meal earlier." Then she moved to one of the animals and turned its head to her. "A snack, then." And she bit, and sucked, till she felt the beast weaken, and immediately stopped.

"Of course, now we stink of farmyard," her new acquaintance complained.

"I've done this with people," she said, "but it didn't fill me and I was afraid I couldn't be with them, couldn't control... be able to be with them without..."

"Yes, I know; without wanting to eat them. The secret is not to let yourself get too hungry, and to fill up on the animals' blood. No need to eat them, either, and sometimes, oftentimes, the owners don't notice: They're weak for a bit but then they make more lovely blood. And there are circumstances when you can nibble on a human too, but best to fill up on these first."

"Otherwise?"

"I think you can guess. Ask anyone who's tried a reducing diet. It's easier to eat in moderation if your food's not very interesting."

Simone wanted to ask more, but she sensed that her companion had said all he was going to on the subject, for now anyway. He reached out.

He took her hand. "Come, dawn is near, let's hurry."

They sped up the drive, hand in hand like lovers, and Simone was content to let him lead her, God knows where. It didn't take long until a quite decently sized chateau hove into view, and she wondered if it contained Germans, as most of them did now. But why would he take her into danger?

The drive was long but they covered it as fast as a motor car would, and before long they were through an arched gateway with no gates, into a courtyard. The walls around were covered in ivy and other growth, and the place had an air of decay, not uncommon now in occupied France.

Her companion found a door, studded as if it led into a church, and turned the handle. When it did not open right away he shoved at it, and thought the wood looked old and hard and black as stone he must have broken the lock, as the door then swung open.

They stepped through into a corridor that was unlit, empty, and stuffy with dust.

"Where are we?" asked Simone.

"We are in the home of a very old... acquaintance of mine. Come, I'll introduce you."

He took her hand again.

"Wait," she demurred, "Hold your horses. You haven't introduced yourself, yet."

65

He stopped to look at her. "I am most dreadfully sorry," he responded, with a smile that demonstrated not the slightest bit of sorrow. "I like to take my time, not to rush things, and it's different for us, you know, we have all the time in the world."

He bowed, and although he wore unexceptional clothes, she somehow could easily imagine him in – what were they called? Gaiters? – rather than trousers.

"How old are you?" She blurted, suddenly needing to know.

"Don't you want my name first? It's Philippe, if you're interested."

He might have added more, but a door along the corridor opened, and a face peeped out from behind it. It was a face that not even a mother could love, Simone felt sure. It grinned, but that may have been due to the largeness of the teeth, which would not allow the mouth ever to properly close. The hair was wispy thin and grey across a blotchy scalp, and the eyes were pale and set close to each other. The impression was that the owner was a simpleton.

Philippe grimaced. "Hello Pierre. Where's your pretty brother?"

"Oh, Monsieur, you are funny! He's here."

The speaker came out from behind the door, followed by his brother, who looked like a twin. Both were, and reminded Simone of grisly little humpty dumpties, being more or less round, as if they had an equator where the waist should be.

"Don't be fooled, dear lady, these two are no country Quasimodos, simple yet kinder than the average. These little horrors are as we are. Without the scruples. Or the self-control."

Simone shuddered inwardly. By what means then did they keep themselves alive? She realised that she knew.

But she did not allow her expression to change, unlike Philippe, whose lip curled as if he were tasting rancid milk.

"Where is your mistress?' he demanded. "Take us to her."

"Of course," replied one of the twins. Simone chided herself, ashamed of the conclusions she was jumping to. She was not her father, who would have...

What would he really do? Surely not kill living human babies? Would he have smothered them? Or exposed them, as the ancients did?

No. Rigid and cruel though his philosophy was, he had outlined his thoughts to her when she was old enough, which in his mind was when she started at university. He wanted to sterilise the likely parents of such children, and abort those already on the way. How, she had asked, would they know who was going to have handicapped babies? What if they grew up all right after all? Would he differentiate between physical and mental handicaps? Surely someone whose intelligent mind was stuck in a faulty body must be allowed to live? What about those slightly simple children that families often described as being loving, and a joy to be around? Couldn't he see what would happen, police going round to people's homes where neighbours had reported a child had been born... a child that was not quite right, but the family was concealing? As for sterilising unwilling citizens, it was surely unthinkable. And at that point, the conversation was over, because news from the continent had for quite a while now featured the Fascists doing just that sort of thing. Her father drew back from saying, even to his only child, that Hitler was on the right track, although she suspected he may not be as circumspect with his cronies.

So then her father would declare that she was a sentimentalist, and she would get upset, because he was a loving father whom she loved back. The thing was, he was just not imaginative. So he could not imagine what might befall other people. It was strange. Probably his education had beaten out of him every vestige of imaginative sympathy.

A little voice in her head attempted to whisper that she was just making excuses for him, but she pretended she hadn't heard.

Philippe and Simone followed Pierre and the other, indistinguishable twin back through the door and into a room which had once been comfortable, even luxurious, but now was a perfect illustration of decayed glories, with great windows the height of the room, whose existence one was forced to assume due to the massive but slightly ragged curtains in red taffeta, shot with gold, along one wall. The room had four doors off it, including the one they had just come through. Decrepit chaise-longues were pushed against the walls, and above two of them, great ornate mirror frames hung, empty of mirrors, on either side of which were wall-mounted candelabras, most of their sockets empty but for a couple of tremulous flames. In the middle of the ceiling there was a magnificently ornate chandelier, not one of whose sockets boasted candles, or if they did, contained mere stubs, unlit.

They crossed the room to the opposite door. Simone thought the room was laid out like a very badly kept museum, and when she went through the next door the sense of antiquity haphazardly preserved was even more vivid.

Across this room, on a dais of some kind and in front of the door that would otherwise have faced them, sat a woman, on a chaise longue, with her legs curled beneath her, posed like the Empress Josephine might once have been, and wearing a dress such as she would have worn. Her hair was dressed similarly, too, and at first Simone thought she was looking at a painting rather than a person.

The illusion dissolved as Philippe approached. The twins hurried to place themselves in front of him, chattering and tutting. It seemed Philippe was breaching protocol.

"We must present you!" they fussed.

Philippe elbowed them out of his way as if they were brambles that had a hundred years' growth around this beauty but were still mere brambles, and worthy of no more attention. Unless they scratched with thorns grown big as daggers.

"Madame Edith," he began, "after all this time, your beauty remains undimmed."

The person dressed like an empress in a painting extended a languid hand, and Philippe bent over it.

"May I introduce my companion, Mademoiselle Simone?"

He waved an arm towards Simone but Madame Edith did not so much as glance at her, so Simone saved herself the trouble of a greeting. So she was *that* kind, woman or vampire; the sort who took no interest in members of her own sex, except to ensure they took nothing, especially not attention, from her.

"What do you want, Philippe?"

"Madame, I am desolated that you think only of what I might want, when I am here visiting you," he responded.

Madame rose from her couch, and Simone saw that she was extremely tall for a woman, slender and very pale, with hooded eyes and delicate bone structure, with a high-bridged nose quite unlike that of Napoleon's empress.

Suddenly Madame's attention switched to her.

"Yes indeed, my dear, I can read your mind a little, and how uninteresting your thoughts are! But for your satisfaction, yes, her nose was flatter and broader, but then she was Creole, you know, which explains it. Horrid scheming little thing. She begged for the secret of my eternal youth as her beauty waned, but I pretended not to know what she was on about. Now look at me!" And she laughed, but it was an old woman's cackle.

Simone was stunned. Clearly Edith could read her mind, and if she was deliberately dressed in Empire style then perhaps Simone's train of thought was not especially opaque, after all... but was she serious? She was clearly a vampire, then... but alive since the Napoleonic era? Or at least, not quite dead.

Of course her train of thought at this point was particularly easy to follow. Madame made no comment, perhaps deciding it was too easy and that she had nothing to prove to a nobody like Simone.

How old was Philippe, then, she wondered.

The object of her interest seemed as adept at mind-reading as the beautiful vampire on the couch, but they seemed to be old acquaintances anyway. He turned to Simone.

"She is telling the truth. It is possible for us to survive indefinitely if we are careful. And it is impossible for us not to get good at reading minds, since people are so transparent. It gets easy, then it gets tiresome, and then it gets so one can hardly be bothered being with them. I am older than she, if you want to know."

"Indeed, my little Welsh dwarf," Edith sneered, "and back when you came on this earth they didn't have much spare to feed you." She seemed to be alluding to Philippe's height, although it was average. Napoleon himself had suffered similar diminishment in the popular idea of him. Perhaps that explained Philippe's shrug.

"While you were a pampered darling, a parasite. Just as you are today. Some things don't change."

It seemed Philippe was abandoning his courtly manners. Simone couldn't blame him. This was a horrible woman. She wondered how many people Edith had killed. And how much, or how little, it had bothered her. She also wondered about that witchy laugh, which sounded as if it issued from a much older throat.

And he was about her height, on the short size for a man, but certainly not a dwarf.

And anyway, why had he brought her here? Was it because he just happened to be going this way?

Edith laughed again. "Thank you, I like my laugh. It has been called adorable."

"Not lately, I bet," responded Simone, who was getting fed up with her.

Madame snarled, like the elegant predator she was.

"You want to know what he came here for? He's trying to bury it in his mind, but he can't. He doesn't have the self-control... or perhaps he has, but it's always in use, controlling his taste for humans. I know what he wants, it's screaming in his mind. He wants to kill my servants! My loyal servants!"

At this, she threw herself on Philippe, biting and scratching, and the twins began to shriek.

"Run, Pierre, run," cried their mistress, and devoted herself to impeding any move Philippe might make.

Can they both be called Pierre, thought Simone. Well, why not, she decided, they're pretty interchangeable.

"Help me," cried Philippe, who was wrestling with the tall vampire. It didn't take Simone long to decide to go to his aid. He might be all kinds of betrayer, a villain, with who knew what designs on her, but the vampire named Edith was a shamelessly nasty being. Between them they subdued her and pinned her down.

"Now what?" asked Simone.

"I kill her," was Philippe's reply.

"No, no..." she replied, shocked as much by the matter-of-factness of his tone as by his intention.

"She's a conscienceless killer. Like me. Do you want this roaming the world?"

"Like you?"

"Yes, but I'm different. I'll tell you later."

"Please..." whimpered the woman they were kneeling on.

Philippe removed himself, leaving Simone still kneeling on Edith's chest, pinning her arms down. As soon as he moved, Simone could feel the strength of her opponent. She herself was growing in strength, and she was aware of it each night that passed... but if this one here was a lot older it could mean she was a lot stronger.

"I've got a job to do. And it didn't include killing her, till now, else she'd have read it from me. But sometimes things become clear that were hazy before... Still, if you want to preserve this antique a bit longer..."

"Well, you don't want her interfering do you? Help tie her up or something."

"Christ..." he swore; an unusual exclamation, Simone supposed, for such as he. Philippe grabbed at the bit of Edith which wasn't pinned under Simone; fortunately it was her legs, and they were kicking against the fabric of her dress, the bottom half of which he ripped away. Between them they shredded the fabric enough to tie Edith's hands and ankles together behind her back.

"It won't hold, so you'd better stay here and mind her till I get back. I'd advise you to stuff her mouth too."

"What are you going to do?" Simone asked, thought she knew the answer.

"I'm going to exterminate some pests," he replied.

She said nothing in reply, as he left. She wondered at her defence of Edith, and her contrasting silence on the subject of the fate of the twins. It was unlikely that they had done anything worse than Edith had. Perhaps they'd even done whatever it was for Edith. And yet... They were not well formed, unlike their mistress. Simone had been brought up to despise disability and to think that even wearing glasses was a weakness. She had always thought such opinions cruel. But the twins were not just formed oddly. Inside – well, he'd said, hadn't he, Philippe had said... they were sick inside; mad, or retarded – or both...

"You hypocrite," said Edith, trying to turn her head, the better to berate her captor. "Just because you think my little fellows are ugly, you won't plead for them. How will I manage when they are gone?"

"Shut up," exclaimed Simone, giving her a kick. "You'll have to get by like everyone else, your ladyship."

"What, hunt? Myself? Like a common poacher?"

"Oh. So your servants poach do they? What, animals?"

"Oh yes, of course. Animals. That's why I can't do it. Beneath me."

"Why do they serve you anyway? They don't need money from you, do they?"

"They are imbeciles. Stupid and wicked. Whereas I... am only wicked."

It became clear that she'd been faking helplessness. She tore at her bonds with sharp teeth and though Simone leapt it was too late to stop her releasing her hands. They rolled across the floor, like dogs fighting, as Edith tried to free her ankles and Simone tried to prevent her. At one point Edith was on top, banging Simone's head against the floor so hard and for what seemed like so long that she felt it would crack open. But Simone managed a punch that sent Edith flying and left her sitting for a brief moment, a little stunned, against a wall.

Simone was about to jump on her opponent but paused to think how it could end. Would she kill Edith? How? Would Edith kill her, or would they just fight till exhaustion set in. And how long would that take?

The pause was a bad idea. Edith suddenly jumped up and hared off, jumping nimbly over her sofa and through the door behind. Nothing could have been further from the bitchy aristocrat she'd portrayed, languid on her chaise longue, as they had walked in. She was like some giant insect, one of those famous for lifting several times their own body weight or jumping their equivalent of a mile in one leap. And she was no helpless, enervated madame waiting in the dark for her revolting servants to keep her fed. She was extremely dangerous, not to Simone and her new acquaintance, but to everybody else.

She didn't follow Edith through the door, but went after Philippe. She couldn't take Edith on alone, she realised. Two of them were needed or else there'd be stalemate.

She would have been bewildered by the corridors and rooms, but for one thing. She could smell him. It was not unpleasant, but to her enhanced senses it was distinctive. As she went on she could smell something else; Pierre. Or perhaps... the Pierres. They smelt indescribably horrible, rank yet sweet, oily and redolent of a sick room where someone has lain ill for a very long time, and nobody has opened the windows.

Then she heard a high pitched wail, which was suddenly cut short, and she ran the length of a dusty hall to an archway from which steps led to what must be a lower floor. And then she smelled the unmistakable smell of death – old death too, not related to that scream.

She stopped, and saw Philippe's face emerging from the darkness below. It might have been the light, but he looked yellow and moved slowly. He looked up at her.

"You probably don't want to go down there."

"What is it?" she asked softly, although she knew the answer.

Suddenly she saw his mind, like a picture spread out. The basement was a charnel house. She saw what he had seen, rotting corpses, bled dry, some dead a long time but not old when they died. Some children.

She shut her eyes, but she could not stop seeing.

"Were any…"

"Left alive? No."

"How did you… oh."

She saw through his eyes, and saw him kill the twins. He had used chair legs, which he must have acquired while pursuing the creatures, and they had not resisted him, which was strange, as it was two against one. Perhaps they wanted an end to it, their horrific existence, or perhaps they knew Philippe was stronger and they didn't want to prolong the pain. He'd plunged the splintered wood right into the core, not quite into the heart, which lay to one side, even of those twisted forms, but into the very centre of the chest. The first Pierre had made not a sound as he disintegrated into dust. The second, on seeing his brother's fate, had emitted the wail she'd heard. He was even easier to kill than his brother.

"I suppose Madame Edith got away from you?" he enquired.

"You can read me, you know." Simone was curt, embarrassed by her foolishness.

"Actually I usually refrain from that kind of intrusion unless I'm invited," was the response.

"I'm sorry, I should have listened to you. How could they have got away with it? The villages round about here… Didn't they want to take vengeance, somehow? Could they take vengeance?"

"There is so much you need to know about this half-life you have embarked on. Yes, if they organised they could destroy a nest of even three. She likes to put on airs, but she and her creatures have only been here since just before war was declared. Vampires don't settle down. It's too hard to get variety in one's diet. People notice if their family and friends disappear. So cities are best. But Edith swore she was only going to dine on animal blood, and the country was the best place for that; with the aid of Pierre and the brother…"

"I think they were both called Pierre…"

"Er, right. Perhaps. Anyway, the idea was to keep cattle, use them for food, and lead a quiet life. The truth was that Paris was getting too hot for her, we knew that. She liked the taste of human too much, and the word was getting out among the human population that something crazy was hunting them on the night streets…"

"'We' knew that? Who are we?"

"I'll have to tell you using the slower, clumsier method, I suppose. You'll get the hang of reading the pictures in people's heads, it's quite easy, you just look – in a sense it's not reading at all. But where there's narrative, and explanations, it becomes a bit tortuous, and the old-fashioned way is better. Best way to tell you who 'we' are, for example.

There are not many vampires in the world at any one time. There is one major reason for this. We are sad and desperate creatures. The life of a human springs from the heart centre, awakened by the tides of breath. All that is suspended for us, so we do not die, but we don't experience joy, or real laughter, or lightness of heart, because that dances in the living core of a person and ours is still, and brittle, and cannot dance. This awful heaviness and lack is such a burden that most of us commit suicide."

"But that's not true!" exclaimed Simone. "I felt happiness in my heart... well, like you said; not exactly my physical heart but right in the centre of my chest. It was like a fountain, bubbling up, and it made me want to laugh: It was when you said we didn't have to kill to survive, not even animals. I felt so happy!"

"I'm so sorry. That was a residual response, as you are so recently changed. I suppose you could compare it to water, yes, as if there was a little water left in the fountain after the main supply had been turned off."

Simone suddenly felt terribly afraid of the future.

"You still haven't said who 'we' are, or why you said you were different to Edith."

"'We' are vampires based in Paris and England. There are just a few of us. Well, three and just four including you, now that Edith and the twins... Ah... we refrain from killing humans. It's not so hard to just drink a little... And you're going to ask me why didn't Edith do it. I could be flippant, and tell you to ask her yourself... Perhaps I will, at that. Come on, let's finish the job, then I'll finish my explanation."

At that he strode back the way they'd come; back to Edith's reception room, and through the door indicated by Simone.

The rooms were gloomy, large, and mostly empty. They explored them together, but it soon became clear that anyone who wanted to could hide in the massive house for as long as they liked.

But they didn't have to wait long after all: They were retracing their steps when Edith emerged from the shadows to confront them. There was no need for a verbal explanation, as she was easy to read, desperation and anger almost making her glow as if about to ignite.

Philippe's explanation was helpful, as far as it went, for Simone could read something else too. Gruesome thought the Pierres had been, they had been Edith's companions, and she really didn't want to have to cope without them. She was not consciously suicidal, but Simone knew that she had suddenly stopped caring whether or not she survived.

While she was sensing this, Philippe had already leapt, brandishing the chair-leg which had recently seen service as an instrument of execution. It was not sharpened, just snapped off, and its ragged end was in no way pointed, but the strength Philippe possessed was enough to drive it through steel, or so it seemed in the vision Simone had of him killing the Pierres. She gasped as Edith blocked him and leapt back, and then into the air and back again.

She had no weapon, but still Simone leapt too, missing her moving target as Edith grabbed a bit of curtain and shimmied up its length. Simone jumped after her and heard Philippe cry 'Careful!'

Edith was just above her but the great swathe of curtain had been doing duty in this room for a very long time indeed and the material began to tear beneath the vampire's scrabbling fingertips. Simone felt it go beneath her grip as well, then a big strip parted from the rest and they both began to fall as it peeled away from the rest of the material.

Dawn had broken a little while ago. Sunlight streamed through windows that were filthy but above all, big. The female vampires screamed as they collapsed onto the floor, but were quickly covered in the falling curtain, which was only briefly their saviour as the ancient material obeyed the inexorable laws of entropy and, telescoping centuries, swiftly collapsed into dust.

Simone rolled away into the shadows beyond the pattern of light now on the floor and the mighty stream of it coming through the window. She didn't see what was going on with Edith at first, but then she heard the screams and still lying on the floor rolled round to see what was happening.

Edith's route away from the morning light was towards the further end of the room, but Philippe was blocking it, wielding his chair-leg. The scene would have taken a lot of explaining to anyone who'd just walked in on it, for here was a tall, elegant yet delicate beauty, dressed like a Jane Austen character if she'd written about the French aristocracy, the ones who'd survived the Revolution, who was trying to get up as a vicious man prevented her from doing so with a battered bit of chair. Then suddenly the woman's arm seemed to catch fire, for no reason, then flames started to engulf her feet. She made it onto her feet and tottered towards the safety of the dark, but just as she was nearly there Philippe flung the makeshift stake at her from as near the sunlit area as he dared to go, with such force that it knocked her over. There was an incandescence and a pillar of flame, a glimpse of bone and smoke and then, like her servants, Edith was dust.

The flame that devoured her had been very hot. There were burns on the wall behind. Simone felt like she too was on fire and she looked at Philippe across a large patch of sunlight. He gave her a smile, but it was rueful rather than happy, which was to be expected after what he'd said earlier.

"Go back into the dark," he said, "Cool down as quick as you can. I'll find you: I'll go round the long way."

Simone followed his advice. She understood it had been a near miss for her, and she felt stupid. He had conquered the other vampire without endangering himself, yet she, despite all the careful training of her instructors, had not learnt the most important lesson they had tried to impart: you're no good to anybody dead.

Chapter Seven

A house of bones is this body

(Dhammapada)

So they met up again, eventually finding each other in the depths of the house. Simone felt as though she'd been scorched, although there were no marks on her body at all by the time Philippe appeared.

"We heal fast," he said. "But that was too close. The sunlight doesn't burn us like a fire would burn a human. It burns very hot, more like the temperature needed for a cremation than anyone would normally encounter; outside of the newer weapons of war, or in a steelworks, perhaps, I don't know."

"Well you wouldn't, having been born before the Industrial Revolution," Simone retorted.

"You don't believe me? Read me, then."

Simone looked at him, and as clearly as if someone had painted a picture of it in front of her, she saw a bucolic vista, a hazy skyline with distant towers, peasants pushing carts in the middle ground, and in the foreground, people sitting looking at the view, dressed in elaborate style considering the topography.

"That's not real, I've seen that! It *is* a painting."

"And I can make you see it, which is quite clever of me. But you're right, the last time I thought about the past I thought about this picture, not my old memories, just a reminder of a memory. I can make it more real for you than that, but not yet. I'm sorry. Perhaps it's just that I have to know you first, and hopefully, trust you."

"Look, I don't care about how old you are. Teach me how to be a vampire without being a killer. Teach me how to live this strange life. Half-life. Were you looking for me? Or just her? You don't want to kill me too?"

"No! At least, I don't think so."

Simone wanted nothing more than to leave this horror of a house. She didn't like being there, thinking of what was in the basement, still. Humans did not die as cleanly as vampires did. They left a corpse behind.

"Yes, I want to get out of here too," said Philippe, quietly. "But we're stuck till nightfall."

"Tell me then, why are you here?"

"To kill two birds with one stone. Well, kill three, help one. I was sent from Paris. I was to find you, help you, maybe kill you. Sorry. We sensed your birth into our world, we always do. Edith would have sensed it too.

My task was to find you and try to convince you to refrain from taking life. Any life, ideally, not just human."

"Why? Are you vegetarians? How weird, for a vampire clan!"

"It makes it easier all round if we don't kill at all. We do use butchers if we need to. But you know the Bible says Thou Shalt not Kill. It doesn't say who, or what. It doesn't specify."

"Are you so religious, then? Isn't that also strange, for vampires?"

"Maybe if you stopped interrupting..."

"I might learn something. Sorry."

Philippe paused, gathering his thoughts. Simone could almost see them, like a complicated sky with lots of different cloud patterns, cumulus, mackerel, nimbus, all at once.

"I have taken human life, as have many, humans and vampires, in this war. I began many, many years ago. Yet only a couple died at my hands, before I repented."

Repented. Such an old-fashioned word, which wasn't so surprising. If he were indeed of Welsh origin, wouldn't he be non-conformist, or something? Simone didn't know enough about history, but she was sure everybody was a lot more religious in those days, whenever those days were.

"I repented and vowed to never kill again. But the weight of one murder is equivalent to that of many. Ordinary rules of arithmetic do not apply. A person is a universe. A person is a Christ. A person is oneself. So repentance is futile and redemption impossible. The other members of our... club – all two of them – think as I do. They do not feel as I do. They cannot feel, and nor can I. However, we can mimic feeling and can even live with ordinary human beings. We can train ourselves to be both kind and rational.

I have researched my situation and studied religions other than the one in which I was brought up. They all have a core of truth surrounded by a fog of lies. One eastern religion has a holy book that states that there is something called Atman, a little man no bigger than your thumb, that sits enthroned within the heart, or more properly, the heart centre in the middle of the chest. Don't laugh! It is true, but also a metaphor... and no, that is not the same as a lie, quite the opposite.

When that little man departs, nothing is left but dead flesh. Except in our case. The little man departs, but the breath is captured, like a beautiful princess in a tower, always at the moment of departure but not quite gone... so we survive, oxygen coming to our brains via the blood of others, preferably our own human kind. But we cannot feel. I have no empathy or kindness in me. I feel as if my heart were a glass cage in which I have preserved a flicker of life. The thing is, I have trained myself to behave correctly, by an effort of will. I act, I hope, kindly. It was kind to remove those three. I benefited the world and they were dead anyway. Their lives were not precious. They did not have lives, so I did not kill."

"But I feel! I do! I felt joy! Today I felt it..."

"It is residual. I told you. And I know what you'll ask next. Feelings of dread or anger are from the solar plexus centre and are properly sensations, or even emotions, rather than the feelings I mean. They are the fight or flight reflexes that are part of our animal nature, only modified, of course, by the human mind. We retain these. But we do not feel kindness or joy, although we can be kind, when appropriate, as I have explained. We are cut off from God."

"Cut off from God! How mediaeval!" But Simone felt – or sensed, or emoted – scared of what he spoke about, the loss of the ability to enjoy... anything.

"I'm sorry if I am not communicating the way you want me to." He spoke stiffly. "Perhaps I am explaining it badly. People these days are more... literal minded. I didn't think I needed to explain to an educated person that I don't actually think that there is a little man camped out in the middle of my chest. It is both a metaphor and real at the same time."

"I didn't say anything..." But she didn't need to, of course. He could read her sceptic sneer. Actually, so could most people, she suspected. It was hard to keep a poker face, and a certain kind of statement made mind-reading skills redundant.

"It is a very loose quote," he went on, "From the Upanishads, which are books in the ancient Indian Sanskrit tradition. The Atman is one and the same as the Adam Kadmon figure in the Hebrew religion. It represents the real human, the indwelling divinity in each person. It is the same; in everyone. The other personalities we have are constructed out of culture, family, and experiences. They are subject to death, but the Atman is eternal."

"Wait... what? What are we then? Without an Atman in us, are we just rubbish on a roadside?"

Philippe looked weary. Whether it was because of her daft questions or because he was tired out from killing vampires was debatable, and after all the need for sleep did not go entirely, though she noticed it had dwindled since her transformation. She could not let him doze yet, though.

"Would you kill me if I started killing people?" she asked.

"Yes," he answered. "Once I would have argued with you. I would have tried to make you see reason. Now, I know that people don't change much."

"Well, read me. You know I am intending to kill someone, and you know others will probably get killed while I'm trying. This is a war, Philippe, a great big one. I was trained to kill, and I accepted that I would have to. Doesn't it make any difference that I'm not *preying* on people?"

"I know you doubt my claim to be older than Edith, and she was fond of claiming she knew Napoleon. She was that old, but vampires are name droppers as much as anyone and as far as I know that bit was fantasy. The trouble is you get very old and after a point you can't be sure if your memories are real or if you read about 'em in a story. That problem can afflict humans too, and we get a lot older than they do. It's not all about the brain in senile decay either. We avoid that but there is still the sheer weight of years. But you don't need to know my birth date and I don't doubt my own memory. Believe me when I say I remember a big war, too, the war to end wars, they called it. But look at us now."

Simone felt the tug of impatience. Which bit of her did that spring from, she wondered. Well, OK, not the heart. But nothing to do with animals, either.

81

"Your restlessness; it's the desire nature, thwarted, and channelled through the negative mind," said Philippe wearily. He'd read that, easily enough. "No one is immune from that. An animal is not able to choose, and is controlled by instinct and desire, which is correct in them. In humans there is mind, negative and positive. Like blood."

"You speak in riddles and embrace superstition."

"We're the stuff of which superstitions are made! And we're real, aren't we?"

"Stop this, let's just speak and ignore the mind pictures. I want to kill Hitler, you know I do, and it's completely in line with what I joined up to do. It's not personal, it's an extension of my job. How can it be wrong to try?"

"First of all, it has been tried before, you know. Many times, actually. The failures were not down to stupidity, on the whole, but to extraordinarily bad luck. As some would say. Me, I think it's fate."

"Fate, clever. Well, we moderns believe that we make our own destiny. Fate! You needn't worry that I don't believe you're really old. In fact, I think you're even older than you let on. You hint of Napoleon, but I think you're pre-enlightenment. Fate! You really have a mediaeval outlook, you know that?"

"I know of vampires of that vintage, but I am not one of them. I will travel with you. I will neither assist or prevent you from your goal. After all, he is not prey. As you say. But the fact that it's not personal is neither here nor there. 'It's my job' is not an excuse. One thing I am convinced of is that no one gets a free pass to kill by saying they were told to do it by some superior officer or whatnot. There is a reckoning. We vampires have seen enough death to know that."

"What if I don't want you to come with me?" asked Simone, exasperated.

"You cannot stop me, and trying would take all your resources. You'd have no opportunity to assassinate him then."

And he'd read everything I intended to do to try and lose him, Simone thought.

She shut her eyes. She felt tired, just a little, but it wasn't her body but her racing mind that needed rest. When she awoke it was evening; Philippe had drawn a curtain in this room back just a little, very gingerly no doubt, and she could tell by the light that came through that it would not be long till dark. She felt hungry and thirsty all at once. She looked for Philippe and he entered the room almost immediately. He must have sensed me waking, she thought. He held a beer tankard which he proffered to her. She could smell the blood.

She grabbed at the tankard and drank as if she'd been crawling over desert sand for days.

"There is more in the kitchens. Cow, since you ask. Bloodletting might be a bit mediaeval for you, I suppose, but it's a useful skill to have. The cow still lives."

"Thank you," said Simone, as gracefully as she could. Manners cost nothing, her mother used to say.

"You know, you can't drink water. You do know?"

Well, makes sense, thought Simone, remembering the seawater that felt like jelly.

"It would choke you, most unpleasant," Philippe went on. "You get everything you need from blood. We can eat, a little, for show… We can even drink water if it is mixed with other substances, but never try it by itself. That's where the story about holy water hurting us comes from. Mind you, some say it is because all water is holy, because molecules of it touched the body of Christ – and Confucius, and Buddha – all the holy ones. No vampires are atheists, though, so maybe they bring it on themselves out of sheer religiosity."

Simone did not reply to this. None of it made sense. Religious vampires? What. Graves, and Edith? And the twins?

She might have known there'd be a reply to the thoughts she could no longer keep to herself.

"They were religious, all right. They just believed they could not die. They're all terrified of dying, because they know they've offended the Divine by sundering the bond between It and Its creation. But you, you could die now, clean. I know, I can feel it."

With what, Simone wondered. Heart, mind, or that hole in the centre of the chest where what should probably be described as his soul used to be?

"If you killed me, would it count as a human murder?"

"Count with whom, or what?"

Great shivering Christ, she thought, this fellow's going to wrap me in the philosophical knots which I think make him happy in some way. Keeps him from the utter misery he's told me is my vampire birthright. Let's keep him practical, if I can.

"So... we can cross water?"

"Yes, we can, but not by wading or swimming. By boat, or plane, or bridge. Wading takes ages. "

So that was something less to worry about. Simone and Philippe went down to the kitchen garden when the sun finally went down, where a placid cow was chewing the grass. They each drank, in turn, till Simone felt the heart begin to slow, and stopped. Philippe nodded and no words passed between them. She could recognise that he was approving her restraint, because it was a necessary habit that she needed to acquire. It was only a cow, but one day the habit she was trying to form would save someone's life, and perhaps her own soul, although despite Philippe's ramblings she wasn't convinced that she had one. Anyway, he was wrong to say no vampires were atheists. He'd left her out. She was a lapsed Catholic who rejected all the mumbo jumbo. And proud of it.

They left the chateau, and immediately Simone felt cleaner, although she could do with another of those strange showers with water like jelly blobs. The filth of the chateau and the horrors they'd uncovered were for others to find. The building might have been a fine piece of architecture but she would have liked to burn it to the ground. But if it caught alight properly, it would draw attention from many miles around. And if it didn't burn fiercely, and very few fires would be that all consuming, there would be a terrible mess for someone to find. And there would be some who'd attribute the massacre in the basement as her doing, and if they knew of him, Philippe's.

They hit the main road, and Simone turned east to continue her journey. Philippe reached out and took her hand, and they moved through the air in literal leaps and bounds, hand in hand. It was almost romantic, and for the first time she contemplated Philippe's profile... and instantly drew back from the thought. Dammit, is nothing private anymore, she thought. And she was annoyed to find herself flushing, something easily spotted, she supposed, by the night vision of a vampire, although for a vampire, biologically inexplicable. Perhaps it was residual, a reflex, like her feelings of happiness were alleged to be.

It was a fine night and the moon was slightly fatter than it had been; the clouds skittered across the moon playing games with its light. Nocturnal creatures, like themselves, went about the business of survival, some of which entailed the death of other creatures. Simone considered this, but reached no conclusion. She knew that Philippe was probably picking her thoughts up, and it was an easy, comfortable awareness that she didn't have to speak, though slightly less comfortable was the growing conviction that he had learned to hide anything he didn't want her to perceive. Of course he had, he was maybe centuries older than her in vampire terms, although only about half a decade older than her in human years.

"How did you become a vampire?" she asked breezily. And then another thought occurred to her. "Where do you live? When you're not inspecting new converts and killing old ones, I mean."

Philippe dropped her hand and alighted on the road, slowing to a walk as he did so. Simone joined him.

"We shan't get on quickly if you insist on demanding my life story," he pointed out. "Which is fine by me. It's your self-chosen mission, not mine."

"Knowledge is power. I'd like to know about the Fuhrer's security arrangements, but I doubt you have that knowledge. But you know about what I am, what we are. And what we can do."

"Very well. Most important stuff first. You are immortal so long as you stay out of trouble, which for us means sunlight, even through glass, unless it is tinted. You can sustain the most terrible wounds yet recover quite quickly. But you know that. You cannot recover from a beheading. Or a stake, not through the physical heart, but through the core of you, into the centre of the chest. That is known as the Wheel of the Heart in India – in Hebrew lore it is Tiphareth, the heart of the cosmic Man – the very definition of the phrase 'the old Adam.' The stake must be of wood. This is because Set trapped his brother Osiris in a wooden chest – the eternal godhead was imprisoned in the coffin of the body, it being like death to be born into this world- from the perspective of eternity."

"Right, so is that it? Stake, sunshine, beheading? And I heal quickly. The other stuff you said... Doesn't make much sense to me. It's just confusing."

"I am sincerely sorry," said Philippe, "I was a teacher once, but not a good one. It seems I have not got any better." He sounded very sincere, and she looked into his sorrowful brown eyes, to see that he was. "And I want to say," he went on, "That I am terribly sorry for what has happened to you, and I would not have wished it on you. I wish you could survive the war as a human, and have a happy life, perhaps with babies and husband, if you want, and a life spent serving humanity, as the doctor you were training to be, with a place in the world, and a place in the sunlight."

He looked so mournful she thought he would cry. But he wasn't feeling sorrow, was he? Oh wait, yes, he's said we can be unhappy, but not happy... That was it, wasn't it?

"Sort of, yes," he answered, and she realised it was in response to her thoughts. This alarmed her, and for some reason she herself didn't understand she thought, very deliberately, somehow – almost *loudly* – what about desire. Yes, that kind of desire!

He did not blush, which was unsurprising, given how old he was. He'd probably grown out of it by now.

"Yes, "he said gravely, "but it is unleavened with feeling. Sensation is present, of course. Loneliness may drive us to seek the fulfilment of that desire, but when it is sated we are still alone. Emotions of fear arise in what you might flippantly call 'the Gut Chakra".

"What emotions? Aren't emotions the same as feeling?"

"Fear of loss comes from the agitations of the gut feeding into the human mind. It is foolish for vampires to indulge in feelings of loss, or worry about potential loss, as we have already lost everything."

"Our lives?

"Our souls," he replied.

"You are such a merry companion!" Simone exclaimed irritably.

"Oh, I am sorry. Please, let me make it up to you. I'll tell you my tale.
I was born, not in mediaeval times, as you like to joke, but in the eighteenth century, in Wales, the son of a good man, but one much troubled by religion. We were better off than most around us; my father managed an estate for an English milord, who didn't visit often. So we were well fed and clothed, and even schooled. When we fell on hard times, it was a huge fall. My father ended up being transported to the colonies for the so-called theft they call poaching, and the man who sat in judgement was also the supposed wronged party. The rest of

my family died out, not long after, of poverty and disease. Cholera, actually, from standing water drawn from an unclean source shared with many others.

There was a revolution about to explode in France, and its effects were being felt all over Europe. It scared the daylights out of our putrid rulers, hence their mad over-reaction to any dissent. We should have chopped their ghastly aristo heads off as well, in solidarity with the French.

I left England and was soon in Paris, at the centre of things, and huge upheavals were taking place. I was afraid, yet as my friend Wordsworth wrote: "Bliss was it in that dawn to be alive, but to be young was very heaven."

"What! You are claiming acquaintance with Wordsworth now?" Simone pretended outrage at this claim, but she was secretly entertained.

"Certainly, but it is no matter if you disbelieve me. Be that as it may, I was soon caught up in the Revolution and witnessed it decay into a blood letting, for all the world as if the Aztecs of South America had all been reborn at once, and wanted vengeance for the seizing of their hearts from their bodies, by demanding heads!"

"Is that possible? I don't know about these Aztecs... are you saying we are reborn? En masse?"

Philippe sounded apologetic. "Please, I am making a creative connection that probably does not exist. And I have only recently become acquainted with scholarship dedicated to the Aztecs. Theirs was a spectacularly unpleasant civilisation. And since I did not know about them at the time, this is a post hoc comparison, a whimsical thing, I assure you... only God knows why the beheadings got so out of hand! Let me continue, I promise to be less fanciful during my story..."

"Oh, don't worry," responded Simone. "I quite like it when you're fanciful. Better than sorrowful, anyway."

"Well. There was probably justification for the blood fever of the Aztecs: There was undoubtedly justification for the sacrifice of so many to the guillotine. By which I mean, someone thought up a reason, and others pretended that there was a reason behind it all, because they wanted a good excuse to kill lots of people.

So when I was made a vampire..."

"Hang on," exclaimed his companion, "'How comes before 'when'!"

"How – I'll tell you later… I just couldn't resist it. At first I was only drinking from people whose death was scheduled by the revolutionary government. But once I followed a woman home… a bit of comfort, I thought, a moment or two out of the frightening chaos around us all… she was pretty. Her home turned out to be a mansion, whose owners had just lost their heads. She was a squatter there, so I understood, and why not. They weren't coming back.

I played with her stupidity, as she lured me into the bed they had so recently vacated. It added to the thrill, the fact that I was still alive and enjoying what they would never enjoy again. But then, I grew hungry and I let my guard down. The desire in me grew, and it was too relaxing: I lay just a little too long, and felt my kisses turn to bites and my greed overwhelmed me. But I gave her the choice…"

"Ah" said Simone. "Not much of a choice though, is it?"

"I could have drained her dry. So that was my choice. She was an unhappy, empty creature. She wanted a comrade. No! Don't ask me about the others, it'll become clear in due course. Anyway, she chose life. Like me, she was young. We had seen a lot of death. I showed her how to survive and taught her to kill. It was easy, then. I made sure to bribe the guards to let those who might be interested believe that there were many deaths in custody.

Belle laughed at me for being particular, and not just helping myself to anyone I came across. They're all dead anyway, she said. If it's not the guillotine that takes them, it'll be plague, or hunger. And for those that survive till old age… if they make it that far they'll be begging you to put them out of their misery, for that is the worst of life, when you are subject to daily torture from your own body. And she would shudder at the thought of growing old.

And I would answer and tease her that she'd never grow old. Then, one day, we went to the house of our most recent victims, who were unwise enough to tell where they had lived before their arrest. Of course, those who snatched them for the guillotine were first into these houses, and had helped themselves to any desirable loot which the occupants had been fool enough not to hide away in the country. But, having put the householders out of their misery, we decided to stroll along and see if there were any pickings left.

She was experienced enough, and should have thought, but everyone slips sometimes. In that house we encountered a large mirror. I beg you, do not look in mirrors. It is said we cannot see a reflection, but it is worse than that. The mirror gives a true reflection, because we are supposed to be dead. I saw myself as a corpse looks when it's been dead a few weeks. And I saw her, a rotten bag of bones, flesh and hair flaking off, and empty eye sockets... you cannot imagine.

But when we looked directly at each other, I saw a pretty woman, and she saw a well set up young man."

Simone stopped, and turned to him. "What do I look like, then?" Her voice was tight, and she felt like she was being strangled, so hard was it to get the words out.

"You will look like someone who has been dead for... as long as you've been dead. A few days, is it? But only a mirror shows it. To me, you are a very fine looking young lady."

Simone thought of all the times she'd thought she was too fat, or her eyes were too small, or she was too masculine looking, or her hair was too fine and *would* just hang there. And now... all those thoughts had been a complete waste of time, her time, her extremely short time alive in the world. She felt something all right. She felt utterly cheated.

"Don't," said Philippe. "you were trying to help the Resistance. An early death was always on the cards for you. Why did you choose to seek it by doing something so inherently dangerous? And there are plenty who have had very short times on earth, thanks to the war, even if they chose to try and stay out of danger, instead of running towards it."

"This is your story you're telling, it's not my turn. And if you were born in Britain you're really called Philip. And stop reading my mind!"

"I'm sorry, but I had to comment. The pain was coming from you in waves. I recognised it. It was too strong to ignore."

"Pain? How do you know? You can't feel... feelings!"

"I can see it in your face. And I know it's bad. I didn't want to cause you suffering but you have to know about this, especially since you could be caught out this way if someone looks in the mirror when you're in front of it. I'm so sorry."

"I am revolting, disgusting, a foul thing walking. I…"

Simone wanted to die. Philippe stopped and took both her hands in his.

"It's hard, I remember that moment like it was yesterday, and since it wasn't yesterday, I am sure I look even worse now. Or maybe not, maybe it's been so long that there's only clean bones, or dust. I am not interested in finding out.

Anyway, it was from that moment that I ceased killing human beings, even those facing the executioner. Let him be the one to bear the weight of sin. I had a heavy enough burden. As for my little Belle, I could no longer allow her to kill, either. I told her this, and she laughed in my face. I had no compunction about killing her. Not only was she dead already, but I had seen with my own eyes. When I determined to kill her, I made it easier on myself. I set up a mirror, and concealed it. This was only a couple of days after I had first looked into one. I pulled away the covering when she and I were in front of it. She screamed in horror, of course, and I withdrew the sharp stake from within the waistcoat I wore and thrust it in her heart chakra…while looking at the vile apparition in the mirror. I was fond of her, you see."

"*Fond?* Chakra?"

"It's an Indian term, means wheel, refers to the energy centres in the body, which, like all of creation, are constantly moving."

"And fond?"

"We were lovers."

Simone tried her best not to think 'Well, that's answered *that* question' but she suspected her efforts could only fail. Philippe just looked down and was quiet for a moment, either in memory of his dead love or embarrassment because he knew what Simone was thinking.

She quickly changed tack. "You killed your lover? And Edith and the twins? Am I next?"

"You don't have to be. Just don't kill people, that's all."

Simone was thinking of a snappy reply when they heard a distant sound, the sound of an engine, that was getting nearer. By silent mutual consent they backed off the road into the scrub that lined this part of it. As the vehicle got nearer, she was aware of a new phenomenon, which seemed to be the ability to hear distinct and different sounds more clearly, as if they were louder than in her pre-vampire days, and for some reason the engine sound did not override the voices she could also hear, which could only come from within the vehicle. What was remarkable was not that the sounds were enhanced, but that the louder did not drown out the softer.

"It is because you are tuning to the wavelength you want. It's automatic, if you think about it, it makes it harder. It's like a wireless, with interference from adjacent channels. You must be used to listening to signals that have some interference."

"Sssh!" Simone said. "And don't think it can't be heard. We don't know who is in that! You know who made me, of course you do, you know all about me, it seems. There may be someone with hearing like ours sitting in that... car."

There isn't, said a voice in her head. You'd sense it. She shot her companion a filthy look. She didn't want him invading her mind, even to be helpful.

Now they could see with their night eyes not only the shape but quite a bit of detail of the vehicle: It was no mere jeep, but a purring Mercedes, and both of them could distinguish the voices as speaking in French, only one spoke it heavily accented with what was surely German.

Simone tensed herself to go to the rescue of the Frenchman, whom she immediately presumed to be a Resistance member going to his death or torture at the hands of the Boche. Already she could foresee problems, like how not to kill but just to disable the Germans, and how to free the prisoner without word getting everywhere about the existence of vampires... but Philippe put a hand on her arm.

She listened to the conversation. How... she wasn't sure, but Philippe, she knew without asking, was not fluent in German, though he could follow it. He was like a native in French and of course, English and Welsh. He had had plenty of time to pick up a few other languages, too, if he'd wanted to.

She half expected Graves to be in the car, but as it drew closer she didn't hear his voice, and in any case she knew she would have sensed him, miles off. But the conversation was interesting enough, even so.

From the two vampires' perspective, they were privy only to the middle of it.

"This is extremely irritating. The papers will be in the name of Jean-Pierre for the first name? But you can't tell me the second. How many of you people are called Jean-Pierre, and will be boarding the train that day? Hundreds, the trains are running all day! I've never heard of such a thing. Seems to me they suspect someone. You must have given the game away."

The other voice was that of a native Frenchman. As she listened, Simone was shocked more deeply than she could have thought possible.

"No, no, I have given away nothing. It is a precaution. Clearly they have learned from the last time. I delivered for you then, didn't I? Obviously you still need me and my friends. People always get more careful when there is a failure and that is it. It makes it more difficult... for us all, of course."

"You want more money, then, I suppose? Well, for the sake of German lives, we'll pretend to trust you. For a while."

As the car passed directly in front of where they were hiding the voices went silent, but Simone found she could sense the minds. There were four in the car, including the driver and another passenger who had not spoken. Three were German, and their overwhelming, shared thought was of superiority over the fourth occupant, the Frenchman, who was either Maquis or well acquainted with them, and was busy doing a Judas for the sake of a few francs. The driver was thinking about Dante, and the bit in the Inferno where Satan continually eats Judas and Brutus, the archetypal traitors. Simone was too, but she didn't expect it from the driver. She chided herself. You're a snob, she thought, but you'll never be an Edith.

She thought then that she would eschew and avoid all thoughts of superiority towards any human being... or vampire for that matter. The Germans in the car were right. They weren't as bad as the Frenchman. But it gave them succour, that thought, it gave them an unholy pleasure. There were, she thought, holy pleasures. I'm not sure what they are. Probably now I'll never find out. But it's definitely unholy to look down on others, even if they're begging to be despised, like this chap. It's bad for the soul. She glanced at Philippe and sure enough, he smiled back knowingly. He'd read that from her thoughts, and yes, he liked that she was thinking that way. Souls and stuff. And she was impressed that she'd picked up the fact that his German was not very good.

But the car was past them now and she wondered what to do. This Jean-Pierre or whatever his real name might be, was perhaps a saboteur, and he was being betrayed. It was not beyond the Germans to search all the trains they needed to, and probably the fellow had already imparted information about what day the sab would travel, and what station he'd take the train from, and what his mission was.

"We'll follow them," said Philippe. "We can travel that fast, and we can keep to the side of the road."

"But I'm hungry," Simone murmured. I sound like a child whining for food, she thought, but I am dangerous if I don't get any.

"It's all right," he answered. "We'll snack."

So they followed, and when a fox crossed in front of them, Philippe leapt. Luckily the fox crossed from the other side into the shadow of the bushes where they skulked. Less luckily, it tasted rank. Simone complained, but she drank with gusto, shamelessly. He was the same, she knew: Neither of them were fit for polite company, or any company except each other's.

It was exhilarating, though, this travelling through the night, following a traitor and his contacts. Oh, yes, there were irritating bits, like the infernal bushes and undergrowth in the shadows of the road where they had to conceal themselves and move fast at the same time. But there was a technique whereby you could land very gently and push off from an unpromising surface, like a branch, or the top of a bush. You didn't have to hang around, although gorse was a bugger to land on, even if you didn't stay long. Their night vision helped. Even with the moon, it would have been very difficult if they hadn't some inkling of what lay ahead of each step.

"About twenty miles, thirty kilometres or so..." Philippe suggested, in response to an unspoken question regarding the speed they were travelling. "They're in no rush. It's more of a mobile meeting place than a car, and from what I just caught they're actually returning from an outward journey."

So they'd driven their informer out of town for their meeting and were now driving back.

The car slowed still further as the nearness of a town announced itself. There wasn't much in the way of lights, but the road suddenly developed tributaries and large, looming buildings announced the presence of factories. Simone knew that if those factories had been making anything of interest to the Allies they'd even now be in danger of dying in an air strike but although many factories had been forced to change over to war work these weren't among them; it was more than likely that they no longer operated at all.

The car drew quietly to a stop, one of the back doors opened, and someone hurried out. The individual in question wore a hat and a muffler, even though the night was warm, and an ill-matched suit and jacket.

The question of what to do next resolved itself as they realised they didn't want to lose either party. Simone didn't need to say a word. She would follow the traitorous Frenchman, while Philippe went after the car. She wondered briefly how they'd find each other again, but she hadn't got round to asking him that yet. She hadn't asked him about loads of things... she hadn't had time. But she was sure they would, even though the telepathy ceased to work as soon as Philippe moved off.

He was able to follow his target immediately, but she would have to cross behind the car's back windows and it was possible she'd be spotted. She waited, seething with impatience and anxiety lest she lost her prey... Hang on, even in her thoughts that was a word she'd probably be better off not using.

At last the car vanished down a side street, some way down the road, and although she couldn't see him she knew Philippe was on its tail. She broke cover and went as fast as she could across the road without drawing attention to herself in pursuit of her... quarry. Yes, that was better.

She couldn't believe it when she made it to where he had been and he'd vanished. There were no side roads now, just looming industrial buildings, possibly unused, clumped together in the least desirable part of town. There was no undergrowth now for her to hide in, just weeds, which didn't provide any cover, and lots of broken fences; no wire netting, so maybe the occupiers had requisitioned it. The broken fences looked like an excellent source of sharpened stakes, ideal for the enemies of vampires, who, to be fair, seemed so far to consist solely of other vampires.

She tried listening, trying to focus on the heart of the sounds of the night, but all she heard was the reproaches of female cats against their males' rough mating. They always sounded like witchy, possessed children, to her. The noise stirred the not-quite-satisfied hunger till, very fast, it rose up, trying to possess her. She had to drop her pursuit because she dared not catch up with the man feeling like this. It wasn't just the hunger and thirst wrapped in one that she was experiencing, but also her eager mind, tripping over itself to persuade her that a delicious meal, free of guilt, could be enjoyed if she caught up with this man, who emphatically deserved not just to die, but to die in suffering and indignity.

What, asked her mind, are you playing at? Before you were turned into a vampire you would have regarded the killing of a traitor as absolutely the right thing to do, and moreover, necessary. It is still the right thing to do and it is still necessary. He is a danger to the Maquis, and to the Allies, and to an unquantifiable amount of innocent people. To remove him from this world is a good and worthy deed, and you will enjoy a wonderful feast at the same time.

All that was true. She couldn't argue with it. She'd helped kill a vampire, because it was a danger to innocent people and could never be trusted. They were at war, not arguing philosophy in some university college. What am I to do, imprison him for the duration? And feed him till the Germans are driven out of France? And if I don't kill him, and instead hand him over to the Maquis, they'll certainly kill him, so does that make me just as guilty? Possibly, and I wouldn't even get a good meal out of it.

She took a break from pursuit for a swift snack of cat blood. She quite enjoyed catching them, and although the first bite into animal skin and fur was disgusting, it was also exhilarating, and when the blood gushed it was more; it was intoxicating.

She killed the little animal, but she hadn't meant to. It was just so small, that it was hard not to drink too deeply. She felt a kinship with it, because it was another living thing, and that delighted her, because it meant that she still had a heart, or whatever Philippe was pleased to call it. He had compared her human feelings to water left in a hose; a residuum that would eventually dry up, leaving her either a soulless, vicious killer or a guilt-ridden shade walking the earth begging for its meals of blood.

The cat did not die in vain. It took the edge off her hunger and allowed her to regain control. But the villain of the piece was out of sight. Even with her enhanced senses, she'd lost him. She spent some time trying to catch a sound, or a scent that wasn't cat, peering through a night that was twilight to her now, when once it would have been pitch black. Eventually she gave up, furious with herself for losing the man, and went back to the junction to pick up Philippe's trail.

She wasn't sure she could do this. After all, it wasn't as though she had become a werewolf. But following his scent proved easier than she'd anticipated, because although her nostrils were filled with cat, the smell of the fox's blood was different, and like a wine connoisseur she could identify its essence: Some drops of blood must have clung to Philippe, and they left a fragrant signature in the air.

It was a fair-sized town, all blacked out and gloomy now, of course, but in what must be the town centre there were a couple of bars, as well as hotels.

She traced the fox blood scent across the square and it stopped in front of the largest hotel, from which came the sound of laughter as well as that of a piano, on which someone was thumping out a lively tune. There was no sign of Philippe, and she wondered what to do. She paused outside the front door; should she hide? Would he find her?

Then the door swung open and a smiling uniformed German came out, swaying slightly. Simone stepped back into the shadows, as he was followed by a young woman. She was smiling too, and they looked like any young couple in love.

They wandered off into the darkness. Simone tried to be disapproving. The girl was whoring herself to the enemy. Yet she hadn't seemed to hate the fact. Perhaps, in the middle of all the insanity of war, these two had really fallen for each other. But ordinary infantry would not be allowed in hotel bars. The fellow was an officer, and that made a difference to his culpability.

Well, what the hell, she had more important fish to fry. She was swiftly reminded of this when she noticed that the door remained slightly ajar, and, peeping through the opening she saw her companion. He was the one playing the piano.

He saw, or felt, her presence at once. "Cherie!" he cried.

So we're a pair of French collaborators now, she thought. Good, I can do that. My German would never pass, though, and neither would his.

But what do I look like? Last time I washed was yesterday and I've been in a fight and a fire since then, and my clothes are too tight. And any French woman would surely wear lipstick on an evening outing. And have I got blood on me?

Philippe wore the same crumpled shirt and tweedy, rather autumnal suit as he had when she first saw him, although she hadn't really thought about his apparel at the time. He did look a bit on the casual side amongst the uniformed Germans but it didn't stand out as odd. He could have passed as a professional musician in his appearance, but also in his playing, which was really very good. Simone supposed he'd had more time to put the practice in than is given to most people.

"Darling!" responded Simone, which would do as a reply till she had worked out what was going on.

He got up as she walked to him, and embraced her, which would have come as a surprise, except that he took a moment to wipe a finger along her jawline, and she knew he'd surreptitiously removed some cat blood. He must have dealt with any fox blood on himself, somehow.

"Let me get you a drink," he said, but a nearby German, definitely an officer and perhaps with experience of the first world war by the look of him, shouted his intention to stand the two of them drinks.

"Your man is an excellent player," he said. "He just came in here and sat down at the piano stool and magic flowed from his fingers!"

"You're a lucky woman, then," said another man, in much poorer French than the previous speaker. Someone guffawed at that. Philippe looked fierce, and leant forward as if to make a retort. It was an act, of course, but the innuendo was unmistakable and the code of masculinity demanded that he react appropriately, or be despised. This kind of situation could get nasty if the occupiers decided to assert their power by humiliating the man.

Not that that was how it would go.

Fortunately, the first speaker cut short Simone's speculations about exactly how things were about to go.

"Silence, you animal!" he bellowed. The whole room went quiet. This gentleman here," and he inclined his head in a little bow towards Philippe, "has played some popular tunes for us, out of the goodness of his heart. Unlike the rest of you peasants, I can tell that he is in fact a virtuoso, a maestro of the piano. You will respect him!"

His underlings looked sheepish. Simone idly wondered what his rank was.

"Thank you," said Philippe, which sounded heartfelt, but couldn't have been, if what he'd said about himself were true.

"Any requests?" he asked the room, and then played a bit of the first movement of what Simone thought of as That Tchaikovsky One.

She had no idea how difficult it was to play, but it sounded terrifically hard. And terrific. And exuberant, which didn't chime with Philippe's claim not to 'feel', whatever he meant by that.

Philippe's admirer applauded like mad as Philippe switched back to a popular melody, and begged Simone to join him at his table. She was concerned. The fellow might ask questions, basic ones like 'where have you come from? Where are you going?' And... 'how did he learn to play like that? At which conservatoire did he study?'

She had just swiftly concluded that it would be all right, that they could get their stories straight even though they were physically apart and had had no time to cobble a story together, because this wonderful faculty of vampire telepathy would help them make sure they were singing from the same sheet music, so to speak, when she realised something. There was a mirror.

It hung in a corner, along the wall against which the piano lived. The senior officer and a couple of other similarly important looking types sat at a table pushed against the wall at a right angle to the piano. If she walked towards them she would be reflected.

She beamed a smile at the officers, but made no move. They'd be getting impatient. She sent her thoughts to Philippe. She felt a strange sensation: He was pulling away from the music in his mind. She could hear it become less intense, something she'd never experienced before.

Can you see the mirror? She asked. She felt his shock. Can they all see what we see? She asked.

Yes, he responded. Go around. You'll be a glimpse by a drunk. It'll be OK. I probably won't show up at all.

She moved away from the piano, towards the door. Her would-be hosts looked puzzled. She smiled again, as flirtatiously as she was able, hoping they'd think a circumnavigation of the room was standard French behaviour when invited for a drink.

The mirror now was far enough away that she could move across the line of vision, a background figure there for less than a second. She took the plunge.

She was past the danger zone incredibly quickly, though she didn't know how or if she could move over such a short distance with the sort of speed she could muster over longer ones.

It was a pity she hadn't mastered the technique yet, as it happened, because she heard the most terrible yell. One of the Germans sitting near the door leapt to his feet and screamed something in German that she didn't understand. But she didn't need to, because the translation was immediately fed into her brain by Philippe, who understood more than he could speak.

"There is a ghost here, a devil!"

Everyone rose, cursing, she presumed, and shouting, and pulling out guns. It was no surprise they were jumpy, and no surprise they were armed; foreign invaders in a resentful land, their lives would be in jeopardy as long as they remained in France.

It was chaos for a moment, but the piano fan was no fool. The variable tonight was the arrival of mysterious and talented strangers. So if something happened that seemed like a potential threat to the occupiers, then it probably was caused by them.

He turned a different face to Simone then. Her complicated manoeuvres around the room had preceded this outburst of strangeness. Nobody seemed to be linking the vision of death to her though.

"You have an explanation, Madame?" And he pointed his gun at her.

We have to get out of here, said a voice in her head.

Or we could have a bloodbath, she thought back.

You'll have to do it all yourself, was the response.

"This place is haunted," she cried. And then, she had what she thought was a moment of inspiration.

"By us!" she exclaimed, and ran to Philippe. He immediately knew what she had in mind and didn't demur. He let out a manic laugh and played a few bars of the Sorcerer's Apprentice, which he speeded up, while they both laughed wildly.

It was dreadful, hammy acting that would have raised sneers at a Hallowe'en party, but in this context it was just the trick.

There was a pause full of bewilderment, then one officer shot at them, a few bullets each to make sure. And they kept on laughing, and Philippe kept playing, while a look of total horror came across their would-be killer's face, and he stumbled backwards.

This was a signal for gunfire from all directions as everybody else shot at them, while of course none of it had any effect, although Simone began to fear for the safety of the bar staff. Some of the bullets were ricocheting. She didn't worry about the Germans, oh no, of course she didn't. They were all, without exception, evil; they were officers, for goodness' sake, they had chosen to be here.

A picture came into her mind of what Philippe planned to do next. She understood his reasoning. After the guns proved useless, the Germans might go in for some unarmed combat, which would be dangerous, not least to them. Part of her wondered if it mattered but concealment was the vampires' friend. If it became known that monstrous, strong and invulnerable (as far as anyone knew) creatures were attacking Germans then Hitler's security would take steps to protect him, obvious target for monstrous etc. Allies supporters that he was.

Philippe picked her up in his arms, as if she was a wee weak girlie ghostie, and he was the stronger. Then he made towards the door. It was potentially difficult to defend himself against blows, hampered like that, but it was another way to throw people off the scent, and mislead them as to what the vampires really were. Fortunately there was a hesitancy about their attackers, not surprisingly, and unlike the novice Simone, he had got to grips with whatever was needed to cross short distances at speed. They were out of the door in a flash, and in another step he had jumped right up onto the roof, with Simone still in his arms. It was an impressive leap, and enabled them to 'disappear' in a more effective way than if he'd just run to a road leading off the square, which might have given the Germans a chance to spot them. Not that they couldn't have outrun them, but a disappearance fitted better with the ghost personae they'd adopted.

They looked down to see pursuers tumble out of the hotel, the first one taking a surprisingly long time to get out there into the square.

"I hope this hotel has a ghost story attached to it," murmured Simone.

"If the proprietor has any sense at all, he'll be making one up right now," Philippe replied.

"There's some hard-headed soldiers down there. I know they can be superstitious, I've met some. But those officers are seasoned old boys, they can't be falling for this."

"Listen, said Philippe. "You can almost hear their minds."

Simone listened. "I *can* hear their minds."

But the detailed thoughts of the senior officers were impossible to distinguish amidst the white noise of the crowd that poured out of the hotel.

"It's not vital," said Philippe. "I picked up that you lost the traitor, but I was able to keep tracking my car."

Simone could not hear the least trace of blame, or gloating, or self-satisfaction at her expense, either in his voice, or in his thoughts. He was either training for sainthood – an odd goal for a vampire – or he was just totally pragmatic, uninterested in wasting time on what could no longer be helped. Or both. He gave her a slightly stiff smile; probably he'd picked that thought up.

"The traitor has told them there will be a bridge blown up tomorrow... today, actually; it's way past midnight. The explosion will take place as a train loaded with arms crosses it. There will be no civilian casualties, as even the driver and his mate have been warned to jump clear. My fellows were debating whether to arrest them and replace them with their own, or whether to arrest them once the bombs had been removed from the bridge. They came to the hotel and started busily sending messages. Word came back that the most important thing was to arrest the bombers, as many Maquis as possible, because they were making life very difficult. So they're already sending key people to the site. Then they decided on a little relaxation in the hotel bar."

"What are we waiting for, then?" demanded Simone. "You might have said earlier instead of entertaining the bastards!"

"I had to wait for you," he replied gently.

"How far is it?"

"It's in Lorraine."

"But that's hundreds of miles!"

"No, about a hundred. Don't you know where we are?"

"I thought we were in Brittany!"

"You're underestimating the speed you've been moving at. And we can make it, but we're hitching a ride. There is a night train; actually a very early morning train, and it goes our way."

"How do you…"

But he took her hand, and they jumped from roof to roof, unobserved by the Boche running about below. He led her to the station without much trouble. His facility with mind reading was so much more advanced than Simone's, she realised as she worked out how he did it. He was scanning for some mental chatter about having to get to the station and he found it; a couple of members of their former audience were bidding farewell to their colleagues because they had a train to catch.

The train in question was sitting in a station that was a glorious confection of glass and steel with some fetching art deco touches adorning its nineteenth century sturdiness. The locomotive emitted a little steam as its drivers prepared it for the journey.

"Let's catch it on the way out, that'll be the easiest thing," suggested Philippe.

So they sprang upwards, running up the walls at full pelt until they encountered girders they could hang on to. There they perched, like nesting bats, chasing the pigeons away. At last the train gave an ear-shattering whistle, and they moved along and down, until they were just above it as it moved. Light as dandelion seed on the wind they floated, rather than jumped, onto the roof of the slow-moving train.

The top of the train was curved, and not easy to hang onto, unless you had the easy balance of a vampire.

"We're heading into the sunrise!" exclaimed Simone.

"Well, you're the one who wants to involve yourself in the wars of the living. It's not without risk."

"What will we do?

"I wasn't intending to travel all the way like this."

So after a while they lowered themselves down over the edge, peering through windows. The first one Simone tried had people in it. Given the time of day, they were asleep, and she quickly withdrew her head without them waking.

The next compartment was empty, so she just hit the glass with her elbow. She was loath to make a noise, so she held back, and the first blow failed to break the glass. Annoyed at herself, she put a lot more strength into the second blow, and the glass shattered. Philippe was behind her, and the two of them stepped through the window and into the compartment.

"This is a mess," she said. "Let's go somewhere tidier." So they left the compartment and peered into the next one. A man sat alone, staring out of his own, intact window, into the darkness.

"It's him!" said Simone in a loud stage whisper.

"Careful, you're reflected in his window," began Philippe, but it was too late. She saw it, this awful, upright, days old corpse, and next to it, some very old-looking stained brow bones, crowned by a skull with a gap-toothed rictus grin.

The man saw it too, and screamed like a schoolgirl having a giggle with her friend. But this was a scream of terror. He turned around and saw them, his jaw dangling open, then back to the reflection. He drew a gun.

"There is no point in shooting," said Philippe, opening the compartment door. The fellow pressed himself back against the window. He had evidently decided that there was no point in speaking either. He just fired his gun at Philippe, trembling in terror as he did so; but the tremble didn't matter, there was no way he could miss.

He fired five shots into Philippe. Each one must have hurt, but he seemed stoic about being used as a target. One shot in particular made him grimace, and as the gunman watched, he dug it out of his chest with his hand, covered with blood.

At last the man found his tongue.

"Are you here to drag me to hell?" he cried. "Demons!"

Ruth Lewarne

"Isn't that what you deserve, traitor? The world will be your hell when we tell people what you've done!"

"Very well, I'll leave it; by my own hand, though!"

And he put the pistol to his head. Neither vampire made a move to stop him. Simone didn't know what to do with him, certainly she could think of nothing resembling justice that wouldn't result in his death anyway. She wanted to ask why he did it, but his time was running out... and Philippe just looked on, his face registering no emotion, in line with what seemed to be his policy of non-interference in human affairs, unless his new vampire colleague insisted on dragging him into them.

Then their quarry pulled the trigger.

The noise was very loud, and even though the train was quite noisy Simone was sure it would be heard. Meanwhile the man's body slumped back, and from his mouth came the final breath, visible to the vampires like a small, gently pulsing cloud of light. It spread through the compartment and somehow they heard it through the sound of the train. Simone could hear the sound of its passing. It seemed to fill her ears, for a moment, but she hoped that no one ever asked her to describe it: There were no words that wouldn't sound wrong. Something washed over her and she felt ridiculously humble. She wanted to kneel to it; the soul of a traitor!

She stole a glance at Philippe. He was smiling very softly, his head bowed, and his hands pressed together as if in prayer.

The light and the beautiful, still sound faded.

"That shot must have been heard by the whole train," said Simone, and her voice sounded like someone else's to her ears, as if it came from far away.

Chapter Eight

Thou bleeding piece of earth

(Shakespeare)

Time does not stop, even for eternity. Trains don't, either. The soul, if that's what it was (though even to give it a name seemed a blasphemy) had departed the body of the man in the corner, and as a consequence, all that was left was carrion. Simone, having been struck silent, was now was back to her more usual state, full of questions.

But now was most certainly not the time to voice them. Philippe didn't say a word but she knew his mind. They'd already made such a row that it was pointless trying to be quiet, so rather than drag the body into the compartment whose window they'd broken, he just smashed this one, ripping stubborn pieces of glass from the frame to which they clung with his bare hands, and making nothing of the wounds they gave him.

The scent of his blood was intoxicating, as if she'd inhaled some powerful drug. She moved to help him in the task he didn't need to explain to her, but he was so fast... and heaved the body out through the window.

If they'd had time they'd have buried it, though even the man's disappearance would alert the occupiers that something was wrong. And members of the Resistance would be questioned, and would suffer. This was probably inevitable, but making the body vanish might buy them some time, enough to conclude this business.

"Back on the roof?" she asked, for the sake of hearing a voice again, though she knew. He didn't reply, and didn't need to. They could hear shouts.

They swung themselves out through the window and onto the roof of the train once more. There was a commotion below but it no longer had anything to do with them.

Still exhilarated from the perfume of Philippe's blood, Simone stood upright on the train's roof, and positively danced along it towards the engine. They silently shared their mutual regret at not drinking from the dead renegade, but Philippe walked briskly, and the late moonrise behind him set him off as though he were something both mad and yet very sober and solemn as he paced the length of the train.

Anyway, they told themselves, a living animal was almost as good a drink as a dead – very recently dead – human, so they had not lost much in their haste. This was not quite true, but close to truth, and hence, good enough in wartime.

When they reached the engine and lowered themselves down the cab's side Simone, still full of glee and mischief, hung upside down.

"Hello!" she cried cheerfully. One of the two men in the cab was shovelling coal and nearly missed the furnace, but all things considered kept his calm remarkably well. The other staggered back, bracing himself against the back of the cab.

Philippe just lowered and then swung himself into the cab in one efficient motion.

The man without the shovel had something else in his pocket. He made to reach for it, so slowly it seemed to Simone that he was in a trance. She felt Philippe enter her private thoughts and caution her that it was she that was moving too fast. Cheek, she thought, but he wasn't dallying either.

"Pardon me," he said. "You are going onto the 3.32 out of Orleans after this job?"

Simone had read them too. They were the team that were taking the train full of arms. One of them must be the saboteur, Jean-Pierre, so they knew about the plot to blow up the bridge. They were planning to slow right down and take their chance to jump, just before it hit the bridge. Their thoughts were easy to read, because there was nothing else going on in their minds at this moment. They weren't distracted: They were obsessed, not surprisingly, with what was likely to happen in their very near futures.

She had the gun wrested from the hands of the man before he could even raise it, and she wondered again how fast she was, or was it that he was slow? It had become hard to tell, but now was not the time, so she stored it away to ask Philippe when this was over.

"Listen and don't be afraid. We have come to take over from you, understand? We are friends. You will not board the 3.32. We will take your place. Everything is taken care of." Philippe continued.

Like a man poised at the top of a cliff, the two men almost let go of the terror that the vampires could feel radiating from them. One of them at least was probably an ordinary driver, told it was his duty by the local Maquis, and was reluctant, not because he didn't hate the occupiers, but because he was afraid. Simone felt pity for him. Yes, she thought, pity, but you probably can't pick up on that, Phil dear, can you? Or only theoretically.

There is nothing wrong, she thought, with being afraid. Only people with no imagination aren't. It's the trembling animal in us.

"If you're friends," said the one who till recently had had a gun, "What's the password?"

Simone read it from his mind right away. It was the type of information which, with some practice you could, if you wished, hide from a vampire. But these two did not have the practice and didn't know they were vampires.

"Lavoisier," answered Philippe. "one of the greatest Frenchmen, by the way," and he winked at Simone, then in her head he whispered, "I knew him!"

The drivers both relaxed. The tension flowed out of them like air from a gently deflating balloon. One of them crossed himself, and Simone was surprised to see Philippe take a step back, though he quickly recovered. More questions for later, she thought.

It wasn't long till they reached the train's final – and only – stop.

The station was full of armed soldiers. The vampires hid in the small crowd of passengers as the latter alighted from the train. There was a lot of muttering about strange events and sounds like gunfire, but nobody wanted to shout about it, or even mention it to the on board guards, two of whom were soldiers and one a ticket collector with a very anxious expression. The three of these quickly got in a huddle with the soldiers on the station, and Simone caught their conversation, after some initial difficulty tuning into the sound and separating it from the hubbub of the place. They'd checked it, they were telling their colleagues, two compartments with windows smashed, blood all over one of them, no sign of a body or bodies. A fight which ended with the wounded victim and his assailant jumping out the window? Or the villain of the piece going back to mingle with other passengers, having disposed of the body? But why two broken windows? Shouldn't they stop the passengers from leaving the station?

This seemed the obvious move, but the guards were hanging back from implementing such a plan, because it was almost inevitable that whoever the assailant was, he'd have a gun. It was truly shocking slackness on their part, and as if they too could read minds, specifically Simone's, the guards started over to a small knot of soldiers, whom she guessed to be here to board the next train. She could read a certain impatience from this group as the others approached. They had a job to do, an important and dangerous one, sabotage being as common as the Maquis could make it. They were not likely to be interested in what went on other trains.

Unless one of the group was the ambitious type, on the lookout for opportunities to shine by doing that little bit of extra thinking…

No, thank God. Yet it should have been a massive warning sign, given the nature and purpose of the next train out. These men have given up, inside. They won't win, and they know they won't win, and all they want now is what common soldiers always want: to survive.

Still stupid though, as this incident could have been, in fact was, something that could have threatened that laudable and quite understandable goal.

While the group ummed and aahed or whatever they were doing the driver and his mate disembarked and headed across the concourse, to a door in a rundown shambles of a building that housed all sorts of railway miscellany, including a room for drivers to rest and generally hang around in between jobs. They entered and then the driver stuck his head out and nodded to the approaching vampires: The coast was clear. Simone and Philippe entered and admired the fire burning in the hearth, a sudden reminder that there was still a world of warmth and comfort, not just war and night and cold hearts yearning after the vanished inner flame.

"We need your clothes," said Philippe.

"And what am I to wear instead of her skirt?" quipped the smaller of the two.

But he was joking. He had a change of clothes in a locker: They'd been planning to take them on the next journey, because it would be difficult to come back and get them, at least till the Boche had been thrown out of France.

"Turn the other way, please, Mam'selle," requested the driver, to Simone's amusement, and they politely returned the favour when she put on the sweaty, soot covered garments lately worn by his colleague. Philippe adopted a brave face as he put on a pair of well worn overalls. Nothing wrong with soot, he thought, it was clean dirt; that is to say, it did not carry infection. It could kill you quick enough if your lungs were weak, and the air was full of it, Simone countered, just for his benefit.

Not if you don't breathe, was the silent reply.

"Wait," said the driver, and wiped the soot from his face, rubbing it gently over Simone's. Philippe used a hanky he'd found in the overalls' pocket which he hoped would be stained only with soot. Simone chuckled.

The two train drivers left, followed slowly out of the door by the now disguised vampires. Simone still wore her stolen shoes but the skirt and blouse she'd taken from Martine just had to be left behind. At least she could keep the rather pretty underwear on, although it could do with a wash, like the rest of her.

"You can wash, with some difficulty, but you know you can't drink water, don't you? It feels like choking. Oh, and... have you urinated yet?"

Simone had, but in the dark, and although she could see well at night, hadn't really bothered to look... oh.

"I thought it was... the last of my..." She felt ridiculously shy.

But Philippe was as matter-of-fact as a Dutchman.

"Your menses? No. You piss blood now. And you're better off not crying."

"Let me guess; tears of blood?"

"I'm sorry," he replied, but she felt no wave of sympathy from him to her. In fairness, he did say that he didn't feel sympathy at all, or indeed anything much.

She tried to bury the thought in the deep layers of her mind, although it was probably futile. Even so, she could not help but promise herself that once her self-appointed quest was over, she'd walk out into the sunlight for one last time... for who could live like this?

Philippe gave no indication of having listened in on that thought, but perhaps it was just good manners on his part.

The drivers had disappeared into the night beyond the station. Philippe and Simone made their way to the platform where their new train stood. It wasn't hard to find, as it was bristling with soldiers at this point. Simone felt a frisson of worry: Was there a station master? Would he identify them as impostors?

But as soon as they stepped onto the platform a personage dressed in a German uniform with an old fashioned moustache that looked more in keeping with the Franco Prussian war, and would have been outdated before WW1, marched up to them.

"Where have you been? You've got ten minutes to fire her up! Go!"

This lack of ceremony was just the job, as any further conversation might have drawn the moustache's attention to the delicate looking, boyish co-driver who looked too young to hold a position involving responsibility for people's lives, and even more importantly, Germany's arsenal, or part of it.

The pair climbed into the locomotive, and started to shovel coal. Simone found it exciting. Her strength was a voluptuous pleasure. This must be how supremely fit athletes feel, she thought, including the men. Never mind athletes, I feel like Hercules, and he was a demi-god!

"Herakles. He's Greek," said Philippe aloud. Simone wanted to laugh with pleasure, even at his pedantry. It was… cute.

"You'd find Hitler cute in your present mood," said Philippe.

"Stop it! Don't listen in!"

Sorry, he thought at her.

"Now," he said aloud, "Don't argue with this. You're the trained operative, so you've got the hard bit. But I know you can do it. You're going to jump off the train as soon as we're out of sight of the station. You won't get lost, with the railway line to follow. Then you're going to go as fast as you can to the bridge, where you will detonate the explosives attached to its underbelly, having first despatched the Germans heading there now as well as intercepting the Resistance people on their way who currently still believe that they'll be the ones to do it."

"Is that all?" said Simone, still astonished at her volatile emotions. In the mood she was in, she felt she could do anything.

"Stay with that thought," said Philippe, clearly unable to resist listening in, even now.

"And your role is?"

"I can't say I always wanted to be a train driver, can I? I certainly never wanted to drive a coach and horses. But this might even be fun," he said, wistfully, as a man might for whom fun was but a distant memory.

He looked at her and she saw a mental picture of him driving the train and then leaving the controls to walk down the roof of the train, jumping through windows and doors, and hauling out guards, then heaving them out the way he came in, to take their chances at the track side.

"You can't!" exclaimed Simone. "There'll be loads of them! Anyway, what about the dead man's hand?"

"You took a souvenir? No, seriously, that's easy to disable, look: the shovel will keep it pressed down."

"Why are you taking such a risk to save German occupiers? It's ridiculous. They shouldn't be here, they can't expect anything else."

"Because of the holy thing within them. You saw it. You know the wedding service... 'whom God hath joined together let no man put asunder?'"

"Yes, yes, and I can read you. Marriage is a metaphor for the wedding of the immortal and the mortal, and that's what those words refer to: Don't sunder flesh from spirit. Yeah, yeah. Well, you're not doing it yourself, are you? They're passengers, and this train is headed towards death. Should've checked the destination board before they joined the army."

"Well I'm giving them a chance to disembark, even though our intelligence reports of literal death trains carrying not just German outcasts to death camps but France's and everywhere... and I've got my own debt. Which I cannot repay. Listen, stop arguing, this is how I'm playing it. Maybe I want to put myself in danger to keep up with you."

Nonsense, thought Simone. But he's stubborn.

"Try to keep in touch over the distance. It'll be hard, especially as you haven't been at it that long. And you'll have to feel out the minds you're going to be

111

dealing with, and somehow make sense of it all. But don't worry. As long as it's done before dawn. Good thing it's nearly Christmas, eh? Unseasonably warm but the nights are getting longer and we can..."

"Go out to play?"

She couldn't help it. It was partly the sort of black humour that gets one through hard situations, but also it was joie de vivre, or more precisely joie de mort... He frowned dutifully.

The whistle blew. They were the only train, so it was time to go. They had a good fire going, and Simone kept shovelling coal while Philippe did the honours, and the train started to move, and then to get up speed.

They soon left the station far behind. It was time to jump. Dressed like a chimney sweep from a Victorian novel, and with no other clothes to her name, Simone leapt into the dark.

She thought her vampire agility would make for a comfortable landing but she somehow ended up rolling over a bed of stones, down an even stonier embankment and into a wilderness of brambles. She lay at the bottom, feeling like she'd broken something. The pain was intense, but she heaved herself into a sitting position, then sprang to her feet. Maybe she had broken something, but it was healing already. She could feel the deep scratches of the brambles, and she knew that as well as looking black with coal dust she was now probably bleeding in many places, although not for long. She jumped forward into a smaller patch of undergrowth, and by dint of moving very quickly indeed, was able to just touch the tips of her toes onto something, some branch or twig or even leaf: The flimsiness did not matter unless she stopped moving. Her first job, of course, was to overtake the train. Could she? Had Philippe *thought* about this?

But the train seemed slower and she was getting faster. Then, to her disbelief, it stopped. So, that's how he's going to do it. Unless something's gone wrong? She was so busy moving she hadn't established a mental connection with him.

This train had one carriage full of soldiers, with the rest full with the deadly freight. She passed it and as she did, saw a couple of men climbing out, to see why it had stopped. The others were moving along inside the carriage, but there was no corridor to the others, so they had no option but to get out. She could see pictures from their minds, even as she hurtled past where they were. Then she felt Philippe.

It was so strong, it was as though he'd got her on the telephone.

"Slight change of plan. I'm slowing it down to help you out."

She could not stop, or do anything more. For one thing, she needed to scan for the minds of the Resistance workers, as well as the Germans coming to intercept them.

The plan was to follow the railway track, clear enough to her with her vampire vision. Now she was ahead of the train she headed back onto it, since that seemed the simplest thing. Then she felt something, coming from the road. She kept moving, still on the track, which at this point was parallel to the road. The track was doing her thinking for her: She didn't have to consider her steps, and this freed her up to try and feel the minds travelling, all unknowingly, to the same destination.

There was a car with five in it, she estimated, and an open-backed transport lorry with, gosh, ten maybe, excluding the driver and any passenger in the cab. Cripes, she thought. How am I going to do this?

She wasn't armed, except with her dark power.

Well, that would have to do.

She left the railway track and did battle with brambles and other, less vicious vegetation, until she reached the road. She weighed up her options and came up with a plan. It wasn't a great plan, but it was all she had.

Her soot stained overalls were topped off with a cap, while around her neck was what they call a kerchief, a sort of scarf. It had been in what she thought of as the railway dressing up box, although virtually everything in it was just overalls, except for this thing, which happened to be red and unexpectedly cheering as a result. She waited for the vehicles, and when she saw the lorry appear first she took a breath and thought, after all, maybe this'll be easier than I've been expecting.

She stood in the middle of the road and waved her kerchief. The lorry slowed and an angry head stuck out of the window.

"Get out of the way!"

His voice was full of fear, rather than anger. Nobody waved down military transport in Occupied France, why would you? Unless you were Resistance trying to trap them. The driver put his foot down harder and the lorry jerked forward. There was consternation behind the cab. She could hear it. Through the babble of voices, heard with the ears and the mind both, she picked up the lack of information they had about where they were going and what they were doing. Presumably all that knowledge rested in the car travelling behind.

She couldn't let them past and they weren't going to stop, so that made her course of action clear. She leapt onto the bonnet of the lorry and punched her fist through the window, then moving faster than she ever had she grabbed the passenger by the neck and sank her teeth, which felt huge in her mouth, into his flesh. It was as though she'd injected him with powerful anaesthetic, which was indeed what she'd done, except she didn't have time to hang around while he counted down from ten.

She turned to the driver, blood dripping from what now had to be called her fangs.

"Drive this into the ditch if you want to live," she said. He didn't need a big debate about it, and the vehicle swerved into the ditch which had been her last obstacle between railway and road, although she'd jumped it with ease. As the lorry started to settle into its new parking spot, it lurched sideways, and the men in the back started jumping out, shouting. It didn't quite turn over, in the end.

Meanwhile, as soon as their new course was set, Simone was on the driver, and took the time to treat herself to a quick gulp of his blood, as well as knocking him out. I need the energy, she told herself. Then she set to work on the troops, who were variously falling deeper into the ditch, or climbing their way out, and having difficulty seeing in the dark. Some were making noises as if in pain, having landed badly. None had used their weapons, so far, because from what little they could glean from their seats in the back of the lorry this could be an accident. Before they could discover anything to the contrary, Simone was on them, fast and terrifying.

She didn't need to work too hard, as fear did its job. The much vaunted German discipline collapsed. By the time they'd noticed the strange wounds they were aware that some kind of monster was causing them. A couple of them just ran off into the undergrowth. Then someone fired a shot. It was a dangerous move, in a melee of people, in the dark, and Simone hoped no one was hit, which was just ridiculous, really, as these were the enemy. She took the opportunity to grandstand, jumping onto the now slanting roof of the cab and screaming in her best banshee voice: "Shoot me then! I cannot die!"

It was shameful histrionics, but the shooter, guided a little by the headlights of the car behind, took a shot, and then another.

Fortunately he did not miss and so the remaining conscious soldiers were treated to the sight of Simone bleeding from gunshot wounds yet showing no ill effect while still looking incredibly dangerous. And nightmarish.

At this point the car drew up. It had gathered speed once the driver spotted what was going on and now he stamped on the brakes so hard it almost skidded to a stop. The four doors flew open and the officers piled out and started shooting. Some of those shots found their mark too, and Simone started to get fed up with being a target, as she was not impervious to pain. Then she saw someone grab an automatic, and decided enough was enough. She launched herself at the officer whose mind obligingly kept at its forefront the thought that he was the most senior, and disarmed him by breaking his wrist. It would heal.

She grabbed him around his head and pulled it back, facing what was left of his fellows. There was a pause.

"I can snap his neck in an instant. Do you believe it?"

Her German was adequate and as she had just demonstrated she was superhuman in one respect at least, they were predisposed to accept the claim.

"Take off your clothes, all of you." This was a bit cruel, as it was very cold, but Simone was not aware of temperature, and never would be again, except for observation, up to the point where she would be consumed by the heat of the sun.

"All right, stop at your underwear. Now use your belts to tie each other up."

"Don't listen to her," screamed the man she was holding. "Kill her!"

Idiot, thought Simone. If you could have killed me, you would. Whereas I could have killed you several times over, but I didn't. Losing patience, she sank her teeth into his carotid artery and drank deep. She could have swooned with pleasure, but she needed to be alert, so she let the unconscious man drop to the ground. The men getting undressed might have taken advantage to attack again, but instead just watched the woman with the fangs apparently kill their leader. They were wise enough by now not to disobey.

"Now don't be afraid. I'm not going to kill you unless you fight. All right? I'm going to have a little taste of each of you, and you're going to get some nice rest. All right?"

One man was trying to back away: He'd survived the tipping of their lorry and come to help the officers from the car. Simone decided another little demonstration would cement their understanding of her power and help dissuade them from any further action till well after sunrise. So she summoned her speed and went for him so fast it seemed like she was there already.

That did the trick. They'd seen her dance on the edge of a piece of metal, seen her get shot several times, and seen her drink the blood of their comrades: Now they saw she could move faster than any living thing they could imagine; maybe a snake darting forward to poison and eat its prey. Maybe *that* could move so fast.

They surrendered. They were already bound, but she felt their collective defeat, and their desperate hope that they wouldn't die that night, mixed with superstitious terror, for this wasn't the death they'd all dreaded, this was something else. She couldn't comfort them. They had to fear her, at least for tonight.

She drank from them, a pint each by her reckoning, which they could easily spare. She wondered how the anaesthetic effect worked, and how long it lasted, and if it were possible to run out of whatever it was that worked this little miracle, but although she had a dozen or so of the enemy to deal with, it seemed to keep working. What a gift this is, she thought. I don't think I could have killed them. It's not about hearts and souls and feelings that you suddenly can't feel. It's this mind-reading thing. That must be why Philippe is such a pacifist. You feel like you're them. He's lying if he says he doesn't feel something, when we're so connected to everyone by this strange gift.

Her last job was to find a lighter, after she'd dragged the unconscious men far enough away from the car and the lorry. She went through their pockets in a desperate hurry, found what she wanted, just punched a hole in the petrol tanks of both vehicles, then lit the fuel.

The flame moved fast, but she was faster, and was over the horizon before the lick of the flames lit up the night.

She toyed with the idea of letting the Resistance come to set and detonate the bomb, without any interference from her. She'd removed the danger to the operation, and she was, honestly stunned at what she'd managed to accomplish, and all without killing anyone. In the back of her mind she's been worrying, a little, about Philippe, but he was older – much older – and more experienced, and she was already discovering how much more powerful vampires got as time went on.

She moved onto the railway track again. Behind her she could hear the rails humming with the approach of the still distant train. Philippe had got it going again, and there was no time to waste.

Never could she have imagined moving so fast. The fuel provided by all that German blood was high octane human, not dead, not animal, and all human blood was utterly delicious and wonderfully energising to her. And she wasn't just running, but progressing in a series of long jumps, as though on the athletics field, but running to build up power between each. When she was feeling more leisurely it was all a lot more floaty, from jump to jump. Sometimes she'd almost hover in the air, and descend like thistledown, but this was no time for drifting.

Meanwhile, it seemed that the road was trying to converge from the parallel to join the railway line. She realised that the bridge must carry both rail and road across a river, something she hadn't grasped before. She caught the scent of humans, and then the mutterings of their minds. They were already in place, of course, and were at the base of one of the great arches that carried the bridge high above the river. She got the mental picture and the next minute she was almost on top of the saboteurs.

"Wait," she called, and raised her hands above her head, although they probably couldn't see her in the dark, "I'm a friend with news."

She heard someone come up from behind and read his intention to grab her. Fine. He grabbed her round the neck. He wore no coat and his shirtsleeves were rolled up.

"We're not expecting any friends," he snarled.

"Wait," she said again, "You may need to know this. Your plan is betrayed by one of your own."

"What!" exclaimed another voice. She could feel that three of them were present.

"That wouldn't surprise me, and I think I know who," said the one holding onto her, without slackening his grip in the slightest. "And who are you? What is the password?"

"Lavoisier," she said. He snorted. "You could have tortured him for that."

"Think what you like. Now he's killed himself and my comrade has taken over the train. There are plenty of Germans on board guarding it, but he... and some others... have taken care of them."

It would have been frankly unbelievable to have told the unvarnished truth. And she was ready for the next bit, though she was getting a little irritated with having to put up with a hairy forearm around her neck.

"We set an ambush for the rest. They were sending cars down here to catch you but we... er... eliminated the threat for you. But others will follow. It's safer for you to go now, be far away with an alibi when it happens. I'll detonate the explosive."

The man with his arm around her neck laughed at that, and let go.

The other two laughed as well. "Never in a thousand years!" said another of the group. "It's too late to establish alibis, and we're under suspicion anyway, so they're not going to worry about little things like that. And the idea of you doing the job... who are you, anyway?"

"I'm SOE trained. I've been operating in Brittany," said Simone, pleased to be frank about something.

"Tell you what, let her do it," said the third saboteur, a woman, "No, hear me out. We'll be right there with her, looking on, so what can she do? It's safer for us to watch her than for her to watch us."

"Safest to kill her," objected hairy arms.

"Easy on the killing," said the woman.

Simone concluded that she'd have been better to have just let them get on with it, but there were too many things that could go wrong if she were not present.

"I'll do it, as planned," said the other one, who may or may not have had hairy arms, but was keeping them covered up. "Keep a gun on her. Everything's set up, anyway."

"It's coming, listen," said Simone.

They looked dubious, but then they nodded.

"Put your hands on your head," instructed her armed guard, and she obeyed.

The train hove into view as they stared back at the railway line. Simone felt Philippe's intention, which was to get the train to the middle of the bridge before jumping out into the river below. If he were a human, it could be viewed as very high risk. The original drivers had planned to jump off just before the train went onto the bridge, as a leap from the centre would be likely to be fatal: It was a long way down, and although the chasm was wide, the river at the bottom was fast, made so by the channelling effect of a lot of big and nasty looking rocks.

"The driver will take it to the middle of the bridge and then stop it," she told them. "Wait till it stops and he jumps."

"We won't see him from here, it's too dark," was the response.

I will, she thought. But it would open up a world of questions and explanations if I tried to tell them.

"Just wait until it stops, then," she asked, but she could read in their minds that they were not going to do anything of the sort. The job needed doing, and it was their priority.

She sent the thought to Philippe. She knew he'd picked up on it. Then she sent another. Do vampires die of explosions?

I've never known a vampire die in an explosion, came the thought. But it trailed its own little addendum – either Philippe couldn't or wouldn't block it – and it acknowledged that the thinker had never actually seen or heard of a vampire actually being in an explosion, so it was uncharted territory. Let's add to the sum of our kind's collective knowledge, he teased.

Or rather, she thought he was teasing. She was never sure how much of a sense of humour Philippe had. Perhaps he meant it: Perhaps he cared so little about his continuing existence that he was as content to die as he was to carry on with it.

Perhaps he wanted to die: Perhaps he wanted to sacrifice himself, and this was an opportunity to do that.

Her mind screamed at his: No, no, don't… I need you, you can show me how to survive with this condition, together we can achieve more good things, we can help humanity more that if I'm left… alone. Don't leave me!

But there was no answer borne on the night breeze, or however this mind-reading thing worked. Philippe's mind was silent, but she knew he'd put up his wall so she could no longer read him. That was a trick she needed to get good at, but the learning would be quicker with his help…

They had no intention of letting her detonate the bomb, she realised. Her captor tied her up, tightly, with a length of rope the woman went to fetch from their vehicle, hidden even on this night behind bushes. Simone hoped that all the Germans on the train had been dealt with, and early on the journey, too. She didn't want any of *them* jumping out of the train, as they might end up too near the saboteurs and shooting would definitely happen. She judged that Philippe had kept the speed pretty slow the whole way, probably so he could throw people off the train without them being killed, although there might be a few broken limbs among them.

The moon was finally rising, just ahead of the dawn, which was something Simone was going to have to start worrying about soon. Meanwhile there were more immediate concerns, for, as the train approached, she saw two figures on the roof of one of the carriages, making for the engine. It looked like two of the guards had escaped Philippe's attentions, and were making their way towards the engine in order to kill him. She was not concerned about this as far as his safety went. Explosions were one thing, two men against an ancient and powerful vampire was quite something else. The whole thing might go awry, though, simply because Philippe would try to save their lives.

She yelled at the saboteurs, "Look! You can see the Germans on the roof: They're trying to kill the driver! I told you we were on your side!"

"Looks like she's telling the truth," said the woman. "Let's give your friend a helping hand," and she raised a rifle. "This thing is good over quite a distance," she boasted. "And it's quite lit up, this train… almost as bright as day… just a little closer… a little bit more…"

Philippe burst into Simone's mind. "Tell her there's tons of explosives in here. She might miss and the whole thing'll go off before we hit the bridge."

Simone swiftly pointed this out. The woman reluctantly lowered her rifle. It must have been hard for her to see anyway, and much as she might enjoy taking potshots in the dark, the mission could have failed if her bullets set the munitions off.

The train was almost on the bridge. The road bridge ran alongside, separated by huge steel girders but fundamentally part of the same great span. There must be a massive cache of explosives up there to cause any serious damage. These maquis were no rural amateurs. They must have been stealing this stuff for months, at least. They must have heard the rumours about the Allies landing in France again in the spring. They wanted to stop German troops and ordnance heading west. Never mind they'd lose their bridge. The defeated Germans would be made to pay for another one.

Simone was not helpless, and could easily escape her hastily tied bonds. But any display of unnatural strength would upset her captors, and they didn't have any trust in her as it was. She was better off being a passive observer, this time, or so she felt. But her resolve was shaken when she saw a figure climb out of the cab of the engine and onto the roof, and the train stop, a few feet shy of the bridge.

There were cries around her. "What is he doing! Your friend; why is he going back to them?"

Because if he doesn't, they'll die, thought Simone, miserably. But deep down, she definitely felt another emotion, and it was pride. It would have been a lot easier to drive onto the bridge, and then jump, leaving the Germans to their fate. And, all right, he was probably just worrying about his immortal soul... oh, wait, didn't he say it had gone and left a hole behind? No, she thought, judging by this it's not gone completely, or if so, then he wants it back.

The sabs were swearing, including the woman. After all she'd done and seen, and been, Simone was still shocked to hear such words from a woman's mouth. But they were helpless, unless they wanted to blow up the bridge alone without destroying the munitions on board. It would be good to destroy them too: It was one of the aims of the original scheme.

By the light of the moon, they saw Philippe make his way along the train roof, and one of the Germans fire a pistol.

"He's missed," cried Simone, hopefully. It didn't look like a miss, even from the sabs' awkward vantage point, especially as Philippe's body jerked from the force of the bullet hitting it.

"He's still standing," exclaimed hairy arms.

The German pumped more bullets towards Philippe, and it was hardly possible to pretend that at least some of them did not connect. Then the second German started shooting, and they could hear him yelling as well.

"Don't let them know we're here," warned Simone, and earned puzzled looks: Those Germans were going to die one way or the other, so why worry about them? Simone, on the other hand, knew that her friend was making every attempt to make sure they didn't die, and he was a very determined... person.

At last Philippe reached the pair, and grabbed first one and then with the other hand, the other, as if he were a strict schoolmaster and they were two naughty boys. Then, he jumped down from the roof and out of sight on the far side of the train.

"He's dead, got to be. Brave fellow, though, tough as well," said the third saboteur.

"He's an idiot. We've got to get up there and get that train on the bridge," said hairy arms.

But Simone knew that Philippe had made sure the two Germans had landed safely on the other side, and moreover were enjoying a pleasant rest. Hurry, hurry, it'll be dawn soon, she thought.

It seemed like forever, but he must have made his way along the far side of the train back to the engine, and that wouldn't have taken long. Just as she feared her new acquaintances were about to take over the job – and certainly kill at least one of their number while doing it – the train coughed clouds of steam in the air and then began to move.

"The bastard's done it!" exclaimed hairy arms. "He's alive!"

"Of course he's alive!" said Simone excitedly. "It's a prototype bulletproof waistcoat we're trialling, and it works!"

"Very strong, isn't he? "said the woman. "Are you trialling supermen, as well?"

Simone made no reply. Now she couldn't take her eyes off the train as it chugged into the middle of the bridge.

"We have to go now," said the woman, urgently. "He's just at the spot."

"No, wait for him to jump," cried Simone, seriously worried at last. In her mind she was shouting, jump now, jump!

"He may be too badly injured," said the third man, "Sorry," and he paused for the tiniest second before pushing down the detonator. In that pause, Simone battled with herself, almost but not quite shredding her ropes and throwing the man aside, but then, what would happen?

The bomb went off, behind the locomotive, under one of the carriages carrying God knows what in terms of weaponry and explosives. There was an enormous bang, and then some more, and a plume of smoke so high it almost obscured the moon. It was one of those explosions that never stop: Every time you thought the bangs had finished, something else went off. Flames and smoke poured from the carriages and then the bridge began to buckle. Nothing could survive that: They could feel the intense heat even from their hiding place back under one of the great pillars.

And then, silhouetted against a backdrop of moon and smoke and fire, a figure jumped from the engine, flames trailing from it like the tail of a comet, and as it fell towards the unforgiving rocks and white rushing water far below, it twisted through a somersault and turned the jump into a dive almost as elegant as if from a sprung diving board into a calm blue pool.

Bloody show-off, thought Simone. He'll expose us. He's slowed himself down a little to perform that move. Will they realise? Have they noticed?

"Fucking hell," said hairy arms, in French, of course.

"What spirit! To die like that, "said the other man, and the woman just murmured, under her breath, "Bravo."

They untied Simone without another word. She was benefiting from Philippe's display, as the saboteurs were now giving her respect by association, but she had other things on her mind. His jump that turned into a dive suggested total control of the situation and perhaps he would have liked to sustain the charade for the sake of impressing her as well as them, but there were circumstances in which he could not put up walls, and intense pain was, Simone discovered, impossible to hide. She felt it as soon as he landed, the unforgiving smack of the water, so far down from the bridge that the impact would have been enough to despatch most people to the afterlife. And he had slowed his fall as much as he could the twisting from somersault into dive gave him the opportunity, given only to vampires, to tread air, just for a little, almost as if one were treading water. Even so, the air was not buoyant, unlike water, and any attempt to try and make it behave as if it were would have appeared ungainly to watchers, and wouldn't have made a lot of difference to the outcome.

Simone would have tried anyway, which might be because, as a new vampire, she didn't yet know where the limits were, and also she disliked pain and didn't care that much about looking good. The dive cost him, it must have done. He should have fallen feet first.

Suddenly she was overwhelmed with pain. Her body was tuned in to Philippe's agony via her mind. He had no strength to put up a wall of any kind. He was broadcasting the impact of his horrific injuries, which, when she thought about it later, she decided must be worse than those that would've killed an ordinary person. No one could endure such suffering without dying, except vampires. This was the flip side of the gift of immortality. She screamed as she felt what Philippe was enduring.

Then she blacked out. When she came to, she was in the back of a car with the woman driving the little group. And she could have sworn the sky was now dark grey.

"I've got to go to him," she said.

"I'm sorry," said hairy arms, "he's dead. No one could have survived that."

"I don't care," said Simone. It was good that they were getting away from the scene before the Germans woke up, and before higher-up Germans woke up too, in a metaphorical way. She didn't want vengeance visited on anyone. But her priorities were elsewhere. She opened the door of the moving car and jumped out, rolling in the prescribed manner and making her body soft. They all knew the techniques for keeping oneself in one piece in various trying situations, but in truth she didn't care. She hit the road, it hurt, briefly, and her body was already healing the bruises.

The car stopped, and the woman opened the door and shouted to Simone to stop. Simone blew her a kiss and ran as fast as a fit young woman could run, and no faster, till she was out of sight. Then she sped up.

They hadn't gone that far. She was soon back at the great arch of the now broken backed bridge and from that standpoint could see where Philippe had gone down.

124

She made her way down a steep embankment to the bottom of what was really a gorge with a river full of rocks, the water still quite low for the time of year.

Right at the bottom she saw him, at the edge of the river. Without her excellent and improving night vision she would have thought it was the remains of a bonfire. She ran to him and turned him over. He was horribly burnt, and his eyes rolled in his head. His limbs lolled at odd angles.

He opened his mouth and she saw a gruesome cavern, seared and sooty. He wouldn't be able to talk for a while. She asked him in her head what was happening to him, but when he opened his mind to her she felt his agony and put her hands over her ears; a useless, stupid gesture but it told him enough.

The moon had again played trickster with her perceptions, but time was not behaving normally either. So much had happened during the long night that she had no idea what the time might be. But the sky was brighter where the moon was, and so she bent and very, very carefully she picked him up. She could almost feel him healing, but he needed something essential that made all vampires feel better.

He was too awkward to carry in her arms so as gently as she could manage, she put him over her shoulder. There was a moan, but no protest. Then she ran, trying not to bounce him around, up to the road. Once they were travelling along that, back the way she'd come, the short journey was smoother.

They arrived at the scene of her battle with the German soldiers. They were all still unconscious. Tenderly, she laid him down by a dozing soldier, and turned his poor burnt head towards the man's neck. She watched him drink, and swiftly said 'enough', before moving him to the next one. By the time he was on his third, she felt she could leave him to it while she fed, always being careful not to take too much. It seemed to work well enough, as she could feel the heart and the pulse begin to slow, and instantly she would stop. It was easy to control oneself here, with a buffet of dishes to sample, but she wondered what would happen if she were really, really hungry and thirsty and there was only one human to nibble on. Still, she'd done it, and hadn't gone on to suck the victim dry, so she could do it again, and again, as long as this existence continued.

At last she was replete, and looking at Philippe, she saw him transformed. His wounds had healed, and even his hair, which had been burnt right off a blistered scalp, was growing again. He smiled at her, and she could have sighed with relief, if she had any breath. All she had was the simulacrum of breath, a forced and pointless effort that felt unpleasant, and she could see no point in faking.

He was virtually naked, and filthy with soot and earth.

"We have to get back to the gorge really soon. Morning is almost here," he said.

"You need clothes," said Simone, "and this lot are near freezing," she added, indicating the Germans she'd made strip.

He put on one of the hated uniforms. "This feels weird," was all he said.

"It's certainly not ideal for meeting my new friends," she said, and sent him a mental picture of the saboteurs.

He smiled at her. He looked quite cheerful, for him.

"They are cold, "he said, indicating the sleeping Germans, "and we owe them for our dinner."

So the vampires piled the Germans close together and threw their clothes over them, covering them as best they could. They put the one whose clothes Philippe now wore in the middle of the huddle of bodies so he could keep warm as he slept. The oddness of their behaviour struck Simone more than once. Her country was at war with these people, and moreover they would not hesitate to kill her if they were able. For some reason, it just didn't seem to matter.

"It's been a mild winter here, so far. But they'll be found soon. In fact this road's going to get very busy. My fellows weren't all knocked out, some I just pushed off the train when it was going as slowly as I could make it. They've got a long walk back to town but they'll get there eventually. And that explosion will have been seen and heard a long way off'. As he spoke, Philippe was taking Simone by the hand and starting back again along the road to the gorge.

"Where…?" but before she got the question out, he sent her a mental picture of what he'd seen at the bottom of the gorge; caves. Cold, uncomfortable, but most importantly, dark.

"It wasn't so bad," he said as they hastened to safety. "The water cushioned me, remember? It's not the same for us."

"The rocks didn't though, did they?" replied Simone tartly. She doubted she could ever forget how he looked when she found him.

At last they arrived at the bottom of the slope where the river ran at their feet. The sun was almost up, but it would take a while longer to reach out into the gorge. There was a series of caves, carved out of the soft rock by the busy river over millennia. The caves were big enough to have provided shelter and a home for their early ancestors, long ago. They didn't enter the first one, being wary of pursuit. The next ones showed signs of being occupied, probably by maquis. But beggars, choosers... it was too late to look for anything else. Luckily the days were short.

They went into the cave, deep into the comforting dark, which wasn't so dark to them. The walls were damp and green, and the floor of the cave was chipped with bits of rock.

"Not exactly the Ritz," she said ruefully. "And... do we need sleep? I mean, I *have* slept... not for long though."

Philippe sat with his back to the wall, making himself as comfortable as possible, although the wall was unforgivingly lumpy.

"Not exactly need, no. Probably force of habit, that recent sleeping of yours."

"Like my feeling compassion, you mean?"

"Umm. I seem to have upset you by mentioning that. It is possible for a vampire to express compassion and be committed to a compassionate way of life. Perhaps I should only speak for myself, but that impetuous uprush of sympathy with which even the manliest breast must sometimes swell no longer happens. The tears which are the signs of that sympathy for our fellows which exists because deep down we are one being – the pattern of God – they no longer flow. We are bereft of the divine. We are empty temples, with our deity now overthrown."

"I won't have that!" replied Simone. "It's probably just you: You say you've been a vampire since the Revolution. You've grown cynical. I find myself kinder than I've ever been; too kind, maybe. And I don't have to theorise about it in order to express it."

"Well, as for sleeping... it is good for us, psychologically, in my opinion. If we try and maintain a link with what we were, it can help us survive temptation. Oh, dear girl! You have no idea how terrible this fate of ours can be, or how easy it is to become feral, feeding off brutes, never going near houses for fear of killing the inmates... or just catching a glimpse of oneself in a mirror... never washing or changing our clothes, till we look like demons thrown out of hell, and forget that we were ever human."

"You've experienced it, haven't you?"

"Yes. And don't try looking at my mind, it's not how I wish to be seen. You need to learn the etiquette of mind reading. But I tell you what, I'll show you some pictures no one living's ever seen. That'll entertain us."

Simone sat back against the lumpy wall and prepared to be entertained. She didn't need to mention her blackout, which had probably occurred because it was happening to him, at his moment of terrible pain. It seemed they had grown close, then, perhaps too close... He acknowledged her with a smile and a nod, and let his mind flood with memories.

She was not disappointed. She was shown pictures of Philippe's memories, and he began with the Welsh hills, back before cars and electricity and telephones, or even proper roads. And he included moving pictures too, of a cart with a lot of hay, pulled by a great horse, and people harvesting wheat without any aid but scythes. And then, perhaps as a counter to what she'd seen, he showed her a hovel, with skinny little children and a woman probably too young to look the way she did, and a man bringing in game for the pot.

Then there was the arrest by the constables, and the man tried before the very owner of the land where he had trapped the bird that day; this owner possessed a face whose pockmarks were the prettiest thing on it, topped by a dusty wig; his face pouched and coarse and his nature worse than any vampire, for according to her instructor, this creature carried, enthroned in his heart, that divine presence which enables us all to feel what others feel.

It was the eldest son of the poacher who sat and watched, speechless with horror and disbelief, and whose vivid memory of the face of the little local tyrant who stole his father away and had him transported to the colonies, had lasted nearly two hundred years. She was surprised. Wasn't his parent some kind of estate manager for the landowner?

He was, for several years, Philippe told her silently. Then, he defended someone from injustice, and lost his employment and any chance of more. They were a wicked bunch, the landowning classes, and they stuck together.

Philip, he'd been then, and he led his family away from the village, which was, for all its beauty, a place of hunger and enduring serfdom, where his family were as enslaved as the blacks were, over in America. The rulers of the country did not argue with those reformers who said the poor of that nation who lived in the country were literal serfs, still, long after the middle ages. They weren't bothered what was said. But how can a nation tolerate every bit of turf underfoot being owned by another?

They went to London, where at least a man could walk free, even if he starved. For a moment she saw a picture of London, seen from high ground, but it looked so different viewed across fields that now were surely covered in houses and roads and factories, unless the Blitz had devastated the place.

Then he spoke. "I'm not going to show you the next bit. I'm going to tell you. They died. The water was unclean. That's all."

"I'm sorry," said Simone, feeling helpless.

"Sorry! They'd all be long dead now anyway, and so would I. I wouldn't be what I am now, if they'd lived, for my life would have taken a different course."

But he saw in her eyes the knowledge that it still grieved him, else why was there no picture?

The next picture he showed her was of a crowded room, with men and women too, leaning forward to catch the words, not of a preacher, though the place seemed like some sort of chapel, but of a man who preached something else. She heard the words, clearly this time, as though the BBC had been there with equipment and microphones and the rest of it, and the accent sounded strange, almost foreign, yet not... but she understood a little of what he said, and it was about the rights of man to a decent life. She felt as though she were pushing forward, and realised that it was Philippe's memory of pushing through the crowd: She could smell the people, and they were really rank, and dressed in a variety of odd ways, and talked in a great many accents, some of which did not register with her at all. Probably those rhythms, those dialects no longer existed.

And she felt along with Philippe, that surge he talked about as having lost; a surge of feeling, in this case, idealistic feeling, and hope of something better, not just for himself, but for everyone who suffered oppression, and his desire to work and serve toward that end, at the cost, if necessary, of his life. And her heart responded, proving its existence, she thought, for she felt tears running down her cheeks, at the pity of it all, when after all this time, war and suffering and the cruelty of man to man – and woman, and child – were still bestriding the world, like tyrants in a bitter old Punch cartoon.

"You're crying for me? That's who I was."

That's what we all were, she thought. Once. Already I am no longer the eager adventurer, ready to lay down my life, because I know now that that is the easy bit. The hard bit is laying down someone else's life. And then living with it.

"I was Philip back then," he said aloud. "And no, it wasn't Thomas Paine, because you don't automatically meet every famous person who's alive when you are, and however long you live, you'll find that's the case. In fact, you can hang around at the back of a crowd heaping praise on someone you all believe is a key figure in the great changes taking place in society... then in years to come you'll find your hero forgotten, a marginal figure, either proved wrong about everything, or worse, ignored, although right. And the best of our heroes don't actually mind their lack of fame. Sometimes it gets in the way of the work."

It was a good thing he was speaking aloud, for those thoughts would have been the devil to translate into pictures. He leaned forward, looking positively roguish.

"That's not to say I didn't meet some people so important to history that their names are known today. But I've had a long... existence. This was an important man to me: I was looking for a father figure, and he persuaded me – once I'd learned to elbow my way to the front of the crowd – to be his eyes and ears in Paris. He was one of a group of men who wanted the revolution to cross the Channel, and there were more of them than history, as we are fed it, would have you believe. I was there when the Bastille was stormed, and it was wonderful, although there weren't that many prisoners in there at the time. Shut your eyes!"

Simone obeyed, and then she was watching it unfold as it had been for him, a chaos of shouting, fighting; but not much, mostly surrendering, and the odd shot, which seemed shockingly anachronistic but clearly wasn't, as she then distinguished muskets, discharged by the guards over the heads of the crowd. Then she heard the slogan being shouted, probably on one of its earliest outings: Vive la Liberte, Egalite, Fraternite!

Although there were few prisoners to release, those that were there were soon hoisted onto the shoulders of the crowd, but Simone wondered, as she saw his memories unfold, how the poor rebels managed to lift them, so thin and malnourished they seemed to be. Indeed, as she looked from Philippe's eyes she realised that he was taller than most of them, though just above average height as things went these days. However, the plight of those they lifted was much worse, and they were mere skin and bone, not much of a burden. Everyone seemed poorly clad and shod, if they had shoes at all, and many of them seemed crippled or sick in some way. Yet their shouts were triumphant – joyous even – at what they had achieved, and even just watching from her vantage point in the far distant future she could sense the wonderful feeling of possibility that ran through the crowd like a flame leaping from heart to heart. And she remembered Shelley's poem, the one that went 'Ye are many, they are few…'

She had always thought it a cruel poem, encouraging people to sacrifice their lives for a collective, notional good. Throw yourself at the walls of the tyrant's castle, be slain by his armies, and when your bodies have piled high enough those of you that are left will simply climb over them to the very towers of the tyrant, and finally topple them. I'd like to see Shelley live by that principle; as if... she thought.

"As if, indeed," said Philippe, reading her mind. "But you are assuming revolution, or war. These are people demanding the vote, and it will come, as you know. Then we'll outweigh the brutes, and outnumber them, and take our land back."

"We have had universal suffrage for fifteen years, and all that's happened is that the Germans voted for Hitler," said Simone tartly. Then she felt sorry.

"But it was a cause worth dying for, the dream of freedom from hunger, from cruelty and injustice," she said.

And then added, "Worth dying for, yes. But worth killing for?"

"Well, you've changed. Strange, given that the heart is cold ashes now. Yes, yes, I know, you still feel it... you say. But I say logic is making you wiser than your confused passions ever could. "

The pictures were fading. Simone called up a picture of her own, from the recent past. It was Edith, baring her teeth with their catlike incisors, and her eyes like slits. . . . she looked like a lion, or a feline of some kind, and mercilessly single-minded. Killing Edith still seemed like the absolutely right thing to do.

"Yes, it was. We are not human, and we present a danger to humans. All of us, any of us, can be overwhelmed by the beast. The lower passions overwhelm the rational mind. That is what eventually happened in Paris, as paranoia and dread found their fertile soil. And I, heartbroken. I determined to return to England. I met up with an Englishman, similar to me, or so I thought, one who had sought a better society, where brainless aristocrats did not live like they were vampires on the labour and rents of the poor. That's not my analogy, by the way. Here is the man who first suggested that analogy to me."

The picture that came to her made her splutter for the words. "It's... him! It's Graves! The one who made me!"

"God is the one who made you, Simone," said Philippe reprovingly. "Yes, I know. We all knew when you were changed. We felt the second death, and I, because of my history with him, still have a connection, and so I knew more than simply that another was of our number: I knew you were from England come to France to fight an undercover war, I knew where this happened, and I knew you were a woman. I agreed to come to Brittany and search you out, and I caught your scent the second I arrived in France... by boat, at night, like you. I also undertook to destroy Edith, whose evil polluted the elements and was also easy to trace."

"So I stink out the whole of France? Joke... So why not destroy Graves?"

"He is an exceptionally old and powerful vampire. Edith was never a rational being while she was alive, always ruled by her whims. She could never think through the consequences of her actions. She'd make a terrible chess player. Graves, as he calls himself, may have a schoolboy's sense of humour, but he is a very good chess player, very good indeed. And unlike the civilians, he knows what we are and he knows how to kill us."

"Civilians? Oh, you mean as opposed to us. But, if you – we – are all so good at picking each other up on the airwaves – you know what I mean – why isn't Graves after us now? He wouldn't even have to search!" Simone felt alarm, but not terror. With no breath to gasp or over breathe with, she was never going to have a panic attack. Still, she had the animal part of her, and that had not been killed, apparently. Perhaps that part, being wise with respect to its own realm, could only react in the physical presence of danger.

"I am sorry, but this is what you wanted, isn't it? To continue to take part in this war? And not only have I gone along with it, I have participated. Enthusiastically, I might add. As soon as I knew you were changed, I wanted to save you from damnation. As for Graves – ha! – he cannot follow us today, unless he travels cowering in the back of a van or something. He won't want that. And he won't send men to find us, even with instructions on how to kill us, because if there's glory to bask in, he'll want it. So I think we're safe, till nightfall and probably beyond."

"Why beyond?"

"Why beyond? There's more to even a vampire's existence than drinking blood, although that's essential to it. He has a mind, and it needs to be entertained. Graves is surrounded by civilians... our definition of civilians. He is intelligent, but utterly mad. He won't want us killed yet. He'll want his money's worth. Why do you think he changed you? And if he retains any of the instincts of a mortal man, he'll want to save you from extinction but he'll certainly want me dead, as a rival for your affections."

Simone was left speechless by this last claim. Did that mean Philippe retained the instincts of a mortal man?

"Show me what happened next," she demanded, before her thoughts embarrassed her.

"Shut your eyes then. It'll be clearer."

Simone had wondered whose those emotions were, when she had seen the Bastille being stormed; those idealistic thoughts, that romantic side of revolution. She had thought it was the crowd, but now she felt that they belonged to him whose past she was looking at. If she saw through his eyes, then she must surely feel with his heart; the heart he had then, even if he possessed it no longer. Now she stood, not at the forefront, but at the back of a crowd, and she was watching one of history's most famous spectacles; a small cart with dirty, weeping people in ragged finery, waiting in front of the guillotine for the merciful death its designer had intended, although perhaps he had not anticipated that it would become celebrated for its efficient despatch of larger numbers than ever before.

Night fell as she watched, and the horrid show was packed away till tomorrow, but still her human film camera was fixed on the same place. He hadn't moved for hours. The numbness disclosed itself for what it was, and she felt a terrible sorrow; the regret for the dream that had foundered on the reality of human nature, or that part of it most easily expressed by a mob of hungry people who'd led brutalised lives and were now manipulated by an increasingly paranoid leadership. His thoughts, too, now shared by her. Not that she disagreed.

As he wept there, in the darkening square, some were arguing over the clothes of the deceased, with the gaolers loudly asserting their right to decide on their distribution. As no one had much money and what there was could barely buy bread, they were demanding the time-honoured fee required from women, at the tops of their voices, without a hint of shame. Some people did not trouble to leave the place, having nowhere to go, and soon there were fires lit where groups gathered around for warmth.

A voice on his left spoke in a familiar accent, close to his ear, and it felt to Simone as though she were more than just a witness to this episode in Philippe's life: She was a participant; though since the past is unchangeable, a helpless one.

"They execute Robespierre tomorrow," the voice spoke, so clearly Simone jumped, as though it were in the room.

It was Graves. It just had to be. She felt like she was choking, but it was not fear of the demon, but Philippe's grief at the death it had just announced.

"A great pity, of course. He could have been a great leader, but he went mad with power. So few men are suited to handle power, don't you think? And women too, of course, though fewer get the opportunity," he mused.

Philippe recovered himself, and his manners. "Sir, you are correct. That is why I am leaving tomorrow, home to England, and, if I am not mistaken, your accent betrays that it is your home land too. I swear that my heart is broken on the rack of disappointed hopes, and what I shall do there I do not know, but devils are at large here."

"Indeed they are. Come, let me buy you some wine, as you are a fellow countryman, and we can talk in English for a while after all this damned French."

The next picture was of a squalid bar, nothing like the famed cafes of the Belle Epoque, which she had always thought of as typically Parisien. The only way you could tell it was French squalor rather than English was that there was wine on the table instead of ale. Simone could even taste it, as though she had just had a sip of this near-two hundred year old wine. It was rough and fruity all at once. The table was an empty wine barrel, and the floor was sawdust, to absorb fluids of all conceivable kinds.

Graves's conversation was dazzling to the young man: Even though she, witnessing it, knew what he was, she was affected by the impression he made on Philippe. He talked of philosophy, and compared the Parisian mob to the many-headed beast described by Plato. They must be ruled, he declared, by reason, which represents the human in us... The Lion is the passionate heart of Man, and the passions must follow reason, for if they follow the Beast, the man is lost.

It was the strangest experience for Simone, looking at him again after what he had done to her. His clothes and hair were quite different but he looked the same age. His face was boney – vampires don't get fat – and sombre, and the lies tripped off his tongue. She was as helpless as she'd been when she lay dying in his dungeon, and although it was so vivid that it felt as if she'd gone back in time into Philippe's head, it was not alterable in any way, like a play or a book or a movie.

Opening her eyes to dispel the vision, Simone said: "I am confused. You say that the Lion is the heart, and it is dead in me, or dying, so I must be ruled by reason or end up a slave to... what? Is it the instincts, is that what you mean? Or is it what Plato means? Or Graves?"

Philippe laughed. "I'm so flattered that you want to know what I mean! Plato describes an ideal city state which is a mirror of the ordered nature of the ideal man, who is in command of himself. It is harder to command oneself than to rule a city. And a city follows its leaders. When they descend into their lower nature there is no hope for the city. The mob is the Beast too, because it is always driven by the lowest common denominator; the violent cruel, degraded by poverty no doubt... but not everyone sells their children to devils in human form. He flattered me with all this talk, for I had not read Plato at the time. He treated me as an equal nonetheless, and he told me... well, watch and listen.

So Simone shut her eyes, and heard how Philippe was, in the speaker's opinion, clearly a born leader of the poor, having had the experience of poverty himself, but still maintaining a nobility of soul. Yes of course, he wanted revenge for his family's suffering, but that was only natural (Graves had clearly let him get a word in edge-ways at some point) and he had shown a lively intelligence that would benefit from an education currently bestowed only on the unworthy scions of aristocracy, and which he must develop. Graves would give him a reading list, he'd be honoured to help. Although it wasn't Graves, it was William Kerr, apparently. If he delayed his departure for a couple of days, Kerr would accompany him to England. And so on.

But, Simone remembered, one had to choose. And so it proved in this case too. Now it was daylight, and Philippe was dragged from his grubby quarters by a mob. He was a spy for England, they declared, pretending to be a friend to the Revolution but betraying it. Never mind, Madame la Guillotine enjoyed the taste of English blood as much as French. And so she had the terrible vision of the device in front of her, as it had been in front of Philippe, all those years ago.

Then enter a soldier, an officer from the army, now loyal to the Revolution, greeted with glee by some of those around the guillotine, shouting Stop and brandishing a piece of paper so thick it had to be parchment. He had a rough and ready little militia with him as well, just in case the mob was uninterested in the written word. With these aids he virtually snatched Philippe from Madame's very jaws – and jaw-like they were, devouring lives, only in this case the upper jaw did the moving, and the lower was still – declaring that new evidence must be examined which suggested he may be innocent of espionage.

Philippe stopped. "I need a little rest, I feel, a break from these memories. Shall we shut our eyes for an hour or so?"

Simone didn't feel she needed even that. She doubted he did either. But for now, they had plenty of time.

Chapter Nine

What in me is dark, illumine

(Milton)

Simone's mind was too restless to permit sleep. Even if she'd still been human, her turbulent thoughts would have overridden sleep, and as an almost tireless vampire, she had no chance of dropping off. She stared at the damp walls of the cave, and felt grateful that she was not vulnerable to such conditions. She did feel pain, and even discomfort, but the variations in temperature which are a feature of this existence did not bother her.

Philippe's eyes remained defiantly shut, for all the world as if he were fast asleep, but she didn't believe it. The rehearsal of his memories must have a draining effect on some part of him – his willpower perhaps? How would it be to have three times as long a life as most people? How could he bear the memories; not just because they might be bad, but the sheer weight of them?

His eyelids opened. "I forget much of it, and sometimes I think I've remembered it all wrong. Have you never noticed how tricky memory can be? Try talking about a shared memory with someone and see how differently they recall it. Perhaps it's just dreams and nightmares. All I know that's real is that I'm here, now, and have power and abilities way beyond what I dreamed possible, which come at a dreadful cost. And even that might be imagination. I could be in a lunatic asylum, dreaming this. But one has to have a working hypothesis to deal with everything that happens. So let's agree to act as though it is real. That's the best we can do."

Simone deliberately did not answer. He was procrastinating, she was sure.

He gave her a soft smile. "Very well then. Kerr had me taken to some offices, very well-appointed rooms they were, with tall ceilings and windows and furnished beautifully. Some aristo's, I expect, once. Kerr must be pretty influential, I thought. I knew he was behind this turn of events, though the captain, or whatever he was, was not communicative. Shut your eyes."

Simone did as she was bidden, and she was looking out through his eyes as night fell, and a skinny man entered and lit the lamps. As he made to leave he indicated that the guards should leave also. No one spoke to Philippe.

Then the heavy curtains in front of the door were drawn back, Kerr/Graves entered the room. He sat down, looking serious.

"Well, m'boy, it seems you have enemies. In this atmosphere, it's not good to draw attention to yourself. I am going to have a job to get you out of here and safe to England. But first, I need to know: do you value your life? And secondly: do you trust me?"

It was the strangest experience for Simone, looking at him again after what he had done to her. His clothes and hair were quite different but he looked the same age, almost too young to be a villain. But his face was boney, and sombre, and the lies tripped off his tongue. She was as helpless as she'd been when she lay dying in his dungeon, and although it was so vivid that it felt as if she'd gone back in time into Philippe's head, it was not alterable in any way, and that knowledge made the excursion both terrible and fascinating.

"I value my life, and I trust you," and Simone heard the young man's voice as if it came from her own throat, though they were not the words she would have spoken then, if she could speak.

"Do you believe in God? asked Kerr.

"Of course I do," answered Philippe.

"Well, that's not approved of now, so don't talk about it. I have always supported the Revolution, and I don't believe people should be indoctrinated into a faith, but full grown men and women should have religious freedom, don't you think?"

I am telling you this to explain something very strange. At one time I assisted a priest, one who performed exorcisms, some on the royal family of France. But he was nearly killed by a creature called a vampire, that lived off blood. The vampire bit him, and made him one of them, but the priest, Father Cayzer, knew the secret ways to kill them, and slew him anyway. Cayzer found out how to live on animal blood, and never hurt a human, and when I was very ill and near death, he offered me the chance to survive by making me a vampire too. He told me that I would have great speed and strength, and apart from a few things I had to avoid, I would also be virtually immortal. And, he said, I could help him in his battle against demon possession... which you must believe in, if you believe in God."

"It would be a fine thing to believe in demons and not God... as if one were to believe in hell but not heaven!" Philippe replied.

"Oh," said Simone, opening her eyes, "this is heartbreaking, even if my heart is cold embers. It's so vivid, it's too hard to watch. And your palpable innocence, it's like a child, or a different person, anyway."

"It's always amusing when idealistic types think they've lost their innocence, only to discover that disillusionment is a process that just carries on."

"In God's name, just tell me, will you? This is hard to bear."

"Very well," he answered. "the whole thing was a set-up, as I realised eventually. If there was ever a Father Cayzer he probably schooled our friends in the worst kind of response to being made a vampire.

Kerr had plenty of money, which is easy for vampires to obtain, as you know. He'd bribed the militias to take me to the guillotine's very steps, then pulled me out at the last minute, so I was face to face with death. Naturally I didn't wonder why he'd sent other militia men to do it and not come himself. Of course it was because it was daylight then. He introduced the idea of becoming like him when I'd just been terrified out of my wits, but it was still a bizarre thing, mad even. Remember Polidori hadn't written his tale, let alone Stoker. Nobody had heard of vampires, except people living in certain eastern European countries with a terrible history of being ruled by monsters in human form.

He told me I'd have to live on blood, but not that I could never go out in daylight. He told me there were few ways to kill us, but not that he knew all of them and that gave him power, which he wouldn't hesitate to use if it suited him. He let me believe that it was easy to avoid the mortal sin of killing another, and that there was no possibility I'd fall into it. He said that with his vampire strength he could do much, but it would take two to defeat the militias and the mob and make our way to the coast to head to England. Trying to rescue me alone would be impossible. He would do a lot of damage, but in the end he would be destroyed. But two of us would stand a chance. It might not work, but it was a chance. Whereas as things stood, there was none. He would be destroyed if he tried it alone, he said, but he liked me and he didn't want to see me executed unjustly.

Then he had the guard at the door banging, and shouting that men were coming for his friend, and that he'd better have evidence that I was guiltless of conspiracy against the Republic. Then the men burst in, and handled me very roughly, while he made a show of protesting. They dragged me off, and as I went, told me I would die tomorrow, as the evidence was all against me. They kicked and beat me and called me a spy, while Kerr cursed. Then they turned to him and told him to be quiet, as he was not French, and suspicion might fall on him.

As they dragged me away, I truly believed I was going to die, and I shouted back at Kerr that my answer was that 'I would but it is too late' and he cried out that he still knew people and he wouldn't give up... but you must understand, I fell for this pantomime, and right then I thought it was all too late anyway, so why hesitate any longer? But I was convinced nothing could be done.

And so I was taken through the streets and thrown into a stinking cell. You may imagine what thoughts tormented me. A couple of hours of this, and he came. One of his accomplices let him in. He looked as though he'd been weeping. I told him I would choose his offer if I could, and he said I still could, so there and then in the dirty cell he drank my blood, and then bade me drink his. Right up until then I thought it wasn't real: I thought I was humouring a well-intentioned friend. And then everything changed forever."

"Why did he pick you to change into another like himself?" asked Simone. "In my case I thought it was because I was a woman, and that he wanted a companion. Not that I stayed around him for an instant!"

"I asked him, and he told me. That was before the whole, awful truth emerged... He does not lie unless with a purpose, so I have no cause to disbelieve him. He said he does it rarely because he doesn't want a race of loose-tongued fools spreading secrets that are his as well as theirs, or greedy animals that will disgust him. He said he missed English being spoken, even though I spoke it with what he termed a provincial accent, and I was intelligent, and eager. Most of all he said he sought sincerity.

He said God loves sincerity, because it is the absolute prerequisite for love of Him.

He said that to destroy that sincerity is the sacrifice he makes to the Devil, his master, whereas the blood he drinks is merely to sustain him, and the deaths he causes are mere by-products of his need for it. He said it is his delight to watch the struggle to maintain virtue in impossible circumstances, and the funniest thing, something he never tires of seeing, is how those he changes grow to absolutely hate themselves, beyond reason, and beyond redemption.

It was then that the scales, as they say, dropped from my eyes.

He did say that he was often disappointed that his new friends *would* end up killing themselves. And he told me how to do it, though I vowed I would never be that weak. And then he laughed and said it was a mortal sin, he'd heard, so they were destined for hell anyway."

Philippe paused, though clearly not for breath.

"Did you, I mean, were you together? Colleagues? Partners?"

"No! I got away from him as fast as I could, like you did. Well, not quite as fast, since I was, for a very short time, still of the belief that I was likely to be executed. Finally he finished playing around and told me as much of the truth as suited him, and assured me that I could not live on anything but flowing blood, and that I would kill a human being before long.

As one who fancied himself a revolutionary I was not cut out to kill. I tried everything, even hiring a prostitute to drink her menstrual blood. But it didn't assuage my hunger and thirst, because it was not part of the system, being, in reality, lining for a nest. It only flows when it is finally dispensed with each month, and the chamber freshly prepared. The frustration of this particular error made me dangerous, and I demanded her neck, and the delicious river that flows through the artery..."

"Stop it, don't talk about it! But ... Did you kill her?"

"No, I only took a pint or two. I mastered myself, with the greatest of difficulty, and paid her double. Then I told her there'd be more money if she returned with friends, but only those who could be trusted to keep quiet. This worked for a while. I didn't spend much, except on the girls, so I spent little time robbing people. You've had a taste of that already, haven't you?"

"Yes, and it was nerve-racking. I think I need to do one big theft, so I don't need to do any more."

Philippe ventured a weak smile. "You need not worry about that anymore. I am so wealthy I can make my bankers meet me at night. With no need for explanations. A little bit of fear goes along way.

I started by saving some undeserving aristos from their proper fate; not difficult, even the daylight problem is not a handicap for those whose work is done mostly by night. I'd not organise things: I didn't want that kind of involvement, and I was homesick for the person I had been... and that person supported the Revolution. That didn't stop me from being a thug for hire, and I calmed my conscience by telling myself that others would have killed the aristos' guards, whereas I saved them, by just putting them to sleep.

To compromise is not to give in. To recognise complexities is not to lose one's sincere desire to be a better person, and make things better, if possible, for other people. Take the aristos... I had to acknowledge that they weren't ALL pigs, like the bastard who ripped my father from his family. Most of them were, though. But there were children and young ones, and some who could perhaps be capable of learning. I stopped hating them, and it didn't mean I was betraying my father or my family. Only if I gave up my sincerity... Anyway, I made enough from their payments to me and returned to England. Why not just rob them? I suppose because I thought that being able to do it didn't mean I should... that it could be the beginning of a descent that would lead to my utter downfall.

And you may be sure Kerr knew my every movement. He was lucky to get out of Paris. It wasn't just about following me. He had been indiscreet. He cannot live in an orderly society for long, as he gets noticed. So he thrives amidst chaos.

Anyway, I just wanted to say, I've been investing for a hundred and fifty years or so and we don't need to go thieving any more."

Simone had plenty of things she wanted to ask him about, but she sensed he'd had enough for now. One question, though, needed an answer now.

"So... you're Philip, really, aren't you? You're not French, you're Philippe in France and Philip in England?"

And that wasn't the question. As he nodded, she burst out: "Can you read everything about me, or are you just not interested?"

He almost laughed, she was sure. "Yes, everything, if I want to. But I'm a gentleman. I know how things went with the one you call Graves, for example. But I wouldn't pry."

She couldn't blush. That was now impossible. They were silent for a while, and Simone tried to do that sleep-but-not-really thing. She was surprised when she was woken by his voice, whispering her name.

There was no breath from him to tickle her ear, though he was close. She shook herself and sat up. She wanted to dispel her thoughts, now, quickly.

"Is it daylight still?"

"No, the day is fading. Come on."

They left the cave and headed back up the embankment to the road. They stopped halfway when they saw the soldiers, most of whom were gathered round the bridge. Lights were being switched on, and the place was swarming with other personnel; labourers, construction workers, and who knows who else. They stopped moving and squatted down, hidden by undergrowth. It would be easy to avoid being seen, now the darkness was thickening. It was a puzzle that the soldiers hadn't searched the caves, and Simone wondered if Graves had told them not to. If Philippe was to be believed, Graves/Kerr had his spies everywhere but had little interest in stopping the pair doing whatever they wanted to, and probably…

"Our mutual friend probably wants us to get entangled with the war, and find ourselves maybe killing Germans or… or anybody. Am I correct?"

Philippe nodded. "He believes it pleases what he calls his Master. There is no real Devil as far as I know, it's all in his mind. But he needs a purpose, so he's convinced himself that his is to serve wickedness."

"Well, we all need a purpose," said Simone. "Mine is to kill Hitler, and yours is to save me from killing – hmm, bit of a clash there – and his is to destroy everything good in those he chooses as prey."

"Yes, that's about the size of it," agreed Philippe.

They decided it was time to move. It was tricky at first, returning the way they had come alongside the road, while being sure to remain invisible to the large numbers of people continuing to gather around the site of what was once a bridge. Some of them, Simone could swear, were onlookers, neither soldiers, or construction or demolition workers, and not Resistance fighters, certainly. They were locals, gawping at their destroyed bridge, and probably not all of them were happy about it. There were always people like that, and they were proud of it. If Germany continued its occupation, which of course would mean it had won the war, these were the people who'd thrive. After a few years, they would not bat an eyelid at denouncing anyone still bothering to resist as terrorists, trying to destroy the state of Greater Germany. And they would be self-righteous about it too, that was the worst thing, and they would most certainly describe themselves as pragmatists, who thought everybody else should just grow up and accept modern realities. Actually the worst thing, really, was how often they were proved right, if their prosperity were anything to go by.

At last they were past all the people, but it didn't mean they could travel freely on the road, although car lights would be visible for many kilometres and they'd have plenty of warning. It was still too risky, and although Simone protested at this summation by the cautious Philippe, she had to concede. People travelled by foot, horse, bicycle: Best to play it safe now they were successful saboteurs. So they progressed by skips and jumps, with their necessary springboards being as flimsy as a branch here, a tussock of long grass there. Simone began to feel she'd had enough and when her foot touched something that might have been green but, judging by the suction, was bog, she protested.

Vampire night vision is not all it is cracked up to be, she argued. It's bright, all right, like a cat's (maybe, but how do we know?) but there is no colour. Like a cat, you're a predator, so you don't need to see colour, he responded. It took her a second to realise they were having a back-and forth conversation without speaking. I thought there were limits on this telepathy lark. Yes, there are, he thought right back at her. It's easiest to project pictures, as you know, and simple discussions. Or arguments, she thought. Yes, yes, arguments. But more complex discuss…argue… debates are harder to conduct. I realise that, she thought. It's because of ambiguity, he thought.

"Ambiguity, eh? Isn't that what these charlatans do? Make statements with lots of room to wriggle? I thought – if I ever gave it a thought – that ambiguity was a feature of pretending to mind read, but it seems not. A picture, if it's a true picture, is quite unambiguous, of course."

"Well," he answered, "Even that can be falsified, but if it's a true memory…"

"True memory? Did all that stuff really happen, the stuff you showed me?"

"What do you want me to say?"

"I want you to say yes, and mean it, and for it to be true!"

"I want those things too, but it's the same for us as it is for human beings. It's possible to get things wrong, not just to forget, but to misremember. Sorry, that's an ugly word."

"With an ugly meaning," Simone snapped. "It means we are our own worst enemies, and that nobody, human or vampire, can be sure if their lives are even real, or just made up. Unless you have witnesses, I suppose."

Philippe stopped, and looked at her with a very serious expression. She noticed how brown his eyes were... as if he came from a country further south than he had told her. Melting eyes... She shook herself, desperate not to be an open book.

"Don't indulge in these doubts. There is one who can bear witness to what has happened to us, but he is a monster who will exploit any weakness. Every word he speaks, or thinks, even, is controlled, and if he can spin you around and send you insane he'll think it is a great victory."

"Come on," said Simone, "Let's go over to the railway line. There won't be any cyclists or horsemen on that, and it'll be easier going than all this blinking countryside." She'd had enough of the direction the conversation was going in, and she wondered if it was possible to avoid Graves for the rest of her existence, however long that might be. Why not? Surely she wasn't that entertaining that he couldn't find distractions elsewhere? Philippe was certainly hearing these thoughts but he refrained from offering an opinion, either verbally or just telepathically.

They made good time along the track, and before too long they were back in town. It was no place to stop, though, after the mayhem they'd caused the day before, so they avoided the centre, finding their way to the other side as best they could, considering the street signs had all been removed. They resorted to getting as close to pedestrians as possible, and trying to harvest directions from their minds, which was not easy as people don't usually think about where they're going when they've done it a hundred times. There weren't that many pedestrians out at night in Occupied France, either.

"I'm going to try something I'm not that good at, "said Philippe.

"Oh wonderful," Simone commented wryly. She read it from him. He was going to try and force the information in someone's head out of whatever cerebral back room it was in, and into the forefront of their mind.

They lurked like panto villains in a unused-looking doorway, just off the main square. A man eventually wandered past, and Simone watched as he staggered to a halt, as if someone had struck him on the back of the head, without bringing him down. He held his hand to his head, and then crashed onto his knees, whimpering. Simone grabbed Philippe's arm.

"Stop it," she whispered. You're hurting him!"

"It's fine, he's all right, I haven't hurt him," whispered Philippe in return. "Bet you he'll be laying off the booze for a bit, though. He's drunk, he thinks it's that. And now I feel drunk after wandering around in his head. Which is full of crap, by the way. The man can't think anything through to a conclusion. He's not exactly an idiot, but he has very poor concentration. Lack of use, probably."

They watched the man pick himself up and amble off.

"I suppose," said Simone, "it's different from reading what's at the forefront of someone's thoughts."

"I don't like doing it, it feels like a violation, and it's almost always a bit upsetting. Low level constant anxiety seems to be what people have buzzing in their brains almost all of the time. It's like a dreary cloud, with flashes of lightning when they're really scared."

"How disappointing. Haven't you ever found anybody who's madly in love? Or composing poetry or music, or... I dunno. Political speeches? Thinking about their scientific discovery? Or even planning a crime? Actually, I suppose you must've come across *those* quite a lot?"

"No. No, not really. Who said it? 'Most men live lives of quiet desperation.' Vampires are often planning crimes, that's true. But they are quite different. They are either logical, in which case they can live a long time... exist, I should say. Or else they are driven by instinct, and cannot or don't want to control their appetites."

"Speaking of appetites..."

"Wait till we're out of this town. Then we'll find some harmless livestock, and relieve it of an awful lot of blood."

Following the directions torn from the drunk's confused mind got them out of town and back on the road, this time going east again. The first field they came to had a barn in the far corner, visible to their night vision. They could hear and smell cattle as well, so they leapt and ran like a couple in love and having fun, till they got there and prised the barn door open. It was full of beasts, all of which started lowing in terror, making a hell of a din.

It was too late for the vampires to stop themselves. They were starving, and it was more powerful than hunger or even thirst, like a combination of the two. They were ravenous, and if a farmer had come to interfere at that moment, they would have had a very difficult time, trying to control themselves. They threw themselves on a beast, guzzling like hungry babies at the breast. It took all Philippe's strength to drag Simone off it.

"Leave it alive, don't kill if you don't need to," he said.

"Why not?" she protested. "It's an animal, bound for the slaughterhouse in any case!"

"Perhaps so, but it's not on you. Just in case."

"Just in case what?"

"Work it out! The good book says thou shalt not kill! It doesn't specify what!"

Lord, this fellow's a religious nut, thought Simone, not caring if he listened in to her thoughts. He might have been what passed for an enlightened radical type back in his day, but the old bible waving non-conformist stays pretty close to the surface. Although, to be fair, those types had no problem with meat, did they? God gave us – them, I suppose, as I'm not really a human and whatever created vampires, it probably wasn't God – dominion, that's it, dominion over the beasts. Which you *could* interpret as having them pull carts and so forth. I mean, you could have dominion over servants, maybe, but that wouldn't include eating them, as a general rule, although you did get made tyrants, like Hitler – but even he stopped short, or we'd have been told! – of actually eating people. Probably.

"I think you're pigeon-holing me," said Philippe stiffly, having clearly listened to her thoughts on the matter.

"Can we eat a whole pigeon now? You'd have to suck loads of them dry just to have a snack!"

"You're being facetious. You forget I have explored religions from all around the world, up to and including the oldest, which originates in India and is called Jainism. I'll tell you all about it one day."

147

So they didn't kill anything, and the farmer did not show up, but they tasted several of the cattle, and Simone wondered what the farmer would make of the puncture wounds in their necks, and their weakened condition.

Replete, they left the barn and headed back onto the road.

"The Jains, the really dedicated ones, go about naked and brush the ground in front of them, to encourage insects out of the way, as they dread treading on a reincarnated ancestor. I suppose they're naked because clothes involve animal suffering."

"What, cotton? Or wool even, it doesn't hurt the sheep to shear it. Leather, of course, unless the animal died of natural causes."

Philippe smiled, which pleased her... a little bit too much, she thought. She didn't care about his approval. Or otherwise.

"I think the Jains are interesting. But definitely extreme. They also believe that all creation is a person, with a lower, a middle and an upper region of the body, the lower being the beasts, and maybe demons as well, the middle region being earth, and people, and the upper corresponding with heaven and angels and so on. Their most important belief, though, is in non-violence."

"That IS extreme, in these days. It is regrettable, isn't it?" Simone was not inclined to be dismissive, and on a full stomach she felt able to give the matter her attention.

"It's not that I haven't thought about the matter before, "she said, "but we're at war. What can we do about the likes of Herr Hitler if we don't resort to violence? We did not initiate the war, he did, by invading people. Most of us knew we would fight, or join in the war effort in some capacity. Conchies are spat at; the lowest of the low, yet isn't it a bit weird that a doctrine of non-violence is seen as way out on the fringes of acceptability? And being violent is normal and acceptable within certain obvious bounds, like..."

"Like if someone in authority, an officer, the King, your teachers say be violent in the name of patriotism, or something. But if such behaviour sends us to hell, do they give us a special pass to show Satan? Have we got a licence to kill, if issued by someone important enough? I don't think so, but apparently there are Jain priests who will argue that in certain circumstances violence is acceptable, like if their country's attacked."

"So priests can issue licences to kill? Better stop off on our way to Hitler and find one to bless us then. Catholics and Protestants are capable of doing it too?" Simone was being sarcastic, but the idea was beginning to grow on her.

Why not, she thought. I didn't believe in anything except perhaps science and socialism, and I was a bit concerned about the socialism, it being suited to human beings who are a lot better people than most of the ones I've met. Now there's vampires that live forever, if they're lucky, and I'm one of them. So if there's a dark supernatural world, there must be a world of light, and kindness. I certainly hope so.

"So do I," said Philippe aloud. "Even if I am barred from heaven, if you want to call it that, for millennia, I can endure it, knowing that it's there."

"Hope isn't the same as certainty," Simone muttered. "But I would like to find a priest. Of any religion, but he must be sincere, and believe. I've got no use for these knowing types who only half believe if they do at all."

"My dear girl, we must get ourselves sorted out. Our clothes are smoke and soot stained and those trousers you have on are utterly disreputable. We've got to get cleaned up."

"But... we can't get a hotel room, it's too late, and they're mostly used for billeting soldiers. And anyway they have to inform the Boche about unknown people. Do we frighten the life out of some innocents and take their clothes and money, again? I don't really want to, and I don't want to leave a trail of weirdness behind us, either."

"I'm carrying a lot of local currency. People like money: it makes them very helpful. Can't trust them out of sight of course... but we don't need to. We find an isolated but comfortable looking farmhouse... you'll see. As for a trail of weirdness, it'll puzzle the Germans but the one who knows where we are anyway is the one to worry about. He sired both of us, and that's a permanent connection. He knows where we are."

"Sired us? Are we bloodstock now? Pun intended..."

Simone was content to follow Philippe's suggestions. They kept on their chosen route and eventually came across a large dwelling that seemed to fit the particulars. She wondered why they hadn't approached the owner of the cattle they'd just dined on but then it might take a bit of explanation. They knocked at the door and although the lights were out they kept knocking. At last the door was opened, by a man carrying a shotgun. He looked terrified.

"You're not German? Are you Maquis? I don't want to get involved, I've got a wife…"

He repeated these phrases while Philippe adopted a reassuring voice.

"You're trying to trap me!" was the next thing. They clearly weren't German but they did look like sooty desperados. Either they were Maquis, who must also be placated, or they were traitors trying to trap people into rash talk against their masters. Poor bloke, thought Simone. How awful it is to be occupied by a foreign power.

At last Philippe managed to pull out a wad of money without being shot. It was a mixture of the German franc and the good old French currency. Despite the dubious status of both of these the man did accept the international language of cash, and let them in.

They had a bathtub filled with hot water, one each; a rare luxury, though not as good as in the hotel where Simone had encountered Martine. The water did its usual thing, so it was like bathing in jelly, but it cleaned just the same. They took turns guarding each other while they bathed, although no one in that house could have posed any kind of threat to a vampire.

It turned out there were two women, other than the farmer's wife, working on the land. This was fortunate, for they were stockier than Simone was, and dressed slightly better, even stylishly, which was a miracle given the shortages. Simone chose trousers, quite well tailored to a womanly shape, and a blouse and coat, although she kept her previously stolen shoes, because they were a comfortable fit. They rewarded the woman with enough cash to re-equip herself several times over. Philippe needed to ditch his clothes too, although he'd looked quite smart when Simone had first encountered him. Their recent adventures had done a lot of damage, although he read from the farmer that the clothes would definitely be repaired. Nevertheless he was generous – to the point of insanity – in the eyes of the farmer.

They were offered food, but of course refused, to everyone's surprise.

"We're fasting," explained Philippe, though it was no explanation at all. No one cared, so long as he paid them. They just sipped a little tea, for the look of the thing.

150

Sunrise was not that far away. Philippe demanded a room which they could share, till sunset came around again. Simone read the farmer's thoughts: He thought Philippe was some kind of pervert but he didn't care.

Before they retired to their room, Philippe did a little demonstration.

"I am a special person," he informed a gathering of the two farm girls, the farmer and his wife, and Simone. Their sons had been sent away somewhere, it seemed, to work on the German war effort, but whether they were alive or dead, or runaways trying to join up with the Resistance, no one knew.

"My hearing is like that of a bat," he continued. "If any of you try and betray us, I will exact revenge. Do you understand? Now, you two girls, go to the end of that field. Yes, right down to the end. And then whisper something, something I could never guess, to each other. Go!"

The darkness was still thick and the girls, although alarmed at the demands made by the peculiar stranger, stumbled their way to the bottom of the field, with little cries as they tripped over uneven ground.

Simone listened too. At last they stopped. Simone's night vision was as sharp as ever but the girls did not try any clever stunts, or make rude signs, or any of the things that Simone might have done in their place. She focused her whole attention on her ears, moving her head so that one ear was directly in line with the girls.

It was more difficult than it seemed in theory, because of course she was picking every noise between the bottom of the field where the girls were and where they stood, just outside the farmhouse door. There were the rustling, squeaking, digging, hunting sounds of the French countryside, only amplified. An owl sounded very, very loud, and as close as if perched on her shoulder, like Athene's.

But just as humans learn to edit what they hear so can vampires. It may be louder, but the trick's the same. They can even dampen down the overall volume by pulling their attention inwards, as Simone was finding.

The girls returned. Philippe greeted them with the names of their favourite film stars, their dates of birth, and the popular songs they liked best. This simple display was sufficient to convince them all that their every word would be overheard by this superman.

But Philippe hadn't finished. He wanted to make sure. He bade the farmer imagine a scene and then described it to him. It took a while, as the man was clearly not comfortable with imagination, it not being much required in his line of work.

This impressed his audience more than the first demonstration, to the point where the others were begging him to 'Do me! Do me!', so he was not exactly inspiring them with fear. He obliged everyone, then he got serious with them.

"It's not just me," he said. "My sister here has also inherited these powers. Now the Germans are after us to try and use us as weapons of war. This must not happen, or France will never be free again. And if any of you are thinking of pleasing the Germans by trying to turn us in… don't. We're light sleepers. And we're super strong, too."

There was a clamour as they all protested they wouldn't dream of doing such a thing, even if they didn't know about the mind-reading and the superior hearing. So finally Philippe and Simone retired to their room and the others went off to do farmyard chores, after which they would no doubt catch up on the sleep they'd missed this past night.

"I still don't trust the older two. There's a calculating flavour to that woman's thoughts. But then, I've lined her pockets sufficiently to seal her lips."

"Tell me more of your story, and then I promise I'll shut my eyes for a bit."

"Where did I leave off? After Kerr changed me… when I realised I'd been tricked I got away as far as possible. I told you, didn't I… to England. There I gave money to my family but they were troubled that I saw them only after dark. I avoided killing people, but the temptation was almost too much to bear. And in London animals were driven alive to Smithfield market, where I used to turn up before dawn for living food. It became dangerous because my face became familiar, and people started asking questions. In the country, one could always be on the move, and animals were in fields or barns, so one beast dead from loss of blood with puncture wounds on its neck was just an unexplained mystery. Here, there was a meat market that drew people from all around, and they'd mix with each other and exchange information and stories.

I still didn't want to leave, though. There was money in London: There always has been, alongside terrible poverty. Although I despaired at what I saw as the failure of the French Revolution it didn't mean I'd lost hope for a better life for the poor. I also needed money for my own ends. So I robbed banks, which was quite easy then, and I refrained from robbing individual people, because I made rules for myself.

There's a trick to being a vampire in a new town. You go to the most dangerous part of it, then you wait for someone to pick a fight with you. You beat them up to within an inch of their lives, and you demand they take you to whoever the kingpin is. He hates you on sight, and picks another fight, and you repeat the original procedure. You then have all the local crims pay tribute to you; the sort of tribute they used to pay to emperors, not just stand about singing your praises. People try stabbing you, shooting you, and gradually give up when they realise they're getting nowhere. News of you gets around, and of course, the first people it gets to is the other local vampires. Since they're your equals in terms of strength, invulnerability etcetera, and furthermore, know how to kill you, that's the time to leave town, especially if there's more than one of them, and they decide to gang up against you. Hopefully, by then you've got enough capital to live comfortably a long way away."

"Is that what happened to you?" asked Simone.

"Sort of, more or less. After I had the constables chase me. It was before proper policemen were invented. There were watchmen; old boys who called out the time and other reassurances, and when trouble arose, the beadle would round up a few likely lads, give them a few pennies and turn them into a temporary police squad, which they looked forward to, since they had permission to bash heads in without getting in trouble for it. That hasn't changed much, has it?"

"Hasn't it? I thought our police were the best in the world?"

"Is that irony? Most police forces harbour thugs who like the support of the state behind their violence, so they don't go to gaol for it. And if ours are the best – well the Germans are worst. Probably. And the French… maybe. Plato dreamed of noble guardians of the polis… but then he was good at dreaming. He also dreamed of a philosopher king…"

"You're very keen on Plato."

"I like idealism. But the big exponent of Plato is my friend, Christophe, who apparently knew him. Yes, I like idealism. However misguided. It's another kind of mirror: You can see how far you've fallen. And how far the world has fallen."

"He liked young males."

153

"Well, really, should that be a crime? So long as they are not too young, but old enough to consent. It wasn't illegal, as it is still with us, but quite the reverse, it was the culture. A brilliant but weird culture. It was practically compulsory, during the teenage years. Then you were supposed to get married and change... but Plato fought against himself. He wrote of struggles with his desires, but it was up to him; society of that time didn't mind. But he needed to make a sacrifice, in his own head. The brightest light casts the darkest shadow, although only in the world of duality.

And Socrates allowed him to be his student. Although... Plato wasn't at the deathbed. He was ill. Supposedly."

"Only in the world of duality? What does that mean?"

"The mind is dual natured; on the one hand this, on the other hand that. And the whole world – all created things – are dual natured, bringing both joy and sorrow, night and day, summer and winter, etc. Only the divine is singular: In it... 'there is no darkness at all.'

"Oh. All right then." Simone felt a little stunned. This Christophe knew Plato and *Socrates?* He must be ancient.

Philippe read her thoughts. "He looks very handsome for his age, for any age. Vampire healing powers treat ageing as an illness and fix it. Surely you've noticed how good-looking I am? But you'll meet him."

Philippe was indeed a good-looking man in his twenties, or so he appeared. Age had perhaps laid hands on him, but had been driven away. He smiled, and even winked, to take the edge off what some might feel was conceit.

"Anyway, I saw off the constables, and got away with sleeping during the day because kingpins of crime don't have to get up in the morning. But I still had to feed and it was getting impossible to keep going to the meat market. I was desperate not to reveal what I was. The game would be up. People would start finding things out. When you're a king, even of a tribe of petty criminals, you're always having to watch your back for those who would steal your crown. If they discovered that mere sunlight could kill me, I'd never know peace again. So I couldn't take advantage of the whores, even though I could have rewarded them, and left them alive, enjoying a more comfortable existence than they'd ever known. I would have had a harem, leaving each to replenish their blood, and taken only a pint, weekly perhaps. They would never have had to sell sex again.

But some of them were stupid enough that I couldn't trust them not to spoil everything. It's different now: When shortages bite, so can the vampires.

So I followed a respectable but poor family home, and offered them money if I could feed, just a little blood, off each. The father offered himself first, but the mother demurred, saying she should try, because if he died, who would protect the children? It was so touching that I wanted to give them money gratis, but on the other hand, I was ravenous, and couldn't let it go any longer for fear of losing control.

It worked, and I left them alive, after begging and threatening them to keep my secret. And it would have been a fine arrangement, except that the wretched mother was religious, and of course had to confess her sins. I only discovered this when I was on my way back to my little house, where I lived alone, to wait for morning.

I caught the scent of him as I turned the corner into the street. Vampire. Old. Powerful. Then his mind met mine. I am Christophe, it said. You have left a trail so wide that a thousand devils could walk abreast to follow you.

Christophe! Older than Kerr, even. Eyes that could hold you still, unable to move, as he looked at you. That's what happened when I entered the house. There he was, sitting in my chair, having got in by snapping the door off its hinges and propping it tidily against the inner wall. I noticed that he'd made a fire – we didn't need heat, so it must be for aesthetic reasons, I thought – then I looked at him, and his eyes held me, and I couldn't move.

He spoke. His accent was very slightly French, but it had unusual overtones and I realised it was old French, though I didn't know how old.

"It is very good to meet you at last, Monsieur," he said. "Unfortunately it cannot be a long meeting. Your activities have come to the attention of rich and powerful people, and they are very well-connected."

Simone had been following the story as narrated by Philippe: It took her a few seconds to realise that she was being addressed by Christophe... or rather, she was seeing and hearing through Philippe's eyes, so that it was as if she had entered into his body and was listening to Christophe just as if she were Philippe, long ago. She could not help but exclaim.

"Oh, but this is marvellous! Like time travel!"

The sound and vision faded. "Weren't you the one suggesting that I could be making it all up And I was polite enough to concede that you might have a point? Make-believe or not, if you keep interrupting me I'll lose focus and you can have a mere sequence of facts, if you'd rather."

"Gosh, no, please continue. I don't care if your memory is playing tricks. I know you're sincere, anyway. I might not be able to do what you do with this telepathy stuff but I am learning, and I can tell it's true."

"No, sweetie, you can tell that this is what my memory tells me. I have learnt not to trust even that. So if you accept that, I'll continue. On that understanding, mind you."

Simone was fascinated, and she'd agree to anything to get more of the tale, and especially more of the way the tale was delivered. Pictures in her head had accompanied previous parts of the narrative, but they had been fleeting, and seemed almost like something from her own imagination, but enhanced and very vivid. She realised they had been glimpses of what Philippe had once seen, but probably not paid detailed attention to, or more likely, the pictures had succeeded each other quickly because he was eager to get to the moments that were most vivid in his memory, and most likely easiest to conjure up.

He continued. "I answered... see how you like this bit."

It was as though the voice came from her, but it was Philippe's and she had no control over it. She watched Christophe from Philippe's eyes and felt his voice as if it came from her lips.

"It is good to meet you too, Mr..." And the last syllable was a question.

"My name is Christophe, but you can tell that. I know that your powers are growing. And I know you can tell I am a well-intending individual who wishes you no harm."

"Perhaps I can. But I can also sense you have been a vampire for a very long time and that your powers are either grown or continue to grow, which might mean, for one thing, that you can hide your thoughts from me. You may be able to dissemble to such a degree that I am completely fooled."

"You have been misused by one of us, I know, and I know who it was, too. He is called upon by many who are not vampires, but who need his power. A creature like him is a godsend to those who oppress large numbers of people, since his strength is a byword. And of course, bullets do not stop him. He is usually called upon by certain elements, employed for this sort of clandestine manoeuvring by those rich and powerful interests I mentioned."

"So... Kerr. Kerr is contacted by go-betweens, who procure for their masters a weapon of great strength and intelligence, a being who can slaughter hundreds, including vampires, as he knows their weaknesses. And I have annoyed them enough for this?"

Christophe allowed himself a wintry smile. "You took a little too much. From the wrong people. But they practise a special sort of vampirism, and they can suck the life out of the people and soon replenish their coffers. That is not the issue. The problem is that you have organised a bunch of criminals, just a little, but enough to demonstrate to interested observers that you have a talent for that sort of thing."

"Really? I see. I think I see... There has just been a revolution in France..."

"Precisely. Those who would have you destroyed don't know what you are, although maybe some, those who are used to employing villains, can guess. But they know you've just come home from France, and they will assume you've been trained in the ways of the Terror. If Kerr is after you, you're in danger. Some of us wouldn't... care if we were. I'm assuming you're past that stage. Perhaps you haven't yet realised it."

At this point Philippe bade Simone open her eyes.

"I see... I think," she said.

"You weren't just making money, you were robbing the rich and giving to the poor. Robin Hood the vampire!"

He sighed. "Even that can be accommodated within the status quo. Don't you see? My own needs had turned out to fit neatly with the needs of others. We all needed food, clothes, shelter, medical aid. And an education. The rich begrudged even a farthing wasted on the likes of us, but they could spare that. If they had to. But I was organising them, you see. Our lords and masters were truly alarmed at that. So they were setting Kerr on me."

Chapter Ten

La mort est le remede

(Chamfort)

Funny thing, thought Simone. I somehow got it in my head that vampires were aristocratic, but the second vampire I meet, excluding myself, turns out to be some sort of prototype trade unionist. It's nice that we're such individuals. Better than nice, it's encouraging that our personalities survive the change to such an extent; that we are not overwhelmed by this thing, this disease, although I don't think that's really the word...

Philippe was continuing, but in less intense mode. As she listened, she thought it was like life in general. If you remembered it all with that intensity, recreating each experience with the vividness of Philippe's first conversation with Christophe, it would drain the present of meaning, eventually. But memory had its vivid moments and its long stretches of not especially interesting stuff... or else it was objectively interesting, but somehow didn't make that impact on the brain.

"I was immediately concerned at Christophe's warning, and I didn't doubt he was sincere. My main worry was my contacts, the poor damned souls trying to survive in London. I didn't want to die, I really didn't, and the funny thing was that the reason was them. I hadn't cared about myself, or so I thought. Now I knew that the curse of vampirism could also be a blessing, if one remained master of the ravening hunger. And by never allowing myself to get that hungry, I would be safe around people. I also determined to acquire enough wealth to protect them. Some were mere children, and this was at a time when children were transported or hanged for the most petty of crimes.

I told Christophe what I needed to do. He didn't argue with me. He knew that my desire to improve these people's lives was the saving of me. He knew better than anyone that the attrition rate amongst recently made vampires was very high, due to the loss of the wheel of the heart and the consequent deep depression. Nothing could make up for that, except a purpose such as mine. It was rational, and it was kind, because ultimately, kindness is the rational thing to spread through this world. I might not be able to be happy, but there is a happiness, even if it's not mine.

He even offered to help me, although, as I discovered, he was an aesthete, more interested in art than in people. He was also a very curious, questioning type, a sort of scientist. You'll see: he is always trying to find scientific explanations for the condition of vampirism.

But he liked me. He said he found me 'moving, like a symphony'. I'm not sure I ever understood that. All I could do musically was sing... and that had suddenly grown harder, without the pure, unmanufactured breath."

"You sing? Is there no end to your complexity?" Simone was being flippant, but she meant it. How could someone whose mind you could read continue to surprise you? The obvious explanation was that he kept the thoughts he wanted you to read at the forefront of his mind, and the rest was... filed away somewhere. You had to look harder. And that breath business..?

"Haven't you tried pretending to breathe? Not yet? I thought you'd have noticed me doing it. I like to do a sigh, quite histrionic you know. But one always has to remember to do it, the fake breathing. The funny thing is, it's a meditation done in some parts of the world, concentrating on the breath, and we have to do it, whenever we want to appear to breathe."

Simone had not yet done it. She tried, and it felt odd at first, almost sinful, as if she were somehow forbidden. But there were no angry gods telling her she couldn't fake her breath, so she inhaled as if smoking a cigarette, and it was indescribably pleasurable and comforting, although she forgot about it moments later.

"You've got it," said Philippe, "It's lovely, isn't it? Yet humans take it for granted."

"So do I after a few breaths. Human or vampire, nobody can concentrate."

"Some people can, I believe, but though I've never met anyone better than Christophe, he would be the first to tell you that he's not very good at it.

Anyway, he and I decided to move as fast as possible. I could see he felt that Kerr could be a real threat to me. I was sure it was my sanity Kerr wanted to destroy, for his own entertainment, and I was convinced he would hurt my new friends to that end. So we decided to steal certain gold artefacts which could then be melted down. Vampires turn to theft rather easily, as you know, but the more refined ones target those who deserve a lesson in loss."

Simone wondered if he meant her, and her raids on innocent Germans and shoe shops. She didn't care, anyway, so long as she didn't rob the very poor.

"So you model yourself on Robin Hood?" she asked.

"This hoard," Philippe went on, ignoring that, "was in the possession of a secretive group known as the Lord Mayor's Men, justices and lawyers each and every one; merciless despots who violated the true laws that ought to underpin society and enacted their own cruel tyranny instead."

"Did you know your teeth are lengthening?" said Simone, a little anxiously. She had felt her own grow, when feelings of savage hunger took over, usually just before she drank deep of some poor beast's blood. She hadn't previously made much note when the same thing happened to Philippe, being at that point absorbed in her own satisfaction. She hadn't thought about it. It was odd to see it when no food was around.

"I'm hungry, let's get something to eat." But it was more than that. He was angry. He must have been very angry indeed, because even when tranquilising Germans she had had to consciously focus on making her teeth grow into fangs. It had not been hunger, nor anger, that made it happen, but necessity. This was different.

"Stay here. I'll see to it." As she left the room, Simone reflected on an aunt of hers that suffered from diabetes. It was crucial that she eat regularly and often, or else she might go into a coma. It was like being a vampire, except that it was other people who were more likely to faint, and maybe never wake up again. So in both instances it was important to eat before you got really hungry, and to be prepared with a supply of food at the ready.

Neither Simone's aunt nor her newfound friend Philippe were always as prepared as they should have been, and this peripatetic lifestyle was too chancy. We should lead very regulated, predictable lives, she told herself, keep ourselves and others safe from the inner savage. But this is wartime, and we have work to do.

She called for the family. Madame rushed to her, closely followed by her husband.

"We have been wounded and have lost blood. We need a litre from each of you," she said. "Don't worry, we won't hurt you."

Madame looked unconvinced. The door behind Simone opened and Philippe emerged. The veins stood out on his forehead and his soft brown eyes seemed to have a golden glint. He moved so fast it was almost a blur: One minute Simone was wondering what was the matter, the next his teeth had sunk into Madame's neck, and she went as limp as if they'd been hypodermic needles full of opiates. The man screamed. He sounded like a hunted creature, hardly sentient: The scream had an hysterical, shrill note to it.

"That's enough!" barked Simone. "Let her go now!"

But he did not release the woman so she leapt on him and gave him a mighty blow on the head. To her surprise he let the woman go and keeled over. Simone was astonished that she was strong enough to do that to him, but she spared no time to consider the matter; she caught the woman in her arms as he dropped her and made sure to lower her carefully to the floor.

The man was still shrieking. Now words came out.

"We are true patriots! It is the only way to free Brittany!"

This would have been puzzling except that his mind was laid bare by shock, and Simone could see what it was about. The two sons were fighting on behalf of the Germans. They were Breton separatists who regarded France as the oppressor, and saw the Occupation as an opportunity for Brittany to break free. They had long found support from the Irish government.

Simone had suspected something strange was going on here. Her childhood had been spent in the country but now she was an impatient city dweller, and she'd thought the stoniness and slow-wittedness was just the way peasants behaved. It was alarming that this man could keep his secret till shock broke down the barriers. Perhaps it had been a mental discipline he'd imposed on himself in case he was tortured. And who would torture him? Why, the Resistance.

The whole thing was a confusing mess. Didn't these people go to the cinema? Or read popular fiction? Didn't they know who the baddies were? Surely they did, which meant they were bad for assisting them. Who would want to play the bad guy in real life? Doesn't everyone believe they're on the side of the angels? Or not?

And of course the Resistance tortured people. They had to, but weren't they then the bad guys?

Simone felt her teeth lengthening now. She was angry, at the farmer for being able to conceal his secret till now, at Philippe for losing control, and at the world for being so confusing. A little voice was whispering in her head: It is confusing, this business of right and wrong. Just look after yourself, take what you want and need, and if you want more than you need... that's human nature. Being a vampire won't change that.

She grabbed the still keening farmer and bit into his sinewy neck. The first hit of the human blood was blissful. All the problems in the world just vanished. Then, before she knew it – although in fact she'd had her litre – someone was warning her 'that's enough now' and it was Philippe. She let the man go, gently deposited him on the floor, and silently congratulated herself on not needing a punch in the head.

"You pack an incredible wallop for a girl, even a vampire girl," said Philippe. "So he was hiding his thoughts about his boys in the alternative resistance? A powerfully obstinate man, then."

"Is that the key? Obstinacy?"

"He's a peasant from the Celtic fringe of Europe. Celts are notoriously obstinate. I'm one, so I should know."

"How long before we can get out of here?"

"I don't know. I bet those land girls have gone to summon the sons to deal with us."

Simone could see lowering winter skies through the window, but even though the sun wasn't visible it would destroy them both if they walked outside. But there was a car, a battered looking old thing, sitting outside.

She dragged the man off the floor with one hand, and the woman with another. Philippe watched impassively, seeing no need to interfere when she was doing a good job. She took them to the door, and told the farmer to bring the car right up to the door, as close as he could get. Then she got the woman to get some thick blankets from the room they'd just been in.

The woman was only allowed to join her husband in the front passenger seat once the vampires were settled in the back, swathed in the blankets with the tiniest gap to see from. Simone told them to drive east or they would die.

They got the message. And the vampires were able to read from their minds that they had indeed sent the girls off to contact the Breton group, but that they were a long way off, in the west, and barring miracles it would be a considerable time before they got back and found Mum and Dad looking anaemic.

They drove for a couple of hours, and were lucky not to run into any roadblocks. They were probably known fugitives now, and all roads leading out from the bridge they'd demolished would be being watched, so Philippe had demanded a map from the couple, only to be told they didn't have one in the car.

So they'd taken some minor roads that led off in vaguely the right direction and hoped for the best. Finally, the sun set.

Philippe ordered the couple out of the car, and dug out some more money; pre-war francs.

He gave it to them in two handfuls of notes. "That's for the car," he said, "And that's to keep your mouths shut."

Of course they wouldn't and in fact they couldn't. It was too far for them to walk home so they'd have to go to the authorities. But neither Philippe nor Simone cared about any of that. The presence of the pair depressed both the vampires, associated as they were with Bretons who regarded themselves as freedom fighters yet sided with the Germans.

Simone got in the driver's seat. "I didn't like them," she said. "The whole thing made me realise that just when you think you've got the hang of politics you discover another layer of complexity."

"Think how I feel. I've been involved in two revolutions…"

"Two? You mean the Russian revolution as well?"

"Yes. I'll tell you about it sometime. Riots and massacres, too. In the end, all you want to do is to stop the suffering, and it doesn't matter whose it is. But the suffering continues. And I faked that up a bit, by the way."

"Yes, I did wonder. You wouldn't have lasted this long life – half life – of yours if you get carried away that easily. To frighten them into spilling the beans, right?"

"I sensed something, a battle within them, but holding back their thoughts: They were amateurs but still... and I'd just been talking about my enemy so the fangs emerged of their own accord."

"Your enemy? Kerr?"

He gave her a grudging smile, like the sun in November, all the more to be cherished for its rarity.

"The class enemy, Simone. Even Kerr cannot be everywhere. But the oppressors are. Much more dangerous."

Simone drove in silence for a couple of miles. It had swiftly become apparent that they needed to fill the tank. It was astonishing they'd got this far. The farming couple must have had a very generous ration book.

"It's for the tractors, probably," said Philippe, reading her mind.

"They've got plenty more in the barns, I expect. We're going to have to steal some. Let's see if they've got a can in the back."

They spluttered to a halt. "I'd hoped to find a petrol station, but they probably don't exist anymore, closed down 'cos of shortages," said Philippe. "There aren't many cars about, have you noticed?"

"There haven't been, ever since... I was changed. And before. Look, let's concentrate, we'll solve this."

Simone climbed a tree, which was easy in the land girl's practical trousers. Philippe waited till she was quite high, and then joined her with one powerful leap from the ground.

"You know," said Simone sombrely, there's something insect-like about us now."

"Don't dwell on it," advised her companion.

They spotted some farm buildings in a small group and then, another such complex, in the opposite direction.

"Which one?" he asked her.

"The one with the cars parked outside," she suggested.

So they headed off to the most likely looking farm, and, having no reason to dislike whoever the inmates were, decided not to steal their vehicles but only their fuel. Luckily their recent hostages seemed to have the equipment for siphoning petrol in the boot, which made Simone wonder a little. These were hard times for everyone.

A dog had started its warning bark – but as suddenly, it was silent.

"That's a good trick, isn't it, very useful," said Simone.

"Very useful indeed. I'll show you how. Dogs are very susceptible to mental control. It came in very handy when I was doing a bit of burglary."

"A *bit* of burglary?" returned Simone.

They got back to the car. It was comfortable, better than hiding in hedges, but they'd probably abandon it when it ran out of fuel again, or if they encountered a roadblock.

And this they eventually did. Since it was dark and they had night vision they saw it ahead long before they were spotted, so they just left the car where it was and headed into the undergrowth. From now on their journey would be a bit more taxing, but soon, maybe tomorrow, they would hit the French/Swiss border.

They made sure to feast on some cattle before they moved too far ahead. They needed their own fuel now. Indeed, apart from the odd stumble over difficult terrain they were moving faster than the car could. It was noticeably colder, something which Simone could only determine by feeling the end of her nose, which was the sole thermometer available. She wondered if vampires could get frostbite, and if so, would it hurt, and would the appendage eventually drop off. And if it did, would it grow again?

"Yes, quite slowly," said Philippe, having followed this train of thought. "And just to deal with the next question, which must follow as the night does day, all appendages eventually grow again except the head."

"But…" Simone grimaced. She didn't want to continue, because what was there to say? Yeuch? "Why are you misquoting Hamlet?" she managed.

"Was I? I'm sorry. I was trying to distract your attention…"

"From the weirdness? Thank you."

They started to ascend to higher ground, and as a raw grey dawn threatened to break they found what looked like a shelter for sheep... for their shepherd too, when needed, no doubt. It was a rambling pen, partially covered by a roof. If they hadn't found it, the only recourse would have been to bury themselves in snow.

"We were lucky, finding this," said Simone.

It's not just luck," her fellow vampire replied. "I went fishing in minds. When it was near daybreak, I went prodding about in dreams. There's a small population in the area so it didn't take long."

Simone said nothing. He could read her mind anyway, which saved time. It seemed she was still learning what they were capable of.

Philippe continued his earlier tale, the one cut short by his rage and hunger.

"Well, I did succeed in robbing the worshipful masters, or whatever damn fool name they called themselves, and with the help of certain acquaintances got the gold turned into manageable currency. Then I packed my friends off to the country, and told them to buy me a house, and to live there till I came back from abroad. *If* I came back from abroad... Christophe swore to help them, and I had to trust him with their safety. Who else could even hope to defend them? Except myself... and I was not ready to confront Kerr yet."

"It's odd that you call him Kerr, and I still think of him as Graves. But I suppose neither of those are his real name."

"Nothing he says can be trusted, obviously. And his mind – well, I was going to say it's impenetrable, but Christophe says that's no longer true for some of us... older vampires. I haven't tried for a while. Maybe it's true. Or just true for Christophe, who, by the way, claims now that Graves/Kerr was originally a Crusader. As for Christophe himself..."

"It's rude to ask vampires how old they are, since it's a big status thing. I read that from you, and that you suspect Christophe of being older again."

"I've waited for well over a century for him to tell me, and I will never ask. I trust him completely, since he's demonstrated his love of the good many times over. Like I mentioned before, he has talked about knowing Socrates, so that was probably around his birthdate. I don't enquire further. There's a world of loss there.

Anyway he took care of my protégés and managed to cloak their presence from Kerr. This is something I am only just finding out how to do. I haven't mastered it yet, and I certainly hadn't then, or I could have protected them myself.

"After all this time – people you don't even know – and Kerr would bother with petty revenge?"

"Vampire vendettas go on for centuries and, unlike human ones, continue to involve the original parties to the dispute. Do you want to hear more of my history?"

"Of course."

So they whiled away the day. Philippe described how he took passage on a ship which had transportees aboard it. He bribed the Captain with a tidy sum to give him the best cabin – which wasn't saying much – and told him he was not to be disturbed in daylight. He naturally offered a matching sum of money to be handed over when he'd safely reached Australia – he had some notion of getting as far away from everybody he'd been fool enough to care about and you couldn't get farther than that… and of course, he might be able to find his father and help him. As for blood, he took several cages full of small animals, and informed the Captain that he was a natural philosopher and needed them for experiments. To add credence to this, he brought some equipment, test tubes and the like, and some bottles of coloured liquid, which sadly was not blood disguised as something else, since stale blood is worthless to a vampire. He soon discovered that the animals weren't enough, they were far too small, and he killed a couple by accident. He decided that he'd have to ask the captain to go ashore for a night.

But the ship was not destined to reach Australia. The transported criminals were subject to beatings and short rations and Philippe could not ignore that. It seemed that mostly they were being sick, and then the cruelty really started at the Bay of Biscay. The worst of it was Philippe having to listen to what the captain was trying to do to one of the women… and not being able to stop it because it was in daylight.

As dusk fell on that particular day, he left his cabin filled with a dark rage that threatened to devour him. And he was starving, having had very small amounts of blood, just enough to keep him ticking over.

167

He didn't go into too much narrative detail to Simone, just showed her the pictures, which he hoped would be enough: The weeping woman, the brutish captain, his sailors awaiting their turn with her, and then the eruption, which felt like it came from Simone's own throat, as she looked through his eyes. As he growled like some great jungle beast she felt the sound. It shook her; the overtones in it were not human.

Simone felt as though it were her, pulling the captain off his prey and twisting the man's head till it was ripped from the shoulders, and the ecstasy of complete abandonment to the beast inside coursed through her, a wicked, horrible bliss. It was as though her arms picked up the gruesome corpse, her arms that were flinging it over the side of the ship, hers the arm that brandished the head as if it were some righteous battle trophy... but it wasn't righteous at all, and it was odd, it seemed as though all creation shuddered at the sight... though the sea was calm. But she, she could not take her eyes off it. She was trembling, or maybe her host was, but it seemed she would never see anything else again.

"God save me," she spat, terrified, but it was him speaking, not her... although the boundaries were becoming frighteningly blurred.

"Let's stop," said Philippe, hoarsely. "This is not me."

Simone opened her eyes to the present, which was night in a sheepfold, with no fire or blankets and the snow falling, although on the plus side, she needed neither of those things for warmth. Still, they represented warmth, and she retained a psychological need to feel as if she were warm... but bleak as her surroundings were, they were a hundred times preferable to being on that ship, then.

"Go back to the telling, but you can omit the showing, for now," she told him.

He didn't argue with that.

There were guards with guns and swords who were there to protect the sailors from any trouble from the transportees, although no one had seen fit to give them the task of protecting the latter from the sailors. One of them nearly paid with his life for this shortcoming, after having tried to shoot a musket ball at Philippe, but this time he provided a tasty snack for the vampire, who elected to leave him alive after taking a pint or so.

After this there were no more casualties, as the shot had actually entered Philippe's stomach. Even vampires feel pain, while they are healing, but so enraged was Philippe that it didn't stop him at all, and he told Simone that he just pulled the thing out of his stomach and tossed it overboard to follow the rapist to a watery tomb.

This had impressed everyone, sailors, soldiers, and convicts. Those whose chains didn't get in the way struggled onto their knees to beg for mercy. Philippe embraced the woman whose ill-treatment had been the catalyst for his violent spree, and announced that she and the other convicts should be unchained at once, and that they were all under his protection, and those who didn't like that could take a cold bath.

Simone realised she was watching through his eyes again. It's happening without my control, said a commentator in her head, who for once, was not her. Very well, she thought back at him, but steer away from the worst bits. Please. She felt his half-suppressed irritation, although she doubted that he meant her to. The thought sneaked past his usually vigilant inner censor: He expected that she would have to see, and even do, much, much worse.

Philippe knew that there would be those already scheming as to how to overthrow this new captain. He gestured to the rather shabby figure who still managed to sport a bit of braid and whom he supposed to be the first officer.

The man stepped forward. "I told him it was wrong!" he spluttered. "Did you see? Others were waiting but not I!"

But Philippe had started to really get good at the old mind-reading game by this stage of his vampiric career. Simone felt as if she were the one who read the truth: The man was homosexual, and so had remained aloof, but that was no virtue under the circumstances, for there was no compassion or interest in the fate of others either.

"No," said Philippe/Simone, back there in the vivid past, "You may have refrained from evil yourself, for whatever cause..." and Simone wondered at his delicacy, when even in her day (as she found herself thinking of it) people were casually cruel towards such men, and women, "...but you did not attempt to stop it. Your cowardice has driven me to commit mortal sin."

He got the man by the throat. "You are not completely useless, though, are you?" he said, plunging his fangs in, and Simone felt the exhilaration and horror of drinking human blood.

169

But in line with her wishes, it was not another horror show. The man paid his tribute to the monster, a litre or so of blood, and then he fell, anaesthetised, to the deck.

"He is alive," Philippe announced to the ship. "I will take turns drinking from you, but I will not drain you and you will not die because of me. Now, is there anyone amongst the sailors who is not a filthy animal? Or do you others know how to captain a boat?"

A skinny boy in little better than rags was shoved forward by an even grubbier looking sailor. The boy stood his ground in front of the mighty vampire and held himself straight, even though he didn't know what to expect and instant death was, as far as he knew, still a possibility.

"I'm not a filthy animal," he ventured proudly. "I respect women, like my mother taught me." His accent was West Country, with a countryman's burr that reminded Simone of the efforts of the supporting cast of a pirate story she'd seen at the cinema. Obviously, it being a British film, the stars had sounded not only posh, but Dutch – Simone was what might have been described as well spoken by those who measure such things, but she was not afflicted with the strangulated 'ah's that were warped into 'eh's.

Probably a fashion set by William and Mary, responded a voice in her head. She was now thinking two lines of thought at the same time, hers and Philippe's. It was like people clamouring for attention.

Meanwhile in the past there was a hush, as everyone watched to see what Philippe would do. He reached out and tipped the boy's head back.

In the watching crew were men who would have brought the boy to him as a human sacrifice, and they would have done it eagerly, desperate to show their loyalty and obedience to the most powerful creature on the ship. They were watching now partly to see if he was indeed to be sacrificed.

"I believe you," said Philippe, "how can you have survived so virtuous still?" Simone could see it was true.

"I have only just joined the ship this voyage, sir. But I was raised a fisherman."

"In Cornwall, if I judge right. There's an edge to them that live on the edge. So you can sail a ship this size?"

"Aye sir, with these gents' help," and he indicated the other crew.

The ability to read minds has its limits, as Simone well knew by now. Because she was virtually occupying Philippe's mind and body, albeit in the past, she could tell the boy was sincere in what he said, but that didn't mean he was correct: He could be deluded, with no idea how to sail the ship. But Philippe was ahead of her.

"Then I proclaim you Captain, while I shall be Master. You will carry out my instructions, and you will be sure to make use of the skills of your fellows, asking their advice and putting your pride away to do so, if necessary. If they disobey you, tell me and I will make sure they never do it again."

"And so," said Philippe, in a brisk tone, while the picture in Simone's head faded, "that is what happened." And the boy, Roger, made a good captain, although he was a little concerned when I told him we weren't going to Australia. I realised that, from my point of view, the project was madness. Vampires can't go on sea voyages, it's ridiculously chancy, no blood, lots of sunlight. What could I have been thinking?

One day, I swore to myself, I'll try by land. I had seen maps, I knew there was a way, although at the very end, I'd still need a ship."

Simone was pondering the way Philippe's voice had changed when she heard him speak to the boy, as if mimicking his accent.

"You do get distracted by the trivial, don't you? Is that a women's thing?"

She was about to flair up, but the sly curve of his lip warned her that he was playing her. No need to read his mind when his body gave everything away.

"Don't bother, I am not going to react: I've heard worse, and from people who meant it."

He almost cracked a full-blown smile at that.

"I'm a peasant, remember? There was a time when you'd have barely understood my speech, then I started mixing with all kinds of people and it modifies your accent without you necessarily noticing. And they were different even a hundred, hundred and fifty years ago. The London accent was very different – or rather, wery different – you find it in Dickens. Now... I seem to automatically settle on sounding like the person I talk to.

Anyway, I offered the convicts, first, whatever they wanted. We could return to Britain, find their families, if they had any, and lay low out of the reach of the law. But everyone deemed that impractical. They could carry on to Australia, obviously travelling with much better conditions, but once there, they'd still have to serve a sentence that might very well be fatal, since we didn't know what diseases or savage beasts might be native to that land. I held my peace during that discussion, as I had seen enough of life by then to know that the most fearsome beast and the greatest pestilence on this earth are the same: man. And that is the creature we would do well to fear above all.

In the end, we put ashore in Portugal, and found some middling bit of land no one seemed to want. We paid off the old caballero who claimed to own it, and we cultivated the plants that flourished there, vine and olive, as well as oranges. We bought what we needed until we were an established holding, feeding our own folk, there at the very western edge of Europe. Crew and soldiers were there too, but when the money ran out I asked who wanted to leave with me, and only Roger was willing. The others had all experienced being landless men and women. Achilles might have thought being a serf to such a person was better than ruling over all the glorious dead, but not everyone was convinced.

I see you are slightly surprised that I have benefited from a classical education. Christophe, to whom I owe so very much, was most emphatic that I acquire such learning although I had been trying to teach myself, reading the Rights of Man and serious tracts of that nature, taking it rather slowly to begin with. Christophe recognised that although my life's path had been dramatically re-routed since I was changed, I nevertheless retained my thirst for learning: It was a huge part of my personality, and has remained so since youth.

There'd been a dame school in my village, and of course she charged, and even a penny was a daunting amount to keep spare, for our family. Luckily the dame was fond of me – Miss Ford she was called – because I liked to learn, unlike the hopelessly thick farmers' sons she had to deal with, only there because their fathers and mothers wanted them to improve their lot in life. After a short while, our family fell from favour, but Miss Ford persuaded my mother that she needed my help as an assistant, so I stayed on for free.

To me, then, the other children were rich. Although they were only tenants, they were secure, so it seemed, and there was always enough on the table. How they looked down on the likes of me! But in all fairness, I looked down on them. And Miss Ford, a childless spinster, encouraged me, telling me that I was the sun to their miserable candles – so intellectual was I – and she spared me time after class. For all teachers favour those who want to learn: Who wants to have to try to ram facts into the boneheads who don't want to know? I hold her in my memory in gratitude, and hope and pray that she sits in heaven at the feet of the greatest teachers, having nothing to do but enjoy the bliss of hanging on their words."

"'Their' words?" Simone was half-listening, not thinking about anything else exactly, but lulled by a not unfamiliar tale, until the plural being used struck her as distinctly unfamiliar.

"Indeed," replied Philippe, and she was almost certain that he had followed her train of thought exactly, since he gave a knowing little half-smile. "My first teacher was devout, and held one incarnation of god to be the only one. But my second teacher, if you don't count Kerr, made me see that it was ridiculous to believe that God sent his son to earth for 33 years out of... billions! So everyone who wasn't born in that place and in that time was treated to a secondhand, second rate version of truth? Nonsense, absolute nonsense!"

Simone did not reply to this because it was not something she had ever really thought about, but she knew people who would have been absolutely horrified at these remarks. Still, they would be horrified at lots of things, including her current condition, and it occurred to her, not for the first time, that she really didn't care about the opinions of most people, because they were absolutely stupid and they knew nothing.

Now that was a shocking thought. It meant she was freer than she'd ever been, but on the other hand, alone, or nearly, in a world of idiots.

"I loved Roger as if he were my son," said Philippe, who had either been preoccupied, or thought her current thoughts too boring too comment on. "But there were difficulties."

Simone saw the face of the grown-up Roger, put into her mind's eye by Philippe, and looking at Philippe, saw the difficulty right away. Already Roger looked the same age, if not slightly older.

"Yes," he said. "That."

"We took the ship out again, and found some suitable prey, by which I mean they deserved it," he continued. "Roger and a couple of the sailors he'd chivvied to come along with us decided to play pirate. We were quite cut off, you understand, although some of the older sailors had heard stories of ships out of Liverpool and Bristol bound for Africa to steal slaves and sell them to America.

173

Slaves! I had just discovered their existence in classical times, and I was fool enough to think that's where slavery belonged. And then I thought the Americas were where men – yes, and women! – went to be free. Didn't they sign their Declaration just before the Revolution took place in France? Were they not guided by the writings of Thomas Paine?"

Simone looked sympathetic. Part of her thought Philippe too idealistic too live in the world, and she couldn't help but let the thought emerge in her consciousness. But all he did was give a wry half-smile.

"We robbed a would-be slave ship of its wealth. We practically stripped the crew and all the fittings, leaving nothing with which to buy slaves. The Captain was very upset, especially as we attacked at night. He thought it was unfair, he said, and I had no reply because I was too astonished at such effrontery to speak. I just lined the crew up, and drank pint after pint from each of them until I was bloated as a flea.

They thought I was a demon, and maybe I am. But I left them alive. That still didn't stop the Captain, who carried on maintaining it was unfair, because the sellers of slaves were also black, and sold their own people.

At this display of ignorance elevated to an art, that of self-deception, I nearly cracked, as I had done all those years before, when Roger's captain had turned beast. I could have ripped his head off and drank straight from the neck stem. But Roger was there, holding me back.

"Remember, Phil, you still have a soul," he said, and I knew he was right, even though my soul seemed at a little distance from me, being still attached to this vampire form, yet not wholly one with it.

So that is how we refilled our coffers, and we attacked slavers on their way to Africa on several occasions, robbing them of the means to buy their poor victims. We wounded people, but we did not kill, apart from one individual so convulsed with fear that he leapt overboard... but I do not hold myself accountable for that. And I am very particular about my accounting.

So then Napoleon invaded the Iberian peninsula, but his troops did not find us in our remote stronghold. During this time it was only accessible by water, anyway. Later, when the French threat had vanished, we started to think about building our own roads, one going north, one south. But I was gone by then.

The community thrived, and Roger grew older, while I – didn't. Roger would not marry, nor have children, although he had mistresses... for he would not be tied to supporting a family, as that, he claimed, would make him a serf to some landlord.

I promised him gold a-plenty from our buccaneering, and he would have been well set-up wherever he went, with no need to be a serf at all. I asked him he wouldn't like to return a rich man to his native Cornwall.

"Don't you remember what it's like?" he responded. "They'll all know who I was, and conclude that to be as well off as I'd be I must've led a life of criminality. They'll find some excuse to put me away, and hang me most likely. They won't like some upstart giving their poor tenants ideas. And I would, you know. That'd be my pleasure. Not that the Cornish have much time for revolutions; too busy tipping their caps and yessir, nossir, and turning in their own kind to curry favour with the filth that runs the place. It's a beautiful place, but the lovelier the place, the worse the people. And they don't have no truck with them famous fellows that were transported. They'd turn those boys over to the Constables. They think they're independent minded! Ha!"

And of course, he was right about the peasantry of Cornwall, and most of the rest of the country too. He must have had an experience or two similar to mine, although he was not one to talk about the past. He was like me: We couldn't stand to see cruelty, or injustice, or to see anything caged.

I can't tell you how it felt to see him age. I can't even show you, because I cannot bear to remember. It felt as terrible as you could imagine... and then worse than that. He stayed fit though, and should have lived longer. But he caught some damned cold, and it went to his chest, and became pneumonia... in Portugal, where the climate is so sweet! I sat with him, and I put all my questions in my eyes.

"No," he said. I knew it would come to this one day, but I had never broached it. He had seen enough of my life to know all the difficulties, and I was determined not to influence him, because there were two sides, but when the end was nearer I lost all my will and my pride and knew I would – God forgive me! – try and persuade him.

Deep down I knew it. He wasn't old, but he was no longer in his prime, and if someone were to have a set intention to become a vampire he'd declare it before his final moments, surely. For wouldn't he want to preserve his physical form at its peak? (I'd never told him that it would happen anyway.) Not that this had influenced me, but I wondered. It was always in my mind, though I was afraid to ask, for fear I already knew the answer.

His breathing was a gurgle, and he could barely talk. I wept tears, vampire tears of blood. Through my sobs, I had to ask... Why?

Suddenly the narrative turned into sound and pictures in Simone's head. Philippe had said he couldn't bear to do it but it probably was the easiest way of continuing: It was as though she were being addressed by this man, who'd died long ago, and she was unable to avoid her host's emotional torment entirely.

"I love you as a father, as a friend," Roger choked out the words. "If I get to heaven, I'll defend your good name to God himself. But... I don't want to be... a demon. I'm afraid it would change me too much and heaven will bar its gates to me."

He lay back, almost exhausted. "But I'll speak for you, Phil, at the crossroads, when the time comes."

Those were his last words, and soon I was to know the meaning of the words 'broken heart' even though I knew mine had withered decades before.

"What did he mean by the crossroads?" asked Simone, as soon as she felt a decent silence had elapsed.

"Who knows? He was dying. He had a high temperature."

"So... delirious, then?"

Philippe nodded, in a pre-occupied way, but she thought he was trying to mask his thoughts from her. He doesn't know for sure, she thought, but he believes the dying man had some kind of vision, or foreknowledge, granted to those on the brink of death.

But all she knew was that they buried suicides at crossroads, and hanged people on gibbets there.

"Well," he said heavily, "to conclude this episode, we buried my friend, and at night, so I could attend. I was aware as I had never been before, of the eyes on me, and it was a burden to be able to hear their thoughts. Roger had been a lot more to me alive than I had dreamed. He had protected me. While we had been buccaneering, much had gone on in our community, new people had been born and grown to adulthood, and they only had their parents' tales of how I'd helped them, and continued to help. The younger ones regarded me with wariness. Meanwhile the older ones were free, with Roger gone, to indulge in their resentment towards me, which grew with every passing year, as my hair stayed dark, my face remained unlined, and my strength was undiminished.

I had to have it out with them, so I called on the oldest, who were transported for trying to bring workers together to call for better conditions, like the Tolpuddle martyrs Roger had alluded to. There were three, and they were good men, who cared for their fellows and seemed to have taught the younger ones the value of cooperation and mutual regard.

But we are born into this world with two natures, and even the best nurtures a little darkness, nestling within the breast like a secret too grim to be told. Envy besets us, and these wise ones could not suppress their envy of what they perceived as my immortal youth.

I went straight to the point with them. I asked them if they were aware that one of the symptoms of my condition was the ability to read minds. I think they did know, but had preferred to forget the knowledge. I told them that I knew that they hated me, and I knew why, and that I did not blame them, as it was human nature.

There were lots of protesting noises and denials, but I stood implacable, letting them spill their nonsense into the air, until they ran out of things to say. At last I got them to acknowledge the truth, and it was brutal, but not unexpected. They wanted me to leave, forever, and never return. After all I'd done for them. They never wanted to see my face, not ever. They hated the very sight of me, and it was no use protesting that I didn't see daylight, didn't eat anything delicious, ever, and was potentially a danger to other people, so had to be very careful to make sure I was full of animal blood, or else had to bargain with the desperately poor for sustenance.

The sight of my youthful face wiped all that out of their minds. I looked twenty five or so. My teeth were white, my muscles firm, my belly flat, my hair lustrous. They had once looked the same. Now their hair was grey and thin, their teeth darkened or missing; even the shape of their bodies had changed, growing around the waist, shrinking around the chest, while their limbs dwindled, and they got out of breath quickly. No wonder they hated me.

So I left, immediately after we buried Roger. I could not stay another minute. I could see that they thought I had refused him the gift they craved. I took a certain pleasure in telling them it had been he who had refused, whether or not they believed me.

I had one last confrontation before I left. I was packing a very small amount into a satchel – books, a change of clothes – as I prepared to leave the modest quarters, half hut, backing onto a cave. I picked up my sleeping roll. Into the room strode Michael, one of the ones I thought of as the Elders.

"Well," he spat, "so you let him die rather than share your secret. And we thought you loved him as a so… brother."

I felt then that I had suffered enough. I wasn't in a mood to tolerate any more nonsense.

"Son, you mean son. But you hesitate, because I look more like the son, now. Even thinking of him as a very big brother is stretching it. Perhaps if I had a father with two wives, like the heathen, perhaps then it would work. What do you want of me, Michael? He didn't want it! Understand? He DIDN'T WANT IT!"

Well that was a mistake. I had revealed that I would have changed Roger, if he had let me. Which begged the question……

"Will you give it to me, then?" asked the old man.

Then Philippe allowed Simone to experience the full effect of being there, and it was shocking to suddenly have those eyes, begging, wanting, desperate, staring at hers/Philippe's, asking for something so valuable that could only be bestowed by Phillipe, or, as it felt then, her.

Vivid though it was, overwhelming even, there was nothing she could do but observe what had happened. She could not change nor influence a thing.

It was as if Michael was shouting in her face, although of course it was Philippe who faced those furious, bulging eyes. She could feel her/Philippe's expression, and even if she had not, she could have read it by the reaction from Michael.

"So you will not!"

"You are older than Roger was. It would not work," prevaricated Philippe, but the man was not fooled. (You expect him to believe that?) thought Simone.

"You're lying. He was what? Ten years younger? So?"

Underneath it all, Philippe was a fiery, impatient Celt, fond of music, poetry and quarrels, Simone realised. His was not a patient nature, though he had tried to direct it that way.

"Very well, have the truth! If I changed you, you'd still look your age, but your back would be straighter and your vigour restored, if not your teeth and hair. Although, why not? I've never met a vampire changed at a later stage of life. The oldest I've seen appeared to be about my age, or rather, the age I seem to be. Yes, maybe that would be the age you looked and felt! What a prize, eternal life, and even eternal youth.

And yes, I wanted Roger to stay with me. We were such friends that we would have kept company through many, many years."

Simone usually saw through Philippe's eyes but without the accompanying emotions; just her own, which were intense enough, but this time she felt the wave of grey grief as if it passed through her as well as him. She felt him clutch at a chair, to stop himself fainting, and for all the world she could not tell whether that sorrow existed in the past, or the present, or even whose grief it was.

She felt her heart, or the place where her heart had been, surge with anguish, like a spring tide so high no harbour could contain it. She was shocked: He pretends to be dead inside! She wondered if he had let that past emotion touch her on purpose, to warn her of the pain that awaited an immortal who became attached to a person who was... temporary.

Michael moved to walk out, furiously angry but helpless. Philippe grabbed his arm, and the man could not move, though it was clear that Philippe's strength was a bitter reminder of what he would never have, even as he was forced to submit to it.

"You are a good man, Michael. But though you have known me for so many years, you have either not observed or forgotten the constraints upon me, and the ever-present threat that I should damn my immortal soul."

"Immortal soul? I thought you were modern, a freethinker. All this religious stuff keeps us in bondage, so we will be good little serfs to the rich man."

Michael did not quite say "Pah!" but it was close.

179

"Religion, yes, it serves our rulers, these damned queens and kings still pretending God put them where they are instead of their bully boys with swords and horses! It's too exhausting maintaining monarchy by force of arms, so they employ priests to get in our heads to keep us in line: Saves a lot of effort. But none of that means that there is no God. We can and we must throw aside this secondhand nonsense that is religion; men's stupid opinions about God."

Simone thought they were both going to exclaim "Pah!" at that point, but they didn't.

Michael was not yet beaten, however.

"So why would God care if I became a vampire? I know how you live, I know you cannot walk in the sun, but that's fine, because I've seen plenty of sun. I know you cannot eat, and have to drain animal carcasses, and although it looks disgusting, it is not terrible for you as it would be for normal men. As for the speed and strength, who would not want that?"

"I would have kept Roger by me, and protected him from this dark nature. I would have helped him resist mortal sin. You are a good man but I do not want to be your perpetual shadow, steering you away from murder every night!"

At this, Michael exploded with rage. How dare Philippe suggest that he would be tempted to murder, having watched Philippe murder only one person in forty years, and that the brutal captain of the transport ship! Did he suppose he was the only one with that kind of self control?

Philippe then began to splutter and rage himself. Did Michael know nothing? One life, a hundred lives, a thousand lives; each life was a universe. Number meant nothing. Number! It was an attribute of the created world, but the spirit of a human being was not created, but existed with God from eternity. To kill a person was to kill God! 'Whom God has joined together, let no man put asunder' That was not about the marriage of man and woman but the marriage of mortal flesh with immortal spirit! And he, Philippe, had driven an eternal spirit from its fleshly home! Didn't Michael realise that one lapse like that was enough to ensure damnation? He was a fool! He would die without a murder upon his soul, whereas Philippe could live a thousand years and still be too afraid to die. And didn't the Arabs say that to kill one man was to destroy the world? All right, there had been more than the captain – there had been the doomed aristocrats – but he didn't mention that in his diatribe.

At last Philippe fell silent. All the arguing had come to nothing, neither side had changed its mind. Michael grew silent too, but in his stare was the reproach of a dying man...

"Philippe!" said Simone, as the scene evaporated from her consciousness, "Did you know he was dying?"

"What do you mean? They're all dying."

"He doesn't – didn't – have long, though. Didn't you read it from him?"

"No. Back then, I didn't always pick up on things. I still don't. But now you mention it..."

There was a pregnant pause.

"Did he know?" pondered Philippe.

"If *you* had known, it wouldn't have made a difference, would it?"

"Well," he responded drily, "his health was not relevant to the arguments I made against his being changed, was it?"

Simone wasn't having this. She had just been through an emotionally trying time, although none of it was anything to do with her, and she felt as if her feelings had been put through a wringer, although according to Philippe, sitting there so calmly, she didn't have sufficient in the way of feelings for any of it to register.

He was so full of his nonsense! How could he continue to convince himself as well as attempting to convince others that he was some kind of empty shell? Nothing could be further from the truth, as far as she had observed.

From his explosion at Michael, to his love for Roger, to his killing of the captain... all had been governed by emotion, and not just the instinct driven emotions that were all Philippe would allow himself to claim.

"I did tell you that the simulacrum of true feeling remains with us for a while," he acknowledged, reading her thoughts.

Simone snorted with laughter at such effrontery. "For over 150 years? Come on!"

"That was then. Those experiences – as a vampire, I mean – were new to me."

"Oh, sweetie! It seems to me that being a vampire is not only all about death, and the postponement of it, but love, too! I'm just a kid while you were here before the Revolution but I know that loving someone is giving a hostage to fortune. You're just trying to avoid pain, that's all, it's classic. Yet from your story so far it seems that we vampires feel loss more often, more inevitably, 'because we never die: everyone else does! You can pray that your children outlive you, and thanks to advances in science that will now happen to most parents and that is wonderful, wonderful! And it wasn't always the case."

"Not just science, public health, clean running water. Those who brought that about are greater heroes than any soldier, however brave."

"Yes, yes, slightly off the point but yes. The point being, of course, that one can expect to lose a spouse, certainly a parent, but it is an exception to have to bury one's children."

"Except in wartime, when it's the young adults who die most."

"For God's sake, stop diverting the course of this argument. I don't mean argument, I mean…"

"You do mean argument, but not in the shouting way…"

"PHILIPPE! I'M SHOUTING NOW! I want to make a point that vampires are doomed to feel more pain, sorrow and grief than anybody! Aren't we? That's what makes them sad! And makes them walk into the sunshine, sometimes. We can find ourselves burying generation after generation…"

"Except we don't generate people. We are infertile," responded Philippe, with an air of smugness, as if he'd won.

This was unspeakably annoying, but it was a truly great diversionary tactic, as it immediately started Simone wondering if vampires could have sex. Then, of course, she was immediately embarrassed because he was likely to pick that thought up, so she buried her head in her coat and wrapped her arms around her head, sitting as though sleeping and not to be disturbed. I bet he plays a great game of chess, she thought.

At last, night came, and it wasn't too long a wait, as the days were now very short, and today had in any case been not much more than a slightly paler version of the dark. The night was brightened by a sliver of moon reflected on expanses of white snow.

They left their erstwhile shelter to the sheep, two of which were now drained and dead, the vampires having been hungrier than they thought. and moved across the frozen landscape, travelling swiftly so as not to sink into the snowdrifts and slow themselves down. Eventually they found themselves climbing what must have been the foothills of the Alps, because on the other side of one particularly steep foothill, a landscape feature probably more deserving of the title 'mountain', they saw a shining lake, the moon luring them towards the water with its silver path all laid out for them to walk on. But neither humans nor vampires could walk that path, although one might sail it. A human would die of hypothermia in that water before he or she'd even have a chance to drown: A vampire would sink as if imprisoned in jelly, and have to push and shove against nature itself before it was possible to escape the water's gloopy tug.

"We can cross this if we're fast," suggested Philippe. Sensing her fear, he ran forward onto the water, and by dint of dancing from foot to foot, he demonstrated how they could avoid sinking. But when Simone tried, she could not move quickly enough, and he swept her up in his arms and rushed ashore before he went down too.

"I'm not ready, I'm sorry."

"It's all in the mind," he offered. "You have to be confident that you can do it."

"Well, I'm just not. Can we take the road?

"The road? I suppose so, it'll be safe enough. Who'll be about on a night like this? I think we're not far from Lucerne."

"How far are we from Germany?" she asked, although he probably had no better idea than she did.

"Well, if we avoid Zurich and all the towns, which we'd better do, even if there are only sheep to eat, and then the nights are long, I reckon two days to Frankfurt and another day and a half or so to Berlin. You've been dithering about till now, and so have I, though I have my reasons. Primarily, of course, I've been trying to get out of going to Berlin. And dying."

She didn't bother answering. If he was really interested in what she thought, he could always ask. Although he didn't need to, although it was good manners.

Why should they die, anyway? Except it wouldn't really matter if they did, so long as they were successful.

Stake made of wood through the heart? How would German soldiers work out how to kill them, let alone find out what they were? Or dragging into sunshine? It didn't look like the sun was coming out much at the moment, perhaps they'd just get a bit hot and bothered if it was overcast. Oh yes, and beheading, though that worked for most people. But the first thing guards would think of would be machine guns, and though that would hurt, it wouldn't kill a vampire. The enemy wouldn't think of that. The first time someone shot her full of holes and then watched her get up and carry on walking would probably be enough to scare them off. What about grenades though?

She realised she was afraid.

"As long as they don't wave their garlic sausages at us," quipped Philippe.

"You've been sneaking a look at my thoughts," Simone complained.

He shrugged. "One hardly needs to look. Anyone could read you, you think you're going to die. We can turn back at any time, you know."

"Everyone dies. Let's give our lives… our unnaturally extended lives, at that… a point."

They were fine words, but she was still afraid. They moved swiftly through the snow, which was much kinder to vampires than water was, for some reason. Why wasn't science aware of their existence, so that it could start answering those questions? As long as they kept moving their contact with the snow was brief enough so there was no sinking through the massive drifts, several feet deep. No machinery could have been as efficient, no creature heavier than a bird could have made better progress in those conditions, and on the roads it was not much easier. Visibility was poor, but not for vampires, and so it became like something beautiful and magical; black and white and silver, but that was what night vision saw, anyway. It's like we're in a fairy tale, all the beauty belongs to us, and none of the deadly cold.

All she felt of the cold was the occasional sharp tang in the air that bit, briefly, but that was piquant, like the sting of a hot pepper.

They were a little shy of the German border, just a few kilometres, when the dark began shading to grey and it was time to hide from the dawn again. They thought of building a snow shelter, but a barn loomed up, so they spent their day in that. It was empty of animals, but the smell remained. The herd must have gone to slaughter. Perhaps they had managed to get over the border after all? The Swiss didn't do deprivation, and didn't go to war, being too busy making money out of it. Perhaps this was a German's barn, fallen into disuse since the farmer had been called up.

But they needed food. As night came again, it was the priority.

"We're too high up," exclaimed Philippe suddenly. "I remember now, the farmers move the livestock, when the snow comes. They move them to lower pastures."

"What are we going to do, then? I can't, I just can't go hungry, it's eating me inside," Simone felt panic. This wasn't a normal hunger. Could she control it? Was that thought her own, or was she sharing it with somebody, somebody not just watching and listening, but someone generating their own version of that thought...

"There are ibex higher up," said Philippe. "Alpine goats. They've been nearly hunted to extinction, but I can track them down if there's any left."

That was the thing about speech. It was so less ambiguous than thought. Somebody opened their mouth and noise came out. Whatever it consisted of, you knew who it came from. It came from the one whose lips were flapping.

Simone wondered if they wouldn't be better off hunting something that wasn't virtually extinct, but he was off, climbing away from the guiding road, moving as if he were a speedy but scuttling insect, and she had no better plan so she wasted little time in going after him.

He turned and looked back, making a gesture that suggested she hurried up. He knows not to send his thoughts to me, because he read my mind. Ironic, she thought. Shows he's sensitive though.

Could she control the hunger? As they climbed higher they were committing themselves to this particular slope. What if it was barren of living animals? And they had to head back down, and try something else, with the night slipping inexorably away. What would happen? It was a nightmare. She could feel her teeth lengthening, and there was a snarl, like an angry animal, but it was coming from her.

Stupid anthropomorphism. Animals – some of them – might kill you, but they didn't get angry. That was the prerogative of humans. But the anger was really the fear of death by starvation. It grew from desperation. Could she control it? There were modest pinpricks of light, far away but visible through the darkness from where they were, which was pretty high by now. If she could reach those lights before daybreak, she could find the humans who'd lit them, and...

Philippe turned around and waited for her to catch up. "It's ok, I can smell them," he said, but his eyes were anxious. He *can* control it, she thought.

The view from where they were was incredible, even if it was in black and white and grey. Probably no human, or not-quite-human, had stood where she was. They were three quarters of the way up a mountain, and way beneath was a valley with a river running along the bottom. It was like a toytown landscape, and it was impossible to tell how far away it really was, or whether the river was really just a stream. In the distance, across the valley, another mountain range loomed, making it beautiful yet claustrophobic. Simone had never been so high up, and she understood why Switzerland could remain neutral. It would be impossible for invaders to conquer this place.

The vampires could go wherever they wanted. Simone made an impossible jump over an icy crevasse and as she landed the snow collapsed beneath her feet and she was suddenly sliding away with it, into the hole that had concealed itself underneath. With nothing to grab and nothing for her feet to touch she was helpless until Philippe grabbed her and pulled her out. How, when there was nothing for him to hold or stand on, either?

"I just hovered," he answered aloud. "You can too."

"I thought we had to keep moving?"

"We can keep still, a little paddling with the feet and a lot of concentration," he answered.

And then above them, they saw the ibex, standing under a ledge that gave his chosen spot protection from the snow. Simone took a moment to pity the creature, pity she'd never had for the cattle she'd dined on, probably because the bovine life was so dull and unenviable that an observer was likely to decide that they were better off out of it. The ibex, however, had massive horns and this one probably weighed as much as a small pony. It looked like the master of all it surveyed.

But the pity lasted only a moment, because it was her, or the ibex. And it would be worse than starvation for her, because she might end up so maddened that she would find a human being and in this state, not be able to stop at the civilised sip, which was, to be honest, difficult at the best of times.

Philippe was ahead of her. With an impossible leap, he was on the ledge. The startled ibex tried to escape but Simone found herself jumping onto the ledge too, blocking its only escape route, which was a path only goats and vampires could climb, just behind her. It stopped and began to lower its head to defend itself with those horns. Simone found herself moving faster than she could have imagined possible, grabbed the horns, and twisted the head till she heard the crack. The ibex fell to the ground.

Philippe didn't bother congratulating her, because that would have wasted moments that could be spent feeding. It was hard to tell who was first at the neck. Both guzzled greedily, as if they hadn't eaten for days. Hunger was even more imperious for them than for humans.

At last they lifted their heads, embarrassed as usual at their loss of control, and ashamed at what they were. Still, neither was about to judge another. They each had their own inner judge, who seemed to have survived the transition from human to vampire, and would no doubt be there at the final transition, or as it is better known, the last judgement.

"One step nearer total extinction," said Philippe, wryly.

"Us or the ibex?" Simone muttered.

They descended the mountain. It was still quite dark, and they made good time, and they were over the border into Germany and past the snow when they finally took shelter from the day in what seemed the outskirts of a large forest, where big evergreen trees would block out the light.

Chapter Eleven

If men thought of God as much as they think of the world

Who would not attain liberation?

(Maitri Upanishad trans. Mascaro)

The following night they made it to the border with Germany. Despite the elaborate security infrastructure it was no barrier to the vampires, who simply avoided the road and travelled via pathless ways. The scrubland and the lumpy fields, frozen into parallel lines, like mini earthworks, were a little awkward to travel across, but that was all. An ordinary human would have been exhausted before too long but the terrain was not much of an inconvenience to Simone and Philippe, as their pace and light footedness took them over any obstacle, and in any case, they did not get tired.

"We do," thought Philippe, who'd picked that up from Simone, "but it takes a lot."

Luckily the ibex had been a big meal, and they weren't troubled by hunger, but they took the opportunity to catch a couple of hares. When food was available, it was as well to fill up.

They passed by a settlement and although there was little light, the vampires' night vision was enough to see that it looked as if it had suffered as a consequence of the war. There was a rundown look, even though it should have been prosperous.

"They're probably hiding all the food," said Philippe. "Farmers never go hungry, war or no war. If they let themselves look shabby it's probably just to put officials off the scent."

He needn't have spoken, of course, but it was good to hear speech after so long travelling silently across the bare winter landscape... even if it was clear that he still bore a grudge against anyone owning or working land. Nobody really owned land, he had already made that clear; ergo, those who claimed to own land had actually stolen it.

They were making good time. Another day and night, and they should, with a fair wind, be in Berlin.

And then Simone ran into a wall. She was moving fast, about twenty miles an hour, and the impact was a painful blow. She slid to the ground, shocked and hurting, just as Philippe collided with it as well. She'd shrieked, but his forward impetus was too great to slow down in time. He swore; out loud, of course. No one swears silently. There'd be no point.

And there was no wall, either. At least, not a visible one. They got to their feet, bruised and possibly even broken: Simone's nose was very sore, but already healing.

There's nothing here, she thought. Yes there is, thought Philippe, back at her. This is not natural, which means that it's supernatural. Which means...

'The collective will of several vampires, led by me, has generated a field of invisible force which encircles Berlin, and beyond this you cannot go.'

Simone instantly knew who it was, resounding in her head. It was the creature who'd made both herself and Philippe what they were. It was Graves. Or Kerr, depending.

Hot fury seized her. Her dead heart seemed to palpitate with thwarted rage, if that were possible. She hissed and her nails and teeth lengthened.

'Hello darling, it's lovely to see you again. Pity you can't see me. Tell you what, I'll come in, shall I?'

Suddenly the voice was in her head, chattering like a jungle full of monkeys, showing her visions that skittered by, only to be replaced the next, and the next; too fast to make any sense of. Simone held her head, almost as though she wanted to rip it off. The parade of visions began to slow down, but it was no improvement: They were all pictures, moving pictures at that, but they were of death and corpses; men, women, children. She heard a scream, very close, and knew it was herself. She was out of control.

The visions were no longer visions, but reality, or so it seemed. She was in a church, and a man with a dog collar was cringing before her.

She was laughing. She bent down, and as if compelled, as if a bystander at her own funeral, she ripped off the collar, still laughing. 'Look, it's a Church of England priest, darling,' she said. She felt the words come out of her mouth as though she were reading from a script. 'Don't they help the Tory party say their prayers?'

'So they do. Eat him, quick, or I will!'

She turned around, still holding the terrified man, and smiled at her friend, as at the same moment, her insides convulsed with horror.

For it was Philippe, smiling back at her.

She bent, and bit the throat of her human victim, and it was the best, just like the Germans back in France, or... she was shuddering, and she couldn't stop.

Philippe was shaking her, and calling her name.

"Simone, Simone, it's not true! You're hallucinating! He's showing you his deeds as though they were yours. Let's go, now!"

But she was barely standing, so shaken that her legs were unsteady. So he picked her up in his arms, and holding her tightly he ran back the way they had just come, until they were almost back at the border.

And then Philippe came to a stop. He put her gently on the ground, and looked at her quizzically.

"Don't," she exclaimed.

"Don't what?"

"Don't talk to me without words. Stay out of my head!"

"Of course, of course. I'm so sorry. I had no idea... he could DO that. Such power! He must have been protecting Hitler from the beginning. No wonder he's survived so many assassination attempts... and we're actually easier to repel than some of those who've tried."

"Shut up a minute! That was awful. Did you see it all too?"

"No, he kept me out. He's not interested in me. But he can block me. He's an alpha male. Males are competition, or else to be dominated. When there's a female around, that's who he's interested in."

"To torment, you mean?"

Philippe looked very solemn. "I'm sorry Simone. I had no idea."

190

"You keep saying that. It was awful, and in the end, I was drinking the blood of a vicar."

Philippe gave a little smile.

She turned on him. "So you find that amusing?"

"No, no... but the real incident was probably a long time ago, and it sounded a bit funny when you said it. Sorry."

"And why were you there?"

"Me? No, I was never there. He put that in your head to drive a wedge between us. He probably thinks we're a couple."

Vampires can't blush, thought Simone, but he stuttered a little there. He must be embarrassed.

"All right, he must know we're not, by now, since he's been rooting around in my head." she said. "But from now on, as far as you're concerned, no more jumping into my head. Just normal speech, please."

"As you wish," he answered, "with the proviso that you or I can break that promise if either of us is in danger."

"Oh... yes, of course."

They took shelter from the impending break of day, back to the thick evergreens that gave them the shelter they needed. Simone felt deeply shaken by the fact of the wall, which indicated a power possessed by Graves that her mentor Philippe did not have, and she most certainly didn't, by the horrible visions and the invasion and takeover of her mind, by the reminder of the exquisite satisfaction of the taste of human blood, most of all though, by Philippe's appearance in her nightmare. Of course, it was all Graves's doing. But those little touches, calling him darling... and the reference to the Tory party! Graves – or Kerr – knew his man enough to besmirch his passionate socialism. But really, it was a joke.

She thought of her mother, happily married for the second time, and of her father, to whom her mother had been married very young. She had seen and heard enough to know that although her father loved her, when it came to her mother he was a manipulator, sometimes cold and controlling. He was terrified of losing her mother's love, and ended up driving her away by his behaviour.

Simone felt sorry for him, but at last she'd understood that her mother couldn't, not anymore. She had to choose survival.

Somehow Kerr reminded her of him. Perhaps he sensed that there was a familiarity there, an imprint on her mind, that would make her vulnerable to his twisted game.

Philippe's eyes were closed. He was no doubt enjoying the short, light sleep that vampires have. At any rate, he was not in her mind. And she was glad to keep her thoughts to herself. She liked him, but she was not going to give up her autonomy to any man, or vampire. She'd seen that, and it was not a lovely sight.

What to do now? Why was Kerr so powerful? Would she be that powerful one day? Philippe opened one eye.

"Your thoughts are beating at my brain. If you want to share them aloud, that would ease both our minds."

She wasn't about to share all her thoughts, for sure, but some things they had to talk about.

"What did G... Kerr mean about other vampires? Is he a leader? Does he have a vampire army? Will he kill us? They'll all know the ways in which we can die, and if a mob attacks us..."

"He likes you, so no. Seriously, he does. That is not a good thing, though, believe me. His mistresses usually go mad."

"I'm not about to become his mistress! I didn't know vampires had mistresses..."

"Ha! Only a select few. Listen, I'd heard talk of this vampire army of his. I doubt it's as big as all that. You need to know something: a lot of vampires are simple minded, just bundles of instinct, like animals. That's because they were more or less average to stupid when they were humans. When they start feeding on humans, I mean, not the civilised sip, but the whole thing, killing them, they pay a price for that loss of control, and pretty soon have no control at all. Which means they need someone to tell them what to do."

"Someone with a lot of self-control?"
"Yes."

"But... Kerr... he kills... why doesn't he...?"

"Lord, I don't know. He's intelligent, but then so are we. I wouldn't like to bet what would happen to us if we started murdering humans, but I don't think we could avoid the degradation. They become beasts, like Edith and her ghastly servants. If you ever fancy making a good meal of a human being, remember them. And her. It might help put you off."

"What do you suggest we do next?"

"I suggest we avoid this place, this entire country. Hitler might have vampire protection, but he is losing the war. It can't be too long before the Allies come back to Europe, you know. Well, you should know, that was your job. Kerr can't lose. Chaos is what he loves, he and his associates. They'll be feasting whatever happens. I think we should go and visit my oldest friend... literally oldest; Christophe. You've seen him when I showed you some of my past. He's also the one who changed Kerr, back when he was William – Sir William in fact.

This fellow Cayzer, whom he told me about, and you... remember? He was trying to stay away from killing, but Kerr, who changed him, loved turning saints into sinners and deliberately tormented him till he snapped. You can imagine, he was imprisoned and starved of blood, till at last a person was put in the cell with him and he could not stop himself. When he'd finished, he found the door to the cell swinging wide, and the outdoors beckoning, so he did what Kerr intended him to do, and walked into the sun."

"I swear I would not let that happen to me, however starved... he was weak."

Don't tempt fate, he thought.

"So Paris, then?

"Yes. And perhaps when the time comes we can give the Allies a bit of cover, who knows. That should satisfy your urge to sacrifice yourself in a good cause."

Simone sniffed. "No need to be so snooty about it. How many vampires are... good vampires, then?"

"You want to know? Living? Or you know what I mean..."

"Still with us, yes."

"Well, three. If we count you."

"Thanks!"

"And there's Vampire Dave, in Liverpool, but he's content where he is. Anyway that's why – that's one reason why – I didn't want to come here in the first place. I thought it might endanger you. Most people… they don't make it through the process and come out as people, and if they do, they don't last."

"Don't last?"

"Can't take the constant self-denial, yet don't want to be murderers, so they take the only way out... into the sun, usually."

Simone stopped asking questions. She was finding herself to be not very keen on the answers.

The following evening they got off to a good start. It was less than six hundred miles to Paris and vampires didn't tire, as a rule. They took five days and nights, in the end. Simone was restless during the enforced rest periods, but thanked God it was winter and the days were short, and moreover, often overcast, which was still unpleasant and very, very risky, but not always immediately fatal like bright sunlight. Their meals were basic beasts of the field, and it was possible not to kill them, if one exerted a self discipline, just as if they were human. They might not understand much, but they breathed the same air as people, who were also mammals. Simone was not terribly fond of meat, never had been. It seemed a waste of life.

Simone and Philippe looked pretty scruffy by now, and Simone began to wonder if they should stop in a town and look for clothes. She also felt the desire to bathe: Even though it was a strange experience it ended up making her feel cleaner, eventually. Philippe was clad in shapeless black, with a collarless shirt and a waistcoat. The shirt looked like it had once been white. Its grubbiness came from the outside: In reality the vampires' bodies seemed to be self-cleaning, or more accurately, they didn't really get dirty.

"That's because we're outside the stream of life," Philippe told her, sententiously.

She noticed that Philippe seemed to have his own strange religion. In the baggy pockets of his shabby coat he kept some items that seemed dear to him: a chunky notebook, full of scribbles, a pen with which to do the scribbling, and an ugly little statuette of a prehistoric, headless 'Venus'. He also had a rather exotic earring, the other one of which he must have lost, for it was not the sort that the sailors or the gypsies would wear in one ear, being certainly designed for women only. It showed a winged Isis figure, like an angel down on one knee, with the great feathered wings spread on either side of her. It was clearly Egyptian, in inspiration if not origin.

He showed her these things, although of course there could be plenty more such objects in the recesses of the coat. And he explained, not totally to her satisfaction, exactly what they meant to him.

The notebook was easy. It wasn't a diary, as she'd supposed, but instead it was full of poems, mostly sonnets, which he promised to read to her one by one, as soon as each was finished. But they never were finished, as he kept changing the words, here and there. Most of the changes were minor, but he would keep fiddling with them, and could not contemplate reading them to her in that half-baked state, so she had yet to hear a single one.

The statuette, he declared, was of the chthonic Mother Goddess, who had many names. This representation of her might be either aged or pregnant. If the first, it signified wisdom, if the second, fecundity.

"Maybe they just liked fat girls," Simone suggested.

The earring, he said, showed the female part of the Trinity, the other two being the Father, Osiris, and the Son, Horus. The female is the all giving breath, without which nothing is, and is therefore the most important element. She is also Heavenly Eve, while the archaic fatty was the earthly Eve. She is the mother of all.

One is born once of the chthonic Eve. But we remain children, without much understanding. If the breath is consecrated, and she spreads her wings, one is born again, and attains pure wisdom.

Philippe's religious practice consisted of occasionally kissing one or other of the Eves in his possession, and muttering words which she did not try to hear, either with her ears or with her mind. It was his business.

Once she asked what was the other name of the earthly Eve – the heavenly one was Isis as well as what he termed Celestial Eve. He didn't know, he said, but it was probably Mama.

She asked him what happened to Papa. He answered that it was a very long story, but the Egyptians knew all about it. We mortals all have a little piece of Papa inside us, he said, but he is sad because he's forgotten who he is.

And the Son? Well... once he was a hero, Philippe had said, and now he's Hamlet.

There was probably some coherence to all this, Simone decided, and she would tease it all out of him, eventually, perhaps in the summer, when they were trapped indoors for the long days of sunshine.

In the meantime, the oddest thing about his religion was that he did not benefit by it, according to him, since he could not be 'born again' into wisdom, being dead, and a vampire to boot. He – and she – were beyond salvation.

But Simone knew that deep down he believed there was a way to save his soul, whatever that might be, and not just because of his scrupulous avoidance of killing even animals.

She understood by now that behind everything he did was the quest, always the quest.

And it could be labelled in several different ways, one of which might be 'the quest to prove himself wrong.'

Philippe admitted he had not known for sure about the feral vampires working together under the command of Kerr: it was a new development. He had told her there were three kinds of vampires – the ones who turned into brutes, the ones who gave up trying and walked into the sunlight – and those, like him, who kept struggling, holding onto their humanity.

"And how many of them are there?" she asked.

"You know it is three, and now you make four, plus Kerr. Otherwise it's me. Christophe. And David. In England."

"What side is he on?"

"We haven't been in touch since the war began. I hope he's well."

It seemed that most 'good' vampires didn't last, their hearts broken by the penalties attached to eternal existence, and in any case those that were made were not usually made by other virtuous vampires, because the consequences of making a new vampire were likely to be dire; there was no guarantee that even the most angelic human would be able or even willing to cling on to his or her standards once the deed was done. It was not out of the question; Philippe had contemplated it with Roger, but in his heart of hearts he'd known that it might not be his friend who survived the transformation. He had been saved from finding out what or who would have survived by Roger's rejection of his offer. Since then... he had not been much tempted to offer the chance of that life to anyone. Simone noted the 'much' but did not pursue it. Philippe had had a long life. She would hear more about it in due course. Something else was concerning her now.

"Was Edith... good, once?"

"Not exactly," he said. They were on speaking terms, but only speaking terms – anything else seemed too intimate after Kerr's assault on her mind. Philippe – well, she supposed he was like a gentle lover, who was patient with her after... oh, why was she thinking like that. He's too old for me! She smiled to herself, not because of any desire for Philippe, but out of a sudden happiness that even around him, her thoughts could be her own. What else did she have?

"Tell me about her. Why were you there? How did I come to meet you there?" She had her suspicions, and his guilty look more or less confirmed them. But she wanted to hear it from the horse's mouth.

"Kerr makes vampires whenever he feels in the mood. Christophe says he feels each one's birth. Kerr doesn't make many, as a rule: but he seems to have suddenly become a prolific sire, and because he is their sire, he has a certain influence, which we haven't.

That's why he was able to get into your head like that. I spend a lot of time tracking them. Christophe is not... he doesn't like to travel and he's older. It keeps me busy. We'd let Edith go, kept putting dealing with her on the back burner... so you see, everyone she and her servants killed... it's our fault."

You poor creature, thought Simone. You poor, poor creature.

"I suppose Hitler is your fault too?"
"Please don't. If I live for a thousand years I'll never make amends. In a way, yes, because if it weren't for Kerr, Hitler would've have been assassinated long ago. And I cannot get to Kerr, because of his little army. I can pick off a few, but he is still making new ones. And he seems to be delighting in siring the worst

197

beasts he can find, just for his amusement. And to torture me. And Christophe. I'm sure Kerr thinks I'm the best entertainment, and congratulates himself every minute on his foresight in siring me," sighed Philippe.

"Oh, you know that for sure? Is that really the only way a centuries old vampire entertains himself?"

Sometimes during that journey Simone was unsure whether or not she slept, a lot, a little, or at all. They didn't talk much during the night, just travelled as fast as they could. In the daytime they found caves or abandoned buildings, and Simone dreamed of gelatinous baths... or day dreamed, because at times she couldn't tell one from the other. Philippe remained respectful of her mental privacy, and his restraint reassured her; the trust that had been there from the start was growing, and it needed to, in a shaky reality, which is where she felt herself to dwell. After all she was neither alive nor properly dead, and she could be dreaming, or in limbo, or...

Eventually she raised the subject, on their third night journeying to Paris.

"How do I know what is real and what's not?"

Her fellow vampire smiled at that, though it didn't really suit him. Not that he looked ugly, or anything, just that his features had apparently settled into a glower. His dark brows were usually frowning, as if he had the weight of the world on his shoulders, and even in repose his expression tended to be that of a man counting up every possible misdeed of a long life and worrying about all the conceivable consequences. The smile made him look less like a tortured immortal bloodsucker and more like a man – a bloke, even – enjoying something, something simple and funny, like his companion's naïveté. He looked quite young, too, no more than thirty; possibly younger still.

"Gosh, you expect me to answer that? Know the one about the king who dreamt he was at war and lost everything? Fleeing for his life, he found himself in a forest, a starving fugitive."

"Bit like us, then," suggested Simone. They had been sipping cattle, lately, leaving them alive, but a greedy, insatiable part of her felt as if she wanted to drain some large beast; of course, it was because she wasn't able to enjoy the concentrated ideal vampire food that was human blood.

"Anyway, he came across a hut, and an old lady who lived there. She was nervous of him, but charitable too, so she gave him some rice and lentils to cook, and sent him away. Well, it must have taken him a devil of a time to get a fire going, rubbing sticks together etcetera, but he eventually did, and cooked the food in a thick banana leaf, which was all he had for a pan. Just as he was about to eat it, a giant bull and a lion came crashing through the clearing where he'd made his supper, and as he hid from them he watched as they fought a ferocious battle, and while doing so, trampled all over the food. At this, he wept so much that he woke up."

"So... that was a dream."

"Yes, but it was so vivid that the king called together his wise men and even sent messengers throughout his kingdom to search out others. He wanted to question them on this same subject. Was the dream actually the reality, or was it the waking? If neither were correct – however vivid – then what was real?

Nothing meant anything to him anymore; his servants, his jewels, his choice of the finest food, his rich robes... and so on, because he knew that, just as in the dream they could all be taken away in an instant; not from waking up, this time, but in dying.

To cut a long story short, no one knew anything to say that brought him comfort, just platitudes and words that sounded good enough but failed to bring comfort to his heart, until at last a little hunchback, barely out of childhood, came to see him.

And this fellow, unprepossessing in appearance though he was, in fact one of the great line of teachers through the ages. He told the king that neither waking nor sleeping were real, since both were temporary conditions. Nothing is real that ends."

He stopped talking.

"Well, and then what happened?" asked Simone, surprised by the abrupt conclusion.

"The hunchback showed the king just what was real."

"And you don't happen to know any of these teachers that can do that?"

"No, there's only one at any given time, apparently. And they usually come from India, or somewhere like that."

"Have you ever travelled there?"

"Oh, no. It's a big place. And it's a long way away."

"Yes but..." Simone felt that there was a lot going unsaid here. Words and speech were clumsy tools, in the end.

"All right, "said Philippe, as if he'd been listening to that last thought, "Christophe believes he met such a person – not a hunchback, another – many years... centuries ago. He means Socrates. And when I say 'met', it was probably more a matter of hovering around this individual, at the back of the crowd, trying to listen to what he had to say but without drawing attention to oneself. If Christophe was a vampire at the time, and I don't know about that, he would be seeking shelter from the sun, and probably missed most of the talk. But I guess he felt unworthy. And it was a difficult experience, he tells me. Maybe for a vampire, it's an impossible experience. You find what the whole world wants, the end of searching... and you're not even human, and it isn't for you."

By this time Philippe's face had settled back into its habitual expression, and he was frowning, as if the meaning of life had been within his grasp and then flown away, although, Simone supposed, it had been this Christophe in whose shaky grasp wisdom had declined to settle.

He could be talking about Jesus, she thought. If I'd met Jesus, she thought, I'd have asked him, in the evening of course, if vampires could get into heaven... oh, and if there is a heaven, and what is real. I'm sure I would. I'd overcome my shame, because I haven't actually killed anyone.

And then she set to wondering about the people she might have helped kill as an agent. She'd been turned into a vampire before she could do much, if any damage in that regard. So perhaps being a vampire had saved her from thinking killing was OK, had in fact saved her from being a killer; a thought which as a patriotic English woman had not occurred to her before now.

But that made her head ache to contemplate it. What had the Pope told the crusaders that he'd set upon the Toulouse area, when asked how they could tell heretic Cathars from good Catholics? "Kill them all: God will sort them out." Or words to that effect.

On the final afternoon, before they entered Paris, they were holed up in a scruffy, god-forsaken barn, having dined off rats. There had been a cat roaming about, but neither could face killing it. Simone wasn't quite desperate enough to kill something so like a child's pet, although she knew deep down that if things got very bad she'd kill the child, never mind the pet. Philippe also seemed content with the rats which staved off the worst hunger pangs, but the fur got caught... oh, it didn't matter when the hunger was upon one, thought Simone, but after, when one was sated... It was so horrible to have any reminder of their vile repast.

Needing a distraction, she ventured on to the subject of Kerr and his band of brothers, or rather, sons, if he could be said to have sired them.

Philippe smiled. And then he apologised for accidentally reading that thought.

"It was there, glittering on the surface," he said.

"Glittering? No one has described my thoughts as glittering before... mind you, no one has read my thoughts before."

"Well, I wouldn't want to do your thoughts down, but I didn't mean glittering like Oscar Wilde, more like a spark in a fire that seemed to have gone out... no!! Don't get me wrong, it's not that your fire has gone out. I meant not visible to me, or something..."

"Because I've cut off that avenue of communication. Well, I'm re-opening it, because after all this time, I know I can trust you to respect my privacy, when I need it. And anyway, I'm bored. And I like that seeing-through-your-eyes thing you do. It's interesting."

Philippe looked a little taken aback. "It has an emotional cost for me, you know. It's not a parlour game."

"And," she went on as if he hadn't spoken, "we may die at any time. We're monsters in the middle of a war. And the creature that made us has plans for us, don't you think?"

"Going by his history, yes. After leaving Portugal... well, d'you want to see?"

"Yes..." And there she was, looking through his eyes, at a wide dry track in front of and below her, which was moving up and down. It was either dawn or twilight, she couldn't tell which, and as she was wondering about it she realised that she was riding a horse – well, Philippe was riding one – and that s/he was covered from head to foot, cloaked, gloved, hatted and booted, with a scarf over his face. But his eyes, the only part uncovered, were really sore, almost as if they

201

were on fire. Gradually the sensation faded, and she realised that night was falling.

It wasn't long before she saw shadows hunched or lying at the side of the track, which caused the horse to slow down. At last, she felt her hands and legs gripping and gently directing the animal to stop.

Philippe dismounted, and Simone was with him as he investigated the shadows. This meant that when a terribly wounded man reached up from the ground where he writhed, and called him Senor, begging him to deliver the final blow that would liberate his soul from the tortured body, the poor fellow did not even get out the final words of the request before he was dispatched by the strong hands of the vampire, breaking his neck with one sharp twist. As he stood up, he glanced about and it seemed that the other shadows would require a similar service...

"No, stop! Why are you showing me this?" cried Simone.

"This is what I have seen, and what I have done I did because I had to. These are the Napoleonic wars, this is Spain. May the little Corsican bastard rot in hell, along with all the other warmongers. And before you ask, this man was not the only one, and none of them seemed likely candidates for the gift... or curse, whichever way you prefer. They were a clergy riddled people – still are – preyed on by their church, their nobles, and then by the invaders, but they seemed to know what they wanted; to be left alone, obviously, but failing that grace, to be sent safely home to heaven."

Simone must have looked distressed, because his tone softened.

"It seems that I have witnessed a lot of stuff you don't actually want to see, and I can't blame you. But if you survive for as many years as I have, you will also see how thin the veil is between this world and the next, and how the suffering is like an evil dream, that seems so real at the time, but soon fades... like a nightmare at daybreak."

"But," said Simone, "How do you know that? You are a vampire, who with luck will never die, yet you talk as though death were nothing much, a release to somewhere better. But how can you know that? And if it is true, in that case, why are you still here? Why not walk into the sunshine?"

"Because I may not have a soul, and therefore, for vampires, death might truly be extinction. For one thing. And how I know that for humans, it is really a change of… perception… is to do with my seeing, seeing further every year I survive. As we all do."

So, Simone thought, that's it, the life of a vampire; eating disgusting animals, raw, and sneaking around in the dark, while realising death is nothing to fear, for anybody else but you, who now do have something to fear. And why? Because you were such a coward when the time came, you begged for someone to save you from it.

What a stupid, stupid move that had been.

Chapter Twelve

Work out your own salvation with fear and trembling

(NT)

At last they were in Paris.

Nothing had really prepared Simone for the changes that had come over the City of Light. They were heading to the centre, to the streets and bridges round Notre Dame, but they had to make a detour to the Marais first, and they could not walk freely through the night, as Simone had hoped, because even though it was a city, and ordinary people shared its pavements with vampires, all unknowing and unconcerned, they now needed papers.

Without papers, you would be arrested. And you would have to fight your way out of the situation, because the possibility of being in a cell at dawn was very real. You might survive while indoors, but you were as likely to be let go as to be arrested. And that would be the end.

So they skulked along the streets of the Marais, hiding in shop doorways, in possession of the advantage of excellent night vision, which was a huge advantage now that most of the City of Light was in darkness. They were going to see someone known to Philippe and Christophe, who apparently thought they were spies, or criminals, and did not care as long as he got paid. Philippe had plenty of money on him, and she no longer wondered where he got it; probably from some act of robbery. It couldn't be helped, she thought. Maybe we should have a policy of only stealing from Germans, but then that might be a bit difficult to stick with.

At last they reached the apartment building where the contact was. It seemed possible that he did not actually live in it, as it was very run down. As Philippe reached to ring the bell, Simone suddenly felt tired, which she hadn't done for ages. She slumped onto the step as her legs went suddenly wobbly.

"What is it? What's the matter?" asked Philippe.

"It's a feeling, it's coming from the city, the people... anger, such anger, resentment... the city is enraged, I feel it too, in my gut, but it came all of a sudden. It hurts!"

Philippe sat down beside her and took her hands in his.

"I feel it too, in the solar plexus, like a boiling sea. It's the Occupation, my dear. Accumulated bitter wrath. You need the knack of acknowledging it without allowing it to consume you. Let it go, now, it doesn't belong to you."

Philippe was right. What felt like a deeply felt personal reaction wasn't. She had picked it up from the streets, from the people, not necessarily on the street in these dangerous times, but hidden behind doors, unable to express their rage at the occupiers, even though it flowed like a river throughout the highways and byways of the city. She had enough of her own complicated emotions to deal with; she wasn't immune to the anger, but she hadn't endured the occupation here the way the locals had.

"Is this part of the gift? Our gift?"

"Yes, it's the collective secret thoughts of individuals, even the secret thoughts of cities, which are not real beings but accumulated history; the secret thoughts of generations. So, past this stuff which is happening now is a lot of stuff that has happened before, and hangs around after those who had those thoughts are long gone. But the strength of the thoughts that are happening now is drowning out over a thousand years of thinking, which normally would've outweighed all this modern... overlay. This is a very... vivid situation, and even the old folk are dwelling less on past glories, more in this outrageous present."

That got Simone imagining layer after layer of city, like Schliemann's Troy, only not so easy to knock down, or burn, as the alleged topless towers of Ilium had turned out to be, because they were creations of mind. They were really layer upon layer of thoughts, like invisible scaffolding, or perhaps like foundations.

What would I perceive with these vampire senses, she wondered, if the war hadn't happened?

"Poverty and despair, mostly," said Philippe.

"You're listening to my thoughts again!"

"I can't help it, they're so loud! You can put a barrier up, but no one can explain how to do it, it's something you have to work out..."

I'm an undisciplined creature, aren't I, she thought, looking straight at him. Yes, it's pot and kettle time, mister.

He looked sheepish. OK, we're all undisciplined creatures, he thought, and she read his thought and smiled. On the same side, though, she communicated to him, without saying it aloud.

"Simone," he ventured, "You know I'd kill you if I had to?"

"I've known it for ages. I know you came looking for me, as well as Edith and her twin horrors, and I know you thought it was a good time to make the journey you'd been putting off for ages, since it'd be two birds – well, four birds – and you couldn't let me roam about freely for long. But you were a bit tardy, because of sentiment over that creature, and what seems to have been a whole village died because of your squeamishness."

He reeled back, but did not answer immediately.

"I'm not a gentle girl, to be protected. You recall what I was doing? You think they let shrinking violets do that kind of work? You know what I would have done if I were you? I'd never have let her out of my sight and once her predilections were known I'd have killed her without a moment's delay, to save human lives."

"Things aren't always as simple as you think! How do you think we got our information, especially after war broke out! We have... associates who know what we are, and others that don't... when communication was broken off by Edith we didn't know what to think... and there was work to be done in Paris, which involved helping as many humans to live a bit longer as we could. You realise only two of us with abilities associated with our condition are to be trusted, maybe three, and those that aren't in the least trustworthy try and thwart us at every turn... damn it, we're doing our best! Sorry..."

Simone almost laughed aloud as he apologised, not for any supposed dereliction of duty, but for swearing in front of a lady, and not even a human lady at that, just a lady vampire. And there were much worse words, although to a being of Philippe's vintage, blasphemous cursing probably was more heinous than the sexual kind.

They rang the bell to the flat they wanted, and after a while the door opened, and a skinny, swarthy man, slightly underfed looking, greeted Philippe brusquely and let them in.

"Bonjour," said Simone politely. He had a shock of dark curls, and she recalled that the word was that the Jews were being deported from their homes and put into work camps in Germany. He looked a bit Jewish, but Simone wasn't normally in the habit of noticing and labelling sets of physical characteristics in that way.

Unlike her father, who was unbearable on the subject, convinced as he was that there was an important thing called race, and all the while treating her with the greatest tenderness.

Anyway, it didn't mean a thing to her: The man could've been anything. Deep down, somewhere atavistic, something inside her identified him as what he and all human beings were to vampires: food. In fact, prey.

Maybe he caught a whiff of that, but his hunted expression looked like it had become habitual a while ago. It was hard to tell if she had contributed to his discomfort, so she tried to adopt a facial expression radiating harmlessness; no toothy smile, just a kindly curve to her lips. Fortunately, the man ignored her, except for one sharp glance.

"Yes, she's fine. This one's close enough," he offered. Then he handed the papers to Philippe, who flicked through them.

"Excellent job, Be..."

"Yes, yes, thanks," said the man, clearly not wishing to share his name, even if it was just one of several aliases.

Philippe gave the man a bundle of money: Whatever the currency, the man seemed satisfied. Then Philippe handed her the papers, and she realised that he was already equipped with identity papers, having been based in Paris for what must be most of a long life, from what he'd told her so far. These were for her.

She didn't ask how the man had known he was to prepare them. Presumably it was long distance telepathy with Christophe, who must have placed the order on her behalf. Probably he had known Philippe for so long that they could cross that distance. She was about to meet him, on the Ile de Saint Louis near Notre Dame, in the heart of Paris. Nearby was the Palais de Justice, and other government buildings now home to the occupying Nazis. Why did the fellow have to live there? Why couldn't he be somewhere more discreet? It was like a dare.

"We were here before the war," said her companion, reproachfully.

They were soon travelling as swiftly as they could in a city. Eyes were everywhere, even if they were mostly indoors, looking out. Leaps and bounds were out of the question, and she began to get impatient, glancing at Philippe to signal that he was welcome to read her thought, at least regarding this one.

"Yes, it is tiresome, but inescapable... if we stay at ground level. However..."

He began to climb a wall. He moved quickly up it, his fingers seeming to find the smallest indents, and even his feet flashed between one impossible non-existent ledge to another, till he reached the roof and leant down over the guttering to call her up, in a loud hiss. Simone hoped no-one was watching, or listening. She also wished she'd been more patient, and had just got on with the laborious walking. She'd handled the mountain when she had to, but this was sheer.

He didn't resort to shouting, but she heard his voice in her head. It's a matter of confidence. It's just a little bit steeper than what you've already done. Just remember to keep moving and don't stop to admire the view.

With a sigh, she stood back, and launched herself towards the wall at a run. She shut her eyes, and pretended that the world had lurched sideways, and that the wall was the new ground, and that she had toppled off the original ground as it tipped her off onto the wall. It just came to her to do it that way, and it seemed to work. She appeared to weigh nothing as she danced up the wall, and it was as if gravity no longer bound her with its laws.

She reached the top, where there was guttering, and a recessed slate covered roof, leaving them room to stand. Just don't think you can't be bound by any laws, he thought at her. That way lies...

"My execution at your hands," she said aloud, as the wind whipped her words away.

"This way," he pointed, and off they went, jumping and running across the rooftops, and it was most exhilarating. Why, Simone wondered, we don't need papers, we could live most of the time up here, above it all. Immortal, free... for a few moments, she felt blissfully happy, to be able to play like this, unaffected by all the worries of the world. She ran up the side of a church spire, and then down the other; leaping off it into space, she misjudged the distance to the next roof, and began to drift downwards, just like a feather falling, but she was not a feather, and giving a languid couple of kicks she barrelled upwards as if boosted by the power of some inner engine.

But then, as they drew near the river, where it would be theoretically possible to bound over the water - so long as she kept moving fast on its cloying surface and except for the startled attention such behaviour would draw, she felt the terrible desire rise, as urgent as thirst and hunger, as seductive as sex. And it filled her mind quickly, so that she became afraid it would consume her and leave nothing but a gape-mouthed monster behind

The new etiquette developing between them regarding mind-reading did not prevent Philippe from rushing to her side.

"We must eat, before we see Christophe, he might have visitors."

Nothing was more likely to annoy one's host than dining on his guests and if he was a crusading vampire sworn to eliminate the bad guys it was unlikely that Simone would live much longer after that. She felt helpless. If this was the way it was going to be, she might as well chuck herself off this roof right now. Oh, but that wouldn't work, though, would it? She'd feel the pain – probably, she'd have to ask – but there would be no release. Unless she waited till sunrise.

But the madness was running through her blood and she knew her teeth were lengthening, and in a matter of minutes she would lose control. Then she felt a hand reach out and take hers. The hand was cold, but gentle. Her own blood was pounding in her ears, and for some reason her teeth were chattering.

"Steady, old girl," whispered the vampire beside her. I'm feeling it too. "Just remember not to kill. But when you're desperate, it's OK to steal."

Together they leapt to the ground. It was dark, so they were probably not observed. It was not possible to be more cautious than 'probably': The imperative of their blood thirst saw to that.

A couple, youngish, were walking along the pavement on the other side of the narrow road. A grudging street light illuminated them for a little, until they passed into a pool of shade. Simone leapt and Philippe was only just behind her.

Neither of them could afford to lose themselves in the rapture of feeding: Something had to remain aloof, some part had to keep watch, not for enemies, but for the Enemy within. They had to take a pint or so, no more, maybe two…

Then she felt someone dragging her off her anaesthetised victim. In a fury she lashed out, but calmed down in the arms of her friend and mentor, enough to feel gratitude rather than wrath.

"Never leave me," she cried.

"I won't. As long as you need me I'll be here."

He had already laid the man gently on the ground, and Simone lowered the woman down beside him.

It was enough to quell the ravening hunger for a bit, but it wasn't enough to sate them. So they carried on their midnight hunt, walking towards their goal, keeping to the shadows, benefiting from the ill-lit city. They tasted more human blood, but no one was a meal. They were appetisers, and eventually the vampires had their fill, and nobody died.

Somebody would doubtless take an interest in this mysterious series of woundings, but this was wartime, and the inexplicable happened. The main thing was that nobody died, and this was exhilarating, so much so that Simone felt as gloriously alive and happy as she had ever been. They said human blood was like champagne, but they were wrong. To a vampire, it was better. The idea of walking into the sunshine now seemed absurd. Life, albeit undead life, was suddenly good, not a burden. It didn't matter that she had to drink blood – the right sort was delicious – and never go out in the daytime: Lots of people had constraints on their lives but still enjoyed themselves.

There was a checkpoint before the bridge. Why, Simone wondered, did Christophe stay here? Gaining access was unnecessarily complicated, and leaving would be, too.

It wouldn't be enough to have papers. They had to have a reason to cross the bridge.

But Philippe said not to worry. He led her away from the checkpoint, off to one side and down to the river. He showed her the way by climbing up the support structure and then, hanging like a bat, scrabbled along, almost upside down, using the most minute of cracks to move himself along with his fingers and toes.

He made it look easy, and so it should be, she thought. This is the nearest place to a home for him, along with Christophe; the two good vampires. There's another too, seemingly virtuous, but I haven't heard much about him. And now there is me... so I'd better get good at this. If she fell into the Seine, it would be no disaster, and she might even bounce. But she didn't want to be the one to draw attention. It would be terrible if they had to abandon their home because of her clumsiness, even if it was ultimately not a bad idea.

It was very awkward at first, slippery with damp, and of course there was water at the bottom of the huge struts. At first she tried to execute a kind of upside down jump across the expanse of water, but she ended up with her hair soaking with what she thought of as 'thick water.' On the next strut she tried to lever herself into a position where she could do a delicate jump, the idea being to touch the water very lightly, but that became messy too, with her legs sinking into squelchiness from which she had to free them. Altogether it was an irritating experience, and she dreaded what might be a twice daily repetition, all too likely if they had to hunt for several human snacks a night: They couldn't very well just dine off the inhabitants of the island. They'd soon run out.

As she made her way at last onto terra firma she was calculating possible numbers of inhabitants and wondering if there could be a rota. Blood took what... a week to replenish itself? Two? So you could theoretically design a chart, where no one was fed from more than once a fortnight, giving them time to create more blood... say four pints a night for each of them, that's twelve a night, over a fortnight, twelve times fourteen... they'd need an adult population available of 148. The city on the whole seemed a lot quieter than she remembered from long ago, and she knew that many Jewish Parisians had been deported to work camps, as for some reason the Nazis disliked the Jews. Probably her father would have an explanation, but she never wanted to hear him tell her how inferior everyone but the English were, yet again.

It wasn't just the Jews though, because many of the adult males had gone to work camps too, not because the Nazis had any particular dislike in their case, but for slave labour, German workers having become soldiers. Like ants, she thought. Sort of.

Philippe was there, waiting on the street as she came up from the river. He took her hand, and smiled. He was a serious chap, she thought, basically serious, but when he smiles, it's such a nice surprise.

The street was as ill lit as everywhere else. This darkened city was the ideal place for all sorts of criminality and evil doing, as well as the fundamental evil of the occupying Germans. But it suited the vampires' purposes, at least.

They walked along until they reached a magnificent building, eighteenth or even seventeenth century, but pre-revolutionary, though Simone was no expert. It was clearly a secular building, but its black wooden doors, stony with age, were like those often seen on Catholic churches. They were closed, and no lights burned in any of the many windows. But light was beginning to manifest itself off towards

211

the east, and Simone hoped that this was their destination. They couldn't hang about out of doors much longer.

Philippe led her round the side of the building, where there was a much more modest door, and opened it with a key he took from his coat pocket. At last, they were inside, where the cruel dawn couldn't touch them.

They walked along a corridor, wood panelled but otherwise plain, then there were two doors, one of which they opened, and then another couple of doors, and this time their choice led to a corridor where the wood panelling had gone, and there were tiles instead. And then there was a corridor with ancient, flaking paint, and a door you had to bend down to enter what was basically a cupboard. At the back of the cupboard was a handle, and when you turned the handle the whole wall proved itself to be a door, which it demonstrated by opening.

They entered a magnificent room, instead of the dingy basement Simone had been expecting. It didn't make any topographic sense at all.

Candles were alight around the room, so she didn't need the enhanced night vision she now possessed. They were mostly in silver candelabras, some on walls, some freestanding, and there was even a chandelier, ablaze with light.

So it was by massed candlelight that she observed with some astonishment the height of the ceiling, the size of the room, the huge fireplace, and most impossible of all, the great windows spaced along one wall.

And then she noticed a movement from one of the sofas placed around the other three walls, and watching, saw a figure rise. Christophe.

He was in overalls and it was almost a shock to see him in contemporary clothes, because without really realising it, she had been picturing him dressed to fit the room so to speak... strangely, long before she'd seen the room. But then, she had known that the Ile de Saint Louis contained a lot of seventeenth century architecture, so she was... what was it? Her subconscious, the bit of her that was half asleep: that was it. She had thought of him as being one with the background.

He was tall, with dark hair, and dark eyes that were a deeper brown than Philippe's, whose ancestors had bestowed some green in the colour of his iris, and a subtle glint of red in his brown hair. Her father would consider him a member of the 'Alpine' race, which was almost as good as being 'Nordic', in the twisted pseudo science he and his friends had cooked up.

Christophe was probably categorised as 'Mediterranean' which was darker of hair, skin and eyes, and she had an idea that this category was considered less wonderful than the other two, but perhaps she'd got that wrong, seeing how the ancient Greeks and Romans were pretty bright. Her father had explained it all to her, but she didn't ask questions in case he became angry, and she never knew what would make him angry so her policy was to speak to him as little as possible. He would never shout at her, just rave about useless politicians until he tired, and she soon understood that the quickest way to bring this about was to say nothing. At one time he was suspicious that she was 'intellectually defective' because she was so quiet, but her school work proved that not to be the case and her mother had succeeded in assuring him that she was just shy.

"I thought you were not in the habit of categorising people according to your father's ideas about what he terms 'race'," remarked Philippe, in a slightly disappointed tone.

So he had picked up on that, when they had visited the passport provider, as well as what she had been thinking just now. Why was he so intrusive?

Christophe had risen. I apologise for my friend, he told her silently. Philippe, also silently, said sorry. His thoughts had the same colour as the older vampire's, that was how she experienced the phenomenon, anyway. Only when they spoke aloud were their voices different. There was a pause as they looked at her expectantly.

She spoke. "I'm sorry I echoed my father, even though, you must understand, not really. It's just habits of thought and this is a curious situation..." She tailed off.

"I'm sorry I was listening in, but my feeble excuse is that you didn't tell me not to," said Philippe, "but..."

"He wanted you and I to be friends," Christophe interjected. "He knows I am very opinionated on certain topics. It is not just the Germans who embrace fascist ideas. There are people of all nations who are desperate to prove they are better than anyone else. They will cite great thinkers' theories, and get them wrong. I can see you are not like that at all, with you it's just a habit, which you will certainly shed as you associate with us." He said all this with an open smile, but then the smile became something different, darker.

"Vampires are great egalitarians. There is no blue blood, or we'd have surely noticed; no divine right of kings, no one is born to rule. It all tastes the same, to us..."

Christophe was like an actor; the sort who could be plain one minute and strikingly handsome the next, so you could never make your mind up which he really was. He took her hand and brushed it with his lips, and that truly was an antique gesture; it seemed natural to him in a way that it wouldn't be to a twentieth century man.

"Enchanted to meet you," he spoke in English and his accent was not just French, but where it originated was impossible to guess.

Behind him, on the sofa, there was another movement.

"Maddy, darling, come here and see my friends." He turned and took the woman's hand, and she emerged from the depths of a pile of silk cushions.

"Bonjour," she said, sleepily. On her neck was a snail's trail of blood from two neat wounds, and Simone's newly sharpened sight saw the white scars of older, similar wounds.

Christophe was ahead of her, in her mind and almost anticipating her thoughts.

"I'll have to stop nibbling on Madeleine. And so will this fine gentleman here. It will disfigure her lovely neck."

Simone couldn't help but turn to look at Philippe, and couldn't help, either, the slightly shocked expression on her face. Nor could Philippe completely conceal a guilty glance at her, as though he were concerned at her reaction. And was that a stifled snigger from Christophe?

But the scent of Maddy's blood was still delicious, even after their adventures on the streets of Paris earlier, and had they not taken care to satisfy their hunger she would now be in danger of losing her life.

"I don't mind about my neck! Can't you take it from the thigh? This is... you are good to me. It was terrible before I met you!"

Well of course it was, thought Simone, she's clearly been a prostitute, and all these two want is a pint of blood now and then. Or perhaps they wanted more, as well?

Christophe took the girl's hand. "That's a good idea, sweetheart, and I'll be in touch soon, I promise. He kissed her on the cheek, and gave her something Simone couldn't see, but which she supposed was money. Then he wrapped an arm around her waist, held her to him and ran up a wall. He was nearly at the point where his head would bump the ceiling when he jumped outwards and sprang onto one of the two unlit chandeliers that graced the room. It began to turn around, and as it did, the ceiling above opened like the pupil of an eye adjusting to darkness. The chandelier lowered itself, slightly, and the vampire, still clutching his burden, climbed up the great chain holding it, using just one hand and the strength of his legs. He disappeared through the hole in the ceiling and shortly reappeared, reversing his journey, although it took no time at all now he was unencumbered.

Simone watched the hole above until the chandelier had completely risen again, and there was no sign that above them was a route out of the building.

"Did you acquaint the mademoiselle with the details of our way of life here, Philippe?" Christophe asked.

"Tell me what I need to know," she suggested to them. Tell me how this place is so big, yet hidden away. Tell me where that hole above us leads to. Tell me how to stay out of trouble for a bit, until…"

"Until the Allies return to France and you can help them drive out the Boche?" replied Christophe, lightly.

Simone hesitated to reply. She didn't know when that would be, and probably only two or three people did, for sure. But everyone knew it was going to happen, and even the hapless German people were waking up to the reality of almost certain defeat.

Notwithstanding, her training kicked in and she said nothing.

"It's all right, Simone, we're used to keeping secrets," said Philippe.

"I don't know anything! But yes, one day the Allies will march into Paris, and if I can help, I will." She realised she sounded defiant, and decided that was nothing to be ashamed of, sticking out her chin as if to show she wouldn't be dissuaded.

"She thinks we're sneering, Phil, she thinks we embrace a different philosophy and believe ourselves above the human world's drama and politicking and wars. Was it you who made her think that?" Christophe was still smiling.

"No, he didn't. I worked it out all by myself." God, he makes me sound like I've got a chip on my shoulder about snobby vampires. And he hasn't said or done anything to demonstrate disdain, so why am I reading this from him? Is it my imagination? Simone was annoyed at herself, and couldn't understand why the atmosphere seemed prickly. They were allies, too, surely?

"Sometimes," Philippe said, "People just find themselves feeling scratchy with each other, and it's not clear why. Not immediately, anyway." He selected a nearby chaise longue, and draped himself over it with a sigh of satisfaction. He looked slightly more suited to his environment than Christophe, because his clothes were drab black garments that might almost have passed unremarked in any recent century, albeit on a bank manager type, or an undertaker, rather than some aristo in bright breeches. Christophe's clothes, on the other hand, were paint-spattered overalls; he looked as if he'd come to give the place a facelift, which it certainly needed.

He caught her thought, or maybe just the expression on her face, and laughed, jumping up again to take her hand, in a grip that was almost delicate. He led her to a large tapestry, a wall hanging depicting a hunting scene, faded and dusty and ill-lit, though gold and blue and rose pigments were still there, and the horses still showed the whites of their eyes. He lifted a corner, and behind it was yet another door.

He held it open for her as she walked inside. The place was filled with candles, but most weren't lit. There was no need, unless he had guests who were not vampires, and whom he wanted to impress. The walls, all four, were covered in paintings, and in a corner of the room were sheets covering large objects which, judging by the paraphernalia around them, were definitely sculptures. The place smelled of paint and turpentine and it was clear that this wasn't a collection of masterpieces but one man's efforts, of which he had been delivering himself for a very, very long time.

The room was of a size similar to the other one, which meant that a grand piano could go almost unnoticed... but not quite. It too was draped in a white cloth, and around it other instruments nestled in their cases.

"You see, I have had a long life, but I have made use of it," he said. "And you are wondering if I am any good at these things? Please, look closer."

She saw that some of the paintings were of the same objects. The earlier paintings were easy to spot, because they were darker, having been varnished a long time ago. They were also like the dabblings of an amateur. There were mythological themes, and like his merely human counterparts he had favoured the stories which gave him a chance to paint the female nude. Some of the most famous painters had their preferred models, but several models had posed for these pictures, clothed and unclothed. They had all got old and died, Simone supposed. Had any begged him to immortalise them for real, or were they content to have their beauty made eternal in paint?

She realised when he answered that she was leaking thoughts like a bucket with a hole in it.

"Yes, they have asked me. And more than one died ridiculously young. There is a new world of medicine now, and it will be available for rich and poor alike one day, because that is the next wonderful thing to happen." His eyes lit up at the thought.

She was surprised how much he sounded like Philippe, but she supposed that an idealistic outlook and humanitarian inclinations had helped them stay friends all these years, as well as helping them master their dark instincts. She realised that both must have been good people to start with. Imagine, she thought, the likes of Marcel if he were turned into a vampire.

"You do understand your thoughts are wide open to me?" He was cautioning her. She shrugged. It didn't seem to matter at the moment.

"It's only fair, then, that I should be as open with you. But I won't show you the past, as I know Phil does. Not that I think it's wrong in any way, it's just that if I show you I revisit it too. I accompany you on that journey and I'm just not happy to do that. It's not because it's sad, though... do you understand?"

"No," she said, noting that Philippe was Phil, so presumably that was normal, "Not really. If it's not sad, why would it hurt?"

"Because death and life are the reverse of what you think they are," he said, confusingly.

"Because he's dead and they have gone to eternal life," said Philippe, entering the room. "and some of them are my pictures too."

The paintings got better as she walked around the room. One or both of them had taken time to copy some well-known masterpieces, and these were quite successful. Some were less familiar than others, and some subjects were painted in various styles, after different artists. Quite a few showed card games, and

217

featured people losing money to shysters. The paintings seemed grouped thematically, so that there was quite a collection depicting gullible people, then there was a subtle shift, and Simone was sure that the next work was copied from Hogarth's Rake's Progress, or some such title; or in that genre anyway. It was a line drawing of considerable skill, and depicted a desperate soul entering a debtors' prison, surrounded by a ragged wife and skinny children, whom he'd clearly let down in every possible way. It was the promise first made in the pictures of card games, delivered.

"I am not an original," confessed Christophe, "but I have some skill after all this time. Of course, some of them were painted by actual artists."

Well, why not? If he was old enough he could have met, who knows, the great names of the Renaissance, for example, and given the ease with which a vampire could enrich him or herself, it was all too likely that he owned some authentic works.

Simone was desperately trying to remember what little art history they'd been taught at school. Christophe might be yet another half bonkers vampire, but she didn't want to look like a fool by exclaiming over the wrong thing. Fortunately Philippe came to her rescue by taking her hand and leading her to part of another wall, which seemed to be mostly landscapes. They were also inspired by original works, and were studies of the likes of Constable, and even Turner. She fancied Philippe's style too stiff to ever have his studies mistaken for a genuine Turner, and his Constables were pedestrian attempts. But then, he was younger than Christophe, so she'd been led to believe, and had had much less opportunity to become good.

"Look at that, no wonder he cannot soar with such a subject." opined Christophe. "It is a deeply conservative view of the British countryside, yet he himself knows the suffering behind that cherished image, so dear to the hearts of his monstrous countrymen. He hates it yet yearns for it: He knows there has never been a British Golden Age, except for the rich, for whom it is always golden, but he insists on trying to emulate the fellow who churned out this stuff. As for the man in the cart, Philippe hates his type, forelock tugging peasants, and still complains about them constantly. But he is influenced by the Romantics, and they too worshipped an Arcadia that never was."

"But Turner is the reverse of that," interjected Simone, hoping she wasn't wading in deep waters.

"Indeed!" Philippe chipped in. "Industry in the midst of nature, and though he mourns the past he also celebrates the future, as you can see: Look at this beautiful, broken down ship, where he is mourning the pre-Industrial age, then look at the movement here, with the train travelling at a speed no one had ever seen before. It's a heralding of a new age. Except I am not doing either artist justice, I know that. I just wanted to pay homage."

Simone wondered why gambling was such a popular subject for these two.

She had no need to speak, of course. Philippe nodded, and said, 'both of us, yes', which wasn't an answer.

There was plenty else to look at, but day must be coming soon, and Simone was a little bit anxious in this strange environment. The windows were almost ceiling to floor, and though they were curtained the curtains looked very old indeed.

"Don't worry," said Christophe, reading her mind, or simply gauging what was bothering her by the normal human method of watching where her glance went, and her expression. In less time than it would have taken to explain he ran up the side of one of the curtains, and jerked it from its great rail, so that it fell to the floor, in a cloud of disintegrating fabric and an eruption of dust that immediately covered everything.

Simone gave a little scream, choked off as soon as she saw the brickwork on the other side of the window. It seemed that no natural daylight ever penetrated the room, with or without the barrier of curtains.

"Are they all the same?"

"Yes," said Philippe, "it was done years ago, and the buildings around us block out the sun, and for that matter the world, without anyone noticing we exist in their midst. Now you know why we stay here. And if people do notice, we make sure that no one pays attention to their stories… but I am at a loss as to why you had to make such a mess, Christophe. You could have just told her."

But Christophe merely laughed at his scolding, while Simone wondered who did the clearing up, and why only Philippe was being addressed by the diminutive of his name.

"We have maids," he answered his friend defiantly. "I am creating employment for them, and given our situation – and proclivities – we pay extremely well."

"Do you bring them from the roof?"

Her new associates positively chortled at that.

"Yes, Simone," answered Philippe, "we do. Or to be literal about it, they wait just outside the building, in the street, and we collect them at an arranged time, then jump down from the outside roof, tuck them under our arms, and jump back up again, finally getting them here. We even keep their equipment here, look," he pointed to a corner of the great room, where Simone saw a white sheet and a number of lumps beneath it, which looked like they might be mops and buckets and other related paraphernalia.

Simone was quietly fascinated by the way this pair of utter outsiders seemed to have integrated themselves and their lifestyles with the rest of the community that dwelt nearby, although she doubted that applied to the German occupiers.

"Why do you not use the hidden cupboard door for all this?" she enquired.

"Because the Germans might get too close, and if they pressured our maids they would have a way in here." Philippe looked serious. "We can always move house, but we don't want our friends exposed to any danger whatsoever. As far as they know, they can only enter the building with our assistance. Please keep our secret."

Simone nodded, looking equally serious, she hoped, but in all honesty the effect of the human blood had not yet worn off and she was secretly jubilant, simply because it was good to be alive, even half alive.

Chris and Phil, as she was starting to think of them, whether they liked it or not, continued to show her the contents of the two vast rooms, including their writing desks, situated quite far apart, which she supposed was to help their concentration, and a veritable library taking up an entire wall. Not even the highest shelves were inaccessible to them, of course. She was less impressed by the contents of shelves further along, which contained things pickled in jars, the likes of which, as a medical student, she had certainly seen before, although the vampires' collection included such gruesome casualties of natural selection that she could not bear to look too closely. Less horrible were the beautiful examples of what looked to be mediaeval astronomical equipment, and even some clocks, some supported by little golden gods, others with their innards visible, and all the more wondrous for that.

"You must come up to the roof to see our telescopes," said Christophe, "but let it be tomorrow, as the sky is lightening, and we shall see nothing, anyhow."

It being vampire bedtime they each chose a sofa, placed along a wall. Simone's was more of a chaise longue. It was the prettiest. The male vampires were old-fashioned gents, she thought.

But that might apply to Philippe, who was born well after the high Middle Ages, during what moderns call the Enlightenment, and whose family, despite their vicissitudes, had probably absorbed some of the fundamentals of chivalry, as the stated ideals of the knights that lived many hundreds of years before them eventually penetrated the culture of the common people.

Putting women on a pedestal had to be better than treating them as domestic slaves but it was less common than one might hope, and it still took an unconscionably long time to give us the vote, Simone mused.

But hypocritical and class-bound though the chivalric code was, it was probably invented by a woman, she thought, because before that there was... what? From what had Kerr come? And when? And Christophe? She shuddered. What was kept alive by means of the vampires? The past, that is what. And it was not just another country, but another world.

Her mind felt... not tired, but full up, and she wished she could sleep and dream, and process all that had happened, but she fell into a sort of fugue state, which she did these days, so that she really couldn't tell if she were waking or sleeping. The others were quiet, and the only thing that really seemed different from normal life was that she couldn't hear anyone breathing.

The three of them dwelt in their separate dreamlands for a while, then they returned to each other, and to the distant rumblings of a storm. But it was not the sky gods quarrelling; rather, it was the approach of hunger. Now, as it slowly began to make itself felt, it was like a mere fancy, an abdominal yearning, but in time it would become a tempest of desire and then... need.

It was the huge drawback of being a vampire, this controlling need. But human beings weren't immune, and needed food and drink too. Though truth to tell, it took longer for them to get to the savage state that she had already experienced – didn't it?

Was it getting worse, or was she imagining it? After all, she and Philippe had dined well last night. Shouldn't the satisfied feeling last longer?

221

A voice spoke in her head. May I come in? it asked, politely. She couldn't work out who it was for a moment.

It's Philippe, it added, helpfully. I can't have both of you! she said, and then sat up and said the very same words aloud. The other two also sat up, Christophe raising an eyebrow, Philippe looking concerned.

"In my head," she added. "At the same time."

"Naturally," said Philippe, "I'm sorry."

Simone felt a twinge of regret for the lost intimacy the two of them had had while travelling here. Christophe said nothing, and seemed to have rendered his mind impermeable to any intrusion. Unbidden, the thought came to her that they were both very attractive men, or had been, before they became vampires. Now they were pale, ethereal like perpetual boys. The beauty of youth still clung to them. They were strong, of course, so was she... but they didn't look strong. The bones of their faces were visible: There was muscle but there was no thickening of muscle, or laying down of fat. Christophe's chin even had patchy stubble on it. Meanwhile Philippe had attempted to shave a few times during their journey, rather messily, as otherwise he got stubbly very quickly, and then he looked quite villainous. But truthfully, he could have been a young man, his colouring like that of a sun-starved Spaniard perhaps, one who would have picked up a gun in their civil war. And he would not have been on the rebels' side, she was sure of that... yet this was a being who had again and again insisted on not taking life. Except the lives of other vampires.

"So," she asked, "what's the deal here? We just hide away from everybody except our maids and our dinners, which seem to be one and the same? Do we just stay aloof from world events and lead utterly selfish lives?"

Christophe laughed, and then frowned. "You disapprove? You want us to be fighting with the allies, I suppose? Do you know that the Nazis and the Allies both are developing weapons the like of which have never been seen before? The first ones to use them will face terrible retaliation, so bad that they will all wish, both sides, that they had never deployed such weapons. Well, we, too, are weapons. If we take a side, if we go into battle, other vampires who have chosen to ally themselves with a different side will retaliate against the humans to whom we are giving support. I don't want to see what a mess that will be." And he put a picture in her mind, even though he didn't make a habit of it: Through his eyes, she was gazing at a truly upsetting scene from Goya. He must be recalling a visit he'd once made to a gallery. Unless he knew Goya and it was a present...

"I was in Spain during their civil war, and I was there during Napoleon's time too, as you know." Philippe looked a bit sheepish. "I'm sorry, I caught the tail end of that. It's impossible not to, sometimes. After all, we've been linked."

"You can think more freely around me," offered Christophe. "We've not been linked in the way he means."

Simone flushed. "He means telepathically. That's all."

"Of course," said Christophe, with just the tiniest smirk.

"You wouldn't want to see what I saw then, believe me," Philippe went on.

"Hence his Goya phase," his friend contributed, "which is relevant to the later conflict as well." He gestured towards a section of wall which, upon closer inspection, revealed a gruesome version of a gruesome subject: Saturn eating his children. an unforgettable work, even copied by an enthusiastic amateur, as was the one next to it, with some chap in a romantic shirt was about to be shot by firing squad. The one was reportage. The other told a tale as old as time, appropriately enough, Simone thought, because Time eventually devours all of us, gruesomely or not.

"So, when you were… interfering with human affairs…" she began…

"He's never stopped, actually," Christophe put in. "I just went and looked at the pictures, and hung around being bored while he did sketches of the more palatable ones. The ones I showed you are the worst. I fancy myself fair at drawing and painting but I wasn't about to touch those."

But Christophe's languid reminiscences were not the most interesting things to... "Did you help people? Did you kill people? Both things?"

Philippe sighed, gustily, a borrowed breath of exasperation. "I saved some from their fate, for a while at least. I managed not to kill anyone directly, which was difficult, I can tell you. Especially with the priests. I never hated priests before I met a few. They were like fat leeches, worse than any vampires, more pitiless in extracting the life from their poverty stricken congregations, while raping and buggering their sons. And daughters. No wonder Spain never had a renaissance. Have you heard the story of the women and children massacred in Barcelona? This was just recently. They sought refuge in a church, but the priest bolted the great black doors against them. I missed that. If I'd been there I could have ripped the doors off that church and thrown the priests on the bonfire I'd have made of their doors."

"Let's go and rip some church doors off their hinges now, "cried Christophe, "in homage to the martyrs of Barcelona!"

To Simone's immense surprise Philippe let rip a powerful back handed slap that sent the other flying. Christophe picked himself off the floor and wiped the side of his mouth, where blood had suddenly appeared.

He seemed unaffected by what had just occurred.

"I have been disrespectful to the innocent dead, I'm sorry. And I'm sorry you can't be in a million different bodies and be on hand wherever injustice happens, to forestall it, and maintain the righteous order. But oh, the trouble is that this IS the righteous order. People have destinies and in any case, it's all a turning wheel, and they come back and back, so just wait a while, and they'll come again, and maybe this time, the victims will be the persecutors and vice versa, and nobody has learnt ANYthing. Right?" This was said with an air of infinite patience.

"Well, is that true?" Simone turned to Philippe, who seemed to have finished being violent.

"Vampires grow in power. That includes mental powers. And the perceptions of the senses. And senses and perceptions that most people have no idea are possible. It's like atheists who've never had any kind of direct perception of anything other than this material world. It's possible to be an atheist when human, but no vampire remains that way after they've been changed. But our perceptions develop in a unique way for each of us. I am not sure about this constant rebirth, myself. I like to think everyone gets a rest between lifetimes.

But nobody asks what it is that is reborn!"

"What do you mean?"

"He means that we all have false identities, borrowed ideas, and are nothing but ventriloquists' dummies, most of the time, spouting what we've read, what we've been told to believe by school, parents, governments and blasted infinitum. Like you with your father's legacy of nonsense about race; it's not your fault, we're all indoctrinated as children, in some way or another. And out of these second-hand rags we stitch together a threadbare thing we're pleased to call a personality. And it dies. It is not reborn. But the eternal inside each human carries on. Eternally, of course! And eternally unknown." Christophe paused.

He lowered his voice to a whisper. "But we are different. We are outside the immutable laws that govern human beings. We refuse, we reject death, because we are the sons of Lucifer, the fallen one."

"And daughters," added Simone, rejoicing at the barely perceptible flicker of annoyance that Christophe briefly allowed to cross his features.

"Anyway, there you have it, we take slightly different views. I am egotistical enough to find myself regularly falling into the trap of believing I can help, whereas my friend here thinks that I am deluded, but tolerates my delusions as it gets me out of his hair while I wander about like Don Quixote, only with less discrimination."

Philippe shrugged, while Simone thought he retained more of his humanity than Christophe did, with his coolness towards suffering. At least the older vampire did not cause suffering, although perhaps he had at one time. Was Philippe the instrument of his friend's abstention from killing?

If either of the others picked up on that thought, they gave no sign of it.

At last their captivity was interrupted by the sound of a bell, tolling as if to call monks to prayer. But it was the sound of a gilded clock, with a figure of Father Time, of course, tugging a bell rope while presumably on a break from harvesting souls.

"It's dark enough to walk abroad, "declared Christophe." Although we could always use the tunnels."

Simone was taken aback by that, but her next question was forestalled.

"Very constraining," he added, "And damp. And full of rats, of all kinds. For emergency use only."

With that he ran up a wall, grabbed a shelf, and flung himself onto the chandelier, which rotated to reveal the exit hole. He shot through it, while Philippe waited for Simone to go before he followed.

They landed in a huge attic, at one side of which was a great window, like doors of glass, flung open, with a balcony outside. Simone stepped onto the balcony as

Christophe beckoned her. The sun had just set, to her left, but the sky in that direction was still red and gold, streaked with clouds the colour of steel. Christophe's long hair blew about his face in the wind, and his eyes glittered... with what; excitement, villainy, she didn't know, but she felt a lurching in her stomach, which she recognised from some time ago, before she became a vampire.

She had only been in Paris for a day, and she was already aware that she must not fall, romantically, for either of the two vampires. She knew what was likely to colour their lives together, and was helpless to prevent the rivalry that was going to erupt... or possibly be successfully suppressed by everyone concerned, which would be preferable.

She doubted that Philippe made a habit of striking Christophe, or that the latter devoted much, if any, of his time to needling his friend until he snapped, unless, of course, they were both really bored. The differences between them were probably accepted by now. After all, according to Philippe they'd known each other for nearly two centuries. It was she, coming into their... lives – she supposed she might describe it so – that had awoken the old Adam; still there, even in a vampire.

All that was as maybe. From what she had gleaned, they were the only 'good' vampires, and the rest were little better than savage beasts, (except for the mysterious Englishman with the very unmysterious name) controlled by the psychiatric case Kerr, who embraced the dark with the fervour of a devoted lover.

And Philippe had intimated that Kerr was fascinated with her, aside from any feelings he or Christophe may have had. For all she knew, Kerr had been trying to sire a female to be his mate... urgh. Perhaps Edith had been destined for that role, until Philippe killed her.

She stood next to the two males – 'men' didn't sound quite right, too human for what they were – on the balcony and looked at Paris, bright in her vampire vision although the night was closing over it, and the City of Light no longer fitted its famous description.

She felt the hunger strongly now. Thankfully, it blotted out any attraction she might have felt towards either Christophe, or Philippe. She hoped Philippe hadn't picked up that moment of weakness she'd felt. Human desire was so contingent... upon a chiselled jaw, flowing hair, a broad chest... designed, after all, to make babies and continue the human race, so it had to be a powerful force. But for vampires, surely it was redundant?

Gosh, she thought. They might be picking up on that thought. But neither gave a sign.

"Now, follow me," said Christophe, to her, rather than his long-time friend, who surely would know the way. He leapt, floating like something weightless, a winged seed, perhaps... then, with a graceful turn and a lazy spin, met the ground, landing on his feet. Simone copied him, with more clumsiness, shortly to be followed by Philippe, who glanced at her, rather reproachfully, or so she imagined.

They bounded through the streets as if they had four legs apiece, so swift and eager was their rush, and then across the bridge, with no one seeming to care if it were watched this time. What if it were? Simone thought. What could the Germans do to them? Bullets wouldn't do it, and by the time they'd ascertained who and what they were, and discovered how they could be killed, they'd be long gone. But deep down she knew that their enemies would have had past experience at seeing these creatures rush past, and would have had time to collect information – intelligence, they called it – on who and what they were.

Intelligence is *not* data, it's what you do with data. She found the misuse of the word irritating.

They were on the other side of the bridge. She caught Christophe's eye. She felt his thought... you're so right. She frowned. He shouldn't be doing that. He lowered his eyes, as if to apologise. You are a very dangerous man, she thought. His gaze remained lowered.

No, vampire. She flung the thought at him. Then she looked at Philippe and now he was a closed book to her. He was successfully masking his thoughts from her, and not intruding on hers, either.

"Come on." Philippe took the lead, and at length they were in a rather seedy little street, so full of sad history that her senses wanted to scream. Thank God, the souls that had passed through here had led short lives full of tumult, before departing to a better place, and it was not them that haunted the alley, but the impression left in the very stone, the cobbles, the walls of the tenement buildings; as strong as photographs – almost – to vampire senses. A hole had been dug, preventing any vehicles getting through, and then just left, like a handy mantrap perhaps, whose only other discernible function was to collect filthy water. At last they came to a door in the front of a large grey building, and Christophe knocked.

The door opened and a tired woman with bad skin peered out.

"Oh, it's you, Monsieur," she exclaimed, with a smile that seemed genuine. "And Monsieur Philippe." A puzzled expression crossed her face, but very briefly. "And a lady friend. Do please come in."

She flung the door open for them.

It was clearly a brothel and a drug den, but they were received with warmth by the inmates and their hangers on. Everybody knew the score, it seemed, and Christophe and Philippe were greeted with positive affection. Giving blood via a painless procedure, two pinpricks in the neck, accompanied by anaesthetic, and being paid for it seemed just a wonderful way to make money compared to prostitution. And the anaesthetic was welcomed by those who could not afford the numbing drug they might have preferred otherwise.

The vampires had plenty of money, and threw it around. Simone, recalling her own experiences of robbery, knew how easy it would be for them to get it. They might as well redistribute it to these poor creatures. Sometimes, often in fact, there was no exchange of money for services, as some of the girls were already full of morphia or other substances, and their blood was best avoided.

"We are safe here, these are friends," said Christophe. "But they are unreliable friends, if you know what I mean. They would sell their own children for drugs, and some of them have. And to that knowledge there can be no awakening, you understand? The soul cannot bear it. They must stay under the influence of the drugs until the release of death. But the effect of drinking from them is to make us very, very careless. I like to be carefree, of course I do, but we have enemies and so it is better to give them the money they need as alms."

Simone looked at the lolling head of a woman who looked like she could be near death, and was suddenly assaulted with a vision of the pain of her childhood, so desperate that it could not be endured for more than a moment. She reeled.

"Try not to do that," advised Christophe. "There is nothing you can do to fix it, not for her. But if we see children here, we take them."

"Take them? Where?"

"To wherever people are kind to children. We test out their minds and we're good at that. Away from the war, of course, and away from other kinds of savagery, too."

Another, healthier looking woman approached Simone, smiling rather shyly.

"My name is Peridot, Mam'selle, and I am clean. The gentlemen will tell you. I would be happy to be of service."

Another moment and I'd have been chewing babies, thought Simone, not caring if the other two overheard her thoughts. She took Peridot's hand, and the woman led her to a mattress on the floor, which Simone realised must be where she did business with other vampires, and probably with humans too. She was shocked when the woman lay back invitingly and undid her dress round the neck, pulling it low enough for Simone to see her neck. She sensed that the others had paused their own activity to watch her and her mind screamed at them: "Don't look, you lechers!" She was not a fool, and she was pretty sure now that even vampires retain the vestiges of the natures they once had.

But she could feel her own eager heartbeat, so strong she was almost deaf with it, and her own lack of breath was compensated for by the woman's fearful breathing as she bit down on the neck. Then there was calm, and quietness from Peridot, with only the sound of Simone, lapping at her victim's neck.

Their all too short communion was a blissful moment, so it seemed to Simone as she guzzled contentedly, and the blow when it came was even crueller and more of a shock than she could have anticipated. It was like being thrown out of heaven by Zeus, as poor Hephaistos was, and as was his analogue, Lucifer, to fall 9 days and 9 nights... to be born as a human. It was the 'nine' that gave the clue that an incarnation into flesh might be what the myth described; that this earth might be a banishment for disobedient gods.

Blimey, she thought proudly, now that's what I call blasphemy. Must be because I feel like God, after blood like that. It was definitely mixed with something.

Philippe it was who had slapped her round the head, and now he was dragging her off the woman. Simone stared at her, lying there, still in a state of bliss, and with a secret smile like that of a Leonardo angel. And when she woke, all would be cold, and harsh, and violent... She wondered if she might just re-anaesthetise Peridot, so that she might stay happy a little longer, before she had to go looking for the drug, but Philippe shook his head, without bothering to speak. He also conveyed to her an observation that he had not made till now, that the anaesthetic in a vampire's fang, like the venom of a snake, needs to renew itself, which it can do within a half a day. Not a good idea to expend it all at once, in case one ran out. Though, remembering the animals she'd killed, she must have used a lot without running out.

"Or caused pain you weren't aware of. You can do that when you're really really thirsty, and drain the blood fast. You can kill them so quickly. But then... it's something that you understand with experience."

Simone wondered if it were usual to fall half in love with your supplier of blood, or bliss, or whatever, and at the same time, when the high tide of feeling began to ebb, and the sea exposed the jagged rocks, the stinking seaweed, and the detritus that humans left behind, to despise oneself for it. There it was again, that falling into illusion. But it would take a heart of stone to despise others for the same weakness.

They weren't vampires. They were victims: The drugs they needed were anaesthetic, mimics of the venom she produced.

The next woman who came up to her was not very victim-like. She had a strong-boned face and an emphatic chin, and her hair was cut short. Her history was easily readable for she had an innocent mind: Her taste was for other women, and indeed in that regard she was almost predatory, and her boisterous adventures had got her kicked out of the family home. She was strong, and would have happily worked as a labourer, but the Nazis were after slave labour, and you were automatically a criminal if you didn't conform to their view of how the world should be. So, eventually forced to endure the demands of the oldest profession, she now actively disliked men, although the vampires had fed from her before and she had welcomed the chance to make money from something else. All this Simone could read, and as she bent for the kiss on the neck she saw the girl's eyes staring into hers, not in fear, but defiantly. She stopped.

"We haven't been introduced," she said, smiling in a way she hoped was reassuring.

The wide blue eyes opened even wider. "Introduced? My name here is Ruby. We are precious stones."

Then she sat up. "I'm not used to this from a woman. It disturbs me. You have no right to know my name."

"But I do know it. I can see it in your mind."

The girl looked horrified. Oh God, how careless I am, thought Simone, suddenly just as horrified at her own dimwittedness. If you must pry into people's brains, do it just to know enough, to protect yourself. Now the silly thing thinks I've taken everything. They're obsessed with the little privacy they can maintain, the rags of identity that flutter around the rawness of their lives. It's not right that I should be able to take their bodies' blood and peer into their secrets as well.

Wait a minute, she thought. Someone planted that thought. It's not really mine. She turned to see Christophe cuddling a sleepy woman with two neat little trickles of blood running from her neck down to her white chest, her neckline having been pulled down till it was almost immodest, although it had probably been done to save staining. Then, holding her gaze with his, he very deliberately bent and kissed the woman's mouth. Lifting his head again, he drew a curtain across the alcove where the woman sat on a narrow bed. She knew he no longer could feed from the woman. He should be moving to another, but he wasn't going anywhere.

Simone was shocked, but not confused, although she didn't understand why Christophe took his pleasures here, from these poor souls. He was a very good-looking man, for one thing, but for another, why make a commodity from an urge natural to the human race if you didn't have to?

She turned again to Ruby. Whose real name was Karin, because her father was Swedish, and who had thick blonde hair as another consequence of her parent's nationality.

"I don't know your real name, Ruby, I was just joking. Sorry. Now let's get on with it shall we?"

Her manner might be described as business-like by some, although others would call it callous. Sadly, Ruby adapted to the new tone quickly, as it was what she was used to. And habit will inure us to anything. She pulled away the clothing around her neck, and the simple movement carried a deliberate erotic charge that Simone did her best to ignore, just as she ignored the soulful stare with which Ruby aka Karin was now favouring her. She had come across this at university, even at her girls' school, though then she hadn't known what it was. Later, she had the discussion with other students; the one in which people agree that everybody is a little bit bisexual, and one makes spurious claims as to what percentage one might be, based on who knew what evidence.

All Simone could honestly say was that she wasn't bisexual enough to even experiment with women, as it would be unfair to raise hopes beyond that. So she snarled, to put the girl off, and sank her now protruding teeth into the luscious neck, delighting in the savour of the all-nourishing blood.

A finger slipped into her mouth and she fell away from the girl. It was Christophe, and he was displeased.

"That's how mothers dislodge babes on the breast. I shouldn't have to do it to you."

"You didn't dislodge me, I am not a baby, you just reminded me…"

"Remind you? I won't always be around to stop you killing out of sheer careless greed!"

"You're just cross because you had to put that girlie down before you were good and ready," she retorted.

Christophe just shrugged. He was too old to bother getting angry.

"You can't rely on us to discipline your appetite. You must do it yourself, because we won't always be around."

Simone nodded. There was a threat there, and she knew it. They would not allow her to kill, and if she did they would dispose of her as they had disposed of Edith. Moreover, it would be the right thing to do.

Philippe was paying the Madam. Her eyes were full of calculations.

"Your friend, the new young lady… she does know when to stop, doesn't she? Because, I have much respect for you, as you know, and I'm sure we'd all sacrifice ourselves if necessary, but a lot of the girls have dependants, and I would have to insist on provision being made, if that should occur…

Simone felt and saw the redness in Philippe's mind, but he was as admirably controlled as Christophe, although the latter seemed not to need to control what was barely there. The redness hadn't coloured his thoughts. He must be much older, surely, than Philippe, to be that much wiser, though he was no saint, given the curtain drawing earlier and whatever went on behind it.

At last they were all done, and they left the place, heading back to the Ile de France and the great rooms where they would read, and paint, and wait for France to be free again.

Chapter Thirteen

Not to be born is best, when all is reckoned in

(Sophokles trans. Fagles)

The pattern of the vampires' lives was as set, in its own way, as that of any bourgeois, except for a few departures: There was no morning baguette with coffee, as a rule. They were home before dawn, of course, and it was the sort of refreshment, suitable for those who had spent the night passed in bawdiness and indulgence, that awaited them, for on that first night Simone had returned to find what seemed to be a butler of some kind, standing guard over a sort of large tray, on wheels, laden with wine and snacks, little bite-sized sandwich things, made with soft fresh bread.

But the two male vampires waved away the comestibles. It seemed that sometimes they ate food, and sometimes they just didn't. Simone took a glass of champagne and it tasted fine, refreshing even. Then she took a bite of a sandwich and it was like cotton wool. It felt as if it could choke her, so she discreetly spat it into her hand, wondering where to put it so the smart-looking butler wouldn't be offended.

But it was too late.

"Madame is not hungry?" His face was droopy: Heavy folds of skin declared him old, very old, yet he moved like a man only just past the prime of life. It gave him a lugubrious mien. Gravity bore down upon him, at least outwardly, but Simone sensed a vigorous nature, and a fire that burned as strongly as it always had. He had equipped himself with a suspiciously blotchy, large-pored nose and his right forefinger was stained brown. This did detract from the immediate impression of smartness, but it was wartime after all.

"So what are you?" she asked softly. "Are you immortal? Do you drink blood?"

But his mind was open and willingly so, at least up to a point. He had been here all the time, discreetly hiding nearby, although his mind masked the location; out of habit, Simone hoped, rather than a lack of trust in her, although for all he knew she could be like Kerr, on the side of wickedness. He might have impressive self control as demonstrated by his ability to conceal his thoughts, control probably developed because over the years he'd had a lot of secrets to keep from some very determined and ruthless people. He might not be able to read minds like a vampire could, so she was impressed that a human could hide or reveal thoughts at will, even with a strong will, but after all, everybody thinks.

She saw that he had been literally facing a firing squad, for working for the Resistance, in the early days, back in 1940. He'd been no innocent, and he had taken lives, but they were the lives of the occupiers, who'd asked for it. She felt this strong assertion from him, which was reassuring, because he clearly knew that it mattered. The Nazis had intended to stage the shooting in broad daylight, 'pour encourager les autres' and had rounded up an unwilling audience to witness and learn what awaited dissidents. But there had been trouble, and the plan was changed: They weren't yet ready to massacre a crowd in the centre of Paris, and that might have turned out to be a necessity after such a public execution. It would be better to do the job at night, and then perhaps... show his head to the mob? Stick it on a spike as a warning?

These last suggestions were those of a certain colonel, a student of military history, and a great believer in overwhelming force. Fear, he maintained, was a weapon of war, and once it had been deployed, and the population cowed, ruling over them would be easy. His superiors were a little more rational, and might be suspected of keeping him around to make them look good by comparison, just as if they really were bringing civilisation to the benighted French, who simply hated them all the more for their confounded cheek.

So the execution was scheduled to take place at night, in a secluded courtyard, and only the participants knew when, and even then, only the most significant ones, which excluded the star of the show himself. He was just fodder.

Charles did find out when he was going to die though, just an hour beforehand. A guard, more humane than the others, had unlocked the door of his cell for long enough to stick his head in and tell him, and ask him if he wanted a priest. Charles had snarled his refusal of such ministrations. He was a communist and an atheist, and he hated the clergy, partly due to his recent experiences in Spain. For Charles was a seasoned fighter of fascism... and once again, his mind, unspooling the story it was telling Simone, mostly through pictures but also with a guiding narrative that wasn't exactly conveyed with sound, but was more of a luminous thread, emphasised that he had only killed the wicked. And furthermore...

"It reminds you of something," he interjected.

"Firing squad? It makes me think of the Goya painting, what's it called – May 15th? I think there's a copy of it here... or it could be there's a copy in the Prado and the real thing is here. But they use a squad so that no one knows for sure who fires the fatal shot, don't they?"

Charles looked like he wanted to spit, like some grumpy peasant with an ancient grudge, but he remembered that he was supposed to be an English butler, for now, and refrained.

"Huh, that's the acceptable side of his work. But the black paintings now, there you see evil portrayed, clergymen sodomising little boys... they're set back in the time of the Napoleonic wars, but priests don't change. The papacy doesn't care, as long as its priests don't breed, because that might produce heirs, and they could fancy claiming some Catholic wealth." Philippe had heard enough.

"Charles, we have a lady here."

Simone was startled at this, but she contented herself by saying that she'd seen enough not to need anyone's protection, after which she promptly regretted saying it, because Philippe's change of expression suggested to her, all of a sudden, that he wanted to be protective of her. It was sweet of him... she closed down her mind very carefully, then, and pulled up the drawbridge against possible invaders.

Charles made the point for her. "She's surely seen it all by now. She might be a lady, but she's a lady vampire. And you took her down the club last night, didn't you? No option, really, unless it's cows, and there aren't many cows in Paris, are there? Not many dogs or cats either... and there won't be many rats left if this lot carries on much longer."

"Have you heard anything yet?" rejoined Philippe.

"It will be summer now, but early summer. That's what they're saying."

Simone knew what 'it' was without using her new mind-reading skills.

"How can we help?" Charles must have links, still, with the Resistance, and they must be in touch with London. Suddenly all she craved was the chance to help the Allies reconquer Europe; all she wanted was to see celebration on the streets of Paris.

"Don't worry, my dear" he said firmly, and there was no Madame nonsense now, "You will help," and he gave her an inviting smile, so she looked at him once more in that searching way. And she saw the story unfold, of how her two fellow vampires had been passing on their way to some brothel or other, and had heard his curses in their heads, loud and fierce, and had stopped to intervene.

The city was full of curses and screams, but they were close enough to feel the mind behind them, and recognised its powerful focus; its ruthlessness and its courage. Unlike Marcel, her dead colleague, there was motivation beyond mere simple patriotism. Defending one's own, after all, was no great stretch for anyone. Apes did it.

But Charles was that most dangerous of beasts, an idealist, a Marxist, to be precise, already experienced enough to be a little disillusioned with the way Marx was being interpreted, yet willing to fight not only the German aggressor but also the French who collaborated and capitulated, and even, in the end, his own colleagues in the Resistance. But deep down, or maybe not so deep down, there was the love for human beings, as well as the love for humanity, that kept him struggling. The two vampires, passing close to where he was to die, had got all that. In fact they'd paused to listen to his mind.

As she learnt about her new, developing self, she had discovered that vampires have extra senses, and augmented powers of appreciation. Only vampires can appreciate the full horror and glory of another mind, certainly not in the sense that an ordinary human might appreciate a fine wine, no, for however delightful, food and drink are not like great accomplishments; not like, say, a symphony, or a play, or a painting or sculpture. It is more the case that the most subtle of minds can be the highest expression of the arts, for all other works of art are made by human beings, but humans themselves are made by...

well, not god, for Charles would dispute that, but call it something else... also, once created, we are co-creators, and we are works of art that are never complete, at least, not until we die.

The fire behind the intellect, and the powerful sense of injustice, as well as what he (at the time) had believed private, such as his own rejection of organised religion while harbouring a secret longing for what could only be called the Divine; the ferocity of his passions, and his gentleness towards the weak. All this had attracted the vampires, ineluctably, but the clincher was his usefulness to the Resistance. So, with a nod to each other, they had turned aside and just barged down the doors that stood in their way.

It had been a simple business, really. The firing squad had been loading their weapons, and Charles, eschewing a blindfold but with his hands tied behind him, had been standing, furious rather than afraid, awaiting the end. Philippe and Christophe had just walked into the courtyard, accompanied by warning yells from those who'd just encountered them, and told the squad to lay down their arms, because "we're taking this man out of here." The usual chaos ensued, as vampire met German, and disarmed them with that special kiss. The key, Simone had already realised, is to shield the human you're rescuing, immediately, or else you'd be blowing your cover for the sake of a corpse, and there was often some smart bugger around quick enough to figure out that murdering the intended rescue would negate your whole plan.

There were weapons that could mess up a vampire's future for quite some time, but ordinary guns, even automatic ones, were the equivalent of a graze. By the time the Germans started waking up and calling for reinforcements the vampires and their new friend were long gone, and when someone finally got round to thinking hard about it, it felt like a departed nightmare, which would vanish at daybreak.

This had been over a year ago, and Charles often played butler, as he liked to eat with the boys, as he put it, even though they were considerably older than he was, and sometimes he had to try and eat all of it, as neither felt like ordinary food. Otherwise he was often to be found elsewhere, playing cards and losing money, which was what he'd been doing when Simone first arrived. Sometimes he was plotting with others, serious people who didn't understand what vampires were. But when money was needed and there was a problem making the connection with Britain the vampires would help out. A bit of robbery in a good cause was an excuse for them to have a little fun.

Christophe was frowning. "Now you know all this, I hope you're not thinking of indulging yourself."

"Who, me? I hadn't given it any thought," said Simone, her hackles rising. "But now I am, and why not? You rob, you rescue people, and it sounds like a good use of our abilities."

"The robbing can be done discreetly, if people make an effort," drawled the elder vampire, with a sideways glance at Philippe, although it was Simone that felt vaguely guilty as she remembered the shoe shop. And the bank.

"But rescuing people more than not requires some sort of confrontation," Christophe continued. "I know you've battled Germans a couple of times, and refrained from killing them, but when they wake up the message goes back. You can be sure they've a dossier on vampires, even if they don't realise the nastiest of the lot is on their side."

It was a topic that leant itself to the medium of speech, for the avoidance of ambiguity. Looking into the mind often revealed feelings, as well as offering the immediacy and the marvel of being present in the past, but there were limitations: it was difficult to dodge the empathy with the person whose mind you were visiting and it was very hard not to identify with their point of view to some extent.

And ambiguity and its cousin ambivalence were features of mind that were luxuries when your country was at war. Commitment and focus and precision were required, and good old speech was best for that.

Philippe snorted. "Well, I might as well say it again for the new girl's benefit, though lord knows I've said it enough already: Kerr by now knows where we are, and could probably guess our exact location within a couple of kilometres. He has doubtless ordered that incidents which have certain characteristics are reported to him immediately, wherever they occur throughout the Nazi empire; like a load of soldiers being rendered unconscious rather than just killed. He may be able to touch our minds, as we've reason to think he's older and hence, stronger, than you and I, at least."

"Stronger? Are you stronger than me, then?" Simone hadn't really been aware of this. She had been too busy feeling her own strength, and glorying in it.

"Yes," said Philippe, briefly.

"But don't take it too hard," said Christophe," You've picked up the mind reading really fast."

"Because I'm a girl?" Simone was getting annoyed.

"Because you're sensitive, and because you're like that already and this augments it," replied Christophe.

It was only too likely that, when the time was right, Kerr aka Graves would issue orders to destroy them, along with detailed instructions on how to do it. And if the mortals he commanded couldn't complete the job, he was stronger and could kill them himself.

"But..." Then she shut down her thoughts, quickly. For although he was guarded, much more than Philippe, and although Philippe must have mind reading skills, he had nonetheless not looked hard enough, or deep enough into the enigma that was his friend. For if he had, he'd have noticed that Christophe had a secret.

And so the days and nights went on. There was more than one house of ill repute that they visited, because you couldn't drink more than once a week from an individual. That is how long it takes to replenish the blood supply. The women were quite jealous of each other, and jealous of the other brothels the vampires visited, because the vampire kiss was a most pleasant anaesthetic, and it was a much nicer way to earn money than prostitution. The vampires were very, very careful not to take too much, even though some tried to persuade them to take more, vociferously claiming that their blood was unusually swift to regenerate, and so on and so forth. Christophe would just shrug at this, while Philippe worried about them and insisted they must be in dire need of money, so the vampires should pay them more. So they did, which was satisfactory up to a point, but then he'd worry that not only the women but their families were getting dependent on them, and what if they were destroyed? Then they'd rob someone, usually a pro-German, well-heeled collaborator, from whom they'd attempt to conceal their vampiric powers so that it didn't get back to Kerr. But Christophe was getting less concerned about that now, as he was convinced that Kerr would not try to eliminate them till close to what was being called D-day, though the actual date was not known to anyone yet.

Philippe took Simone out robbing, as he called it, probably because it sounded like Robin, and the association with Robin Hood made him feel less of a criminal and more of a philanthropist. They targeted the swish nightclub scene, and even the opera. They hovered around, inconspicuous, and Simone had then to lure some couple away from the crowd, which was easier to do if you were a woman, while Philippe would draw a knife and demand valuables. He didn't need a knife of course, but they wanted to seem like ordinary thieves. On one occasion the male half of the couple had pulled out a gun and actually threatened, not Philippe but Simone, and was absolutely flabbergasted to see Philippe shrug and tell him to go ahead, so much so that he'd lowered the gun and offered him cash and his expensive watch, on the grounds that he didn't want to tangle with a man that ruthless.

They did a couple of banks too, but it was surprisingly slim pickings, probably because everyone had hidden their French money under a mattress and had no faith in the survival of the German currency, since everybody knew there was going to be an invasion soon. The air hung heavy with expectation, and spring was nearly upon them. Never had there been such a spring, never had so much hope uncurled itself as if not only nature, but the human world too was about to be reborn.

They did get a lot of money together, as Simone was restless and needed to do something, while Christophe seemed to become more withdrawn, as if now Simone was here he could leave the others to it. Philippe had fixated on providing for half the prostitutes in Paris – or so Christophe flung at him – for the rest of their lives, and their children's children's lives, and Christophe painted, and read books, and played the piano as much as he ever had, nagging his friends gently when he wanted a bit of light relief.

The leafier streets and boulevards began to unfurl their summer green, and early flowers scented the shortening nights, so that the vampires were able to enjoy the annual enchantment. Simone might have wept at the ephemeral beauty of it, except that she didn't cry anymore: The bloody tears were just too repulsive. She'd been astonished, and a little unsettled, to discover that they could be photographed. When she asked how that could be, when they couldn't see their reflection in mirrors, Christophe just shrugged and said it was a different process. He was a great shrugger, perhaps because it was such a useful response when you either didn't know the answer to something or you did, but you couldn't be bothered explaining it, especially in the case of those shrugs which also conveyed an unwillingness to waste one's time explaining stuff to dopes like one's questioner.

Once Christophe had photographed her and got her to cry by telling her sad stories, just so he could capture a black tear on her sculpted cheek, which was really red, of course. She was thinner than she'd ever been: A diet of nothing but blood will do that. Of course there were Charles's snack days, when she'd eat just to be sociable, but after a while she made a point of eating as much as she could, before she 'lost her figure altogether', as her mother would've put it. But she did look good in the photograph.

Charles and Philippe actually had a few non-vampire friends. They were a select group. The staff of the brothels they frequented, for instance, who were sworn to secrecy but mostly well-bribed, and furthermore had been warned in no uncertain terms that the flow of money would dry right up if the vampires were exposed to the Germans, or their puppet government enforcers.

Then there was the journalist and photographer Daniel Aubrey, who'd started doing his photographic social diaries of France in the early thirties, which featured the poor and the outcasts. The vampires had found him, beaten senseless by the Nazis and given shelter by one of the Madames whose house they were visiting. It had looked like he might die, and, moved to pity, Philippe had offered him the Gift. He'd laughed in their faces, told them not to lay a finger on him or he'd kill them (since they were vampires and he'd been badly messed up this was just bravado) but he hadn't disbelieved them, and further evidence, like watching them drink from people's necks, had confirmed their offer was real. Still, he'd rejected such a life for himself, and declared that he expected to die in the arms of the ladies of the night, and furthermore he was sure that death would come soon.

But some of those ladies had clearly missed their calling. They should have been doctors, or nurses, for Dan had pulled through, much to his and everyone else's surprise. Now he came to visit via the passage through which Simone had first entered what she thought of as the crumbly palace, the same entrance Charles used.

Simone met him when he came around with a series of Christophe's photos which Dan had developed, including the one of her. He was persuading Christophe to rig up a darkroom, and maintaining that the photographer's eye had not completed its work at the moment of taking the shot, but that developing a photo was an art as well. Something like that. What was strange to Simone was that he could not, apparently, take his eyes off her. It got embarrassing in the end. He was raving at the beauty of that single shot of her with the treacherous tear.

After he left she didn't pause before exclaiming that he was a weird bloke, at which point her fellow vampires laughed, apparently at her lack of self-knowledge. You haven't realised how lovely you are, thought Philippe, then started to cough, as though to draw attention from his remark.

"I'm so thin!" she said.

"Look again. You've no mirror, or at least none that'll serve you, so make the best of it," said Christophe, a little snappishly, she thought.

She studied the photo again. She was all bones, including in her face, but they were quite elegant bones. She'd never really seen them before, and they did make a difference.

A few days later she'd been trailing behind the others, and was about to drop into the room, when her hearing, which seemed to get better all the time, was acute enough to pick up a fragment of conversation from below. It was Charles that was speaking.

"She's still an innocent; must be, or she'd have surely noticed by now that you're both besotted with her."

There'd been a snarl from Christophe, and a muttered 'ridiculous' from Philippe, and then no more. She tried to mask her thoughts, then waited for a diplomatic minute or two before descending. How much use that was, she wasn't sure, because you wouldn't have needed telepathic powers to describe the air as something that could be cut with a knife.

Just before the waiting and watching and hoping began to become intolerable, something changed, and the dreaming started. Simone dreamt that she was flying over a vast flotilla of boats, but they were fleeing, and they were British, so she woke up and supposed that it must be Dunkirk she was dreaming about. This filled her with despair, until pointed out that vampires, though telepathic when awake, were not renowned for prophetic dreams, and this was probably her fears for the Allied invasion and its likely fate, fear being a common cause of certain kinds of dreams.

Philippe reported dreaming his own death by fire, which again, could qualify as subconscious fear, or indeed, prophecy. And Christophe would sit, gazing quietly ahead, sometimes shutting his eyes, claiming that he was reaching out all the way to British shores, trying to make contact with a British vampire, if any, other than their acquaintance Vampire Dave, existed; failing that, trying to touch the minds that would be organising the invasion.

Then it was the fifth of June, just before dawn. They were coming back from their haunts, and Simone was brooding on that word, thinking how great it was that they didn't have to actually haunt anything, and instead had access to light and warmth and company, instead of what the word suggested, which was hanging about in graveyards, or creepy abandoned churches, or abbeys like those reduced by Henry the Eighth to skeletons of stone arches, like giant ribs.

Suddenly Christophe stumbled, which was unlike him. He was usually sure-footed and even graceful. Now he was clutching his head.

"Stop!" he cried, "Someone's in my head!"

"We can't wait here, it'll be daybreak soon," said Philippe, and between Simone and him they helped their friend stumble home. When it came to scaling the walls of their crumbly palace Philippe didn't hesitate, but flung Christophe over his shoulder and leapt up to the roof with little sign of effort. When they were finally inside he remarked to Simone that she could easily have done it too, because the only thing stronger than she was, was a male vampire, and even then, not one more recently changed.

"It's your habit to assume males are stronger. You haven't tested your strength much. Christophe weighs nothing, not to me... or you."

But Christophe was gripping her arm with excitement. "It's him! It's him, I know it! The one I've been trying to touch... but it's so far, it's been so hard..."

His head jerked back, and he lowered himself into a chair. At first it seemed as though his head was controlled by another power, as it lolled backwards, but Simone saw that he was absolutely in charge, and was actively seeking to arrange his body so that the contact could more easily come through. It was as though the jerk backwards had allowed an opening of the mouth, chest and windpipe. Now the head moved forward into an upright position, and Christophe's eyes, though open, looked unfocused... or rather, focused within him.

Then his lips moved. "Greetings from Britain!" they said, rather boisterously, and with a definite northern English accent. Neither Simone nor Philippe could disguise their astonishment. Christophe spoke French like a Parisian, and English without any regional tinge, though it wasn't like an old Etonian either; his 'ou' sounded closer to 'ow' than 'eye'.

"Your contact is from Liverpool!" Simone exclaimed.

Philippe looked dubious. "There's mostly Welsh and Irish in Liverpool," he objected.

"In your day, pal," said Christophe's lips, in his new accent. Philippe acknowledged this with a slight bow. Liverpool had been a city of immigrants when he'd been a young man, but it seemed that the disparate accents had eventually come together and given birth to a new sound.

It was not usual, as far as Simone had experience of the process, for a vampire to act like a medium for another vampire, but she guessed that the distance made it difficult to do it any other way.

"Listen, we're going to lose the signal soon, like the wireless, so pay attention. I want my country to win, and so do you, or so this joker tells me. You're not Nazis, I know that. He offered me the tour, so I know."

'The Tour' was what the vamps called it when someone let you into their mind to explore motives. It was only offered by people with absolutely nothing to hide who needed to demonstrate their utter integrity. In practice, Philippe had told Simone, citing his long experience, people usually declined the Tour, as such an exploration was time-consuming and often a little embarrassing. The feeling was that offering it was enough to demonstrate truthfulness.

Simone had asked him for examples based on his experience, but since Philippe had only really known two vampires, and now three, with her arrival, he hadn't been able to expand much upon the topic.

"We can vouch for him, too," she said, and then instantly wondered if that were true. Then she thought of Christophe's secret and decided that she would never, ever understand him... at which point she shut down her mind as best she could, so as not to alarm their invisible guest.

"I offered the Tour to him as well, of course. No, lovey, it wasn't a game of double bluff we were playing. If he were the cause of losing one Allied soldier I'd come over there and do for him myself. Anyway, listen, it's tonight, after sundown, it starts moving. It's top secret till it starts, but they'll be listening in. I'm down here already, south coast, all along... that Billy boy fella... sorry, I always call him Bill... Kerr? Same vowel sound... as in air. Aha-hah. Joke. But he'll send troops as soon as he knows... get over here if you can, escort them. If you fall in the sea, just walk out, takes ages but you can do it. Signing off... I'd go to church to pray for them but they won't let me in! Ahahahaha! Stay in touch."

Christophe blinked several times.

"Yes, of course I heard all that, I'm not deaf," he replied to Simone's unspoken query. Fellow's been sucking drugged necks. Amphetamine, probably. Or he's a manic depressive. Anyway, he's got plenty to get excited about, although if it were me I'd omit the mad laughter. We've made contact in the past and I was pretty sure he is on the side of the angels. The city of Liverpool has suffered aerial bombardment and we all hate the bombing of civilians. "

"So what do we do?" Simone asked aloud.

"We head to the coast at dusk, should be there in time if we put our skates on, then we put the German army to sleep. Whatsisname will probably join us, somehow: He'll hitch a ride on some big boat is my guess. When he gets close enough, we'll feel him, so we can work as a team," answered Philippe, sounding a bit excited himself."

"And what about Kairrrr?"

"He's called David," Christophe began, "oh, that one, Care. or Kerr. Very good. Yes, he'll show up, won't want to miss the party. I can't wait to meet him again." His eyes narrowed.

"It'll be to the death," he said, sombrely. "We should have got rid of him, the two of us, long ago. He might be strong, but against us, fighting together... now he's their secret weapon and he knows how to kill us. I didn't want to get involved in human affairs, but Kerr loves it, and who else is going to exterminate him?"

"But… aren't you older than Kerr?" Simone could keep silent no longer.

"Sir William was a Knight in a very secret order," replied Christophe. "The wealth of the order was mostly obtained, at least at first, by pillaging what is laughingly known as the Holy Land. Funny that, how things often have a name that is the exact opposite of the reality. Sir William has boasted at his skill in obtaining secrets from people who were very loath to give them up. He became an asset to the Order. Eventually, the Pope of that time envied their wealth and had all the knights executed. Except for Sir William, who escaped in time.

I wanted to broker peace between Christian and Arab, but there was too much wealth for those bold enough to snatch it, and peace didn't suit their purpose. He assured me that he'd been a dupe, and I didn't know that much about his past when I changed him, so he said he had seen the error of his ways; convinced me I needed him, and promised that he would do as I did, if I saved him, and drink from people who were willing, or else from animals. He lied. But I wanted to be lied to. I wanted to believe I could have a friend. Mea culpa, mea maxima culpa."

"Well," said Simone, "I got that you were older than Kerr, but I didn't pick all that up, and I didn't get how far back you both went… to the crusades, but you're older again? How…"

"Old enough to know better," he said, and that was that. Simone could not connect with his mind at all now: it was as though a fortress sprung up around him. But it seemed he had been letting her see only what he wanted her to see, and had put everything else firmly behind the walls of the fortress she was only now beginning to recognise had been there all along.

Chapter Fourteen

He who overcomes himself is mighty

(Tao Te Ching)

It was infuriating to have to wait till sunset, but they had no option. They occupied themselves by sitting quietly, as if in deep meditation, letting their minds wander in the hope that they'd pick up some signal. It was like turning the wireless on and trying to find someone broadcasting. Then Christophe again made contact with Vampire Dave, the Liverpudlian. It seemed that he had been misled and the boats were not departing from the Pas-de-Calais but from further down the coast, and that the airborne troops would set off to France at midnight. The invasion had already been delayed by bad weather.

They discussed what they'd actually do, and it was probably not one big dramatic intervention, but little things, or so Philippe, who'd been on battlefields, maintained. Christophe may or may not have been on literal battlefields, but in any case was currently keeping that information to himself. It looked as if they'd be most use protecting the troops that were flying in. They could do nothing to help the ground troops, not in daylight.

At last they left for the coast. The journey would have taken Simone's breath away, if she had any. They left Paris via rooftops, jumping large distances, larger than she would have thought possible, and at a speed she had not guessed she'd be doing. If I fall off, she thought, it'll hurt loads, but it won't kill me, so why be afraid?

You won't fall right off, said a voice in her head. Look at me.

It was Philippe, who then deliberately stumbled off a roof. She almost screamed, then saw him rise above the roofline as if the ground was a trampoline.

Try it, said his voice, still in her head. She had no wish to try it, but she thought it might be a good idea, in advance of when there might be a real need. So she did a little fake stumble, just as he had.

As soon as she fell she felt her body seem to shift a gear, and slow its descent. Her hand reached out, somehow automatically doing the right thing, and touched the side of the building. This slowed her more, so she was floating now. Her body had uprighted itself, and she landed on tiptoe, as if she were as lacking weight as a feather. Even so, there was a huge bounce, and she sprang up to the roofline just as Philippe had.

It's great. Isn't it? Philippe smiled at her as his voice left her head. She didn't have time to ponder the physics of it. She just wished she could have put some time into mastering these new rules of time and space, but the abilities that went with being a vampire didn't arrive all at once. All she could do was hope to be of use to the brave boys who were finally coming back to the same beaches they'd been driven from. Or nearby beaches, anyway.

When they reached the suburbs they dropped onto the ground and began to travel across the flat lands of northern France. There were people about, but not many French people, and at this stage the vampires were loath to engage with the enemy. They didn't want to get bogged down when the landings were about to begin. There were trees, in some places, and then they jumped from tree to tree, although it was a bit slower than travelling on the ground. But they got faster and faster, running on roads and fields too, although it was more like tiptoeing at great speed, with the occasional phenomenal jump. So, they were mainly jumping, and by midnight they could smell the sea.

Then they stuck to the road, and now they forswore the jumps because the flat surface was so easy to just run upon. Faster and faster, distance running faster than any sprint, so to an observer who happened to be able to see in the dark as well as they could, their legs would be a blur of midnight blue against the darker night.

And then, a roadblock. Either they'd have to take on the enemy, or dodge the road and go cross country. To her immense surprise Simone found herself thinking those pointed sort of thoughts she had, that were quicker to convey by thinking them than via the medium of speech, but unambiguous enough to hold the shape of their meaning. And she wasn't receiving but sending. The others were much, much older, and they were male, which usually was synonymous with thinking you knew all about warfare, even if you'd only ever seen a picture of a battlefield. And Philippe had told her of his pirate years, when he must have masterminded a good few fights.

Let's disarm this lot, we're getting near now, she thought. We need to disable any of the enemy we see from now on. She felt the others' agreement. It wasn't, in any case, a particularly controversial view. After all, these soldiers were in communication with their command, and as soon as the airborne invasion began they would be told to kill as many would-be liberators as they could.

Full pelt frontal assault, chaps, take them by surprise, she thought. But they felt it before they heard it: They were acting almost as one.

One minute the soldiers were looking out into a dark and quiet night. The next, they were attacked by what seemed like people but moved like trains. A couple of soldiers were knocked out by flailing arms as the vampires barrelled into them. Some began to shoot.

Simone felt the stinging sensation as bullets penetrated her clothing and then her skin. The sensation was not pleasant, but what was worse was when a bullet hit what was usually referred to as a vital organ. The skin of a vampire was cold to the touch but still felt like that of a human. However, it had certain properties, one of which was that it acted like an especially ferocious immune system, pushing the bullet back out of it before it could penetrate too far. And all this happened with such speed and force that it was as though they bounced off completely. Because of this bounce, it was as though an opponent had returned a ball in a tennis match, with force equal to that with which it was served. So of course, some of those bullets were returned to those that fired them, often with fatal, or at least painful, or disabling results.

When the bodies were found later it was a puzzling scene, and one officer observed that their soldiers appeared to have been shot by their own bullets. But this was no crime scene, and nobody was going to be investigating further, even though this was not by any means the weirdest feature of the encounter.

Some of the men were unconscious when help arrived, and these had puncture wounds on their necks. The observant officer thought they looked odd, and indeed, who would inject someone with anaesthetising drugs in the middle of a war like that? He tried out an hypothesis for size; that women had offered them sex and they'd accepted, only to be knocked out by the treacherous seductresses, who then alerted their fellow Resistance members. But as they slowly awoke from slumber and told their tale this theory was binned. It was rubbish anyway. The dimmest of sex fiends would say 'not tonight Josephine' to women appearing out of nowhere, and apparently overwhelmed with desire that no one but German soldiers could satisfy, and besides they were on duty, busy occupying a country that – mostly – hated them, apart from a few collaborators and the Vichy government.

No, went the explanation, they had been jumped on by an army travelling very fast, and it was likely that this army was drugged to make its soldiers like the berserkers of old, for they moved really, really fast and didn't seem to care about being shot themselves, although perhaps that was because they did have surprisingly good body armour. And of course the biting could be part of the maddening effect of the drugs they were given, which must have gone into the bloodstream of those who were bitten, although how could the same drug turn the enemy into berserkers while rendering their own soldiers unconscious?

But after all, the book was closed on this incident pretty fast, as events overtook everyone involved. And later, when there was time, other minds started collating information and drawing conclusions that the officer was unable to come to, even though he encountered other phenomena that night that could only be described as strange, because he never uncovered the whole story. He didn't get the chance, for the following day he joined the millions of souls forcibly expelled from their bodies by war.

Meanwhile the vampires moved on as the landscape got wetter. They caught their first glimpse of a plane, high above, but coming closer. Then they saw the parachutes, one by one, leaving the plane, not white but some shade of grey, as camouflage, Simone supposed. This was it, the airborne invasion. The vampires stopped their headlong pelt to the coast, in case they could be of help. Simone suggested they be cautious, as they might be a bit of a shock to the arrivals.

But they dispensed with caution when they saw that one of the parachutists was descending way too fast and the chute wasn't opening. There was no way they could reach him, it was too far and what would they do? By the time this thought had coalesced in everyone's head it was out of date, as all three charged to the scene. Christophe might be as old as Notre Dame itself. He was the fastest but Simone and Philippe were right there. He jumped into their ready arms, linked together to make a little trampoline, and they threw him up into the air.

It was quite a throw but the parachutist was still too high. Christophe came down but their linked arms were waiting and he thrust his feet and bent his knees and they threw him into the sky once more. As he flew up he twisted his body to the right and with one outstretched hand, caught the parachutist, pulling him in towards the vampire's body.

Christophe wrapped him in a tight embrace and manoeuvred his own body beneath the man. There was no time to fiddle with the 'chute. The other two leapt towards the descending pair, arms still linked to break the man's long fall.

He had been screaming for quite a while, and as they caught Christophe and the soldier in his arms he was still screaming. They fell in a heap, all three vampires wriggling to position themselves below the vulnerable human.

Simone could hardly bear to look.

But he was all right, and started to babble thanks.

In wartime rules are suspended, including the ones that we make for ourselves. After the thank yous came the questions, or they would have done, except that Christophe didn't have the patience. The languid aristocratic demeanour, the suggestion of perpetual ennui which he liked to cultivate, even when clad in paint-spattered overalls; these airs were gone. There was work to do and it was really important, and only they could do it, which was the point he made to the soldier.

"We have special powers," he told the man, "because we are vampires. We are on the side of the Allies. So don't tell anyone, because keeping this little secret means we can carry on helping you all. Alright? Ok, as you people say? Right then, let's get you to your lot."

With that he slung the man over his shoulder with little thought for his dignity, and headed off as quickly as he could – which was very quick – to the area where most of the parachutes had come down.

The more speedily they acted, the more lives were saved. More than one parachute failed to open that night, and this situation could be salvaged by three of them working together, sometimes even two, while the third was elsewhere taking down a nest of Germans. They evolved a technique: It didn't take long because it was very simple, a matter of charging headlong or more usually, sneaking up from a neglected angle and then going for it. The drawback was the pain, as even vampires found automatic guns a challenge.

Philippe had little time for battlefield reminiscences but nevertheless found time to mention that having a sword in your guts hurt too, but there was also an added danger in that one's opponent might know that vampires could be finally destroyed by beheading, and swords were far more convenient for that sort of thing.

"So that's a blessing," muttered Simone, in response to this.

She found herself facing a heavily armed deployment of Germans, and the others were out of sight. They weren't holed up in what she thought of as a nest, mounting a last ditch attempt to repel the airborne invaders, but marching towards the sea, which she saw was no longer far away. The allies would be landing on those beaches soon, straight into the arms of death. She called for her friends with her mind, and the answer came that they were facing a platoon. She didn't question it. She was in the secret service, and had been given a job a long time ago, or so it seemed, to help save her country and her countrymen and women from the Nazis. The other two vampires had accepted no such duty, which didn't stop them being brave and determined, so she could do no less.

She found a high place; a bit of raised ground in that mostly flat countryside, and when the Germans were directly below she leapt as high as she could – and was surprised at how high that was – coming down into the middle of the column of soldiers, screeching and flailing her arms and legs to cause as much confusion as she could. Once she was among them, there was little time for anaesthetising people, and it became a matter of kicking and punching, but oh-so-carefully, because she didn't want to kill what were probably ignorant conscripts.

It was no easy task, fulfilling one's duty in the midst of war by trying merely to temporarily disable the enemy, and she knew she hadn't always succeeded, but then, ricocheting bullets from the gun fired by an intended killer which then killed their originator weren't really her fault. This was a situation she hadn't thought enough about, but it became clear quite soon that she really didn't know her own strength, which seemed to have increased mightily since she first became a vampire. The screams around her bore witness to that, and in her heart she prayed she would not cause any deaths, because she feared that she could pull arms and legs off, or send someone flying so far and so forcefully that they would never get up again. No one was shooting, in the chaos she'd created, because they would more than likely hit an unintended target.

At last, to both her relief and trepidation, the soldiers backed off and raised their automatics.

The shooting wasn't anything as painful as she'd feared. It just went on a long time. At first it was like heavy raindrops in a driving wind, then it felt like hail, and the force of it was strong enough to blow her over. Then the soldiers came towards her prostrate body, slowly lowering their guns. She waited until they were just outside touching distance, then sat up and said 'Boo!' opening her eyes wide and smiling a skull's grin.

Even conscripts have courage, and only a handful of them fainted. Most of the rest ran away, and since they were running back the way they came Simone made no effort to stop them. But some stayed, including a couple of older types, professional soldiers. These last were admirably cool. One of them leapt onto the truck and jumped behind a machine gun, and as he pointed the thing at Simone the soldiers still in her vicinity scattered. She braced herself. She would give them one final demonstration then she'd disarm that clown. She was beginning to get a little annoyed at being shot.

It really hurt. Her vampire tough skin was penetrated, and she felt the bullets penetrate what would be termed her vital organs, except for her, they weren't all that vital. Blood, black blood, flowed out of her wounds but only for a short time as they healed up, to be breached again and again. Sometimes they healed so quickly that escaping blood came up her throat from her lungs, bubbling from her mouth like someone had found oil down there. She would have choked had she needed to breathe. She felt blood pouring from her nose, then, unmistakably it began to exit her vagina and backside, which was absolutely infuriating, as her clothes would be ruined. A frisson of fear, social fear – that fear of the humiliation that might attend any woman who wasn't adequately absorbing and disguising her monthly flow shivered through her – until she reminded herself it was all black, and would not look like blood, and anyway, blood was bound to get everywhere when you're in a war... and who cared what these soldiers thought, for God's sake.

The pain of all her wounds, even the pain associated with healing them, was surely as bad as giving birth. She sank to the ground, for a rest at least. She lay flat, one eye open, watching as bullets exited her arms, and the wounds closed behind them. The gunner climbed off the flatbed vehicle, and cautiously began to approach.

Simone was very angry. It had hurt. A lot. As he approached she tried to read his mind. Fear. She sent him a thought, hoping he'd think it was his, which of course he did, never having given a moment's consideration to the idea that others could influence him to the point of believing their ideas were his own. Possibly that explained why most people's thoughts and utterances sounded like second hand, warmed-over nonsense. Her nonsense was as good as any, so she told him he needed to run away and never fight again.

She stood up, snarled at the man, and flew at the gun. Then she started to tear it apart. She twisted the barrel as if it were clay rather than steel, and finally ripped it in half. She felt the rage consume her, rage against being shot so much and so hard, rage at war, rage at those who designed the instruments of war, and then made money out of mass death. The gun was turned to smaller and smaller fragments as she howled her rage. At last it was pulverised, and she took the time to look around and saw that no one was left. They had all run away, back in the direction of Paris.

Give me but world enough and time: Simone recalled the poet's regret that he did not have time on a geological scale to woo his coy mistress. She could spend eternity though, on what she wished to accomplish, which right now was the destruction of all the world's weapons. Perhaps it was worth living forever, with such a goal, and now with the means of achieving it: her growing strength, virtual invulnerability, and the speed as well as the heights she could reach.

But there was never a chance that she could forget the weaknesses that were the other side of the coin. Even now it seemed to her that the sky was lightening in the east; it was nearly midsummer, after all. Soon the vampires would be of no use to anybody.

She called them with her mind.

Out of the west came Philippe, and Christophe followed.

"That's not the dawn, Simi," said Philippe.

"Well, not for us," said Christophe gently.

But the most important thing remained unspoken, because there was no need.

It was the most wonderful, most marvellous of sights, hardly a sight at all, trembling on the very edge of perception, and invisible to anyone who hadn't become a vampire; even then, it would seem that they had to have been a vampire for several months for the visions to kick in.

Impossible to speak about or to describe; nevertheless if Simone were ever to try explaining to someone she would probably say it was like wispy clouds with moons in the middle, hundreds of them, ascending from the earth like sea mist, with delicate light trails behind them. Almost like Jacob's ladder, but not really, just that when she turned around, they were all over the heavens, and when she looked she could see faces, turned upwards, looking at the way they were going, not to find which way to go but to look at something that seemed to be illuminating them, like the sun illuminates the moon. And then it was just clouds, wispy clouds, lit by distant stars sculpting the night.

What a hopeless description that would be. And how to explain the utter conviction that she had in that moment that everything was right with the world, with the people in it and the people currently out of it, even at a time of world war, yet it was and always would be just fine, whatever scares the future held.

And of course, there was also the conviction that she was seeing the souls of the dead.

Which was correct, according to Philippe and Christophe.

Simone had had a scientific training and she was by nature sceptical, but changing into a vampire had put quite a strain on her previous world view. However, there were laws of physics, and just because vampires were odd and anomalous that didn't mean there weren't rules to explain how vampires worked.

But when it came to death... well, there were probably laws, just different from anything modern science imagined.

It would be too obvious to say aloud what they all thought; that there were no uniforms in heaven, not countries, not even religions.

But soon it would be dawn, not for the departed but for all those still fighting and living on earth, and that included vampires, for whom dawn was a threat rather than a promise. They needed to find shelter. Fortunately while attempting to save some of the parachutists whose 'chutes had failed they'd had time to survey the landscape and Philippe led the way to a copse they'd seen, well away from any potential fighting. Once there they found nothing in the way of rocky outcrops and certainly no caves, but it seemed that Christophe and Philippe had been expecting that to be the case, so with a resigned air they got down on their knees and started digging with their bare hands. These flew, without injury to themselves, at a fast pace and the diggers seemed very accomplished, even without tools. Nevertheless Simone joined in, thinking it politic, and was astonished at how powerful she was, like some badger or similarly well-designed digging beast. In a few minutes they had made themselves a burrow, partly dug into the roots of the trees, where they could cover the entrance with leaves and branches and the sun could not penetrate. Once that was accomplished, they amused themselves by digging deeper. Soon there were passageways off the main burrow and Philippe was wondering about shoring up their temporary home to raise the ceiling.

The source of vampire energy is not glandular, otherwise they might have been described as high on adrenaline. They had taken the opportunity to feed on any stray Germans that came their way, being careful as always not to let themselves go, so in a way they had quenched their thirst, but there had not been time to sample much Boche blood, nor to explain who and what they were and negotiate with others on the field of battle. Not that they wanted Allied blood: they didn't want their favoured troops to be weakened in any way. As a consequence, they were energised but not quietly sated, and the burrow was always going to be too small: There was nothing with which to shore it up so they were like nocturnal animals; underfed, restless, powerful ones.

It was a couple of weeks till midsummer, and the days were interminable. This day was one of the longest ever for the vampires. Somewhere, not far from here, above their heads, the course of the war was turning, for good. Brave men were jumping from landing craft, some getting slaughtered before they even made it ashore. Vampires don't sleep much anyway. None of them even bothered to try, because when they shut their eyes they could see it all, beaches stained and tides coming in and washing away the blood, only for more to be shed... whether it was feverish imagination or a psychic connection with the events of the day Simone could not distinguish, perhaps because she was still new to her condition.

She did not pry into the thoughts of the others. At least they could lie flat. Even so, the frustration seemed to emanate from them in waves. At last Philippe began thumping the ground beside him, making quite a hole. He was snarling too. In the shades of violet and silver and indigo that coloured the vampires' night vision Simone watched as he sat up and punched the unstable ceiling of earth, so that it rained down on them.

"Cut it out, twerp," said Christophe, also irritable. "You might want to eat dirt but I prefer beetroot juice." 'Beetroot juice' or occasionally 'beetroot gravy' was vamp code for blood, Simone had learned.

She saw Philippe's face, as she'd never seen it before, streaked with earth, the whites of his eyes red, but looking purple in the dark, and his fangs grown and bared.

"Cut it out, I said," repeated Christophe, "you're scaring her. She doesn't know what you get like. We can't fight in here, there's no room. And we can't go out."

Tentatively, Simone reached out and touched Philippe's shoulder. He stiffened, and then slowly the whites of his eyes began to look a little clearer.

Simone seemed to see by way of her hand: she could see that Christophe and Philippe had fought, physically fought each other many times, and she could feel it too. She felt that sometimes their lives were full of painful frustration, a mental as well as a physical agony that arose from the constraints of their condition. And she felt that they had long ago decided it was a lot better than fighting humans. She heard as well as felt them telling her that it was necessary, that it kept them going.

Then Philippe spoke. "If it weren't for him, I'd be dead. And a murderer. I would've snapped, fed off a human and not bothered to preserve the life. And then I would've walked into the dawn. Couldn't have lived with it."

"Well, what about you? You're the elder vampire," wondered Simone as she turned to Christophe.

"Maybe my conscience is less delicate," he shrugged. "Accidents happen. Just as we are stronger than ordinary humans, so are our desires. We cannot always conquer them, even if we want to. There are wicked humans."

He showed her a mental picture, or more accurately, a little movie. She was behind his eyes, and he was walking a street, purposefully... She could feel that. The street was dingy, covered with muck. There were no proper street lights, but light spilled out of open doors, so it was not a wartime blackout, but perhaps no one had street-lights yet... a woman and a man came out of a door from which there came laughter as well as light, their arms wrapped around each other. The woman had a long dress, longer than her, so that it was astonishing that she didn't fall over it: It was low cut at the front to display the goods. The man wore clothes that could have been part of the wardrobe of any working man for probably hundreds of years. They ignored Christophe/Simone and melted into the shadows of an unlit, narrow lane at right angles to the larger street. The observer that was an amalgam of the two vampires' consciousness waited. It wasn't long before the pair emerged again. They seemed quite friendly and the man gave the woman a coin before returning, presumably content, to the bar from which he'd come. The woman stood, waiting, then another man came out, but this time he held his hand out, and she gave the man her hard won coin.

He went mad, or so it seemed, screaming and ranting, and finally landing a massive blow to her head so that she fell, or would have done, except that Christophe was there, moving out of the shadows swifter than could any ordinary man, to catch her in his arms. He was already old, and certainly he had seen people die whose killers had not meant to murder them. But the crack of a skull on stone often undid both killer and victim, forever. The delicate cranium is not designed for such a blow.

Having caught the woman before that could happen, he lowered her gently to the ground, pillowing her head in the crook of her arm. Behind him the outraged pimp pulled a knife and before Christophe had removed his arm he had stabbed him right in the middle of the back, still ranting.

Having made sure the woman was as comfortable as possible without an actual pillow Christophe straightened up. The pimp pulled the knife out and stabbed him again. Then Christophe turned.

Simone felt the swell of passionate feeling, but it was more than that. It was glee; an unnatural, terrible glee that frightened her. This was why they were here, or rather, he was here. Christophe had come to this place where prostitutes operated because he was looking for predators and not just pimps but some of their clients could be described that way. Although Simone could not read the thoughts of a man long dead she knew Christophe could, and had, and she knew that the pimp had struck the woman without the slightest care whether she would live or die. He had other women.

But Christophe was the biggest predator of all and now he faced the pimp. His joy was palpable: He had his target in sight, he was his own moral arbiter, and filth like this was lawful prey. Simone enjoyed the moment quite as much as its rightful inhabitant. The pimp did not die, but he gibbered, and there was not much fun to be had with him, she found herself thinking, and was promptly horrified. Surely that thought did not come from her?

"It was, naturally, much more intoxicating than the memories I can convey. Each time I got closer to taking life, and deep down, I was giving myself permission to go further."

"That's why you sought people like him out, so if you lost control it would not matter," said Simone, still shocked at her own reaction.

"And then I met this fellow, this Welsh gabbler of prayers, always worrying about his soul, and for a hobby, he took up worrying about mine," said Christophe. "I don't play those games with myself any more. We do fight, you see, but he's my friend... because he's the friend of my better self."

So they passed the seemingly unending wait till sunset.

At last it was dark enough to creep from their burrow and survey the scene. The smell of death, though emanating from quite far away, was palpable and would have made a human gag, though vampires do not find it so unpleasant. Philippe gestured to the others to follow him. His senses seemed the keenest of the three of them but they all felt something bad was about to descend upon them.

Travelling as fast as they did they soon came upon a heap of dead men, though dead boys would have been more accurate, as most of them looked to be in their late teens. Horrible though the sight was – and the fact that the uniforms were British didn't seem to make it less or more horrible – worse was the evidence that their deaths did not involve guns. They didn't need to turn the bodies over to confirm the reason they'd died: The smell of vampire was all over them.

"Kerr," muttered Philippe.

"And not alone either," said a voice they all knew too well.

Kerr had dropped by, literally: It was as though he had fallen from the sky. And Simone could almost hear the steel doors clanging shut, as their minds, including her own, sought to armour themselves against possible invasion by the only being they had good reason to fear.

She didn't have the confidence to speculate on how he'd seemed to plummet into their midst, or whether his vampire abilities were greatly augmented by now, as he must be some age, although probably Christophe was older... a lot older. She'd been convinced of that, after a glimpse of something, buried away and unfathomable – a language learned and stored away – memories that couldn't be interpreted easily, because they made little sense to a modern mind.

And then a voice whispered, "Thank you, that's very helpful" and Kerr was grinning at her.

From the pitch darkness around them, shapes coalesced, framed by the softest of glows. This was the vampire aura, which vampires themselves didn't need to see by, but came in handy if their intended victims wanted to know who was about to kill them. As for the three vampires, they saw perfectly well; they could distinguish every shade of night, and what they saw was that they were surrounded by more vampires, Kerr's own army.

This time no attack was launched by Kerr upon Simone's mind. She hadn't been able to stop her thoughts about Christophe's likely age from leaking out of her mind, but she felt slightly better protected than the last time she'd encountered him.

"What do you want?" asked Christophe of their leader.

"Well," said Kerr, sounding amused, "what I want is for a lot of people to die, or nearly die, and then beg for their lives at any cost. Like this lot did," and he gestured at his vampire platoon.

"Well indeed," said Christophe. "And what I want is for people not to die in the first place, at least not until they're old, in the natural way of things. So our desires are incompatible... run!"

This last was directed at his two friends, who needed no further encouragement, having observed the circle of vampires begin to close around them, some of them jeering. That was one thing – sticks and stones, etc. – but Simone was alarmed to see some of them brandishing sharpened bits of wood. Some of the wood looked as though it had been picked off the ground, little more than twigs, and some of the vampires were wielding fence posts, but all had pointed ends, which is what Simone and Philippe would have, and very soon, unless they got out of there quickly.

Philippe took her hand and they leapt over the heads of Kerr's vampires. Simone asked a mental question as they stormed through undergrowth, and he answered the same way: Christophe was distracting Kerr and there was nothing to worry about regarding him, since he was at least as powerful as Kerr. Neither Philippe nor Simone could kill Kerr, since both had been changed by him. Philippe had told her that it was not just the lore, but that there was a danger that vampire patricide could cause the killer's body to somehow unravel, as if someone pulled on a loose thread. So that was yet another way for a vampire to die.

Simone looked back and saw the two older vampires fighting. It was virtually an aerial battle, from what she could see, and neither of them were armed, but then neither needed to be. They used teeth that had become fangs and hands that seemed almost like claws; kicking, biting, trying to choke each other, they seemed like great cats fighting for the harem. Something about the sight suggested to her that Kerr was trying to break away, which wouldn't be surprising. He wanted to catch up with the younger ones, but Christophe was preventing him. He was giving them time to get away.

But then she had to focus on escape. Philippe was a lot older than Kerr's vampires and that meant he was stronger, faster, and could almost fly across the landscape just by touching something solid with the very tip of his foot every now and again, and pushing off. She was able to do the same, but more slowly; slowly, the way she picked things up... like now, for example, she was beginning to understand that both Christophe and Philippe had kept to her pace when travelling, and that they could have gone a lot faster. Simone was beginning to suspect that Christophe and Kerr didn't even need to do that, but she wondered why, if that was so, Christophe seemed content to get around the same way she and Philippe did. Perhaps you had to save the moments when you truly flew for when it was needed. Maybe. Well, she'd find out one day, if she survived for long enough.

Simone looked over her shoulder and saw that most of the crew pursuing them had dropped out. Presumably they were younger even than she... but she kept tight hold of Philippe's hand, and he at least could outrun the pack. But she began to stumble, and that was odd because she didn't feel tired, it was almost as though she wasn't ready to keep up, yet, not for long... Philippe picked up on this, but so did the pursuing vampires. She was catching their thoughts. She could block them, which she couldn't with Kerr. But that was something she could do with all the vampires, despite her lack of several lifetimes worth of experience, except for the one who'd sired her. She didn't have to hear their gloating threats...

But she did. They were threatening to pierce her heart with a wooden stake, and watch her body turn to dust and fly away, carrying her soul with it. Perhaps some of them had been polite, once, even educated, for they used metaphor to describe what they would do. It must have been an eclectic education, though, for the metaphor they used was vulgar in the extreme, and she would've blushed if vampires could blush. It seemed to provoke Philippe enough to make him turn and tell her to keep running.

But he was no longer running. Four of them were left, but they stopped when Philippe did. Simone couldn't see his face and body become more feral, but she knew he was turning full-on vampire. She ran ahead as he had bidden her, hearing yells of rage from him. She prayed, though not sure whether she was allowed to... prayed that he would somehow beat them, though he had no stake and they did, and they might be almost as old as he was, enough, combined with their numbers, to bring him down. She didn't want to run away. Then the choice was taken from her as she realised that one of the four had left the circle and was coming for her. He was faster than she was. She could hear him gaining, so she turned and waited. She had to fight.

He didn't jump straight at her, but paused a few feet away, trying to assess his chances. Then he grinned, which was unnerving. Simone could see nothing resembling a pointed stick in her immediate surroundings, but she knew he was carrying one, because he waved it in front of her, taunting her with the prospect of death.

"Come on baby," he cooed, obviously enjoying himself. Simone leapt in the air as high as she could and descended on him, delivering a two legged kick with enough force to knock an ordinary man's head off. It did knock the vampire off balance, but it was not enough to detain him. She turned and ran, the way vampires run, which includes being in the air much more often than touching the ground. Behind her was the enemy, keeping up, but not quite catching her. Well, that was something. Perhaps she could get all the way back to Paris like this.

She felt angry, furious in fact. This devil Kerr and his devil's army were keeping her and her friends from saving lives, while his plan was probably to find as many dying men on both sides as he could, and offer them the gift of eternal life, if gift it was. A battlefield was a happy hunting ground for Kerr. And most of those he turned into vampires seemed to succumb to his control. Or perhaps he just killed those who showed signs of holding on to the things that were associated with being human; the good things, anyway.

Why was she allowed to escape his influence?

A shout came from behind her.

"You're female, that's why!" explained her pursuer. "The old one needs a wife! So I won't kill you, don't worry! Come with me, stay: you'll be a queen!"

This was said in the most creepy, leery way imaginable, and Simone could have kicked herself for leaving her mind so open that he'd picked up on her thoughts. It was hard to keep watch over her mind and run and leap at the same time.

She bade herself focus and kept running but she could not lengthen her small lead. It was scary, how close he was.

Then she felt the approach of Philippe, and she knew her pursuer felt it too, so when her heart leapt in hope she didn't bother to try and hide it. He must have beaten the three…

The vamp behind her was readable too, as he cursed himself for his impatience in wanting to impress Kerr. He'd become a vampire after Simone had, but had imagined that as a female, she'd take longer to reach her full strength.

He knew he couldn't take two of them, and Philippe had just – somehow – defeated three of his kind, older than this one. The Kerr loyalist wore a dishevelled uniform that identified him as a German officer. Capturing the female for Kerr would have put him in favour. Perhaps he would have been elevated to second-in-command of the vampire army…

"Kill him," said Philippe, aloud. "don't let him get away."

The vampire turned and ran, and Simone chased him, wondering about the stake he held, but she need not have worried. Philippe's injunction must have been to himself, for he moved so fast he seemed to flicker, like a broken movie reel, and pushed the fellow onto the ground, pinning his arm with a strength the other couldn't match, and crushing his wrist with a grip that ground bones. His opponent became his victim, and his scream of agony was cut short as the stake fell from his broken hand, enabling Philippe to use it on the vampire with instant, fatal effect.

"I've been slowing you down," was all Simone could think of to say.

"It's been necessary to er... play down what we can do. Kerr doesn't know for sure how it all works, because there aren't that many older vampires. We don't last very long, as a rule. Look at that idiot over there... oh, you can't: he's dust. But that's my point. Stupid doesn't make it. Kerr knows his strength and abilities have increased but he doesn't know for sure how much that applies to us. His arrogance is a big help. He assumes that we avoid taking human life because we're weak, soft, haven't got it in us... you know. Christophe is really the only one who can kill him, but won't in case he himself becomes monstrously arrogant. That is not just an excuse. We live on the edge of things."

"How did you hide it from me?"

"I'm sorry, but you're new to this. It was simply that you have to get a bit better at hiding your thoughts before we can share certain things..."

Simone considered objecting to this but she knew she was on rocky ground, having just had the recently staked vamp replying to something she had not said aloud. Her thoughts were definitely liable to leak out to anybody with vampiric abilities, that was undeniable.

"How is Christophe doing?" she asked.

He shut his eyes. "Can't tell. Come on, you and I must get back to Paris. We have work there."

He's lying, thought Simone, trying as hard as she could to hide what was going on in her mind. He knows where Christophe is... And so do I, now.

For a picture formed in her head, and Kerr and Christophe were still fighting, and though neither was winning it was clear that Kerr wanted to break free and return to his main business, harvesting souls. It was clear, too, that Christophe was determined to stop him.

Christophe had to keep Kerr busy till dawn, to save those poor soldiers from making a choice they'd regret for eternity. Meanwhile his vampires were leaderless, and would be reverting to the beasts that only lived to drink blood, and most were overwhelmed with that desire from the very beginning.

She held the pictures of the countryside they had just left in her mind. On its horizon were the bright wisps that looked like clouds, glowing... They spiralled up, billowing as if a goddess were using her silver gown as a net to catch souls. There were more than before.

Well. They went to their deaths, and others would live through this, but who could tell which was better? Didn't Socrates say something along those lines? What would he say about vampires? Even good ones? At least Christophe was there, preventing the approach of the hunter. Exactly how old was he?

It took less time to reach Paris than it had to travel to the coast, or it seemed to: it is the case for everybody that it always seems longer on your first trip somewhere, and shorter when you retrace your steps. Yet it seemed to Simone that she was also getting quicker, already.

"Practice," was Philippe's response. "speeds up your development." They'd reached home before dawn, and now all they had to do was worry about Christophe and the progress of the Allied invasion, in that order: Christophe was their friend.

"We'd know if he had gone," Philippe assured her. 'Gone'; appropriate word for one perpetually hovering between life and death, just as Simone was, just as Philippe was. When the time came they too would be gone, and quite likely with nowhere to go; heaven wouldn't take them, and they'd battled against the forces of darkness so hell would reject them… probably… if there were such a thing as hell. A human goes to dirt; a vampire to dust, and perhaps that's all that happens, to anybody, living dead, or living dead.

But then she remembered the glowing veil of cloud around a bright centre, which seemed to be what left the body behind at the point of death, rising upward like a once tethered balloon with its rope cut. And then as these rose higher, they seemed to dissipate as real clouds do under a hot sun. Was there another death, then, a dissolution more complete? Simone remembered something from the New Testament, probably Revelation, promising that followers of Jesus would not be hurt by the 'second death'… what did that mean? It sounded as if it might apply to vampires.

If Philippe had bothered to, he could have picked up on these speculations, perhaps even supplied some answers, but he was utterly distracted. Despite what he'd said, he didn't seem to have convinced himself that they'd know if Christophe had 'gone'. Vamps could communicate over distances, especially if they were tuned into each other. Simone had no idea what limit there was on this, and anyway she felt sure that Kerr could mount interference if he wished.

So they spent the day feverishly impatient to get back to the front line, and when night started to close in, they were off again, so fast they could have beaten a train, although the trains weren't running; not normal ones that carried normal passengers, anyway. Paris was also feverish with impatience and the grip of the occupiers was loosening as they dispatched as many men as they could to Normandy. People who broke cover too early would probably not see their city set free, though; they'd be dead. Timing is all, they told themselves. But the bloodsuckers were already busy.

As the vampires neared the front they disabled two separate German units, one about to blow up a bridge in an attempt to hold back the invaders for a while longer as they waited for reinforcements. Philippe and Simone picked up the thoughts of their quarry shortly after they'd identified their presence, over a distance of a few hundred yards. Further than that, and the hunters wouldn't have noticed the Germans, so there was an element of luck involved, but there was also the sense that the tide of affairs was in full flood, and it was favouring the Allies.

Simone and Philippe proved to be an efficient team, delivering the vampire kiss with speed and precision to a unit of twelve men, cutting through them as if it were harvest time. There was no time for a decent feed, but both took long draughts from the necks of a couple of them, to keep their strength up. As for the weaponry, the quickest way to destroy it was to throw it all in the river. They made sure to include the soldiers' hand guns.

That left the explosives on the underside of the bridge. There was a detonator, guarded closely by a soldier who now lay on the ground next to it, deep in a dream of bliss. Simone had no idea how to dismantle it. Her training had touched on the issue of explosives but they scared the hell out of her and she had switched off her attention during that part, vowing to specialise in wireless, instead, as wirelesses rarely blew up. Still, what could go wrong? If no one used the detonator Philippe could remove the explosives and deposit them at the bottom of the river, far away from the bridge itself, where they could either blow up or gently moulder for decades. Or they could wait for this chap to wake up, and force him to disassemble the detonator, but they couldn't wait and he'd be out for hours.

"I'm just volunteering for pain beyond the ability of even a vampire to imagine... again." said Philippe. "Only this time I don't have to imagine, as it has happened before, quite recently." He was jocular about it, so that's something, thought Simone. She liked his style, and she was grateful beyond words that she didn't have to face this task.

"Good luck," she whispered.

He left the channel of mental communication open between them, so that as she kept watch on one side of the bridge, she could see through his eyes as he approached its centre. She had two sets of images and neither of them was reassuring: with her eyes open she could see as she normally did, but when she shut her eyes she could see what he saw. The explosives were underneath the bridge at the very centre. Stop worrying, said his voice in her head, without the detonator I won't blow up.

But something was happening. Simone knew that some explosive substances or certain combinations thereof could be very unstable, and to her horror she saw that this was going to be one of those occasions when instability was fatal. Perhaps this stuff was old, or something, but she saw Philippe jump over the parapet and then swing himself under it, and he was too relaxed, too casual, not cautious enough.

Whether the stuff was indeed too old, or too unstable, or Philippe had flung his weight around too nonchalantly she didn't know, but she could see what looked like tiny lightning flashes coming from beneath the bridge via Philippe's own close up view. And when she opened her eyes she was far away, but she could still see flashes and that could not be good.

Something went bang and then Philippe was in the air, then he was on the water below, holding a ball of lightning, or so it seemed; faster than a train he was running along the water, so fast he didn't sink, but then it all happened and the bright fire of death was blossoming noisily along the river. Simone was too scared to shut her eyes.

Why did he run with it? Did he have to be a hero? So what if the bridge blew, at least it didn't have the Allied army marching across it at the time. They'd find it an inconvenience, that's all. They'd just have to go around... but the bridge still stood, and already the fire was turning to blackness and smouldering as the water put it out. And at last she dared to shut her eyes.

The consistency of the water was like jelly, of course, to a vampire, and the jelly had seemingly acted protectively around Philippe. She was staring at water, filled with bits of charred trees, blown off the bank, and quite a few charred fish, too.

The water was like a force field around him, and had protected him from the full horror of the blast. Nevertheless, he had sustained damage, since he'd been virtually on top of the explosion. She looked down at his hands, as if they were her own, and saw they weren't there any more, and at his stomach, and it had a big hole in it, leaking black like an oil well. She felt like fainting.

Stop that, said Philippe's voice in her head, it's not helping.

She went down to the river, and waited for him to wade ashore. It would be pointless her entering the water. To leap across it, pushing off from the lightest touch of her foot on the river's surface would be feasible for herself but trying to drag him ashore would only pull her down. So she had to wait until he emerged, looking like the dead man he really was.

He howled at the night, a cry of unbearable agony, and collapsed on the ground. His eyes rolled in his head, and spittle foamed at the corners of his mouth. No one alive had endured so much and still lived, Simone was sure. It was utterly horrifying to watch his writhing. If she'd had a stake handy... But she hadn't.

Thank god, or whatever, for that, for before her astonished gaze the black stumps began to swell and what looked like little pink buds appeared on them. Fingers, she thought. Philippe was still howling, but then healing often hurts before it doesn't any more.

The explosion had blown a hole right through him. You could have seen daylight, if there'd been any. But the huge abdominal wound was closing. Bit by bit, new skin and new organs were forming, as tissue reached for tissue. Muscle waved around like some blind deep sea life form seeking food. Ligaments extended themselves like baby creepers in a forest of fleshiness. It was both wonderful and revolting, all at the same time.

At last it was done. Philippe's body had regrown its damaged parts, the way very basic creatures regenerate themselves. The agonised sounds stopped.

He sat up, and smiled, although it was a rather forced smile. That had been an ordeal, and they both knew it, and although Simone could have stayed close to him mentally, she chose not to, on the grounds that someone needed to keep lookout when it was going on. She'd opted out of the suffering, and he couldn't blame her for that.

They had time to hunt for more Germans to disarm, but it was more difficult to find them over those distances than they'd imagined it would be, and when they eventually caught up with another group they were pleased that they seemed to be using only guns, albeit machine guns. There was no river nearby for them to dump the guns, so they had to call on their vampire strength to rip the guns apart.

Simone found herself tearing steel as though it were cardboard. It made her hands hurt, but not for long. They took some of the ammunition away, and on their way back to Paris made sure that it went to the bottom of the Seine.

At last they reached home, and they knew already it would be a happy homecoming, because they could feel the warm glow of reunion before they were in the city. Sure enough, Christophe was there, smiling with unaffected pleasure at seeing them again. They caught up with each other by means of mental pictures: Philippe and Simone's account was really vivid, and made Christophe wince more than once. His own tale was no less interesting.

Kerr and he had fought for hours, but neither had finished the other. Kerr had been armed with steel sword and wooden stake, one for the heart and one to remove the head, but clearly he had managed to do neither. Christophe was pleased he'd kept Kerr busy, but it meant he couldn't deal with Kerr's vampire army either, and they had been recruiting. It was imperative that they be stopped.

"The curse of vampirism is very old," Christophe said, "Very old indeed. A very, very gifted man, an inventor and benefactor of the human race, was envied by the gods for his abilities, or so they say. They infected his son with such hubris that he died from arrogance: One of his machines killed him, and it may have been different had he enlisted the help of his father with its design. So the devastated father made a dark bargain with the god of the underworld, and was granted the secret of eternal life... for humans.

The lower nature of man is what was made immortal, because the higher nature cannot be constrained within the flesh once it is united with its true home. And the higher nature is immortal anyway. Yet the son was brought back to life, but as a beast whose only desire was to drink blood.

Soon he had made many more of his kind. That was the genius of his father, that the thing he made was able to reproduce itself. This was an act of great hubris, greater than the sin of his son."

"And hence," interrupted Philippe, "he got a visit from Nemesis. He and his son created new beings from those who should have been dead. They gave life without the aid of a woman, too, which offends the feminine principle. Which is present everywhere, intertwined with everything."

"The son waited till the father was on his deathbed and was able to change him before death," Christophe added.

"How is that possible?" asked Simone. "It has to be at the desire of the dying person, surely?"

"Some sort of bargain with the gods," said Philippe.

Simone lost patience. "What gods? We don't believe in gods anymore! Not in Europe. And if we do, it's just one... big one!"

Christophe laughed. "One big one is no more believable than several smaller ones. Not smaller, really, just with different realms. You can anthropomorphise them if you want, but think the essence of Venus, or the essence of Mars... you know what that means, don't you? The laws of the universe, sort of, that control us, as well as the world. Gods."

"But... that's not exactly holy, is it? I mean, they don't care about us, like Jesus is supposed to? They're just powers, "said Simone.

"Well, they're immortal, or at least they live till the end of the universe, which is about the same thing."

"You know what I want to ask now, don't you?" asked Simone.

"No," said Christophe," I am neither the father nor the son from this tale. It is ancient, pre-Atlantean..."

"That's a myth," she said.

Christophe was emphatic. "No, it's an island near Crete that blew itself apart over three and a half thousand years ago, with a very advanced technology. Volcanic eruption it was; sent them hurtling back into savagery, took the rest of the Mediterranean on the same trip. And perhaps that's the real Nemesis that was visited on the vampire progenitor, and I suppose you could say, on humanity."

"Look at this war. The last one was labelled the war to end war, another lie from our leaders. War is a way of trying to grab resources from those you think, and certainly hope, are weaker," said Philippe. "The people who benefit are the ones who make weapons of war. Think how that would have developed if we'd had civilisations that didn't destroy themselves periodically. It's as though there are natural forces that topple us before we can blow up the whole world, some sort of self-righting mechanism that kicks in when there's too much cleverness and too little wisdom."

"That wasn't the question I was going to ask," said Simone, "I'm not ignorant, I know you're talking about the myth of Daedalus and Icarus, with added vampires, but I can't believe it was as literal as that... that the myth actually happened, I mean. I was going to ask how it is that we are not reduced to animals, like Kerr's army."

"Neither of us can give you a definitive answer to that one," replied Christophe. "We're not different, or special, or anything set apart, that I know of. It's a continuum, like sanity. It's like if you succumb once, you're finished. So we kill vampires, because they're..."

"Dangerous to people," Philippe came in, as if to emphasise their oneness on this. "But we don't – we daren't – kill a person, because we don't want to be some drooling carnivore, slave to the likes of Kerr... and before you ask, the intelligence usually exits with the humanity, and I have no idea how he is the way he is."

And so they waited for the night, impatient to help liberate France while not actually killing any of her occupiers, not because they were innately more virtuous than other vampires, but because they were terrified of losing their souls to darkness, and falling into a degradation so complete that it would be better not to have been born.

They got out to the battlefields more quickly than ever, moving faster than any car or train. Christophe was not much use, as Kerr showed up within minutes, and they started to fight. Neither of them got tired, so Simone, watching, knew it would go on till dawn, when Kerr would retire, hoping that he'd left it long enough to prevent Christophe seeking shelter. He would be out of luck, as someone of Christophe's experience would make sure he wouldn't be caught out of doors. But it meant she and Philippe would have to try and assist the invasion without him.

But that night they got to see their quarry, whose lives they had protected, die because of something they had done. It was a small German battery hidden in a copse, waiting to pick off some Allied troops. There were six of them, three each for Simone and Philippe. The Germans managed to get off a couple of shots against them, but as usual the soldiers were shocked and easy to subdue by the insouciance of these two, whom they had thought seriously wounded, even dead.

Simone was just thinking, as they left the scene, of how convenient it was that you could disable the enemy and enjoy a few cheeky nips of type A or B at the same time. Then she heard a cry from her companion. They hadn't bothered to switch on the inner antennae that tuned them into anyone approaching, because there'd been a mental cacophony from the soldiers they'd just despatched into the arms of Morpheus, and the quiet following their falling asleep had been so peaceful, they'd just forgotten.

So it was that Allied troops had come across the sleeping Germans, and broken the rules of combat to play the triumphant warrior. It was too late to do anything:

they were just that bit far away, and hadn't been scanning for the mind noise of humans, so it meant that the first the vampires knew of it was the sound of a machine gun.

Simone began to cry. "Macbeth hath murdered sleep," quoted Philippe, "We should have..."

"Don't!" she said, simply. Everything seemed more serious, suddenly. It had been a game to the vampires, especially to her, still new to war. She saw that it wasn't flippancy, but the lack of fit words of his own that led him to quote Shakespeare.

The mental state of the soldiers was all heat and madness and the stink of a killing fever. She didn't have any trouble reading it, but it was unpleasant to her and she backed off, but not before she had understood. They were Americans, young, never travelled before; simple minds. They probably saw themselves as rational, but they were governed by emotion, in the absence of anything else. They had witnessed the horror of the large scale slaughter of their fellows as they landed on the beaches, some mown down before they'd walked out of the water. They needed to do some killing in return, and the fact that their targets were unconscious... well. All that play up, play up and play the game was an attempt to make war look manageable by those who led battles, a pretence that it could be conducted according to rules. War was filthy, wicked, dangerous and the very opposite of manageable, and certainly, never civilised.

She took Philippe by the arm and drew him close so he could cry on her shoulder. If vampires need new clothes, she thought, watching the black tears dribble down her shirt, we can always get them. And that's a very useful thing, even though I rarely bother.

"What are we doing?" Philippe murmured. We set that up, she thought at him, rendered the enemy helpless. So what, he answered, his thoughts hot with anger. These two groups would have skirmished anyway, there would have been casualties and given what these boys have just seen, definitely fatalities as well. We just accidentally stacked the odds in favour of the Allies. Isn't that what we set out to do?

"You're the one asking what we're doing," she said aloud. "Now you've described it. But it feels bad. Not just because of this."

"Quick, shutters down," whispered her companion, which meant, she knew, she should block her mind from invasion: this made her head feel like a sea anemone on a rock, closing its fronds so that it turned into a tight ball.

The reason for this advice immediately became clear. The Americans cleared off just as a figure in civilian clothes wandered across the scene. It was soon apparent that he was no wanderer but clearly had a purpose. Unerringly, he walked over to one of the Germans. This one would have looked as dead as the rest at a careless glance, but he was not, though he looked badly wounded.

Simone and Philippe were mirroring each other's shock. They'd been too preoccupied with guilt to pick up the flickering life force of the dying man – or rather, boy – now they looked closely.

The vampire surely felt their presence, but he was very focused, and must have decided to take the risk. Later, Simone would think about it, and decide that there weren't vast amounts of suitable candidates to be changed, even on a battlefield. Those that were lightly wounded would expect to recover in the normal course of things, and those already dead were out of the picture. Religious types would expect to go to heaven, and would surely regard the vampire's offer as against the will of God.

So the intended recipients of this great gift had to very seriously wounded, yet conscious enough to make a choice, with no philosophical objection strong enough to outweigh the animal instinct to survive. This combination was surprisingly rare, even on a battlefield, and that was why the vampire was taking a chance.

It was likely that he underestimated the speed at which Philippe could operate. The older vampire waited for a few seconds, listening. Simone was impatient to get over to the wounded man, but the other put his fingers to his lips, and with their augmented hearing they heard the whispered proposal, familiar although it was in German this time: "Do you want to live? I can save you so that you can live forever. Just say yes…" and they heard the dying man, whose physical pain they could almost feel, saying yes, as they both had done in their time.

They let the ceremony begin, with Kerr's minion biting into the neck, and releasing the merciful anaesthetising dose that immediately silenced the groans. But Philippe immediately moved, so fast he was but a blur, and forced the other vampire to the ground. Meanwhile Simone, having left that to him, assisted by tearing a branch from a nearby tree. Green as it was, it was still no match for her strength, and the break was ragged, which suited their purpose. She threw it to Philippe, who was kneeling on the other's chest. He caught it and plunged it into the heart.

They watched in revulsion as the vampire's flesh decomposed before their eyes. It did not turn to dust, though. It was a slimy, stinking mass. Philippe had helpfully explained that 'killing' a vampire caused its physical form to revert to what it would have become had it died normally, and spent the intervening time between that point and its ultimate death going rotten.

Simone worked out the months since her death and subsequent life as a vampire and decided she had better stay alive till her remains were well past the sticky stage. Becoming dust would be favourite, although being a skeleton wouldn't be as grotesque as the spectacle before her. Perhaps. She saw Philippe, grinning. He'd read her thought.

"It's all right for you, dusty," she said aloud.

And then their attention shifted to the dying man, blessedly unconscious thanks to whatever it was that vampires secreted from their fangs; some kind of opiate, Simone supposed, useful in war but also in medicine. As they stared his lips parted, and with a last sigh the light flowed out of him, visible to the watchers with their vampire sight. It was shimmering, cloudy as a cauldron of stars, glittering through mist, and rising gently towards the heavens. It would have been as coldly beautiful as the night sky beyond it, but there was something more, something that was as hot as the centre of the sun, and as balmy as a summer day on a Mediterranean beach. And then Simone turned away, this time not from disgust, but from a feeling of what she could only think of as her own unworthiness.

And then it was gone, seemingly risen, and at the same time as if exiting the scene into another, more real place; gone backstage, so to speak, which was one of the things Simone felt had happened, although her feelings were in confusion, and a longing for something she dare not name, along with a sense of its loss, shuddered through her.

"That's what we need to concentrate on," she said aloud. Philippe nodded, and she knew that they were of one mind on this, and there was no need for debate. They were on the side of the Allies, of course, apart from their love for country, which Simone felt was fast diminishing, just because it didn't seem relevant, not really... apart from that, the Germans had, after all, started it. It was their leader who had begun this war, and invaded other people's countries, and was rumoured to have tortured and murdered large numbers of people for being communist, or crippled, or homosexual. And he had even targeted Jews, rounding them up with the help of their neighbours, in some cases, shipping them all off to work camps where it was said they were worked to death, and worse.

So it was right to fight the Germans, but perhaps it was not right for the vampires. Both of them had been feeling uneasy for a while, but their interference, meant to save lives, hadn't helped. The war was something begun by humans, and it was humans who ought to bring it to conclusion. They shared that thought, with a feeling of relief. The acts of Kerr, however, and his foot soldiers, could only be understood by his own kind. They were the only ones who could oppose him in his wish to steal the souls of the dying and prevent what seemed to be a beautiful thing, an apotheosis. It followed that the vampires ought to fight on the supernatural front, and leave the battlefields of France to the living.

The short summer night was already preparing to give way to sunrise, and the dawn chorus had started, the earliest avian risers all ready to sing a hymn to light. They made their fastest time yet back to Paris, and fretted once they were there, as they waited for Christophe. It was hard to turn off the human propensity for worry, although it was highly unlikely that he would allow himself to be stranded by the dawn. At worst he could always burrow into the ground. At last they felt him in their thoughts. Nearly home, he told them, then the next thing they knew he was dropping from the ceiling, smiling and hungry, grinning like a wolf.

"Yes, he's still alive," was the first thing he said. "I need food, I'm starving. Come on."

They too were hungry and it was stupid of them to let it get this far. They needed a couple of pints a night to survive, more or less, which were basic rations. Without that minimum, they needed immense self-control. They moved as fast as they could travel to their nearest brothel, where the tired but unprotesting staff made themselves available. And they were just in time, throwing themselves through the door.

"My arse is on fire," said Philippe, but it wasn't quite. It was close though, and it was fortunate they had all got a lot faster.

At last they were replete. Christophe thought rather than said, (so as not to disturb the still unconscious ladies), that he agreed with the direction of their thinking, and moreover, he felt that Kerr just wanted to tie him up in endless scrapping so that his vampire army could get to work harvesting souls without his interference. At this Philippe sent him a bit of emotional breeze, pretending offence at this assumption that he and Simone were unable to do much to stop them.

Christophe just let it go. He didn't care for transient emotion at the best of times. It felt like weather because it was weather, and would blow over tomorrow, although some people, like some places, had climate rather than weather: the perpetually angry, or the ever-depressed.

There was no denying that his great age gave him the greatest strength.

"You're like a queen on a chessboard," said Simone lightly, "and we're like rooks."

Not exactly, he reproved, while Philippe stifled a grin. Hobnobbing as they did with the ladies of the night, they knew all the latest slang, although this term was one of the older epithets for an effeminate homosexual.

The vampire males did not appear to indulge in all the silly play acting common to ordinary human males when homosexuality was touched on, Simone noticed. Not that they'd touched on it much, but nevertheless she got the impression that neither of them had a problem with it and were quite matter of fact on the topic. There was no need to demonstrate that they were not queer. She was pretty sure they weren't, partly because they always chose women's necks to dine from, when there was a choice, although there were young men available at some of the dives they visited. Hinting that Christophe was a queen was just a little tease to draw him out, but he wasn't to be drawn.

They were stuck at the brothel till sunset. They purchased further nourishment from fresh ladies as the day went on. Might as well fill up, as Philippe said. But it was torture, waiting for the night when they could be useful at this time of crisis in human affairs. There were tunnels under Paris, even catacombs, but none came near to this spot and in any case, Parisian tunnels would scarcely take them to the battlefields miles away.

At last they were free to go, as the sun dipped below the horizon, a manmade horizon of buildings giving them protection to at least move to the edge of the city before the final disappearance of daylight. They left Paris, moving at an incredible speed, and it was impossible for Simone not to rejoice at the thrill her vampire body delivered to her, and the feeling of power and immortal strength.

There is a figure in most mythologies called a psychopomp, whose task it is to escort the dead to their future home. Simone knew this, because she had started to take an interest in a rather recondite branch of psychology, founded by a disciple of Freud. In the Divine Comedy Virgil is the psychopomp for Dante, although he has to give way to Beatrice when it comes to Il Paradiso, because he's not pure enough to visit, or something.

The vampires were not really equivalent, but they did keep a lot of dying people safe from the Kerr vampires' contagion. Simone hoped that once they were dead, they were guided into invisible worlds by beings more angelic than she could imagine; worlds in which she was not worthy to travel. Hoped for it but failing that hope, wished them gentle into the night.

Or perhaps the soul was merged with the divine, and lost all awareness of its separateness. Better than non-existence, but still...

Each night for several weeks they made the journey out of Paris. And each night it got shorter as the Allies approached. Kerr's crew did succeed in creating new vampires, both Allied and German, but the three that came from Paris undid as much of their damage as they could and slowly the ranks of Kerr's army diminished, until what was now a tiny band were unable to change any more dying soldiers, harried as they were by Christophe, Philippe and Simone.

July came, and the vampires' threat seemed to have passed. Christophe told them that now he intended to end Kerr's existence, and acknowledged that he'd been afraid to try, in case he took on the mantle of 'the Dark one'. After all creation worked by means of duality. Nazis and Allies, black chess pieces and white ones: gods and demons, summer and winter, male and female, a 'chequerboard of nights and days'. Before creation, Christophe said, all was one and we were pure, but for the world another number was needed, for the interplay of creative forces, and that was two, the number in the shadow of the light. It was something to do with Jewish mysticism, according to Christophe, who had read everything, having had plenty of time. What he meant was he'd feared being recast in the Kerr role of chief baddie, by inerrant destiny.

Once Christophe's mind was made up it tended to stay that way, so this was a seismic shift. He was under no illusion that he'd driven Kerr over death's cliff or even out of northern France but nonetheless he was glad when the fellow seemed at last to have disappeared, along with his remaining vampire force, if there still was one. Perhaps Kerr sensed his change of heart. It would explain why he was keeping quiet.

Then it was August.

Chapter Fifteen

Comes the blind Fury with th'abhorred shears and slits the thin-spun life

(Milton)

Souls were still leaving their bodies in great numbers as the Allies advanced, but there seemed to be nobody left to lure them into the brutal but theoretically eternal life offered by the likes of Kerr. The three musketeers, as Simone inevitably thought of herself and her two colleagues, were feeling unemployed again. She began to roam the night streets of the city on her own. It wasn't as though she needed anyone's protection, but she wondered if she were strong enough to defeat the one enemy that mattered – Kerr – since his greater number of years as a vampire gave him strength beyond hers, and, even more conclusively, he had been her sire. It seemed that this was enough to render her helpless against his mental invasion. He was a spiritual and mental rapist, and she had a violent desire to destroy him, by fire perhaps, but it would have to be the fire of the sun's light. Or, she fantasized ripping off his head and tearing his brains from his skull. It sometimes felt as if only that would satisfy her hunger to see him destroyed, and unable to touch her anymore.

Meanwhile she didn't care if the others could read her thoughts or even wanted to, they all knew that they would help liberate Paris, but how they hoped to do that without taking life was not clear to any of them. Simone tried to experiment on the locals, who were just as much inclined to fighting and general criminality as they'd always been. She'd beaten up a few pimps, as had Christophe, many times, and taught the more rowdy of brothel clients a startling lesson, long overdue, about not thumping girls, although in her case it was in case they thumped you back, harder.

But being a bouncer at a brothel was not a long term goal of hers. It wasn't even much good as practice, because none of the low forms of life she dealt with carried a machine gun.

The Germans, meanwhile, were edgy, although terrified might have been a more apt description. Rumours came to the ears of vampires as well as everybody else to the effect that the Occupiers had started rounding up people suspected of Resistance sympathies and executing them by firing squad.

People were starting to collect material for barricades. Paris has a very old tradition of street fighting, and this generation was more than ready for its turn. Simone and Philippe had got used to each other's company as they'd wended

275

their way across France and a very craggy bit of Switzerland, and so they'd go out as soon as the sun set, seeing what they could do under cover of the night to assist the locals, while keeping a low profile. That often meant lifting heavy stuff, but not in an obvious way. So the need for concealment held them back, a little.

It was an art all of its own; how to manoeuvre massive old bits of block, (usually rendered a bit more moveable by being smashed up by heavy artillery fire) without causing surprise. The cleverest thing to do was to allow strong men to think they were even stronger. Simone's favoured technique was to be slightly ahead of the barricade builders, seizing the thing, which might be, for example, an old pew from a damaged church, and pretending to try to lift it, but making certain not to succeed. The men would swagger over, and Simone or Philippe would try and help, feeble as they seemed to be, and of course the item would be moved, with the chaps congratulating themselves. It was time-consuming, but diplomatic.

They kept a watchful eye on the Hotel de Ville, as well; it was where German command was based. But that was not all. Christophe was long used to a solitary existence, enjoyed wandering about, and liked to refer to himself as a species of nocturnal flaneur. Philippe, on the other hand, put this down to vampire instinct. In his view this wandering was the night prowling of the predator, and it was only by the grace of God and his conscience that Christophe observed his former brethren, rather than dined on them.

Once, Philippe had acknowledged to Simone that he and Christophe had led rather a pleasant life between the wars, and even before that, passing in society as comfortably off minor aristos when they were required to, but equally at home in the dingiest of drinking dens, even betting on fighting animals, and sometimes, fighting humans, enjoying the opera as well as the rowdy musical theatres, and communing with the great artists of the past by visiting the Louvre, and other galleries, as well as sharing scandalous stories regarding the artists of the present.

Now, there was a different emphasis. Christophe would go over to the Hotel de Ville as soon as it was dark, and climb about on the roof, feeling with all his vampire senses for what was going on within. He'd usually enter via a chimney or sometimes a slightly ill fastened window, and, being unable to stand aloof from suffering, would try and get to the basement, where he could feel that a lot of it was going on. But he only got there once, early in August, and intervened in the torture of a member of the Resistance, saving his fingers for him, and whisking him up to the roof while the hue and cry went on below. The lucky street fighter, tough as you like, had been rendered speechless by this event, and Christophe could not think of any rational explanation for what had happened. So when he finally set the fellow down in a safe place, he just told him he was dreaming, and left the scene. The next time he tried something like it, he found someone waiting on the roof.

Kerr was there. He meant business, because he wasn't alone. Several vampires stood beside him. Christophe was especially sickened to see the Allied forces uniforms that some of them still wore. Those brave boys deserved better than to be turned into blood sucking demons. Even the Boche were, after all, mere boys compared to a person in sensible middle age, let alone a vampire who'd spent an undisclosed amount of centuries on the planet.

Then, as he was thinking of the pity of it, every one of those facing him drew a sharpened wooden stake, and began their advance. Christophe was deeply affected by this shocking turn of events, as those who knew him well would have immediately spotted by the slight lift of one of his eyebrows. He in his turn drew a sharpened stake from a concealed pocket, at which point the vampires, apart from Kerr, flung themselves at him.

He was a very old vampire, was Christophe. He had no problem in concealing his mind from fellow vampires, when he wanted and needed to. This he did, being wary, not of the lost boys who were fighting him, but of the watching Kerr. If Kerr had been able to penetrate his mental defences he would have known that Christophe realised why he stood aloof: Kerr was afraid of the older vampire, because he did not know what he was capable of. Since he was his sire, it was surely only by his, Christophe's, whim that Kerr could attack him without a mental storm that would send him crazy. The explanation was a simple one: Christophe wanted to take him out of the main fighting and keep him away from the souls of the dying, so he allowed him to defend himself, but surely Christophe could kill him? Why didn't he?

They had fought, night after night, back in June, and always Kerr had wondered. Now he had heard the story of Christophe's reckless rescue, and had set a watch on the roof. He was not intending to fight himself, this time. He had soldiers for that.

So he watched as his latest crew were despatched by someone with speed and strength beyond that of any vampire he'd ever seen. He studied each movement Christophe made: Sometimes there was a certain clumsiness but that didn't matter, given the power implicit in even the most casual seeming move, so once more he wondered why Christophe hadn't finished him off before now.

He disappeared before Christophe wiped out the last of his latest recruits. If he had stayed, he would perhaps have learnt something about his enemy that could have proved useful. Christophe was weeping, great bloody tears of regret for the wasted young lives reduced to carrion. They lay in a festering pile, in various states of decomposition around him. Some were now showing the signs of what had killed them, and the limbs that had been blown from their bodies and regrown whilst they were vampires had reverted to their wounded state, so Christophe got to see the mess, the charring, the burnt flesh... and how he cursed those who had invented these weapons that made such a horror of the human body, created by God to be beautiful; beautiful but temporary, but even more beautiful because of that.

If Kerr had guessed Christophe's thoughts, he might have realised that something was holding him back, although he might not have comprehended what it was, because the truth was that Christophe dreaded being the most powerful one, the strongest vampire, as he feared what that knowledge might do to him. He knew he already was, in his heart, but having a deadly rival filled with hubris somehow kept him from developing the same disease.

Kerr didn't and couldn't feel like that. What could be undesirable about being the strongest, most powerful... *anything*... good guy, bad guy: It didn't matter.

Christophe discovered, after that, that there wasn't much torture anymore. Everyone knew what was happening, which was that the Allies were approaching Paris, coping with the poor roads from the north east, and that when they got there, which would be soon, the Occupation would be over. The Germans would be dead, or gone, but in any case, beaten. So they contented themselves with firing squads, not bothering with the torture. They also took the time to send a lot of people off to concentration camps, which was perturbing: it was whispered that no one came out of those places.

"Maybe we should start doing our own torturing," complained Simone. "then we could prevent these things happening. The trouble is that we only find out after it happens!"

"Now, I know you don't mean that, because you wouldn't be the person I know you to be," said Christophe.

"The vampire you know me to be," replied Simone.

"Yes, and vampires have extra talents. Which is why Philippe is up on the roof, trying to pick up German thoughts. He has a bit of a problem, though."

It wasn't funny, but Christophe smiled anyway. "He doesn't speak good enough German."

Philippe had an answer for that, so they left him to it. He reckoned that he could read emotions, because they were similar everywhere, enough for him to understand. He was kidding himself, really. Emotions on their own might hint but nothing useful could be read from them, as without words they told you little. You could feel the fear, all right. In fact it was mostly fear, but that made sense in the circumstances. Sometimes the fear was intense, sometimes, more rarely, it dissipated as the subject was distracted by more pleasant thoughts. But that was only temporary. The Germans were afraid. They were more afraid than ever now, and therefore very dangerous.

Philippe would scan the city, heading towards where there were concentrations of Germans, especially at the Hotel De Ville. He returned with snippets, like Hitler wanted Paris trashed, but some of his officers would rather save the city's architecture. He'd got the first part from eavesdropping, which was often more fruitful than trying to read minds in turmoil. He'd taken to climbing up the outside of buildings, or more accurately, jumping up, from window to window. Any irregularity in the surface of a building was as good as a stepladder to a vampire. And when he could, he listened, even though he understood at best every other word of German. He was very rusty indeed, to his surprise, but the accent had changed, the vocabulary had expanded or shrunk, he wasn't sure which, because it had been many years since he'd tried to learn it, and like everyone does, he underestimated how much time had passed since then.

He'd got lucky with this particular bit of news, as the matter was discussed in French, due to the presence of a certain gentleman, a collaborator whose very name was anathema to all patriotic Frenchmen. Yet on this matter, he seemed for once to be on the side of the angels, pleading with the German officers present to save Paris. It was frustratingly difficult to make out what they thought of his plea.

Philippe picked up feelings of rebelliousness, or so he read them, but that could have been either rebelliousness against the fellow's pleading or against Hitler's command. Christophe was not sanguine about it. Hitler was a man who terrified his subordinates, and with good reason. Surely they would not dare defy him?

The other means by which the vampires gleaned information was the most natural and basic. They looked, when they could, and when there was little danger of being spotted. So Philippe, hovering round that particular window, peered into the room very carefully, and watched the men within as they drank brandy and made incomprehensible jokes, pretending as they did to forget that their guest wouldn't understand. They clearly despised him. It wasn't looking good for the City of Light.

So Philippe relayed this part of his reconnaissance with a heavy heart. Yet, in the end, Paris was not annihilated, and it was Simone who returned to the invading armies to find, and bring back, intelligence that had somehow passed them by when they were busy saving souls. The rumour was that the Americans weren't bothered about liberating Paris, but were intending to bypass it and drive into Germany. Paris surrounded would soon be surrendered, so the thinking went. And General Eisenhower and his advisers were loath to fight in the streets of a city, because of the terrible casualties amongst soldiers and civilians that would be the likely consequence. He thought Paris had little strategic value, and didn't want to be seen as kingmaker when De Gaulle went marching home. The Free French of the Interior, aka the Resistance, naturally took a different view. As did the locals, most of whom assumed that Paris was worth fighting for.

The vampires made sure that word of this got out and the febrile atmosphere ignited. People went out on strike, starting with the railway workers. The Americans may have wanted to bypass Paris but the French troops, although under the American Generals' command, desperately wanted to free their capital city. Meanwhile, the passage of thousands of troops through Normandy was taking longer than expected.

The strike widened to include almost everybody, even the police. There were skirmishes on the streets and quite a few people lost their lives, including a lady friend of the vampires. But there was no time to weep. The vampires decided at first to split Paris into three parts and spread themselves across it every night, watching, listening, even fighting, a little, but always avoiding the curse of murder. That was how Simone thought of it now, and she was vividly aware of the contradictions in her thinking, as were the other two. For instance, she could and did disable German teams of gunners, by sneaking up or even jumping down on them. The surprise lasted long enough to give her the chance to anaesthetise a couple of them, and then she'd have to go through the tedious experience of being shot at as she went to work on the rest, and that was usually quite messy, though mostly it was her own blood being spilt.

She knew, though, because there was no escaping the knowledge that knocking the enemy out in this way left them vulnerable to reprisals from the city dwellers who'd had to endure occupation, curfew, and too many indignities in their own country. She never stayed around to find out if the same fate that befell the first artillery unit she and Philippe had attacked was a typical one for those whom she'd put to sleep. She didn't want to know. And, to be honest, the quick snack that she got a chance to grab every time she did it was very useful, and meant she didn't have to waste time looking for sustenance when she could be helping the struggle.

But the immutable fact was they could only go out at night. And although there was fighting at night, there was always going to be more going on in the day. Then the brief armistice, sought by the Free French of the Interior, as the Resistance now styled themselves, and granted by the German Von Cholitz, who seemed to be keen on not destroying Paris, contrary to his master's orders, had to end. And it was then that the Americans entered Paris from one end, while the French General Leclerc sent a much smaller contingent ahead to eventually arrive at Notre Dame in the city centre.

The suburbs were entered by night, and the sleepless population greeted the dawn knowing they were at last free men and women, while the vampires caught sniper bullets in their own bodies when they could, and there was enough German resistance left to make that a pretty meaningful contribution. They took turns: one would look for the sniper's nest, the others were shields and that hurt.

"We're not even human shields," Simone complained.

"We're vampire shields," said Philippe. "And proud of it."

It was not pleasant being shot, though, and Simone felt more angry than proud. When it was her turn to track down the location some of the shooting was coming from, she faced the little group of gunmen with rage boiling in her heart. She shouted at them "Cowards!" she cried in English, "Cowards!"

This only made her life more difficult, as losing one's temper generally does. Instead of being able to take at least one unawares, all four were alerted, and things became an unseemly mess as the vampire girl tried to disable without killing the men. She had to knock two out, and as they fell to the ground she agonised about her strength; had she hit them too hard?

As she was wondering another of them had turned his rifle on her, and had a clear target once she had disencumbered herself of the pair now lying at her feet. He shot her, at very close range, right through the heart. She fell to the ground with a scream that even to her own ears sounded unhuman.

There was a short pause, during which nobody moved. She sat up, and undid her shirt. Then she reached into her chest, and pulled out the bullet. It was the quickest route to healing: dig the bullets out yourself, don't wait. It wasn't always the most convenient move, and tended to alarm the locals, but when speed was of the essence...

The two snipers that were still conscious stared at her as though hypnotised. Faster than their eyes could follow, she moved and sank her teeth in the throat of the one who'd shot her. Now all the self-denial Simone had practised since Kerr had changed her proved its utility. She was habituated to not letting go of the reins on her appetite, even when sorely tried.

She sipped the man's blood, and dropped him, sleeping like a baby, while she grabbed his whimpering associate. As he, too, fell from her arms onto the floor she heard footsteps on a staircase just outside the room. A man rushed in, dressed in civilian clothes, wielding a pistol.

He glanced at the scene. It didn't make any sense.

"Are they dead?"

"No, they're your prisoners," replied Simone. She didn't feel up to explaining matters, and he didn't look as if he even wanted an explanation. That was just fine by her. She turned, and jumped out of the open window.

Why should it matter if people knew of them? There were quite a few Parisians, and Germans too, that had witnessed the vampires taking bullets to what must be vital organs, and getting up again with nothing more than a grimace. War brings upheaval and unusual events, but that was the sort of thing that made you question reality.

Simone decided that was one thing she was not going to concern herself with. She looked around for her friends, searching for the next useful thing she could do.

But as the glorious morning approached the three were almost glad to leave the humans to it. The bullets, some of which were still buried in the vampires, had hurt, every last one of them, and it was an onslaught that wore them down. Eventually even vampire stamina was on the verge of giving out, at least that of the younger pair. After this latest event Simone just wanted to fall to the ground, and roll around screaming for it to stop, but then an arm swept her up and her rescuer sped away from the scene, carrying her as a child does a doll of whom it is especially solicitous. It was Philippe; not as strong as Christophe, so they said, but Simone couldn't tell. He was strong enough to save her, that's what mattered, and she certainly needed saving, since it was almost daylight.

They were very near Notre Dame, and Christophe was ahead of them, scrambling up its mighty walls without worrying too much about who saw him, so it seemed: there were a few upturned faces goggling at what they saw, but he was in a hurry and it was wartime. Philippe stopped to reposition Simone into a fireman's lift, while she whimpered in pain, then up he went, for all the world like the ape in the King Kong movie, although much smaller. People were probably watching that too, but it was still early, and it could have been a trick of the light. At the top there were the bell towers, and as they heaved themselves into Quasimodo's domain Simone recalled that there were more local precedents for chaps with women slung over their shoulders, and that thought, making its way to the front of her brain, was already a sign she was recovering from her ordeal by bullet.

"Next time," she managed, "next time I'll be carrying you."

He deposited her gently on the floor and she stayed upright. The clothes she wore were ripped and barely hanging together, and blood stained, though not as badly as she'd thought, since the body healed so fast. The blouse she wore started to bulge across her stomach in a peculiar way, so she undid a button in time to watch a bullet being expelled, quite slowly, back through her organs and skin and finally out into the world again, where it flopped to the floor.

Meanwhile Christophe was there, to share this experience, which happened to all three of them, several times, and it was as painful and unpleasant as could be imagined. They speeded it up by tugging the bullets out as soon as they could get a good hold on them.

Down below them people were gathering in the pre-dawn light. It was quiet down below the towers, although there was a lot of shouting, too distant for them to hear. The penetrating sound of gunfire seemed to have ceased. The occupation of Paris seemed to be over.

Christophe was a very long-lived vampire, that was clear, and he hadn't survived through the years without paying attention to what was going on around him. He heard feet pounding up the steps to the towers.

"They're going to ring the bells," exclaimed Simone, hearing it too.

"There are too many feet," Christophe answered.

Sure enough, the door onto their level burst open, and, constrained as they were by the narrowness of its opening a horde of people managed to come through.

Only they weren't people anymore. They were Kerr's latest crop of new vampires.

Without wasting a moment Christophe attacked them, but he wasn't armed to kill vampires. All he could do, and all the other two could do, was to hurt them a lot, while casting around for long pieces of wood that might do the job of stakes, a quest in which they proved unlucky. There was one other thing the male vampires could do, and that was to get the enemy in such a grip that they could wrench their heads from their bodies. This was extremely unpleasant to do and to watch. Nevertheless Simone wished she were strong enough to do the same. But Philippe and Christophe had had hundreds of years to get strong, and even thousands, perhaps. She was certainly stronger than the new vampires, some of whom were civilians or Free French, while some wore German uniform. So she had to just do as much damage as she could, keeping some busy as her two colleagues decapitated the rest of them.

But it was a sickening task, and Simone wondered if it were really true that she and her two associates were the only decent vampires that existed, or even could exist. What about the Vampire Dave, as she thought of him? Wasn't he on the side of the angels? Or at least the Allies?

Maybe if there were time to persuade Kerr's ravening hordes that one could live as a vampire without taking innocent human lives, rather than slaughtering them like this. Nobody really wanted to be a vampire, after all. It was forced upon them, usually in the form of a choice that really wasn't a choice.

She saw the delicate mist of a departing soul from the recently beheaded body, and she caught the scent of it, through the blood and carnage; a familiar scent, a bit like the stephanotis in a bride's bouquet. It was like an assurance from the Divine – all is well – but faithless as she was, the scent evaporated for her, and she wondered if the spirit likewise dissipated into an unregarding universe.

"Don't think," muttered a voice in her head. "Just fight till they're dead. And don't let them drive you outside shelter." It was Christophe. And it seemed that this was the fighters' goal, to sacrifice as many of themselves as necessary to drive the three of them out into the dawning day.

The new vampires had weight of numbers on their side and were still coming through the door, two at a time. Philippe slammed the door shut and kept his weight against it, although cracks in the ancient wood were already appearing and it would not last for long. Meanwhile those who were already through were pushing with their combined weight against Christophe and Simone, trying to force them backwards away from the shelter offered by the towers.

Christophe was like a whirlwind as he wrenched heads from shoulders, while bodies dropped around him. The mindless creatures just stepped over the headless corpses, some of which remained upright because of the press. The door was splintering behind them.

Simone seemed to herself to be getting stronger even throughout the fight but the three of them were getting overwhelmed. She bit the throat out of one new vampires. His head lolled to one side, but he kept coming, so she bit the other side, tearing through arteries and gristle. It was both horrifying and tasty, and she was appalled at herself and the others too. Her opponent's head was now hanging by a thread of stringy tissue, and with an animal roar of satisfaction she bit through that, and he was gone. There was something like a breath, and the sweet spirit was free to depart, but Simone didn't catch a scent this time, as every other smell was drowned out by the symphonic stench of death and decay.

Simone tripped over the head, and lifted it up to drink from the artery, still dripping blood. It opened its eyes and mouth and spoke.

"Why have you killed me? I am just like you," it said, reproachfully, and she dropped it, horrified. Whatever or whoever had animated it swiftly departed.

Suddenly it seemed as if the battle had ended. Nobody was battering the door any more, and all around were headless corpses in various states of decay. The smell was now indescribable.

Simone saw that Philippe and Christophe were safe. There was still some time before sunrise. There would be room within the cathedral, somewhere, for her to sit quietly and contemplate all that had happened. It was going to be a wonderful day, as Paris celebrated its liberation, but there would be many for whom it had come too late; fighters who had kept the struggle against the occupiers going through the dark years, but had died before the final victory.

Some had died beneath them, on the bridge nearby, or in the square, in the very last days of the occupation. Amongst the vampires they had just fought there may have been some brave warriors, dishonoured by the use Kerr had made of their bodies, though he was able to do so only because they loved life and wanted a little more of it. Just as she had.

She turned her back on her two friends and went through the door, now free of vampires shoving their way through.

She descended the steps and then drew herself back into a recessed bit of the wall as she heard footsteps. But her sharpened hearing was misrepresenting the

285

closeness of the sound, and there was a strange effect, that she was still not used to, where things that were far away seemed near. Her judgement of distances would sort itself out as she continued to adapt to her vampire body. Nevertheless, she stayed where she was until finally the approaching footsteps rounded a final corner, and she was suddenly looking into the eyes of Kerr.

How did she not sense his mind? Easy, he answered the unspoken question. I shrouded myself in a cloak of darkness. You don't know how to do that? Your so-called friends do it all the time when you're around. But then they have to, they're still men as well as vampires.

I do know about it, she thought. I know I'm no good at it.

And slightly below conscious control a little voice said 'men'?

He looked at her with his blue/green eyes, that altered colour according to background and light, not like camouflage, but like the ever-changing sea. He didn't need to hide from anything; he was at the very top of the food chain.

The muscle that lifted one side of his upper lip twitched, and she knew he'd put that thought in her mind, because of the self-congratulation. That didn't come from her, and it was distinct from admiration, which of course, she never felt for him…

He allowed the twitch to become a smirk. "Gotcha," he said aloud. So he planted that one too. Very clever.

"What do you actually want? The war's over, your side has lost."

He looked surprised. "I want you," he answered.

"I'm a man, as well as a vampire, just like those two you're living with. I'm not jealous: I don't need to be. I know you haven't slept with either of them. One of the advantages of telepathic ability."

"What do you want me for?"

At this he laughed, although it sounded as if he was somewhat out of practice.

"Who should I want? Prostitutes? Women I've anaesthetised? Or changed into blood-suckers? It's not just me, your two paramours are the same. Like me, they succumb occasionally to the lure of the night girls, but unlike me, I hear that they always pay. Whereas sometimes I have no change."

His expression was odious, but familiar: He sounded like a typically creepy type of bloke. Only times ten.

He was right in her face, but she was against a wall. He'd pin her arms... don't think... think lots!

Chanting the alphabet in her head, she kicked him in what she'd have thought of as the family jewels except he would not be able to breed in the normal way, however much lust he still felt, and however potent he made himself out to be.

She hadn't expected to connect; hadn't had time to think it through, so scared was she of his ability to read her. But she'd connected all right, and the immortal vampire lay on the floor, rolling in agony and clutching his private parts. She hadn't yet learned to cloak her thoughts in darkness but her strength increased daily and his genitals were mince from her kick. He would recover, of course. It might take a while, though. But she called up the steps for her friends to come. They would help her drag Kerr to an open window and push him out into the dawn.

Philippe and Christophe came running, but Kerr leapt to his feet. He ran over to the window, which had no glass, and jumped out. The sun was not up yet. The males moved to go after him.

As they reached the window Christophe turned and gave Philippe a mighty shove backwards. Neither Philippe nor Simone needed to ask why. Their minds were full of it. Philippe was a younger vampire than Christophe, whose actual age Simone still didn't know, and Simone was younger than them both. The longing to kill Kerr was raw and intense, but he could probably overpower them both, physically and mentally, via the connection that he'd made when he changed them into things like him. But most emphatically they were both Kerr's changelings: possibly they could overpower him, possibly they would both be destroyed via the power of that connection.

Christophe begged them to stay behind, safe here from the direct light of the sun. Sure, they could all go after Kerr but it was dangerously close to sunrise. The villain might want to take them all down. If self-immolation was his game, then what could be a better outcome than dragging them through the doors of non-existence alongside him?

Simone wondered if Christophe was tired of a half-life, lived in darkness and candlelight, which latterly had evolved into gas lamps, and then electric lights. He was as likely to fry as Kerr was. They could both die...

No, I don't want to die. I really, really don't want to die. I want to live, so I can greet someone who may well not be born yet. The Messiah will come again.

Surprised, Simone thought he was the last person she'd have thought would believe slavishly in Christianity and the Second Coming.

I missed Jesus, couldn't find him, heard about him afterwards. Christophe thought.

"Oh, in the name of whatever you think is holy," Philippe said, getting up from where Christophe had pushed him aside, and sounding peeved. "He doesn't mean Jesus. He means Socrates."

"Which means he has not tasted death for nearly... blimey." Simone screwed her face up as she did the sums.

So you see, thought Christophe, I'm much older than Kerr and much stronger than any living thing.

Did you hear about the kings of old, thought Philippe, who'd have a man follow them everywhere, accompanying them in their chariots and carriages, sitting nearby at their vast banquets and so on, whose sole job it was to whisper 'Remember you must die'? Well that wouldn't work with him, so...

But Christophe had grown tired of explaining himself and leapt through the window. Simone moved to follow him, but Philippe held her arms.

"You'll die out there. Please don't kill yourself. If his ancient lordship doesn't return you're the nearest thing to a friend I've got.

He loosened his grip on her arms, and leaned forward, and to her immense surprise, Simone found herself kissing him. Then she dealt with him as she'd just dealt with Kerr – but with less force – and the next moment he was on the floor, writhing in pain, and Simone was jumping through the window.

288

Chapter Sixteen

Now hast thou but one bare hour to live

(Marlowe)

The rim of the sun began to rise, behind cloud for now, although soon it would be a beautiful day. Simone had jumped, breaking the jump in a cursory way, one foot casually touching a wall on the way down, just to be sure... but she knew she didn't need to. She could have descended in one unbroken leap, as Christophe clearly had. In fact she wondered if he had not been holding himself back, trying to keep to limits that he didn't have... Why?

To be less... apart, said a voice in her head, and she really couldn't tell if it were his or hers.

He was in front of her, blowing like a Botticelli cherub, but it was no tender Zephyr he was exhaling: It was nearly knocking her off her feet. He lifted his eyes to meet hers as he kept blowing, and she was surprised to find what looked like anger there.

Guiltily she remembered Philippe's kiss and she knew Christophe was aware of it too. It was clear that vampires were subject to nature as well as to the dark longing for blood. She remembered what her mother had told her, more than once, when she reached her teenage years: "Never make a man jealous, they cannot deal with it in a civilised way... and if they can, that's not a man."

It seemed really unhelpful advice, however accurate it might be.

Well, three men competing over me! Pity we're all dead. Simone savoured the irony.

The tornadoes, if that's what they were, became one large one, dark grey now, as if freighted with water, spinning round the cathedral and the square. It was as if the wind had drawn down water vapour from high cloud, but Simone had no idea how Christophe had done that. It was like winter, gloomy, dark and cold, though beyond the dark, the summer's day was dawning.

Christophe was maintaining the enchantment, which was the only word for it. He was no mere bloodsucking insect. This feat declared him a great sorcerer. It was a little worrying that he seemed to be feeding on anger. He was still glaring at her, then he raised his face to the invisible sky and shouted Kerr's name. His voice had the resonance, depth and command of a Robeson without the overtones of kindness and humanity. It was deep enough to speak to stone and furthermore, to demand a reply.

There was a great groan that seemed to arise from underfoot and spread to the walls of buildings, including the great cathedral itself, so that mighty walls nearly a thousand years old seemed to shudder as if in terror, demonstrating their willingness to let the stones that made them fly apart into chaos, rather than defy the sorcerer. Heavy doors, made of ancient wood, creaked and flew open, and at last a figure came hurtling through a doorway as if regurgitated by the building that had sheltered him, like something indigestibly rotten.

It was, of course, Kerr. He showed no surprise at the scene before him, nor at the absence of the sun: He must have been following what was going on, through a window or just from the noise, which was considerable, like Nature shouting angrily. High winds are noisy, and high winds picking up and dropping things, especially things made of wood and metal, are very noisy indeed. It was quieter now though, with the winds steadier and surrounding them with cloud. Kerr looked as pleased with himself as ever, though Simone thought that he must know his end was approaching.

"So," he addressed Christophe, "You intend to destroy me. You, the representative of good, will eliminate me, the representative of evil. It will crown the day, won't it? Lots of kinds of evil will be destroyed today. And you are so scrupulous, you only kill vampires... who are dead already."

"Yes." Christophe had clearly had enough of speech. Get me a piece of wood, he asked Simone, via his mind. He didn't seem bothered that his thoughts were accessible to Kerr.

Simone was confused at first but then she realised he meant a stake, or something wooden and stake-shaped.

"You know," began Kerr, looking at Simone as he spoke, "You despise me as a villain, with no greater ambition than to drink human blood and make a few servants to keep me company till they annoy me or get in the way of your friends. But you know how few keep our minds after the change, a very select group indeed. And he," nodding at Christophe, "was the key to it. I have only just understood that, because it was you that got it out of him. His mind is closed to me, but my mind was there, listening to him. And I tell you, it is worth it to know what he revealed, even though he is going to turn me to dust."

"Any minute now," agreed Christophe, while Simone searched for long pieces of wood.

Kerr seemed to be enjoying the sound of his own voice. "Thousands of years ago this man was a disciple of an idle troublemaker who used to hang around public places and distract young men and even women from their duties by preaching nonsense about knowledge and ignorance. However, this fellow had powers beyond that of any sorcerer, and by the time he was finally executed for treason, blasphemy and corrupting the youth, your friend here had developed himself and so had not reverted to beastliness even when he became the lawful prey of our kind."

"Perhaps I should just tear your head off," mused Christophe.

"I had suspected for a long time that this was the cause, not just of his... grasp on his own humanity, but also his shame. For his master famously demonstrated how unafraid he was of death, sacrificing a cock to the god of medicine as though life were a disease he was at last cured of... Showy nonsense! But you" – and he turned accusingly to Christophe – "were asked what we are all asked... you must have been." And unlike Socrates, you begged for your life, and became a vampire. Socrates: the most famous person ever to be emphatically unafraid of death. It's why this fellow here keeps so quiet about his age, and his story. Because he's a disgrace, letting down his teacher and guide. In fact, he should be walking into the sunrise, not me."

Christophe now looked very scary indeed. "One more word and I'll rip your tongue out," he snarled.

Kerr moved backwards, just a little, watching Christophe all the time. Simone realised that it didn't make any difference, not really... If what Kerr was saying was true, Christophe was incomprehensibly old, and, given that she'd seen that vampires grew stronger and more powerful with age it followed that he was so strong and fast that he could crush Kerr in the blink of an eye. Or less.

"Why don't you just kill him?" she blurted.

"Same reason as always," snarled Kerr. "As long as I survive, there's one worse than him. That's the reason he made me, after all."

Lightning cracked over their heads. It was followed by thunder, but that was drowned in Christophe's roar, before which all other sounds retired, defeated by his ultra bass rumble. In a movement so fast it was almost invisible, he swept

Kerr up under his arm and ran up the front of the cathedral, reprising the role of Quasimodo. It looked as though everybody wanted a go.

What happens now? Simone asked silently. What is he doing?

Belittling Kerr and showing who is the more powerful was Philippe's equally quiet response. They'll have a punch-up but there is no conclusion. If he kills Kerr he, as his sire, might die. Perhaps. Or perhaps not.

"And the corollary of that is that you and I are safe from Kerr, who made us both," she said aloud. "Unless he decides to commit suicide," she added.

"Looks like Chris has created a micro-climate in time as well as space," mused Philippe aloud as he appeared at Simone's side. "Look with your vampire eyes."

She squinted, but nothing happened. Then she saw something at the periphery of vision. She tried to focus on it, but it slipped away. Then she looked straight ahead, into the swirling wall of dust and water, and in the corner of her eye, as fast as the lightning that was continuing to illuminate the sky in fantastically short bursts, she saw a scene of daylight, and gathering crowds, all jubilant. And then it was Christophe's dusky world filling her sight, holding off the day itself.

"How...? Oh, don't bother, I'm past explanations. But can I just make the obvious point that if he dies, we may well all die." And maybe, thought Simone, that's a good thing. We're all bloodsuckers after all.

"I did enjoy the film, though it doesn't do justice to the book," said Philippe.

"What are you? Oh. The hunchback."

"Quite funny, tucking a villain like that under his arm, instead of pretty Esmeralda."

"Have you been knocked on the head, or something? Is this the time?"

"No, certainly not, though it may well be the place."

"We'd better follow. I suppose."

I want to hear what you have to say, she thought at him. Did I hear it right? Christophe killed Kerr and made him a vampire?

"It's taken me centuries to tease out part of the story," said Philippe. "I never heard him tell it all in one go. But haven't you seen the Raphael study for the

School of Athens? He would always comment at how irritating it was to see Socrates curled up on a step yet the upstart Aristotle and the boy, Plato were the central characters. Yes, I thought that was an odd way of putting it, but to be frank, I thought it must be just showing off. Waiting for me to fall for it, but I wouldn't, I'd never heard of such a thing. No one could stand it, not for thousands of years. But now I've seen."

"He must have learnt something from the old man then. But he was not a sorcerer. Was he?"

Philippe shrugged. "It's guesswork from now on. So here's my guess: I think that whatever the... er... spiritual equipment Socrates supplied to his followers may have sustained Christophe when others reverted to beasts. It also manifested itself in powers growing, but clearly not just strength in his case. He must have tried to make another like him, though why Kerr I can't imagine. Like me, you were turned by Kerr and whatever made Christophe different must somehow have been transmissible. Kerr caught it from Christophe, and we caught it from Kerr. But while Kerr kept his brains he either lost or never had any humanity."

"I suppose, if he killed him... I mean, he doesn't want to kill people... some might be dying, but..."

"I'll help you out. Even the most cultured, kindly, civilised person cannot be guaranteed to retain those qualities when changed into a vampire. The higher functions just die off, usually, to leave... well, you've seen. Jackals, slavering brutes. I think Christophe took a chance with Kerr and lost, but Kerr somehow partakes of the gift Socrates gave Christophe. It obviously doesn't always work. Maybe Kerr has changed thousands, and we know three who are still... people. You and me. And Dave."

"So," Simone pondered, "Christophe won't make any more vampires. My god! He must have been through a very special hell... he could have turned thousands, hoping for a companion but instead, destroying the humanity of everyone he touched... till Kerr, who didn't have any... to start with. That's why he lets him live! You're not about to pass anything on... nor am I... and it's a chancy and really unethical thing... and Socrates was all about ethics, wasn't he?"

This wall of wind and vapour, there's a lot of water, isn't there? It was Christophe's voice in her head; not different from the way anyone else's voice sounded in her head, not really, but it felt like him. Philippe glanced at her, and the look in his eyes told her he heard it too.

The voice continued. The water is the manifestation of all my tears, which means that it is safe for a very, very long time. And the wind which keeps everything swirling yet contained, well, that's my anger. And when I speak, that's the sound of my despair, and it can move bedrock.

The ground beneath them began to shudder and then split, once right through the centre of the circle of magic, then another at a right angle to the first. Where the cracks crossed each other, the gash they made began to smoke. Then a spike of fire rose and grew, like a pillar in motion. From the fire rolled a ball, which split and proved itself to have consisted of two figures locked in combat, with their clothes still smouldering. One of them leapt into the sky. How, no one was sure anymore; there was nothing for him to use as a springboard. The other stood in front of them, still with flames dancing through his hair and around his shoulders, as though that was his robe of choice.

"And this fire," he said aloud, "is the ferocity of my desire for the divine; the only desire that when satisfied, grows greater. Now it is time, I will do it. I have two of you now, and may you forgive me. Get inside. I will remove this abomination from the world."

And keep me humble, please, in the name of all that's holy, save me from pride, they heard him think, looking at them closely. Then he took off after Kerr, and Philippe pulled Simone into the cathedral, and the protecting embrace of the shadows.

People were pouring into the square, where De Gaulle would be leading the victory march. Soon he would speak from the steps of Notre Dame. Somehow the twilight world of the vampires and the bright morning which was the rightful possession of the humans occupied the same space, neither intruding on the other, at least not currently.

Simone and Philippe hurried to climb the steps to the roof of the cathedral, where they'd have a good view without being barbecued. Others were there now, laughing and excited: young women had baskets of flowers, some of which were paper, some real. Below them, people were gathering, although they shrank back while others pushed forward to see. So they could not see the crowd very well from their place in the shadows but they could feel the minds and knew there were many of them, and they were very happy.

Simone started to smile, and the smile would not leave her face though her cheeks hurt. All that joy was flooding her mind and she just let go into it, as if carried along by a warm river onto a peaceful sea. Philippe had a silly look on his face, just as she must have. She had never experienced the joy of being part of a large populace before… or even a small one, certainly not since the war began and she became a vampire. It must have been during childhood. Had she any memories of joy?

Not really, she commiserated with herself, just an ache, occasionally. A wistful feeling like homesickness, like the Jews and their Zion. Or the black people in America, stolen from their homeland and forced to be slaves in a foreign land. Like the women of Troy…

"Like us all," said Philippe. "like the poem, where shades of the prison house surround the growing boy… or girl."

"You were listening to my thoughts," she replied.

"You didn't bother to hide them," he answered. "You think, along with Wordsworth, that Joy is our home. Makes sense. How can there be a literal place with grass and trees and buildings that we all yearn for? And why cling so to life, when it is an exile from Joy?"

She laughed. It came easily. It's heavenly, but it will pass, she reminded herself. And we have plenty of mourning to do, but if we all die and pass into a joyful state, what does morality matter? Or justice?

"Very good question," said Philippe aloud, and started giggling. "You know what I think? I think we're going to hell, you and me, for disobeying the rules. And at the moment, I really don't care. And if I'm going to hell, then to hell with it…"

He took her hands in his and gently pulled her towards him, lifting her chin with his forefinger and kissing her lips, happy and respectful all at once. This time she responded delicately but they were both aware that great enthusiasm was there too, like a horse getting restless in its stable. They both moved slightly away from each other but their eyes remained locked.

Well, said a voice in their heads, I see I needn't worry about you. You're going to be fine without me.

They looked up. The sky was bright, but beneath it was a dome made of air and dust, coloured with different shades of black, if that could be. Within the dome everything went on as if there was indeed just sky and ground, with people passing through it as they moved around, and out again, with no obvious signs of noticing it was there.

They looked down, and saw that the dome extended to the ground. It was clear that only they could see it. It was growing, too, past the Ile De Saint-Louis now, across the river. Soon it would encompass Paris, if it kept getting bigger, and all the time the population went about their mostly joyful business. There were some, however, who wanted to destroy right up till the last minute, and others who wanted to stop them, and these minds were now so isolated from the mass of people that Simone found she could pick them out, and locate them, as well, like following the direction from which music was coming.

"Conceal your thoughts," commanded Christophe, who was now sitting stroking a gargoyle as if it were a pet, a thing of flesh and blood. Simone shuttered her mind as best she could, knowing that Kerr could get past her defences and hoping that he wasn't aware that it would profit him if he did.

This is the only way we can do it, Christophe thought at them. It's taking a lot. I'm not telling you what I plan to do but I can tell you the best hope is to tear yourselves away from each other and do some vampire killing. You can feel the minds that want to fight on, they can be located. You will have to content yourselves with disabling any that are still human, but then, you know the drill. I'll concentrate on Kerr, who is also tracking them, and trying to change them into vampires, obviously. The dome will hold till nightfall. Now I don't want to split you up, but we'll accomplish more if we work separately.

Simone could see the skin stretched across his cheekbones. Fine as they were, they looked better with a little more covering of flesh. He appeared to have lost weight, which was impossible with the short space he'd been out of her sight. Or maybe not, for vampires. And surely, however old you were, your eyes wouldn't look as if they were trying to shrink back into your head like that.

Go, he gestured. And they stepped off the cathedral's parapet and into the air, which seemed to give slightly, like soft sand, but that was it. They were flying, or perhaps hovering would be a better description, level with the top of the towers of Notre Dame. Don't leave the dome, Christophe thought, but there would be no danger of that until nightfall, as the sun would fry them if they did, and they wouldn't be able to fly through air with this freedom either: It was clearly a feature of the dome.

Christophe was gone when Simone turned around.

Philippe said "Do you know what this is?" He made a sweeping gesture to indicate the dome.

"What is it?"

"It's the inside of Christophe's head, the cranium. Remember your Coleridge?"

"In Xanadu did Kublai Khan a stately pleasure dome decree? Not much of a pleasure dome is it? All dust and darkness."

"That's what his head, physically, is. An ancient cranium, all the other bones crumbled, like something in an Egyptian tomb. We vampires have two lives, running concurrently. Like a prison sentence served twice over, in two dimensions. But all this... it's unbelievable he can do this and maintain it."

"If he doesn't maintain it, we are in big trouble."

They sniffed the air, though what they were sniffing for was anybody's guess, Simone thought, even as she sniffed. It was something altogether else they needed to tune into – something more like a cry, or a shudder – the feelings of those who were unhappy with the events of today. She felt a pang of anguish, and it wasn't her anguish. It wasn't any old anguish in fact, it was being felt over in the Marais district, and she found she could tune into it as if it were a dial on a wireless. She stopped sniffing, and felt the emotion thump straight into her chest, as though she'd been struck.

Ah. The middle of the chest, the heart chakra in Hindu thought – or Tiphareth, the central point in the Kabbalistic model of the Human, and Adam Kadmon, the Prototype; the ultimate Person.

Simone had taken advantage of Philippe and Christophe's massive library. They had suggested a reading list... well, Philippe had – Christophe had long since read all he wished to, except the newspapers – but they had been full of pro-Nazi propaganda over the last few years. There were a lot of fascinating secrets in those books, but the funny thing was, when you dug into it the real secrets were in the most widely available books, unnoticed by most who read them.

She felt the thread linking her to the... prey... and followed it like Hansel and Gretel and the breadcrumb trail till she came to a house near Rue St Denis where she could feel two anguished minds and their black intention to go out towards the parade and blow themselves up, taking as many innocent Parisians with them as they could.

She hovered in mid air, outside a first floor window, which would have been fun were it not for what she could read from the occupants of the room. They were suppliers of women for the Germans, and, as not all the women were happy with this, they were afraid that some would give evidence against them. But they weren't just collaborators. The trade in human flesh is very dark indeed. There is a lot of damage.

As she read their minds, Simone recoiled. Vampires merely killed, after a nice dose of anaesthetic. It was a gentle death, really, as gentle as it could be.

But these men dealt in women who were actually girls, and their minds were filled with too many horrors to dwell on. Simone felt the surge of rage sweep through her body like a scouring desert wind. She wanted, oh, how she wanted to kill them and wipe their evil from the face of the earth. The desire was exceptionally strong, and it almost overwhelmed her. Who would object? Their victims would kiss her feet if they knew she had delivered justice to these two horrors.

Her vampire nature added its weight to the human that still dwelt in her, and both were in agreement, it seemed. She punched through the window and stepped into the room.

They had been about to strap grenades to themselves. One had already done so and he moved to take out the pins. But Simone had already read his mind and was there, wrenching the grenade from its belt around his waist. She punched him to the ground, then spun round to do the same to his partner, whose intended means of murder was not yet on his body.

Then she grabbed their necks, and draped an arm around each. She was hungry, very hungry, in fact, but she was surprised to find herself hesitant about anaesthetising them and enjoying a snack on each. She felt that she might be polluted.

Of course this was nonsense. Was she only to snack on innocents? She bent and sank her fangs into one of them and he immediately collapsed, unconscious. The other she gazed at, and he at her, but his face was a picture of terror.

"Maurice," she whispered, "I am the angel of Death and I know everything you have ever done. Hell has sent me to you to collect your dues." Then she did the same to him as she'd done to his partner, and dropped his unconscious body to the floor, none too gently.

As she was puzzling what to do next, especially regarding the arsenal now strewn across the floor, she heard a door opening on the floor below. She felt the minds coming up the stair, and watched the door open.

There was a young woman, with a face that had seen too much, and four armed policemen, whose loyalties might have been questioned, and with good reason, given that they had served under the Germans. Now Simone was, for the first time, fully appreciative of the telepathic powers that went alongside being a vampire. She read the woman's victimhood, and then the minds of the officers with her, and to her delight, they were honest French patriots, and tired of taking orders not only from the Germans, but from the corrupt go-betweens who made sure the new masters had everything they needed.

Meanwhile four guns were being pointed at her. She improvised.

"They kidnapped me," she said quickly. "They were going to strap grenades to themselves and me. I was too afraid to argue with them…"

"You are not French, by that accent," one of the policemen pointed out.

"This is an English accent, we are your allies," Simone replied. "I am a spy for the British government."

"I'd have thought they'd have chosen someone with better French," sneered the woman. Simone was irritated. At last a circumstance had arisen where she might as well tell the truth, and she had, although vital details had been omitted.

"Undercover operations get you into some very strange situations," said Simone. She decided not to respond to the woman's remark. She was feeling hungry and irritable, and didn't wish to be delayed by some idiot. She had work to do, and moreover, food to find. Soon.

"Take them, they're all yours," she said, indicating the unconscious pair.

"On the day of days, you think we should want to lumber us with a couple of traitors, who are also conspirators to murder, and who'll be sentenced to death anyway, God willing?" enquired one of the policeman.

Simone's mind reading abilities had not deserted her. She knew what was intended, and she also had the ability to stop it, so great was her speed of reaction. And she did nothing, as the gendarmes pumped bullets into the men she'd rendered helpless.

"So," said the most talkative of the policemen, "What are you going to tell your English bosses? That we're an undisciplined rabble, who can't wait for the due process of the law?" His colleagues just looked sullen.

"It's different in wartime," Simone muttered. No one looked as if they were about to argue, and in any case she was more interested in what was happening around the corpses.

The graceful, spiralling cloudy light, with a steady pulse at its heart, was hovering around the traitors' bodies. It was just as bright as the shimmer around the most virtuous of boy soldiers, shot dead as they first stepped off the landing craft at Omaha beach, just as bright as the brilliant luminescence around a child, which miraculously she'd never seen – thank god, thank God – when the soul departed.

She sat there for a while, till after the police had left, wondering at the beauty of the feeling still in the room, as the shimmering light faded and left two lumps of meat behind. It was as though everyone went to heaven, good or bad, and then surely the badness went somewhere; perhaps to enter another lost soul.

She walked down the stairs and out into the street, which was deserted: Everyone was gathering for De Gaulle's speech, or trying to. Bootleg booze of all description was being distributed, and there were those who set off towards Notre Dame to hear the great liberator and never quite got there.

But Simone had bigger matters on her mind than war, even a war which had ravaged all of Europe, and the Far East as well. She was ruminating on the strong impression she'd had, that heaven, whatever that was, received all comers; that when Destiny finally caught up with everybody, up to and including Adolf Hitler himself, they all ended up in the same place.

She turned her mind to the matter in hand. As to be expected, she picked up a lot of white noise as she scanned the minds of everyone she passed, as she headed to the central area on the Ile De France again. All this time she saw the dome, seeming to extend from her as though it were a protecting barrier. She saw it as grey, made of cloud and rain, and dust, but they were spinning, bands of water, circling and upright. As she moved, it moved with her, though beyond it she could see the sunny day. If the dome went now, she'd be fried to a crisp.

That's not where everything's happening, a voice in her head appeared to say, with a sharp edge to it, as if trying to wake her up.

She felt it, too, it wasn't just words in her head. She turned, and as she turned through 360 degrees, she flared her nostrils, oh, so delicately... and she caught a familiar scent.

She made her way out of the crowd, and made for the direction from which the scent had come. It was odd, it smelt like perfumes did before the war, but as if kept in sunlight too long, so they smelt powdery, like the cosmetic bag of an aging diva.

And at last she located it. It was subtle, it was sporadic, but it was there and it was in their home, the apartments in the forgotten palace. It was a bad augury, for it was essence of Kerr, overlaid with old cologne. And that meant he was there, or 'here' as Simone was already thinking of it, having swiftly crossed the distance and, being a bit alarmed, taken shortcuts over the heads of the crowds gathered about, to the point of running up the bodies of the stronger looking men, then leaping off from their shoulders hoping to land on another such, who needed to be within the dome area... although she noticed it was not only aligning itself with her, and her immediate intentions, but apparently, anticipating them. For when she moved, it was already there, covering, enclosing and protecting.

So she ignored it. If whatever was making this operate somehow failed, she'd die, but it wasn't helpful to keep thinking along those lines.

And, as she began to follow the fragrance, a burst of stinking flatulence burst upon her nose like a big wave on a beach.

"Welcome to the world of Christophe," it sniggered. Somehow, Kerr was beside her, and together they were climbing the wall of the palace, although they were really running up it, to the bemusement of anyone watching... and a few were, though the wonder of this day seemed to have inured them to other spectacles. Plus, there were quite a few who had obtained strong drink, and were not necessarily used to it after the shortages of the Occupation.

"What is happening there?" exclaimed a woman's voice, but the man beside her just shrugged, and a moment later, so did she.

The dome was very expandable, but it was something engineered to protect vampires, but it clearly had drawbacks. It didn't discriminate, or loyally hang around its progenitor. So Kerr was under its protection, although presumably Christophe could move it away from him.

She tried not to think. Kerr was laughing as he jumped ahead of her onto the roof, and entered the palace by the trap door. She dived through it after him. They landed on the floor beneath, and there was Christophe.

"Let's kill him now!" Simone shouted aloud. But following them through the trapdoor was a steady stream of new vampires. Beside Christophe's beautiful desk, which looked older than Philippe actually was, was an umbrella stand, which held two umbrellas, and several walking sticks, which had all been sharpened to a point, in readiness for just such an occasion as this. Simone grabbed a couple, and began executing vampires.

"Damn you all!" Simone did not get much satisfaction as she drove the stakes as fast as she could into the cold dead hearts of the invaders. A short time ago, they were ordinary people, even those still in German uniform. Maybe some had still been alive today, excited to be celebrating their liberation. And now, having been blackmailed by a bloodsucker into pleading for their lives, they faced an early death. But they had changed into something so dangerous that it could not be allowed to survive.

It was Kerr's fault. He had done this to them.

And who did it to me, was Kerr's silent riposte.

Then Christophe leapt on him, stake in hand, and Kerr gripped that arm, while his tendons and veins stood out with the effort, and crimson tears appeared at the corners of his eyes.

Suddenly Christophe let go.

"After all these years, you're still afraid to die, Critias!" Kerr cackled. Then he leapt up the wall and out of the roof, his gang of vampires completely destroyed. Simone turned in fury to Christophe. But he took her hands in his and told her that the truth was that the one who had changed him had told him that it was not possible to kill a vampire one had made without it also being the end for oneself. However, being braver than anyone gave him credit for, he had tried it anyway.

If he had succeeded then not dying would have disproved that theory, but it was not guaranteed, and a mistake could leave his friends, and the world with Kerr and no one stronger. So he used his strength to prevent Kerr causing damage when he could, although he didn't follow him around... meanwhile Kerr had told the vampires he created the same story, you can't kill your maker without dying yourself. It was a useful lie for him, since he created many vampires, and who knew when one of them might regard their condition as worthy of revenge.

"But what about vice versa? If the maker kills ..."

"I am pretty sure Kerr has killed any that he made that might have retained enough humanity to want him dead. I was his maker and he has not perished. But it is not because I fear to die. These threats are untrue, they're lies once thought to be useful. But the truth is, we can kill Kerr without dying ourselves, necessarily."

"Perhaps you should," said Simone, sharply, "since you are his creator."

"After a thousand years," he responded, "One gets lonely."

Then Philippe came through the other door, the ground floor one. No need to tell me, he thought at them. I started following this before I got here. Your thoughts are so loud I'm surprised humans can't hear them.

Did you know..? Simone thought at him, with a colouring of accusation in it.

"What's the problem, Simone?" Philippe went for speech when he wanted clarity: it was more substantial.

Yeah, then there's writing, she sneered, that's very substantial. Then he realised she was reading his thoughts at a deeper level than just picking up on bits of mental commentary or even taking a trip down memory lane, which in his case, was a lengthy journey.

Christophe snapped out of what Simone felt as a dreary haze of guilt. "You're moving fast on the mind reading. Must be because you're a woman. They are better at that sort of thing."

"Perhaps that's the way we can get rid of Kerr," suggested Philippe. "though he's got a thousand year start."

"More like five hundred," said Simone.

"Oh, *well* then..." Philippe shrugged.

"Shut up, both of you. It's likely that a brute like Kerr is by nature undeveloped in this ability, even compared to us. Us chaps, I mean. After all, Philippe wants to improve the lot of others, even change society, and as for me... I had the privilege to encounter the greatest of men, and hear him speak on the most profound of subjects, and as for my fellow humans, all I could wish for them is that they might have had that privilege too. But Kerr... has no womanly element of nature at all, nor has life taught him better. He is pure masculinity unbound by any conscience." Christophe looked sombre, but then he often did.

"Why did you pick him for an immortal pal, then? Why not a nice looking woman? There must have been quite a few of them dying of the plague, or in warfare, or something. And there must have been a few who really didn't want to die, surely?"

Christophe looked even more sombre, if that were possible. "Indeed. It felt like it would be a terrible sin. I mean, I had failed to convince anybody I might have wanted to be eternal companions with, that turning vampire would be better than death. You don't realise how religious a lot of people were in those days. I got desperate, and came close to the darkest of crimes, self murder. So at the back of my mind I thought if it went wrong, and he turned out to be a curse on everybody else, I could er... cancel it."

"So you were experimenting, let me get this right, but you didn't want to choose a – for want of a better word – decent person, because I suppose you didn't want to damage their chances of heaven. Surely a child could see the flaws in that plan? But then, after a thousand years one gets lonely, like you said. So why not pick a ruddy psychopath on whom to bestow eternal life? Genius!"

"I told you Simone, it's not so much eternal life as eternal damnation. Maybe, if you keep your nose clean... you can survive as a vampire without taking human life. I thought I could help him, show him what to do. Don't look at me like that. I was going mad. I visited women, bought the chance to drink some of their blood, but I couldn't do *that* to them. They were simple, unlearned, and their lives were hard but they believed in heaven, they believed in God, and it would break their hearts. No, I had to look for another type altogether, and I found a mercenary battling the Moors in what is laughably called the Holy Land."

"What were you doing there? Surely not fighting?" asked Simone.

"No, I went to do good, Simone. What else should I do? I anaesthetised wounded men on the battlefield. There was very little provision for the injured. Also, I would be able to survive on their blood, without killing them, I might add, although sometimes I administered a little too much anaesthetic to the ones who couldn't be saved. In their last hours I showed them some kindness, but since many of them were mercenaries and had lived murderous lives they were terrified for the fate of their immortal souls. People were very religious during that period. Even the mercenaries, while helping themselves to stolen riches when they could, did believe that God wanted them to fight in crusades. They were very interested in seeing a priest to get the last rites, so they could be forgiven for all that they'd done wrong, which was usually quite a lot. I did try to persuade a couple of them, but they were horrified, and moreover, frightened by me, and started screaming about the devil.

In the end I left the scene of battle, which of course I could only attend at night, so that I could do nothing to ameliorate or deflect the cruel wounds inflicted on both sides. By the time I appeared from my tent at sunset what lay before me was a scene of terrible carnage, and I could not even weep, because even in the fading light someone might see my bloody tears."

"So then what?" asked Simone.

"Both of you, look at me. Stand together, you'll see."

And they saw. Simone had her doubts about whether the thing would work when there were two pairs of eyes for Christophe, apparently aka Critias, to communicate with at once. But it did. Then she wished it didn't work at all.

The Moors were winning, going by the cries of the wounded, the bulk of whom were from Europe. The screaming was mostly in various European languages, as well as in no language but the lingua franca of agony. And most of the dying were from the western countries, judging by the style of armour on the few could afford that protection. Still, given the heat, and the narrowness of the aperture through which knights had to peer, a suit of armour was sometimes no better than an upright coffin, with the unlucky man swiping his sword wildly in the hope of hitting something he could not see.

It had been a ragged army, and included those who genuinely thought their souls would benefit from freeing the 'holy' land from the grip of the unbeliever, as well as adventurers who sought wealth at the point of the sword. This latest battle was butchery, as most of the combatants were unskilled and without proper weapons. Christophe, the being who was hosting the other vampires' vision, was engaged in alleviating misery as much as he could. This must be why we have tales of angels on battlefields... or maybe someone sees the light of the departing souls, thought Simone. The air was thick with the smell of carnage, and very hot besides. There would be no coolness as the night wore on. The very landscape, dusty brown by day, was without pity.

An armed man lay before them, a sticky mixture of blood, dirt, and sweat with insects crawling in and out of the narrow slit in his visor. He was moaning still, as the insects dined on his eyes. The sounds he produced were not commensurate with the terrible things that were happening to him, but he had no strength left to express his agonies. He must have heard Christophe's approach, though, as he gathered the last of his voice to beg for a blessing, then death. Christophe recited the last rites, though Simone thought the man must have wondered at his luck – though that wasn't quite the word – at the presence of a priest just at that moment. But then she realised as she looked down at where her feet normally were that Christophe was indeed in a robe and dressed as a priest.

Having absolved the man of his sins, Christophe did not, she realised, want him to imagine his immortal soul stained by a request to die, which was practically suicide, and definitely frowned on. And of course he read the man's mind, which Simone could feel, even watching from down the centuries: There were other wounds, but even if there had not been he'd not survive. So he did not even wait to anaesthetise him, but twisted his head around to snap his neck. From the corpse there arose a bright, glittering mist, pouring out of his mouth, which rose up and disappeared. And what was left would nourish the insects.

Why not him, then? Christophe did not answer, but showed them the field of battle in all its horror; healthy bodies, miraculously evolved, or made in God's image, or both combined... why not? Now they were butchered, and broken, turned into a squalid mess. And Christophe went where actual priests would be too frightened to go, comforting the dying and often helping them on their way.

Simone, and of course Philippe, did see a man begging for his life, crying aloud that he didn't want to die. He was the first they'd seen on that battlefield who did that, and Christophe, trying to staunch a dreadful wound to the man's stomach, was so excited by this Simone could feel it. His hands trembled as he tried to keep the man alive long enough to make the request.

His voice echoed through his fellow vampires' ears.

I can save you, it said. Let me drink a little blood from you, and you from me, and you shall live free from pain and death and old age for as long as you wish.

But already the man was unconscious, and could neither accept nor reject that or any other offer, anymore. His soul issued from between his lips, and there was a sense of relief again, but whose relief it was remained unclear. Then the bright thing arose, as if riding on the back of the last breath, and what happened next was ambiguous: It either went up to heaven, or dissipated into the air.

Simone wondered a lot about that. It wasn't exactly an unimportant distinction. Maybe one of those possible fates befell the good, and the other, the wicked... but on the other hand... maybe all of us just dissolve. Or all of us get to heaven. And good and bad don't matter then. Surely not?

Stop thinking, warned Christophe. You're interfering. Indeed, the vision was flickering, so Simone paid attention again.

At last, they came upon a recognisable form. It was him, Kerr, looking little different than he did several hundred years later: He looked older back then, and filthy. Here, on this cursed field that had once grown olives and grapes but now bore a horrid fruit, he was relatively innocent, although of course he wasn't. He wore chainmail but no helmet and at first it seemed impossible to reach him, as his head was pouring blood. In fact it was the wound in his side that was more probably fatal. Head wounds were often showily nasty, but it was simply all the tiny blood vessels. So it was not that from which he was dying, but he *was* dying. Time was running out.

Christophe knelt by the injured man, and put his face up close to his, which was a strange sensation for Simone and Philippe, as though they were there, too.

"Save me, save me, I don't want to die," begged Kerr, in terrible French. Then he said it again, in another tongue, but this time they recognised it as a mediaeval English accent, and Simone knew that he was an Englishman by birth, like her and Philipp... though not like Christophe, the wandering Greek.

That should have been enough, but Christophe seemed determined to be conscientious.

"Will you give up your soul for eternal life? And the promise of never growing old?" He asked, in the same tongue. Simone felt anxious and excited, but they were no doubt Christophe's feelings. She felt like shouting to him to get on with it, but of course he could not change the past, however immortal he might be, however strong. Not even God can do that.

"Lies, but I'll agree..." panted the injured man, in a voice so weak it was a bare whisper.

There was a very strange sensation for the two younger vampires, piggybacking on the wildly vivid memories from a life led by another, as they perforce bent alongside Christophe, smelt the fear and the blood and God! the sweat of the dying man as his head rolled back, ready to yield up the last breath... but the vampire's fangs were buried now in his neck. It was like a dream for Simone, but so physical she almost believed that she would drink some of the blood. But although the taste was in her mouth, nothing flowed down her throat, and she almost roared with frustration and hunger. As she watched, the burst of strength needed to feed was carried through those vampire fangs and the dying man was able to turn his head enough to sip at the blood dripping from Christophe's own wound, inflicted by himself, and a little drop entered the barely open lips of the man who would one day be called Kerr.

Then she saw the man's colour change. Pale before, his complexion grew ruddy, and as they watched the wound in his side healed with a gentle, hissing sound. He sat up.

Simone suddenly felt uncomfortable, as though too many circles had been completed. Kerr smiled at her, a smile for which the description 'wolfish' had been invented, surely... it was Christophe at whom he was smiling, of course, but she felt dizzy and disorientated, as if it were her. But that wasn't possible. Kerr would have his own memories and what he did now was what he had done then. There could be no crossover. Surely.

But someone close to her was speaking.

"I have saved you, knight, and to me you owe obedience," said Christophe, so close that it felt like his voice issued from the pit of Simone's stomach. Probably she would have phrased that more tactfully, she thought. It was centuries too late, though.

"In return, I will teach you all you need to know to live through this transformation," he went on.

"I am hungry," said the man now known as Kerr. "For blood," he added. "By fortune, there is plenty hereabouts." And once more he was grinning, seemingly straight at Simone and Philippe as well as Christophe.

"I owe you nothing," he added. "I know what has happened to me, I know you did it. I know you have immense power and I too will have it, and I'll get more joy out of it than you do."

And then he laughed, a huge gleeful roar of celebration, rose to his feet, and went off, seeking victims, presumably. Simone felt the wave of despair that passed through Christophe as if it were her own, fresh sorrow.

Kerr, who apparently was originally called Sir William, had just come across a friend who hailed him by that name, and went on to crow that, thanks to God's mercy, this fellow, 'The Butcher' still lived.

That was a bit depressing to hear, but Sir William was clearly not loyal to his old associates, for he wasted little time in sinking his teeth into the friend and gorging himself on the fellow's blood, with no thought of moderation. Then the scene faded, probably because Christophe could bear no more.

What happened next? She thought, and Christophe replied silently that the basic information about being a vampire was all there, in the blood. Vampires just knew what their lives were about, not just the clear need that was obviously for blood, but they knew, once bitten, what the rules were; most of them, anyway. I always thought I could not kill whomever I might attempt to change, not without dying myself. So he knew that right away. Later he kept changing his name, but it couldn't have been to hide from me. He can never hide from me, nor I from him.

"Well." Simone was brisk. "You made him, you kill him. It's easy, because he can't kill you without dying. Have I got that right? And the same applies to you... except you don't, because of balance, or something. I don't quite believe you, I'm sorry. You're unwilling to pay the price because you don't want to die, just as you accepted the opportunity to become a vampire because you don't want to die. You haven't changed, that's all. But you unleashed a terrible pestilence upon the world, so you eradicate it. At the cost of your life, if necessary. And apparently, it is."

"You have considered the other implications, which include the fact that Simone is safe from him, unless he chooses to walk into the sunrise, Philippe added.

Simone would have gasped, had she any breath to do it.

"Is that what you think?" She finally spat out. "There's always a loophole, that's what my old man would say to me, and he was a lawyer, as well as a misanthropist, so he should know. So melodramatic, aren't you! Surely the mysteries of vampire hood are understandable if you accept the basic premise, but this rule can be easily circumvented. It must kick in when you administer the fatal blow yourself. Or there's another possibility, and that's that it doesn't exist, or rather, it's the other way round. You can kill a vampire that you've changed, but he or she can't kill the sire without paying the price. But if we work together that will be someone else. We can connive to destroy him, but it must be by another hand. I think you can kill him, Christophe."

"Yes," offered Philippe. "We have nothing like your strength, even two of us. But he won't kill Simone. So if you don't want to do it..."

"So, he hasn't killed me so far because of the fact that he fancies me, which he would do if I looked like the back of a bus, because after Philippe killed Edith that makes me the only female of his kind in his world."

"And in ours," added Christophe. "that we know of." There was a silence.

"We'll deal with that later," said Simone, quickly. "It is possible you're right, and he'll hold back from killing me. But he has to die. Neither the world nor I will have any peace from him. I knew when I met him he intends to dog my steps. He is the worst sort of... masculine person. His power makes him untouchable, so he believes, and all he encounters from others is fear and awe, so he is vulnerable. He has no understanding of himself or others."

"So: a Judith and Holofernes, Samson and Delilah move on him?" Philippe asked.

Simone shuddered. "Didn't those ladies ... lose something themselves in the process of entrapping their victims?"

"It had better be the first example, as Samson only lost his hair. With a vampire, you need the whole head," Philippe replied helpfully.

"Weren't both those gents sleeping in the aftermath of er... erotic bliss?"

Simone shuddered again, then she thought of the connection Kerr had established with her mind, and she knew the others were thinking too, that it's all right thinking fanciful thoughts but Samson and the other fellow didn't have a psychic power between them. Kerr could not only read thoughts, he could zone in on her mind from a long way away, was probably doing it now in fact.

There was an option, which was to do nothing. The war was not over, not yet, not for everyone. But for Paris, it was. Kerr was a warrior, trained to fight, kill and plunder what he wanted. He would go where there were battles still. Simone could stay here and live a comfortable existence, albeit in the dark... but at least it was Paris by night, not some festering English village full of narrow minds and grudging hearts. Why chase trouble?

Then she thought of the lives Kerr would take, most of whom would go mad with horror. He would choose the young and beautiful, hoping to change a human woman into a mate, but even Edith had not been able to bear it, or so it seemed. She herself, Simone, was some kind of anomaly, and that was just as well, because if Kerr found a mate who could survive the change with something resembling sanity intact, the pair of them would leave a trail of utter havoc across the world.

What is death, she asked herself, that I should fear it? Every one of us humans must face it, except for these. Maybe I should show you that there's nothing to fear, Chris and Phil.

They smiled uncertainly.

Her mind felt clear for once, and purposeful. She must go where that living devil went. You can follow my thoughts, enough to find me when I call, she thought at the two males. Wait for my call.

There was a lot of noise in her head, as if a wireless had been tuned badly and there was cross talk between different stations. It was mostly protests against her plan, or to be honest, idea: It hadn't been developed into a plan.

But she felt an overwhelming feeling that she had to get out of there and away from the other two, to get away from what felt like their excuses, which was probably unfair. For all she knew, Kerr was sending suggestions to her mind persuading her to dump her associates, the better to isolate her for his purposes.

She was up through the roof as she thought that, and onto the parapet, from which she leapt in the approximate direction of the roof opposite, a distance she'd not done in one jump before. Now it was easy, and nearer to flying than ever.

And Kerr spoke to her as she flew on to the next building. It was not as if he were in her head, but as if he were next to her. But there was nobody there.

She made a messy landing on a steep early nineteenth century roof, stumbling clumsily as she came to a halt against some slatey outcrop, a chimney or a vent. Kerr knew everything; everything she thought, everything she had discussed, silently or aloud, all she had ever been, all she was now... an open book to him, and worse, what were her real thoughts and feelings? How could she know what was real and what was a subtle form of hypnosis imposed from a distance... and a threat forever.

They say religion is primarily a means of social control, she thought; more powerful than weapons, and less exhausting than continual violent oppression. You learn to think the thoughts they want you to think, at school, at home, in church. You learn to believe that the rule of monarchs is the will of god. The beginning of freedom is the throwing off the mental chains, joining the mental fight. You may nod and scrape and bow to the church and the upper classes to avoid prison or torture or death, but at least you're free in your head. But how could she escape the will of Kerr? Vampires made other vampires and... hang on, Kerr made Philippe. Kerr. There must be some fading of the connection after 150 years or so, or maybe Kerr didn't bother with the chaps, even those over whom he had a hold.

They're male, you're a weak female, said a voice in her head. Oh right, I'm going to fall for that, she thought back. If that's how unsubtle you are.

Who? Who are you speaking to? They all want to control you, you know. You're a scarce resource. What do you think war is about? Control of resources.

Now that IS you, "isn't it?" Simone said the last bit aloud and added, "come on, show yourself, coward."

"I want you to admire my trick, though," said Kerr's voice, from the empty air, as if he were there next to her.

"Did you know I helped you fly this far? Did you realise that a newish vampire like you has no hope of making the leaps you've made without touching down a few times? It was I that lifted you higher, and further, and stronger, as a token of what I can do for you, if only we can be friends."

"I want only one thing; to kill you. You know that don't you?"

"You know, we could share so much," mused the space beside her. "Only very intelligent people survive being changed into vampires for any length of time. I knew you were intelligent when I first saw you, before you even spoke, and my poor black heart leapt. Then you ran off. I didn't mind, I knew you had things to get out of your system. I was confident you would survive, and when you were ready, we'd find each other again."

"What's so intelligent about you, though?" Simone felt sure that thought was wholly hers, since he was too vain to plant it in her head. "You're a mediaeval brute, good for nothing but fighting."

"I'm a deeply religious being," came the voice, and it had an injured tone. "I was a monk before I was a knight, but I didn't take to celibacy. Or to prayer several times a day, to be honest. But I was very careful of my immortal soul, so when the Pope announced a crusade I thought I'd be in with God."

"Well, I rest my case," said Simone. "who with any intelligence believes that killing other people pleases God?"

"You do, don't you? Or are you trying to please the king? Or your country, which is an idea, not a place? None of that seems intelligent either."

"We know better than that! It's to stop Hitler and fascism. But I don't need to tell you that. You're trying to taunt me, and it's a waste of your time, and mine. I know what's right and what's wrong."

"You don't even know what's real and what's delusion..."

"You mean illusion."

"No, I really don't. Illusion is a posh word for it, redolent of Indian mythology, where they practise meditation until they achieve enlightenment, and they're supposed to rise above the illusion of creation, also known as Maya. Then they don't have to be reborn into the illusion again. Of course, it's much easier to become a vampire, you don't have to go through the rigmarole of birth and death."

"So?" asked Simone of the empty air, although it wasn't, not really. Was he projecting his voice? How was he doing this?

"So, all very grand and cosmic. But most people just have delusions. Not just mad people. They just have the more florid delusions. There are artists, geniuses, who have visions, too, but most of the deluded are only minimally productive. Biggest delusion of all is that there is a person, a self, underneath the upbringing, the schooling, the false identities, the lies. And that there is any truth, even if someone wanted to tell you what it was. No truth, no self. Me, I find that liberating. Most people cannot bear it."

"If you're trying to undermine me, forget it." Simone spun in a circle and kicked at the air, just below where the voice seemed to be coming from. The only result was a burst of laughter.

"You're so clueless. If you want to encounter me in the flesh, follow me to where there's a good view of the city."

"Where?" But she knew he wasn't going to answer. And it wasn't a high rise city. He probably meant the Eiffel tower. She immediately began to move in that direction, and as she did, she felt a little heavier, a little slower, and her jumps seemed more clumsy, and shorter. Was he influencing that; infecting her mind and making her believe she was weak without his help, trying to prove that he'd helped her by withdrawing his strength? Or was she tired? She didn't really get tired, so it must be the former. Maybe.

It would not be long before the first lightening of the sky would herald another dawn. But it didn't matter. As she made her way towards the structure that symbolised twentieth century Paris as much as Notre Dame did the earlier city she decided in her heart and her very permeable thoughts that she would die if it would finally eliminate Kerr from the world. There. If you're listening, I mean it.

Clear as a stage whisper came a response directly into her head.

How do you know that wish is yours and not mine? That I am not tired of life and nurture a longing to die at your fair hands?

"Stop this! How would you like it if I invaded your thoughts?" She spoke aloud in her fear and frustration.

You are most welcome, was the reply. You always have been.

She changed tack as something that felt like truth occurred to her.

"You're afraid to die because of all your evil deeds. You expect to be punished and you're afraid."

But silence was the only response.

To the Eiffel Tower, then. But not right away. First she stopped to snack on a sleeping man, too drunk to even need anaesthetic love bites. He, along with many others, had obtained alcohol, or most likely had a little distillery he'd nurtured through the Occupation, or knew someone who had.

After she'd taken about a pint from him, she thought she'd take plenty of fuel on board, in case it became difficult to obtain, for some reason known only to the future. So she drank from some of his comrades, lying nearby and similarly inebriated.

She cringed a little at the standards of some celebrants' cleanliness, but guzzled their blood anyway. Finally replete, she stood up, and a wave of dizziness went through her.

I'm drunk, she thought. Is that a good thing or a bad? Why am I going to the Eiffel tower? Because an evil creature told me too? What is wrong with that proposition? Everything. Anyway, if I'm the last female vampire on earth, he should be pursuing me to wherever I want to go. And... so should they!

He stopped me going to Germany to kill Hitler. They all stopped me. What good have I done here? Nothing, not really. Bugger the lot of them. I'm going to Germany. They won't stop me this time.

She started to giggle, thinking of how angry Kerr would be when she didn't show up. Phil and Chris would be worried… haha, Phil and Chris!

So she headed east and kept going that way. Her jumps and speed were not quite what they had been earlier but that was encouraging, as it suggested that Kerr had lost track of her. Maybe alcohol wipes out my thought patterns enough to block him, she thought; then decided she was getting too sensible.

She covered a hundred miles or so before it became too light to carry on. She bedded down in a smelly barn, feeling desperately impatient. Vampires don't need a lot of sleep, so she was edgy and bored until the farmer, or one of his labourers, came in. She could have hidden, but was getting to the hangover stage and felt too grumpy to pretend anything.

She leapt on the poor chap and sank her teeth in his neck. She could feel the alcohol still circulating a little, enough to make her imagine draining her captive of all his blood. She stopped, and considered the way one never really appreciated how useful inhibitions can be, especially when they saved one from mortal sin.

She laid her prey down gently, and waited for him to come to. When he did, he was clearly too frightened to say much. So she did the talking.

"I am a vampire," she announced.

"I have just rendered you unconscious and drunk your blood, but no more than you would give in a donation to help the wounded, so you'll soon make it up again. I have no wish to hurt you. I am on my way to kill Hitler, and I'm sure that as a patriotic Frenchman you must approve of that aim."

He did not reply, just looked at her with terrified eyes, so she sighed, slightly exasperated.

"Do you have wine, or spirits? I must have some. Lots, in fact." She considered, briefly, explaining that a mind-reading vampire was probably pursuing her, in fact, three mind-reading vampires were scouting around for her right now, but two were friendly. Unfortunately the unfriendly – or, possibly over-friendly – one had the best mind-reading skills, and was especially tuned into her, Simone's, mind. But she couldn't feel any of them near, so perhaps they weren't, and perhaps her previous drunkenness had confused their vampire radar.

"If you bring me strong drink, I will not kill you or your family, I will be very pleased with you," was what she said, and so he scuttled off, murmuring

315

Mercies, while she waited to see if he would do as she wished or bring soldiers or policemen or vigilantes. But he came back with bottles of wine, carrying them in a sack, and apologising that they were not made from grapes, but from hedgerow fruit and even root vegetables.

The headache hit her after a couple of sips of some urine coloured concoction and even that wasn't as bad as the taste. She didn't let him go till she'd swallowed the contents of three bottles, then she found herself gripping his shoulder and demanding his name, which she forgot as soon as he told her. She remembered she must go somewhere – Germany, yes, that was it – and she kept telling the man to look out and inform her the second the sun went down, and that he must remind her where she was going, and why, at regular intervals. She felt sleepy at last, but now was not the time, she must get on, and she must do it while drunk, for a reason she could no longer remember.

Chapter Seventeen

I'll put a girdle round about the earth in forty minutes

(Shakespeare)

Night fell, and she was away, moving faster, jumping higher, eating up the ground, though perhaps a little less than on the previous night, when that bag of filth, Kerr, had claimed he'd helped. Well, he wasn't helping now, so her strength and power must've grown naturally... though were vampires remotely natural?

She was really fuzzy headed, and in no condition to think coherently about anything, let alone conduct a philosophical enquiry into the condition of a strange subspecies of humanity, of which she was an involuntary member. Except, of course, that it wasn't involuntary, was it? That was the rule, the potential vampire had to ask, or at least answer with a 'yes', and she'd begged to be allowed to survive, at any cost. And there were no goodies, not completely, and possibly even the baddie wasn't completely bad. Christophe and Philippe might be the vampire equivalent of vegetarians, but Chris, as she'd begun to think of him, though not out loud, yet, had been so lonely and desperate he'd gone looking for pals, and with stupendous lack of judgement had elected to turn a crusader, aka murderous thug, into an immortal bloodsucker.

So she could think a little, but it wasn't as though she had pleasant thoughts. She was still drunk when she crossed the border into the Netherlands. For a while she thought she'd got to Germany, but there were too many vowels in the road signs. She had to dine on a couple of Dutch men that were asleep next to a ditch, which they seemed to have been digging out, judging by the gear surrounding them. And they were asleep because, God be praised, they were drunk, and still had strong drink in the shape of a half-finished bottle of dubious looking whisky. She drank their blood, a little of it, but it was enough to intoxicate her... a little. But then she drank the rest of their moonshine, and was grateful she was a vampire, and immune to its more malign effects, which going by the taste probably included blindness and liver failure.

It occurred to her that a human would die or fall asleep, but neither of those things was happening to her. Her last thought was that she was getting more drunk than anybody ever had in the history of the world. Then she stopped thinking. A lot of what happened next was only pieced together much later, as Simone had blacked out, and forgotten it all.

Some part of her must have remained efficient and functioning, because the next thing she remembered she was in Germany, she could tell, perhaps because she seemed to be in front of a building with a great swastika'd flag draped in front of it. On closer inspection it turned out to be the entrance to some kind of massive compound. There were guards all around the place, but no one had spotted her, so she must have been stealthy and careful, while not really conscious, which was quite a feat.

She quietened her mind, which didn't take long, as it was sluggish, anyway, and sent her awareness, ravaged by drink as it was, into the mind of the nearest guard. He seemed to be as thick as a brick, his thoughts like rags, no beginnings or endings, just an inarticulate mumble. She directed herself to another, and although he wasn't much better she managed to discover that they were guarding a top secret weapon Hitler was very keen on developing, because it was a step ahead of what the allies had.

She saw them salute someone who passed by them into the building, which was a sort of façade, really, a deliberate camouflage which gave the impression of a municipal building being behind it; a town hall, something like that. But it wasn't. She followed the officer's mind as he passed beyond it, and she saw what he saw; a huge rocket, pointing to heaven, quite vertical and propped up by metal scaffolding. And she thought what he thought: The prototype is magnificent. We are launching it on London. We are damned by over cautiousness. We should launch several at a time. Then he started to think about his home and worrying about the Russians. We should launch it on Moscow, he thought; anywhere, they would not hold back! If the Allies had something like this they wouldn't hesitate. Then he started thinking dreary homesick thoughts, so she peeped through his eyes until his/her gaze alighted on a senior looking figure, who seemed puzzled.

"Why are you staring at me, man?" enquired the figure. Simone did a lightning flip of her consciousness from one to the other. She watched through her new guide's eyes as her old one shook his head and stuttered a load of ahs and ums and ers. Her current ride turned away with a shrug.

She didn't want to confuse them all by taking charge of their actions again: she just wanted to observe. She didn't want any rumours of unusual behaviour to get back to… Don't think the name, girl, she told herself.

Eventually she discovered that the rocket, which was so secret it didn't even have initials, was fully functional, and armed with a payload of destruction. But the Axis powers were concerned that if it were used Allied scientists would figure out its secret and reproduce it, and the advantage would be gone, quite apart from the fact that it would escalate the destruction and death on both sides. Simone was surprised to pick up this concern from her senior man, as well as from the other minds around the place, which she sampled as if she were at a buffet. She was more rational than this lot even when dead drunk, she decided. They were supposed to be cool-thinking strategists, not stuffed with unfinished, frankly *amateurish* half-formed thoughts. On the plus side, they weren't all brutal psychopaths, which begged the question why follow someone who clearly was just that.

This mind reading lark was pretty incredible. It turned everybody into spies on her behalf. It was a power not to be used lightly. Even drunk she knew that. If she were to talk, all her words would come out slurred. But she wielded such a gift. Sober she was unworthy, drunk she was unworthy, but she was still less of a menace to the world than...

It was useful that currently it was an effort to remember his name, as it gave her a chance to stop trying. If she thought him, maybe she'd inadvertently call him.

It's lucky I don't have to *say* inadvertently, she thought.

Her latest conquest was heading towards the great vertical missile, giving her an excellent view of the thing. Then something began to happen: The metal sides of the silo in which it was housed began to peel back, and it was possible to see that the beast was larger and longer than it first appeared, as a little more of its massive shape eased its way outwards and upwards. She listened to the mind she occupied. It was the mind of a scientist, and woefully uninterested in the impact on human lives on the thing he had co-created.

It seemed that they had been told to stand by after the liberation of Paris. This missile was battle ready, and trained on London. Her agitation at having this confirmed instantly affected her new ride. In fact there was a mutual disturbance: His previous calmness had given way to her shocked reaction, and his heart was beating too fast, while his breath came quickly. Suddenly he was on the floor and hyperventilating, with no idea why, so there she was, too. She scrambled into the mind of the medic who rushed up, and then out, and back to herself and her own body, as it nestled safely in the surrounding overgrown parkland.

Better things to do than cut the grass, she supposed. Or worse.

How did she really get here, she wondered. She was drunk, and heading for Hitler, who was in Berlin. This wasn't Berlin, but it was clearly a key location, where his greatest weapon was being developed. How had she just happened to turn up here?

There was only one convincing answer: Kerr must've brought her here, either physically brought her, or lured her, more subtly. So drunk was she that either approach could've worked. But why would he do that?

And then a thought came into her mind as if it had been sent there.

Because if I can't have you, no one will.

She was on her feet immediately, feeling quite sobered up, although this was probably a bit optimistic. Then something happened; a noise. A menacing sort of noise, although so far still a background sound... and then louder. The deep note sounded like the earth beneath them all was being tortured.

The explanation for the noise came swiftly from the minds around it. The missile didn't need a plane to drop it on a desperate population. It was its own delivery mechanism. It had taken years to develop, and many blind alleys and backward steps had been part of the journey, but here it was, pointed at and programmed to destroy a great city.

A cacophony of chattering minds were giving her this information but she knew from the unnatural sound what was happening. It was going to be launched. Today. Almost now, in fact.

It was no good hovering around out here. She needed contact with a single mind, preferably a well-informed one. She sprang to the topmost branches of a tree, from which it was a very long jump to the roof of the building housing the silo and the deadly missile, and upwards, too, but there was no use wondering if she could make it, and no use entertaining any self-doubt at all. She finally had a mission: it wasn't to kill Hitler, or even to aid D Day or help liberate Paris, although hopefully they had distracted Kerr – Sir William – from killing too many people during his visit there. And it wasn't even to kill the bad vampire.

It was this. She had to stop this. So she leapt from the tree, and to her amazement and panic, fell. She needed to keep calm, to be in touch with her centre while she was being very active and dynamic. And the centre moves, but imperceptibly, while causing huge changes at its periphery.

She wasted no time in picking herself up and taking a run at the side of the building, and did not trouble to wonder if anyone noticed her running up a vertical wall. It was too late to worry about that.

She ran across the roof, which was of corrugated metal, till she reached a pair of opened doors, like trap doors. She was used to those. She plunged through and found herself sliding down the side of the rocket. It must look quite funny, but no one was laughing. Instead there were shouts and a lot of swearing.

She controlled the last bit of her entrance by slowing herself down as if to step demurely on the floor, but she wasn't going to do it that way. Instead, she leapt into a gathering of bewildered Germans, soldiers and scientists, and attacked them with everything she had. She had plenty.

She heard someone make a sound that sounded like 'shoot', in German. Several people shouted Nein. The business end of the rocket, which packed all the explosives, was quite a way from any guns but the space they were in, though large, was enclosed, and who knew what a ricochet would do?

Soldiers were pouring in, and a man was telling them to stab her, and not to shoot her. They piled on top of her but could not prevail. She called on every ounce of her vampire strength, kicking, punching, biting... She could do this indefinitely, she could take on the whole German army, she felt invincible. But meanwhile it was a distraction, and springing into the air she saw a figure moving away and towards a door.

She felt the intention coming from that mind. The debate about the dangers of using the rocket no longer mattered. Someone was taking history into their own hands. In a second the figure was through the door... and she was surrounded, as outnumbered as a Spartan at Thermopylae but just as determined and in her case, likely to survive. For a moment she felt despair, but jumping up again, she ran across the heads and shoulders of those around her and kicked the door down.

A man in a white coat was pressing some buttons, while looking through a window that gave him a view of the melee at ground level. He tried to back through another door.

"Get out of here now," he hissed, "or we'll all be fried!"

She grabbed him. "What have you done?"

"I've started the sequence. Now everybody must vacate these levels."

"Stop the sequence now!"

"It cannot be stopped!"

She grabbed him by the throat, almost crushing his windpipe.

321

"I said, stop the sequence!"

She wanted to hurt him, but it would not help, and if she killed him she'd regret it. Besides, she could read his mind.

"You'd better evacuate that lot, then," she said, indicating the window. Through it she could see panic starting, and she knew it was because they were now in danger of incineration. That's a poor design, she thought at him. She felt him think it too, believing that her thought was his own, although that didn't seem to be too much of a stretch, as it became clear that he was concerned that the order was being carried out too fast: Safeguards were not in place, and they had tests still to do. The control room wasn't ultimately supposed to be where it was, but further away from the site, with cameras to relay what was going on to a safe distance.

They might all die, his mind exclaimed. But Simone was damned if she was going out of her way to save this lot. London was about to be obliterated, and she was the only person who could stop it.

She wasn't as mighty as this awful invention, but she was determined.

The chains that bound the beast to the ground had been released, and lay at its base. She left the room and was gratified to see soldiers pushing and shoving to get out of the room and away from the rocket, because as a consequence they were now ignoring her. Someone was trying to shout orders, including 'Get her!' but no one heeded them, discipline collapsing in the face of death. Simone headed for the chains. They could have stopped a ship, but she picked up a link as though it weighed nothing, then she broke it off: It was redundant. She wrapped the remainder around her waist, and leapt onto the rocket, which although vertical, had handholds not yet folded flat, though they soon should be, else she would have slid down it again. But she had time to wrap the chains around the rocket and herself, snapping two links to make a catch and thereby chaining herself to the rocket for all the world like a suffragist chaining herself to railings. Meanwhile, beneath her the heat was palpable.

She prayed because, why not? Pascal had recommended wagering that there was a God, because if it turned out there wasn't, you would die and never know anything about it, and if there was, well, you'd always been a believer, and could hope for a spot in heaven. Or something like that.

If the rocket blew here, she would die in the fire of the explosion. Probably it would be worse than the ones she'd seen Philippe emerge from, many times worse. As it growled beneath her she whispered 'bye, world', and commended her soul to her Maker, hoping that she had one, apart from Kerr.

And as the growl turned into a roar and as she felt the thing begin to move, someone emerged from the chaos of fire and smoke and yelling Germans, and of course, it was Kerr, jumping from what appeared to be a standing start onto the rocket and hooking his arms into the other side of her chains. A new, prolonged loud shriek that set her hairs standing on end indicated the roof was sliding back. But there was no countdown, because nothing was going according to plan. It seemed likely to Simone that it was Kerr who had preempted the launch. The roof should have retracted fully before the rocket began to move: Something was wrong.

Kerr started to laugh, and then the thing broke the surly bonds of earth, and she found out what vertical take-off meant. Fortunately the roof had opened just in time to let it go to meet its destiny.

She clung to the rocket with the help of the chains and an immense strength, no longer able to hear if Kerr was still laughing, and wondered how she could get the thing off course. Then she got distracted because they were still going straight up and it was becoming ridiculously cold. She felt sleepy, and realised it was the cold making her lose consciousness. She wondered if she could survive a fall from thirty thousand feet. Theoretically, she could, so long as it was dark. But boy, would it hurt.

The rocket, obeying some instruction deep in its circuits – she was a bit vague about how it worked – started to incline towards the horizontal, until it was following the earth's now perceptible curve. The view was incredible: No one before her had seen such sights, unless you counted Kerr, who was squatting on the rocket's body, just as Simone now was, though both still clung to their chains. It doesn't matter, she thought, if I just have a little sleep; strange desire for a vampire, but she'd never drunk so much…

Kerr still looked like he was laughing, but the noise of the wind as well as the roaring sound of whatever was going on inside the rocket rendered his laughter inaudible. But she heard him in her head; just the thing she had tried for so long to avoid.

He didn't want her to fall asleep, as she would fall off, he told her, and most certainly die, and if she'd ever thought he wanted her dead, he didn't. He loved her, or so his mind whispered to hers. She brightened his lonely existence. No other woman…

323

Survived being turned into a vampire while remaining sane, for if one had, she'd run from you, thought Simone. As I will, if I live.

Then I'll punish you. I'll kill everything you love, he responded.

Well, I guessed that, she answered silently, as the rocket dipped its nose down from the horizontal so it was now heading back to earth with its huge cargo of explosives.

It was a good thing they hadn't gone much higher, because a glimmer from the east was already heralding the sun. Beneath then now was darkness, and little in the way of light except for the moon. But they were over the Channel. And the moon was tipping the waves with its light.

Blackout Britain meant that there was little light on land but their night vision was enough to help them see where London was, and Simone knew she had little time. She started to rock her body from side to side, and the rocket began to move with her. Kerr was still on board, astride it now, and still appearing to enjoy himself.

"I'll help you save London if you come away with me," his thoughts promised, though not seeming to take either her or himself seriously.

She had a thought, and threw the available part of her body towards him, pushing him before he'd had a chance, or so she hoped, to clock the thought. It must've worked, because taken by surprise, he fell, dangling from the rocket by a length of chain. Then the rocket flipped back to horizontal and they were no longer heading to the city.

All she had to do was keep him there until they reached... where now, allowing for the curvature of the earth? The missile was travelling on a north-west trajectory... How much fuel did it have?

It was wide enough to stretch her legs across but really, it wasn't that big and it was probable that it had only sufficient fuel to reach the capital. They had altered its destiny already: It would not land on London. Now it would keep going along with the world until it fell out of the sky. Possibly there was a bit of fuel extra to what was needed, strictly speaking, and then maybe it would fall into the Irish Sea. Or maybe it would fall in the Midlands, or else perhaps... Liverpool. And between London and Liverpool there were lots and lots of people.

Lights were visible down below, which they shouldn't have been... but some people would not be told. The impression they gave, of widely scattered, small communities was entirely misleading. Due to the blackout, great cities lay in darkness, more or less.

If they could get past Liverpool out onto the sea she would have to bring it down, fought by Kerr, probably. He was smiling at her, laughing almost, and in a bizarre way she could see why, because this was an experience no one on earth but them had ever had, and the world below was like their playground, as they powered through the heavens like gods. It was exhilarating, and the only thing detracting from the feeling was the fact that they must die. Probably. If they went into the sea it mightn't blow up, and all that would befall them was a long and weary walk through the gelatinous water. Simone, who considered herself a natural pessimist, thought crossly that these were the hopes of the crazed vampire sitting opposite her, now smiling as if he hadn't a care, as if they were kids on a seesaw.

Reading her thoughts, he bounced up and down at his end, then shrugged. Willing to help, he thought.

We don't know if that will help or make things worse, she answered, impatiently.

So they travelled on until it was possible to see the broad silver of the Mersey, fringed by the city. With a desperate twist of her lower body, she just managed to move the rocket into line with the river, because she could feel the power ebbing. With her heightened senses she was aware that the fuel was almost gone. The rocket wanted to follow the coast from here but that would endanger towns and cities along that trajectory. Kerr saw what she was trying to do, and read it in her mind: he too could feel the rocket begin its inexorable descent. For Simone, it was different.

He concealed the thoughts he didn't want her to know, in a way she couldn't manage to do herself, in relation to him, presumably because he had made her. So she couldn't find out why he wanted to help, but she knew he did.

Together they jerked the missile slightly out of its path and sent it following the gleam of the great river out towards the sea. It had proved worryingly easy to do, as they were no longer fighting the full power of the rocket.

We can jump into the river below, he thought. It's a long way, but we'd survive. We could rest under the water till nightfall, then walk ashore. We could even survive a jump onto land from this height, although it would be very, very painful, and we'd soon need shelter.

You jump if you want, was her terse reply.

It was not possible to judge the outcome with any certainty. The rocket was a lot slower and she could see the country, then the city sliding past, when till now everything had gone by so fast and so far beneath them that it was a blur. It was possible that the missile would drop into the river and sink to the bottom, and either the water would stop it from exploding or there would be a minor eruption of water and perhaps a small wave would hit the shore. Or something much bigger and nastier could happen, and this was a heavily industrialised port, just thinking about waking up, with a busy day ahead for its inhabitants. Simone did not feel she could risk it.

Kerr yelled through the noise of the wind. "It's been a great ride," he said, snapping his chains, and he paused while his mind added...

...but it's nearly sunrise and, while the excitement of ending in a fireball with you had its appeal, being so dramatic and all, the most I can expect now is possibly months pushing through jelly at a nightmarishly slow pace. So, see you in Hell, or Berlin, or wherever.

With that, he was gone, and she was way past him before he hit the water.

The rocket was slowing and dropping. She could see the sea ahead, but the now sluggish rocket might not make it, and the sun was about to rise behind her. She was so slow now that she could see early bird fishermen preparing to dig for bait in the estuary mud, and some of them saw her.

A woman chained astride a rocket in flight was not the commonest of sights, and the fishermen who saw it did not share it with their fellows, probably because they feared the mockery, but then fishermen are a taciturn bunch at the best of times.

She felt the sun as it peeped over the horizon. Her back was getting hotter. And then, there was a beach, and they were over it, above the sea. She could not steer the rocket at all, not now: It would go as far as it could, out into the Irish sea. The pain as her back began to smoulder was indescribable. And so she snapped her chains, and dropped into the water, as the missile, freed from its burden, flew a little further and then dropped gracelessly from the air down into the water.

Chapter Eighteen

Lasciate ogni speranza voi ch'entrate

Abandon hope... (Dante)

Months, he'd said... months.

The explosion had been huge, tearing through the water, and ripping a giant hole in the sea bed, hurling Simone and a lot of fish and other sea life and detritus through the sea. But it still seemed like jelly to Simone and did nothing so useful as divide, like the Red Sea, leaving a path; something she'd secretly hoped might happen. If only she could swim through the blubbery substance up to the surface, there might be a ship she could hide herself on till it reached shore. That was the hope, but it turned out that she was virtually buried alive.

No momentum could be summoned in this world seemingly made of blancmange. There could be no swinging of limbs, just an unending struggle against a resisting substance. She walked across the bottom of the sea, one foot struggling to place itself in front of the other, being resisted at every step. It seemed impossible to power her way through, and it was puzzling: How was it that her strength didn't seem to help? In any case, that strength appeared to be diminishing, since she had no nourishment available. She knew that there were plenty of fish in the sea, allegedly, but she couldn't reach them.

She didn't even know, for sure, that she was making her incremental progress in the right direction, but then she wasn't sure that there was a right direction... how wide was the Irish sea? How far had she got before the thing went up? Thirty miles? But that was just a pointless guess. The truth was that she had no idea. She had to assume that the English coast was nearer than the Irish coast, because she'd only just made it out of the estuary and into deep water, hadn't they? Speed and distance had been difficult to estimate when she was riding a missile across England, and down here in the dark it was easy to lose one's bearings. She could be going in circles.

A shuddering panic gripped her cold dead heart. She wanted to scream but her mouth was blocked with jelly. She tried to move, but she was imprisoned in the substance. It was much harder to move in any direction than she recalled from the last time she'd waded through water. It dawned on her that she was in deeper water than she had been that time... so the pressure of the water was greater and it offered even greater resistance.

Of course. Kerr was an experienced vampire and knew how it would be, that's why he'd bailed out above the river, which would be much easier; not so much weight, nor distance, and either bank would be a welcome haven.

Now, though, he was probably hiding out in the shallows, waiting for dusk till he could roam through Liverpool, or some settlement nearby, drinking human blood without a care for whether his victims lived or died.

Kerr belonged in hell, but it was Simone who was battling to suppress the hysteria she was feeling at the horror of her predicament. He'd known what it would be like, but he hadn't made it clear to her. He had accompanied her on her wild ride but he'd known he would jump ship at the appropriate moment, that is, before it had real consequences for him.

Well, he was evil, so no surprise. He had imprisoned her for what could be eternity in a dark, cloying loneliness so profound that not only was she without any human or vampire companionship but there didn't seem to be any living thing down here but herself. She pushed through, one step at a time, each step delivering another faceful of gunk which she wiped away as best she could with a hand also covered in gunk. And that hand was pushing against the pressure of many fathoms of jelly, just like the rest of her.

It was agonisingly slow, but the worst thing of all was not knowing whether she was going the right way, which of course was the shortest way to land. But she couldn't just stand there, she had to do something, however futile.

Simone lost track of time, as well as direction. She envied prisoners, who at least knew the length of their sentence, and knew too that freedom might be behind a wall, but at least they knew where the wall was.

Then, after minutes, or hours, it seemed that something had made some progress, because movement began to disturb the jelly, and the next thing she knew she was surrounded by fish, swimming incredibly quickly through the water, until they were within inches of her, when they would tantalisingly slow down. Seeing them she was inspired to summon all her power and strength so she could reach out and pick one off as though it were an apple on a tree. It was strange, but it was handy.

The blood in the fish's body ran as freely as any other blood, which was odd, as its high water content should surely make it jelly-like. But the same should probably apply to all the water-containing substances she'd come across on land. It seemed that the ratio of water to other stuff in any liquid had to be very high indeed before it went gelatinous.

As the shoal of fish passed around her She guzzled the blood of as many of them as she wanted, and felt much stronger. Well-fed, she was more optimistic. Where fish were plentiful, she reasoned, there should be fishermen. She walked through the fish, but there was no net cast, and it wasn't really a surprise, because she would have picked up the chatter of human minds well before she came across what they were doing. All she could do was hope that one day she'd come to the end of this sea.

She prayed to any God that existed: she wasn't proud. Time passed but she had no way of measuring it. The first time she sensed the nearness of human beings they were too far away for her to reach before they'd moved further, and were lost to her.

They were in a submarine, and they were German. To get at them, she would've had to rip a hole in the sub, which would not have achieved much except kill a lot of people. It would take an enemy vessel out of action, which was probably saving Allied lives, yet her heart was not in it. But she could cling to it, somehow, and then presumably she would travel with it, at its pace – which was very different than that of the fish – at least, those fish that came close enough to her to appear to be almost as slow as she was.

Simone was disappointed with herself. She should be devising a new theory of physics to incorporate an explanation of the vampire's relationship with water, and how it affected objects that came within the vampire's field of influence, which itself was a departure from everything she knew.

But all she wanted was to get out of this mess and… well, that, she thought, was really all she wanted. But the vessel moved swiftly, and she could not reach it. If they scanned the sea bed, somehow, they might see her, making strange gestures as though she were a mermaid trapped in glue, or a person brain-damaged, whose limbs could not stretch as others' did, and who could make only the tiniest movements. Or even, perhaps, a statue fallen from a ship carrying antiquities to somewhere safe from bombing: that was how little headway she was making. Her clothes were modern, and did not resemble draperies, but she was in absolute rags. She could have been a maiden pursued by a lustful god, her lower limbs beginning to turn to bark, instead of a young woman reduced to her underwear, apparently wrestling with invisible spirits at the bottom of the Irish sea.

After that there were no more submarines, though there were, as the saying goes, plenty of fish. And there were, as she'd hoped, fishermen, but she couldn't get close enough to hitch a ride on their boats before they were far away. She tried influencing their minds, but she was no siren, luring men to their doom with her singing, and she was picking up that all she'd done was to generate a deep discomfort in her targets, so that she could feel their fear, their sense that something was calling them from the depths, and if they listened, that is where they would end up too. It happened more than once that fishing trips were cut short by spooked fishermen, who decided that their inevitable mockery at the hands of their friends was worth getting away from whatever it was.

She did, however, get inside their heads a little way, enough to discover that she was going the wrong way, heading towards neutral Eire, which would have been fine except that England was a lot nearer. So that was something. She followed as fast as she could, hoping to stay in the right direction, but a toddler learning to walk could have outpaced her and it wasn't long before the boats were gone again, though luckily the nets left traces of their passing so she could follow for a while, like Hansel and Gretel finding their way.

Her personality seemed to fade, or so she felt, without any company or stimulus, and she became just a creature, a creature like others at the bottom of the sea, though not adapted to her environment at all. She wrestled with the jelly-like water, and walked a little through it, each day, but it was only inches. She tried doing sums. If England is 100 miles away, and I move 6 inches a day, that makes...

But she didn't seem to be able to concentrate enough to work it out. Perhaps part of her was wise enough not to let her brain do that terrible sum, because it was trying to keep her sane.

She tried reciting ancient tales of gods and demons, in her head, of course, or else her mouth would fill with the stuff that surrounded her, but then would find herself remembering some of the shocking punishments these beings would visit on anyone who offended them. Some of the punished deserved their fates, being guilty of some dark, dark crimes, like serving their own kids up to the gods for dinner; nightmare stuff.

So she tried to think of jollier tales. But at last she surrendered to fate, and reduced herself, as much as she could, to her dark world of continual pushing, with her whole body, against the customised coffin of jelly that enclosed her.

Now she felt detached from her thoughts. Next, they seemed to fragment into white noise. She forgot her name. She forgot her feelings, then forgot she'd ever had them. She forgot the world, and all the people in it. She was a zombie, a creature that moved very slowly, here at the bottom of the sea, where there were no storms, or changes from light to dark.

Then at last she became nothing, nothing at all, dumb as seaweed.

And then she heard minds, thinking, and raising her head, saw that some light was filtering through the water above her. She didn't realise that this meant that the sea was shallower now, which in turn meant that she had made progress towards the shore. She didn't realise it because she couldn't think anymore.

If she hadn't been so hungry, if there hadn't recently been a shortage of fish coming within her grasp, she might not even have gone after the boat, which was almost above her, because she couldn't make sense of the world, couldn't cogitate. But she was very hungry, and just as sharks live entirely by instinct, and that instinct was to kill and eat, so now did she.

The boat above was a trawler, not that large. Simone didn't know that. She was empty, in every possible way. Instinct alone remained, and it was communicating to her, in no known language, that there was food nearby. It was a long time since she had been concerned about escaping from the hell she dwelt in. That was too difficult for her to understand now but she understood she needed that food, desperately.

So when the net was lowered, and it was close enough, and moreover, stayed close enough, she grabbed it, and struggled a little at the strange feeling, trying to understand, then trying to thrash, but her movements were too slow, and she got entangled.

She didn't know what was happening but without reason, instinct can be a cruel master: Appetites and terrors rule the being, and so she was panicking and terrified. Then she felt herself being dragged upwards. Fortunately for her, by now it was dark.

The trawler had its own fierce lights, and soon the crew were hauling their catch in, and she was lying on a heap of fish, but more importantly, she was free of the prison that had held her so long.

For a few moments she lay there, virtually naked, a fish in each hand, biting at them desperately to get her nourishment. But as the night air caressed her limbs she smelled the human odour of the crew, five of them, and suddenly she lost interest in the fish.

The men briefly admired her naked form, but mainly just wondered at her presence. Not for long though. As they looked on, she rose and went to the nearest man, moving impossibly quickly, enjoying not only the slow return of vampire strength but the sudden loss of a constant resistance, which had been suddenly removed. A blink, and she was at his neck. A heartbeat later he was dead, and she was replete.

Her vampire nature, untrammelled by reason or kindness, goaded her into more killing. It urged her to fill up while food was easily available, and she had nothing left to resist it. But as she leapt to feed on the others, they did the wisest thing they could do, and jumped overboard.

Simone, full of delicious human blood, felt good, for the first time in ages, but it didn't last. With better nourishment came better functioning. Her memories began to return, and with them, realisation.

It was as if she'd turned her back while a tsunami arose behind her, and then became suddenly aware of the overwhelming despair about to sweep her away, but just before it all descended, felt its first beginnings... but really, no description of what came next would come close to the truth.

All at once, she broke, and she knew then what drowning was, and that she was experiencing it for the first time.

She remembered her name, she remembered what she was, and the restrictions as well as the power that went with being a vampire. She remembered her childhood and youth, and her decision to join the SOE. She remembered Kerr, aka Graves, and what he had done to her... by her request. She remembered her fellow 'good' vampires, and finally arrived at the conclusion that it inexorably led towards; that she was no longer good. She had killed a human being, and not because he was an enemy, nor in self-defence, nor in the defence of others, but because she was hungry. Like any vampire. Like Kerr.

But she did not drown in an ocean of regret: She did not allow herself to do so. The tsunami of sorrow dragged her under, just for a moment or two, but the very desire to survive that had made her agree to become a bloodsucker was still there, still powerful. So she called out to the men who went overboard, who were currently mere minutes from death by hypothermia, but in any case had not got life jackets on, and so were in a parlous state.

"I'm sorry! I'm sorry! I didn't mean to kill him, please, I won't hurt you, I was just so hungry."

She leaned forward over the side of the boat, a little gingerly, because she didn't want to fall into the sea again, not ever. The men treading water looked up at her, terrified. There was a dinghy, but it was on the other side of the boat – she had been between them and it – so their chances of survival were slim and getting slimmer.

She stretched out a hand, and they regarded it without reaching back to her.

"Look," she cried, "Let me help you."

For a spy, Simone was a very open person, and her default was always to tell the truth. Now this was probably because she was too lazy to invent lies, and mostly took the easier option, but she couldn't think of any other approach just at that moment.

"I am a vampire, you've seen it. I can't deny it. I have been under the sea for years, with nothing to eat, but before that I never killed a person. But I was mad with hunger… I swear I won't kill anyone else, it's the first person I've…'

One of the men looked like he was in trouble, already looking tired and cold. His friend pushed him towards her outstretched hand.

"Closer," she said anxiously. She'd do anything to save them except risk falling back into that sea. The man came within a couple of feet of the boat. She stretched as far as she could, and at last had his arm. She dragged him close and lifted him with one hand.

Using both her hands, she hauled him aboard. He lay on the deck, shivering and blue. Then she beckoned to the others, who were still treading water. They swam towards her helping hand, and each of them experienced being lifted by it, and then both hands, and wondered where her strength came from and what she was, as she lifted each to safety.

Once they were aboard again, the bravest of them moved towards the shivering one, and before he could speak, she told him to get a towel and a blanket.

"All of you," she said, "all of you dry yourselves. I swear I won't hurt you. How far to England?"

Before they could answer, she'd read it from them. Less than four miles. The sky was black, so there was enough time.

"As fast as you can," she said, and they rushed to obey. They were thinking about trying to destroy her. She was reading their complicated thoughts; fear, rage, disbelief, and an unsureness about how to act. "And get me some clothes, for heaven's sake."

They got her some fisherman's clothes, but there was no footwear available at anything remotely resembling her size, so she made do with a scratchy jumper and some shiny oilskin trousers that made her feel like a clown, even eschewing the floppy shoes.

One of the men, in particular, was angry and it was strong enough for him to act. Once she was satisfied that they were underway and heading in the right direction at their top speed she moved closer to him, and turned her back, subtly, or so she hoped. She had noticed the axe, resting in its position in the cabin, on a wall. She was picking up on what he meant to do, and his thoughts were so loud she was surprised the others couldn't hear his anxious brain ticking over, like she could.

The next bit hurt. She allowed him to take the axe and made sure, in the instant that she had, that his swing would connect with her back, and not her neck; no need for that kind of risk.

He came in from her right side, and she let the axe touch her, which was painful, but she didn't allow the blow to do more than that. She swung round in a movement and at a speed that none aboard could follow, and disarmed the fisherman, chucking the axe a great distance away from the boat. Then she knocked him down with what for her was a gentle tap.

Perhaps it would have impressed them even more if she'd have let him slice and dice her, then let them see her put herself together again, but it would hurt a lot. Hopefully she'd done enough to impress upon them that they'd better do as she said and just get on with it.

She helped Bob to his feet. She'd got his name from his colleagues' minds, of course.

"Well, now, Bob..." she enjoyed his shocked expression. "I really am sorry that I killed your friend. As I explained, I am a vampire and mustn't let my appetite turn me into a killer. I wasn't myself, I have been at the bottom of the sea for a long time. I won't let it happen again."

Bob looked wildly around, but no weapons were at hand now. He was unreconciled, and going a bit mad, so she bit him and rendered him unconscious. The others looked on, expecting the worst, but with no intention of interfering. Then she drank from him, and then dropped him, gently as a mother, on the deck, still alive but fast asleep.

And then she told them again about what she was, and how this was her normal method of nourishing herself, and how being turned into a vampire involved consent, and usually it was just a small feed, after which sometimes money might change hands. Then she apologised for murdering their colleague. But they just looked blank, and she didn't need mind-reading to smell the atavistic fear on them. So in the end she stopped talking, and was rewarded by seeing a glimmer in the east that she was pretty sure wasn't the dawn, not yet.

Their minds told her it was Liverpool, but it seemed, even from however many miles off, to be dangerously bright.

"Don't they bother with the blackout?" she asked. Then a thought occurred.

"Have we won?"

The noise from the men's minds became a cacophony. It was difficult to make out what they were thinking at first. But gradually something became clear to her, and it made her feel really scared.

The war was indeed over. And then, she had to face the truth they could not help but tell her.

It had been over for more than twenty years.

This takes a lot of digesting, she told herself. How could all that time have passed while I was under the sea? How did my awareness shrink?

And underneath the shock she observed in herself that there was a certain jubilation, because surely her murderous deed could not be blamed on her, but on the terrible circumstances she'd endured, so terrible that she'd mistaken years for days, so terrible that she'd become an utterly desperate, bewildered pawn of her unnatural instincts... terrible, terrible, all of it.

And now the coast was a lot nearer and she was impatient to walk on land again. As soon as they could, they obeyed her instructions to ready the dinghy, and she insisted that Bob rowed her ashore. There was no harbour where they came to shore, but there was a beach, albeit made of mud. She insisted that he dragged the boat up the beach before clambering out of it. She was taking no chances with the sea.

He knew better than to try and run for it: He'd seen her speed, as well as her strength.

"It's all right, you can go back to the boat," she said, and he began to push the dinghy back out to sea.

Not even a goodbye, she thought. Wonder what they'll do when the police ask them about the one I...

But now there was another figure on the shore, and he was coming towards her.

She stood, her legs still wobbly, and before she could even see the approaching Nemesis that had a mission to despatch her, she opened her mind so that he could see the events that had led up to the murder she had committed. It was a he, she knew before he got close enough for her to see. His name was David.

Vampire Dave, she thought, after literally putting him in the picture of what had happened. Then she moved from pictures to thoughts that were more akin to speech. At last we meet. I'm sorry, I must look a terrible mess. I've been at the bottom of the sea.

And now I've been a naughty girl. I haven't had time to let it sink in. When it does, I may just walk into the sunrise. But you can't understand, even when I show you, and if I'm to die it will be when I decide, not you, not those two in Paris...

He got closer, until he spoke. He had a bag, not a rucksack but a patterned bag on a bit of rope, hanging off his shoulder. He had the idiosyncratic Liverpool accent, more pronounced than Philippe's lilting tones, or the generic foreign – to British ears – of Kerr or Christophe, who had both been around long enough to sound a bit like everybody.

"I'm not going to try to kill you. I don't fancy my chances anyway: I know you can fight."

"Could fight," she said, pulling the uncomfortable, oversized oilskins around her. "Back before I was sent to the bottom..."

"Of the sea," he returned.

He had long hair, prone to curling, probably a dark brown in the daylight, almost black to her night vision. Was he sired in Regency times?

He laughed.

"Fashion, love. Perhaps a repudiation of wartime values. It is a very different world, and yes, we won."

He reached into his eccentric bag, and pulled out a dress. Hope it fits, he thought. I had to guess. He turned his back, politely, while she discarded her oilskins and put it on. It was alarmingly short, especially when her underwear was in shreds. Trust a bloke to forget the important things.

This won't do, she thought at him impatiently.

It'll have to for now, he answered silently. It's not long till dawn.

He beckoned, and since she knew by now that he wasn't about to kill her she followed him across the beach and onto some steps which led up to a road, deserted at this time of night. He took her hand and together they ran the way vampires do, leaping from foot to foot almost too fast for the eye to follow. They stopped, just in time, in front of a large house in a road of large houses, opening the front door as the light in the east began to intensify into rays of unmistakable sunshine.

A woman wearing an apron appeared as if she'd sprung out of the floor, and gave Simone an admonishing glance.

"You only just made it," she scolded. "You shouldn't be taking chances, not with your experience."

How does she know about my experience, Simone wondered. Then she realised that the woman was addressing Vampire Dave.

"Oh, don't nag, Doris, there's a love. Do you like tea?"

Simone realised that he was asking her, not Doris. Doris looked as though she loved tea.

She nodded, and Doris went to make it. As she moved past Simone to, presumably, the kitchen, Simone noticed scars on her neck. Old scars.

Simone had known at once that Doris was not a vampire, but she was surprised that the housekeeper, for that must be what she was, had allowed her boss to feed on her. It could get dangerous, if he lost control.

As you have just done, he thought at her. Her fault... she hadn't bothered to hide her own thoughts.

I was in extremis, she responded.

We all have the occasional emergencies, he agreed.

"My housekeeper has a very easy life. No cooking, no washing up, the occasional dusting session. I am very undemanding as an employer, but in the past there have been times, though very rarely, when blood is unavailable. She likes cats, and suggested herself as an alternative when she saw me, once, about to pounce on next door's moggy. I pay her very well indeed, but the blood is given freely. Well, not too freely, obviously. One has to know when to stop."

"And your usual source?"

"The same as our friends in Paris. A rota of ladies of easy virtue. In fact one of them gave me the dress you're wearing."

So presumably that's why there was no underwear, thought Simone.

"Tomorrow evening I will take you shopping. I mean, properly: we don't have to stage a robbery. I did all that a while ago. I have plenty in the bank, but the opening hours are a bit inconvenient. Doris will go for me, although I've got a stash under my mattress. Mind, I think some of the notes may be no longer legal tender."

Doris returned with tea, and two plates, upon each of which sat a piece of toast, buttered.

"I know he likes his tea and toast in the morning after the end of a long night," she said.

Suddenly it became clear. Doris had been Dave's mistress. She had grown older, and he had not. It was less a matter of reading this from her than an explosion of emotion like a fire, successfully damped down for far too long. But her expression barely wavered, and her movements didn't change. For Simone, the woman had nothing but fear and hatred, those well known companions.

Vampire Dave probably ate the toast with difficulty, since it tasted of little to a vampire, and even the tea was unappealing, tasting of hot water... which was more than water did, having no taste at all but a truly horrible texture. Simone wasn't ready to cope with drinking water, but tea was all right. Soon she would have to have a bath and wash away the salt, and it would be like bathing in blancmange; a thought to make her shudder. Meanwhile she wasn't putting up with this sly Liverpudlian, however much Dave indulged her.

"Thank you for the tea," she said, "but I... I can feel your intense dislike of me. We have only just met. I am a vampire like Dave. I will probably outlive you, while looking young as well. Forever, maybe, if I can bear it. That's the situation. It isn't going to change."

Doris flushed an angry red, turned around and was about to stalk away when Dave spoke her name, softly, and Simone saw the tenderness he still had for her. He ignored Simone's remarks, and Doris's glower. He wasn't one to let others' emotions affect him. Quite old, then, enough to be a little bit wise too.

"Have you got any clothes you could lend Simone? She's been lost under the sea for twenty years. I took her that dress but she's tall, she needs more length."

"Come with me," said Doris at last.

The house they walked through was panelled with wood throughout, like a stately home, though much smaller, more of a stately council house, although one with several bedrooms. It was full of books and beautiful furniture. It even had chandeliers in some rooms. Everything looked antique, and probably was, but when the lights were off it was gloomy. The windows were either left to the advance of the ivy, or had thick winter curtains blocking most of the morning sunlight.

Simone could feel Dave, ever so tactfully following her thoughts as she moved through the house in case I go berserk and start snacking on Doris, she knew. Don't give it a thought, she told him silently. I am no danger. I showed you the circumstances, which are not likely to occur again. I hope.

They went up the stairs, and Simone was shown to her room while Doris fetched some clothes from her own wardrobe. She didn't invite Simone in, perhaps wanting her privacy, or perhaps believing that old legend, regarding vampires' need for an invite. Simone wondered if the tale arose from a confusion about the need to ask a potential vampire for their consent to be changed. When Doris returned she asked outright why she had never asked Dave to change her, too.

"He wouldn't. He said that there was no guarantee I would not become a monster. I begged and begged. He feels guilty that because of him, I didn't have a normal life, but I don't regret it. Not for a minute."

Simone thought Dave was a fool to forge this bond and he would suffer terribly when this woman died, while Doris herself was already experiencing a different kind of suffering.

"He showed me his reflection, to put me off changing. And to put me off him. It made me heave at first, but then I just didn't look in mirrors when he was around. What woman doesn't have to overlook her man's failings? Will you take him from me?" she stared at Simone.

"You're one of a kind from what I hear. He's a gossip, he told me you lived with the two of them and had the bad one after you too."

Then, to Simone's horror, she got down on her knees.

"Be kind. Don't take him away, not yet. You've got a world of time. I will die eventually, you'll live forever, take him when I'm gone if you must!"

Simone was horrified. She yanked Doris to her feet.

"Don't kneel to anyone, keep your pride. I promise I have no designs on Dave or anyone else, vampire or human. Yes, I know you want a guarantee anyway, so I promise that under no circumstances will I have any romantic involvement with any of them…"

"No, that would be too hard, you never know what will happen. Just keep your claws off the one I love till I'm dead and buried, you can do what you like with the others."

Simone took Doris's hands in hers, looked her in the eyes and promised.

After that, they were able to sort some clothes out for Simone, who could not enjoy her reflection in the mirror but knew that she looked good. The housekeeper's wardrobe was not at all drab, as Simone had imagined it might be, given the domestic nature of her occupation. In fact it was quite glamorous, almost racey, some of it, which, given that she was a vampire's human lover, was probably to be expected.

No one mentioned that Doris's clothes fitted Simone better than it looked like they would Doris, nor the reason for this, which was that Simone was younger and thinner. No, that wasn't right, Simone reminded herself. She wasn't much younger, if at all. Well, ten years or so, at a guess. She had lost over twenty years under the sea, but that experience and the passage of time itself had left no mark on her, except to make her look even skinnier, which emphasised her bone structure, whereas Doris had carried some of the marks of age. Her waist was too thick for some of the items in her wardrobe, her hair was thinning, and was greying, although in a flattering way… silver streaks amongst the black.

Simone disapproved of Dave's weakness in loving this woman. He had deprived her of a partner in life with whom she could grow old, the two of them together. It appeared that he had robbed her of children, too, for none had been mentioned.

And then she heard someone telling her that Doris had never been able to have children, and that had been discovered prior to her meeting Dave, during a marriage entered into and regretted, long ago.

Get out of my head, nosey, she thought. Sorry, he thought back at her. Then she wrapped her mind up in an impenetrable cloud of junk thought, the sort of nonsense that paraded through the mind without adding up to anything. This was the way to get privacy if you were a vampire amongst other vampires, although some claimed that it all arose from unconsciousness anyway, and one might view it as valuable information, if one could decode it. She had listened as Philippe and Christophe had discussed the matter. She was content to wait till experience informed her views.

Vampires tended toward the philosophical, due to the nature of their condition, unless they were brutes like those whom Kerr, or rather Sir William, had created from often harmless human beings. Simone knew that William was also philosophical, which was no doubt what saved him from the degradation to which most newly made vamps descended, but she remembered agreeing with the lads that it was probably a Nietzchean take on things, while the other two were proud Neo Platonists and in Christophe's case, Old Platonists, given that he had met the bloke...

But he would deny the label, for he had, when questioned on his past by a curious Simone, told her that it was Socrates who taught him what life was about, and Socrates was also the teacher of Plato, which made Christophe the latter's equal, by any reckoning. Christophe, when he told her that, had the grace to look a little embarrassed and had added that he was inspired by her entry into their lives to write his reminiscences, and some thoughts on philosophy, for her to read. But no volume had emerged during the wait for D-Day and the liberation of Paris. He had been busy, to be fair.

Although he must have had some spare time during the last two thousand four hundred years...

It felt good, cleaning up and dressing nicely, although the clothes were a little old-fashioned, according to Doris. Simone thought they were fine, but she had been at the bottom of the sea for twenty years so what did she know? It also felt good to be in the company of a woman after all this time, once Doris was satisfied that Simone did not pose a threat to her... although Simone suspected

Dave now got his human needs met by whoever it was who helped cater for his vampire needs, and it may well be someone other than Doris. That, she supposed, was different. Dave probably kept even his commercial transactions civilised.

Even after her sojourn beneath the sea, when any companionship would have been welcome, Simone could appreciate the difference between female company and male. She was fond of the lads, as she liked to think of them, but it was only now that she realised how much they tried to impress her. It was a Pavlovian reaction to women, but she found it exhausting after a while, because it interfered with everything: it was just in the way.

She lay on the bed, as she used to lie with her mother, having a gossip, and chatted with Doris as if they were old friends. Simone read from her that she was willing to believe Simone's protestations that she had no designs on Dave, and she was really touched by the trust placed in her. She didn't want to go back and talk to Dave, not for a while. She just wanted to prolong this comradely feeling with another woman, especially precious because Doris might realise what Simone understood too well; that she was separated from the experience of being a woman. She was an immortal demon, didn't have periods, wouldn't die, couldn't get pregnant, but then, nor could Doris, apparently.

Doris had told her this, at which she had tried to look surprised. Doris seemed to have ceased to mourn this circumstance, so she tentatively wondered aloud whether it was true, or just an assumption. Then she confessed to Doris that she had been a virgin when she was changed, and nothing had occurred to alter that state since then.

She hadn't been sure about the lads, but there had been a moment when Christophe stayed with a certain lady long after he had dined on her neck, to the point where Simone had started to worry, and Philippe had stopped her from going to check that he wasn't getting carried away with the blood drinking. It's fine, he said, don't worry, leave him be.

She'd wondered at this laxity at the time.

The relationship between Doris and Dave was further evidence that male vampires could be lovers of ordinary women, but what about her? She had nobody to emulate. She was sure William was changing women, but equally that they couldn't last. they would soon perish, caught between their own, newly monstrous appetites and the controlling presence of William.

That's a bit presumptuous, she told herself. I broke from him, so cannot suppose that all female personalities are weaker than mine. Perhaps one day I shall have a true friend after all, someone who is more like me, someone with whom I can be real, and who can be real with me, and not have to compulsively show off all the time. And then she realised that a similar desire had caused Christophe to create the vampire William, aka Kerr, aka Graves. Better loneliness than bring more trouble into the world, if truth be told. The lads'll get used to me and behave in a more casual way, if they don't kill me as a menace to society after they find out what I've done.

She went downstairs to greet Dave, wearing her new clothes. He was reading the paper, which must have been delivered, as Doris had not yet been out, and Dave couldn't go. How domestic. Dave had also drunk his tea.

"Helps keep the water wet," he said cryptically, nodding at the mug. He then nodded at Doris, who had also come into the room. "Let's speak. She needs to be kept informed."

Chapter Nineteen

My son, if sinners entice thee, consent thou not

(Proverbs)

So Dave began telling his tale, which Doris must have heard before, probably several times.

As for Simone, Dave had been made aware of her entire history the moment he had faced her on the beach last night: She had been in no state to put up mental barriers and in fact he had known who she was before she had fully recollected anything, including herself. So it was his turn to tell his story.

"I was made by the vampire Kerr," said Dave, "who was still Sir William when I encountered the business end of his sword. Previous to that, I was not of particular interest, met no one famous and made no impression on history, but I was fighting for control of a petty kingdom in Wales. I declared myself a king, but was never crowned.

It was a fool's task, especially as the English were taking the part of the opposing side. I lost interest in what happened after I was changed. The English won, I believe.

I do wish all the brave warriors that fought that day and every day, on both sides, could for a moment feel the complete sense of futility I experienced, the sudden, 'Where am I? And why? Who are these people? Why are we maiming and killing strangers?'

He raised his voice at that, as if doing an impersonation of someone, but it was himself, Simone guessed, his younger, stupider self that he was imitating.

"Billy boy had wounded me badly. I was already on foot, my horse having been cut from under me. I had been fighting for hours and was exhausted. He came to the battle as it was ending, and the sun had just slipped below the encircling hills when he sought me out. I mustered all my dying strength but he wanted my life as a trophy. I saw that, then, but did not imagine the full truth of it.

The wound he had given me was deep into the side, like the one you suffered before your change... Oh, I'm sorry, I would have held back from looking, but I had to get into your head to understand if and how much of a danger you represented.

Anyway, he had delivered a similar blow to me with the intent that it should be fatal but only after he'd had enough time to tempt me."

"Does that mean it was Graves – Billy boy – who wounded me? I thought it was ordinary soldiers…"

"Of course it was, he couldn't be out in the daytime. That rule is unchangeable. But he will have instructed them as to where to aim their shots. Especially as he would have had intelligence that a woman was working for the Resistance. He must have rubbed his hands when you were brought in."

"I escaped, though."

"And how thrilling that must have been, to let you go while knowing that he would eventually tire of that stage of the game, and that he kept tabs on you and would catch up with you again when he was good and ready. How delightful too, that you soon encountered the Paris vampires, who would want you at their side forever, once they met you… even if you looked like the back of a tram, seeing as you are the only living female vampire that we know of… you don't, of course… he would rob them of you one way or another, so at least if you rejected him they would still suffer from your loss. Which goal he has achieved, if not permanently. They thought you dead, you know."

"And now?"

"Well, I could travel to the south coast, stand as close to France as England gets, and try with all my mental strength to project the news of your escape from the depths as hard as I could to Paris. Or we could use the telephone?"

Simone hesitated a bit. Perhaps, probably, the lads, as she had begun to think of them, would think that they had to kill her.

"Cheer up, love," said the former pretender to a Welsh throne, "We all make mistakes, and in their time they have too. One ought to be let off, for one mistake."

Philippe had killed, more than once, as she recalled. Christophe… no, she hadn't heard him confess to anything.

"Wait. Tell me what happened next. To you, I mean."

"He taunted me. That's no excuse, I know. Funnily enough, he taunted me with the promise of rulership over an earthly kingdom, and how it was all slipping

345

through my fingers, rather as the Devil does Jesus. Only I succumbed. The funny aspect of it is that as soon as I was changed, I lost all interest in earthly kingdoms. I had been brought up to expect to go to heaven. We all believed that, back then. Not so much, in England, now. But most people around the world, the majority believe in heaven, and hell. It's really only north-west Europeans who don't. Maybe the Chinese as well, they pray to their ancestors so I don't really know…"

"And how many people have you killed since being changed?"

"Not enough to turn me into a beast, but I might be tempted if I could get my singing voice back. Don't look surprised, it's a fact that Welsh people have the best voices. But now, there's an ancient stinking void where the breath used to live, and nothing sweet comes out of there any more. God knows, I should have stopped fighting, let anyone who wanted it become king, packed my harp and gone travelling, singing till I was too old, and then died like a natural man."

He looked into Simone's eyes, and let her read him. His memories came alive, very quickly, and died back again as further memories awoke. He was a trophy for William, a vampire who was once nearly a king, but he had kept his head a little through the change, and listened when William passed on bits of information that he understood he would need. This self-control, however minimal, distinguished him from most of his fellow warriors, and if things had gone differently, probably qualified him to be king.

Back then, he had realised that he'd just been feeding on one of these comrades in battle. So much for self-control, he'd not been aware he'd been doing it. He had cursed Sir William and blundered away through the night.

Then came the dawn and he was in a hut, where some frightened people were staring at him. He promised that he wouldn't hurt them, but they must find him some fresh blood. So they went out and came back dragging a badly wounded man whom he knew, Owain, who'd been fighting for his, David's, right to the crown.

The blood Owain was losing smelled strongly and invitingly of life and strength and vigour, so why waste it? Owain could not be helped. Why not save himself? But first, he had asked the dying man if he wanted immortality…

There was no problem, in those days, of convincing people that vampires, and indeed, other demonic entities were as real as the peasant next door, and that one's neighbour might very well, through some unfortunate encounter, be transformed into a witch or demon him or herself. So there was no time wasted by anyone exclaiming that they didn't believe it, what was happening etc. Owain didn't have much left in him, but what he had he used up in damning his erstwhile leader to hell and back. Never, he spat with his last few breaths, never would he lose his immortal soul and chance of heaven to live as a night crawling demon sucking the blood of beast and human... with his last breath, he cursed David, calling on God to punish him for his terrible sin. But David's lengthened canines were already buried deep in his neck, and the life giving blood was flowing out of the dying man and into him.

So he skulked among the poorest, hiding in their hovels, helping them as best he could in exchange for a little blood from their mangy cows or even from them, once he'd explained how he could do it without killing. A fat beast was an absolute treat: you could guzzle and gorge till you were bloated, treating the innocent animal as you would like to treat a human being, but daren't, for fear of degenerating into something worse than a beast; something wrong... something with no rightful place in the world. But so long as he made sure not to kill what little belonged to the poor, the occasional orgy of blood drinking was part of his armoury, a weapon of self defence that kept him from darkest sin.

At last he left the area and like all outcasts from rural communities decided to head for the anonymity of the big city, which back then was London, even though it wasn't really that big. Relative to everywhere else it was huge.

Fortunately he was a good-looking man, or vampire, and women were a source of sustenance, in the broadest sense. His dark curls and sensitive mouth got him regular snacks, once he'd convinced the lady in question that he wasn't about to gobble her up, and he'd get a roof over his head at the same time, like as not. I loved them all, he thought at her. Not my fault they'd up and die.

Aloud he said, "I didn't leave when they got old. I helped them when they were poor, a little bit of threatening behaviour and I didn't need to hurt anyone, just relieved a few unworthy individuals of some of their undeserved wealth, and brought it home to my girls. Fewer desperate women on the streets... I loved it when some lord's whelp wanted to join issue over my little thefts by drawing the sword. That helped me keep my hand in, though it was hard not to kill them... all right, you've read it from me, I killed a couple. By accident."

He took a sharp look at Simone, as she tried hard not to think the thought that instantly occurred to her.

This was a hard thing to attempt, and judging by his hastiness to get off the subject, it had failed anyway.

"Well, that's me," he concluded. I've met a few famous people, but far more infamous ones, and greater still is the number of those I encountered who have no claim to fame of any kind, and are not even a footnote in history. And now I actually am a footnote in history, in the indices at the back of academic studies of the endless wars of the Welsh. Believed killed in battle. Now, we're putting off this phone call... why? You don't want to die, and I don't want you to die..."

The telephone, which Simone had not even noticed, sat on a little table in the living room, tucked away in a corner as if infrequently used. Dave sprang to his feet, as if now his mind was made up to do this thing he was unable to wait any longer.

He dialled a long number. Simone heard a familiar voice answer 'yes, who is it,' in French.

"It's David," said Vampire Dave in his Liverpool/Welsh accent. He might not sing but there was still music in his speech, and an extravagant abuse of consonants. "I've got a big surprise for you. She's here, your lost girl. She's back."

A gasp headed down the line, so loud they all heard. Then a shout and a couple of expletives.

He handed the phone to Simone.

"Chris? Christophe? It's me, I'm alive. But I killed someone."

She summarised what had happened to an almost silent Christophe. He absorbed the information but it was clear he was a little shell-shocked,

Finally he answered, and spoke, quietly enough that he could not be heard except by Simone. But the others could piece together what he was saying by her replies. He was coming to Liverpool, with Philippe. They would either hire a plane or arrange to be transported across the channel by ferry, or perhaps a private vessel. All that mattered was not going outside in daylight, and that could be difficult, especially with customs and passport controls and all the rest of it. In the old days, plenty of hungry boat owners would be looking for extra work.

"Don't worry, no rush, I'll look after her till you get here," shouted Dave in the general direction of the phone, which earned him a dirty look from Doris and a warning glance from Simone, who didn't want some flirty vampire putting barriers of mistrust between her and her new and only female best friend. There were undertones to the phrase 'look after her' but they were easily deniable. It did seem unlikely, though, that Dave would have anything to prove after nine hundred or so years of successful seductions.

So they waited, and for amusement – for Simone could not relate to the square box which invaded the living space with news of the outside world, which seemed all bad – Dave produced a thick envelope that Christophe had sent him.

"Fancy some light relief? I guess this is supposed to be his answer to Plato, or as he'd rather have it, his response to Socrates. I've read a bit of it. Actually, give it back, if he's coming here he might ask me for my opinion on it. Sorry."

So Simone curled up on the sofa and shut her eyes for a vampire doze, which is not as deep as human sleep, while Dave re-acquainted himself with the few pages he'd read, and then handed them over to Simone.

Christophe had a style very different from that of his erstwhile friend.

'We are all slaves!' That was the arresting opening phrase. Even more arresting was the realisation that Christophe had typed the manuscript, which for Simone was a surprise. He was a very, very old vampire. Possibly even pens were in short supply, back when he was a human.

The manuscript continued. ' Let us look at the story of Inanna. She represents our eternal soul. She descends to earth via the planets, which guard the seven gates, at the invitation of her dark sister Ereshkigal. But at each gate she must discard her glories, necklaces, bracelets, beautiful robes, till she arrives naked, whereupon her sister casts her into a dungeon, and where she is visited by the 60 ailments, until a messenger of God comes to rescue her. Some say that the seven refers to the judges of the underworld, which are the dark versions of the planets. Inanna is saved after 72 hours, or years, which is a figure derived from the 72 years which is one degree of the celestial horizon and represents the time taken for the axis of the earth to move one degree as the sun shows at its ever changing rise. This movement is called precession.

It is close to the Biblical three score years and ten and therefore its use symbolises a human life span. From this we can deduce that Inanna's imprisonment represents the soul's incarnation in a body: that is the dungeon. And it is the stable that Jesus is born into, as well, for this world is nothing but a stable or a dungeon to the worlds of glory enjoyed by the immortal soul. He died for seventy two hours and was resurrected, in other words he died into this life but for a certain reason, to which we shall return, he remembered who he was, and what he came from, while he was alive. For that is the chief problem with the central character in these stories of being imprisoned in hell: they do not remember their origin, or only have brief flashes of memory, which just confuses and upsets them and leaves them restless and homeless throughout the worlds. The story does not end with death or crucifixion though. It ends with redemption, but cannot end until the protagonist learns their true origin, and hence, their true identity. There are many, many, many stories of heroes going down into the underworld, very often for three days, and then emerging. 3 lots of 24 hours. It's pretty clear that, at least according to these astro-archaeologists that Marlowe was spot on when he gave the lines to Mephistopheles: ' Why, this is hell; think'st thou that I, who saw the face of God, and tasted the eternal joys of heaven, am not tormented with ten thousand hells in being deprived of everlasting bliss?'

Well, thought Simone, that's dense with information, even if it is just mythology. I think my brain needs a rest for a bit, before I tackle any more.

Doris wandered in and out as she was reading. Simone had heard various appliances being used, and she went out to the kitchen and its utility room to stretch her legs and admire the washing machine. They hadn't really been available when she'd been human. But this one made an infernal noise and it got worse when it began to spin, finally starting to move across the floor. This made Simone laugh for some time, partly because she needed to, to let out the joy she felt at not being under the sea any more. So all right, she'd killed for blood. But at least she was free… up to a point. Perhaps the freedoms and constraints of her condition might be what Christophe's book was going to explain to her.

But as she leafed through the file of manuscript Dave had given her she realised that much of it was in note form and not yet incorporated into a body of work. For example, there were several pages headed 'In the Beginning', but whether that referred to the world in general or Christophe's life and times wasn't necessarily clear.

For instance, the mythical inventor, Daedalus of Crete, was to be credited with inventing vampires. Simone remembered that he was famous for losing his son, Icarus, who died when the wax on his wings melted, while he was trying to fly. According to Christophe's text he was a real person, renowned for his clever devices. He had even made a cow for the wife of Minos, Pasiphae, to mate with a bull that she had been cursed to love. Now that definitely was a myth, wrote Christophe. Such an attempt would be lethal, and the whole thing was really to do with astronomy, the Bull representing the astrological sign Taurus, and Pasiphae being a name for the Moon. Apparently it was all to do with the precession of the equinoxes, and so entirely metaphorical.

But Daedalus was a real person and attempted to bring his son back to life. He was less caring about others' sons and daughters though, as many died during his experiments, while he kept corruption away from Icarus by having ice brought from Mount Ida.

At last, by what means no one but Daedalus knew, Icarus came back to life. But the corruption had already taken hold, and it started with the brain. The thing that came back was not his son, and it was running amok, so Daedalus, whose heart was more broken, and whose pain was more extreme than it would have been if he had accepted the consequence intended by fate, had to kill the creature, which he accomplished with a stake to the heart.

And that would've been all, tragic enough, and a cautionary tale against trying to wrest away God's prerogative, except that one person had been fed a mixture of blood and other substances, not all of which Daedalus could remember, for he had destroyed all his records, not wishing to be reminded of his failure. But this one failed to die.

Daedalus concealed the survivor. The King had forbidden him from any more experiments in this area, and had even held sacrifices and ceremonies to placate the gods, because all who knew about it were troubled deeply, and afraid of divine vengeance, for it was an act of great hubris'

Daedalus aided the survivor to escape to Egypt. It was difficult, for the First Vampire was severely burnt before they realised he could not go out, even on an overcast day. If they had made this mistake in full sunshine, he would have been incinerated in seconds. But the devil has his favourites, and they were able to discover weaknesses and strengths and keep him from dying. Daedalus presented himself to the Pharaoh of the time, and in exchange for the marvels he created to assist Egypt and its rulers he was able to achieve his goal of allowing his creation a regular supply of human blood. It was no worse than the normal method of execution in those days, which was to throw people to the crocodiles.

At length they had to flee even Egypt, and while they were travelling across the desert at night, Daedalus died. He was an old man, so there was no need to assert that there had been foul play, but it has been said that his protege was starving, and such was his love for this substitute son that he allowed his creation to drink his blood, which he did till there was nothing left of the great inventor but a dessicated corpse.

As for the first vampire, he naturally gave himself the name Set. And now we see the number 72 play a part in the story once more.

We do? thought Simone. Why… and where..? For the bundle of papers turned out to be in no particular order at all, and it was a case of a distraction on every page. Chris, my boy, you need an indexer, she thought. And coherence. Bits of it were very coherent, but at the moment, nothing seemed to join up.

Dave appeared, and as soon as she saw him she knew what was on his mind. It took no great telepathic ability to work it out, as Simone too had started to worry.

Dave spoke aloud, which might even be safer.

"He will know where you are. So what. I'm not convinced my strength will fail when it comes to the one who made me. Or yours.

It's just a legend, put about by vampires dreading the revenge of those they've begotten. But what I don't know is whether it is true, or not, that one who has made many others of the kind gains more physical power that way… in which case I'm a slacker compared to William.

You, too. Only Christophe can ultimately best him, due to the great age he claims… probably… and he will not do it, for fear of himself, as I understand. But we should wait for Christophe to get here before we have anything to do with William."

"That might not be an option. On the other hand I think he likes to win… but you don't suppose he could have lost interest, perhaps? He might think I'm dead…"

"Not a chance, you're a prize, only female vamp we know of, and best of all would be if he could steal you from Philippe and Christophe, 'specially Chris, who changed him. So he's a kind of Daddy figure to Bill, but the sort of Dad you can't wait to get big and strong enough to overthrow. Bit of parricide'd suit Chris, though, being as he is, an actual ancient Greek. But a bit of the Oedipus comes into matters when you're involved."

Simone wasn't having that.

"I'm nobody's wife, or mother for that matter. To me Oedipus is just another story nicked by Shakespeare. And the earlier version's more dramatic.'

Dave cracked a smile, but Simone could tell he was worried. He left the room, and shortly after that she heard raised voices. Doris then came into the room, followed by Dave. She was shaking with anger.

"You promised me! And now you're sending me away!"

"No, no, you've got it wrong…"

Dave did intend to send Doris away, it seemed, and when told this Doris naturally jumped to the wrong conclusion. It took a while to calm her. She wasn't too impressed that he might be putting himself in danger, either. Finally Dave convinced her of the truth, which was that he wanted her to go and stay with some relative, but not even think about whom it would be, let alone tell him. As for Simone, she too tiptoed around Doris in case they should pick up her intended destination, and have it read from them by William. He could try and use her as a bargaining tool in some way… and even that, thought about too carelessly, might give an eavesdropping vampire some ideas.

Not that Billy boy didn't have plenty of ideas of his own, of course.

To fill the air with mind numbing chatter, which she hoped would distract them from any properly developed thoughts, Simone switched on the TV. Her first thought was 'why haven't they got it in colour? Cinemas had it even before the war.' Her second thought was more of a feeling of nausea than anything else. A photograph of a man had appeared on the screen. He wore a fisherman's jumper in the photo, and looked familiar.

"Lost at sea," said the newsreader. His colleagues were in shock, apparently. According to them, somehow, while no one was looking, he must have fallen overboard. They had heard no cries for help. They had been working by night, but powerful lights were used on board the trawler. Investigations were proceeding. The newsreader was a master of delicate scepticism: he put invisible question marks after telling his audience that no one was looking and no one had heard cries. The implication was clear. The rest of the crew were as guilty as hell.

Dave switched off what Doris and he called the telly.

"I'm sorry," he said.

"I'll have to confess," was Simone's first reaction.

"No! You keep quiet. Nothing can be proved or disproved, and you don't know what'll happen. You'll expose us all!"

He took her hands in his, and looked into her eyes.

"We've all had moments of insanity and desperation. Only we vampires can understand the sort of problems that, er... can occur. Don't confess, but make redress."

He was pleased with his little rhyme, but it did make sense. Following up his advantage, he began to plan aloud how redress might be made.

"Got it! A fake pools win. His wife, if he has one, can be part of a syndicate. Hubby joined it but didn't tell her. The trawlermen can convince her it's legitimate. They know the truth anyway. Everybody benefits. Don't worry, I've plenty of money. We can tell his family the others want no publicity..."

His eyes lit up as he planned the scheme. But Simone couldn't agree that everybody was benefiting. Her victim, whose humanity she had brushed aside to service her appetite, would not benefit. He lay at the bottom of the sea, fish food... apart from his blood, which had gone to save her and make her strong again. She nodded at Dave's plan, but she was hardly present. Part of her was also at the bottom of the sea, with the thick jelly like substance clogging her nose and mouth and eyes, and everything a dark, dark green.

Chapter Twenty

A woman wailing for her demon lover

(Coleridge)

Doris phoned the station and obtained the times of trains; to where, she wouldn't say. When the time came to leave she had to get a taxi. Dave had no car; he said because he might be tempted to use it when it wasn't a good idea. It might make him too impatient for sunset.

Simone was sorry to see Doris go. She had made a friend who wasn't just there to sell her blood, like the girls in the brothels of wartime Paris, although she did give it away to her lover. And thinking about blood... what would happen tonight? They had to somehow communicate with the trawlermen, and the vampires had to make sure they themselves were fed, otherwise communicating wasn't all they'd be doing.

Don't worry, Dave sent the thought to her, we have many kinds of technology. He led her to the basement – the house would have a basement, of course – and in it was a very large freezer, as big as you like. Dave threw open the door and within it she saw serried ranks of polythene bags, hanging from small rails like miniature files, but full of frozen blood.

He smiled, pleased with himself, and the new world of technology. Fridges and freezers weren't yet that common, but they were getting to be, since they were so useful. It meant you didn't have to go shopping every day, he gloated.

"How do you gloat without articulating the gloat aloud?" Simone wondered.

"I don't really know, but my pleasure that the world is evolving to become more convenient for vampires as well as people just bubbles over, I suppose. That's a commercial freezer, by the way. I've even got a backup generator if there are power cuts."

And so he had. "We can last several days without needing to mingle with the humans. But I suggest you warm it up first."

He got out two of the bags of blood and they went upstairs, where they warmed them in a milk pan, one bag at a time, because even the most well intentioned vampire might get a bit primaeval if they thought that one of them had a bigger share of the available food.

By this time it was growing dark. They had bought themselves a night off hunting, though Simone could have happily consumed more of the little packages.

They decided to cross the city to the Echo's offices. The Liverpool daily would be writing up the details of the stories that had broken earlier today. Simone needed to be convinced by the thinking behind the visit. Dave explained.

"My favourite reporter will be there. Someone, one of the young ladies with whom I have a commercial relationship decided there might be money to be made, even though I always paid her well. She thought her revelations might land her a big payday, pools winner big. All she got was sacked by me, and now her life is shit... I had to get rid of someone so treacherous. She followed me home and gave the address to Stan Madders. Of course I could read her mind, warned Doris, took precautions, and he found nothing. Then I threatened him with legal action, which would have seen him unemployed. The paper couldn't afford that sort of thing. So we shook on it, no hard feelings.

But he is no fool, and he suspects the story may be true. I told him I stay up all night because I'm a writer, and keep odd hours, but I refused to tell him the titles of the books I'd allegedly written, saying I had a nom de plume. And if I told him my secret'd be out. Then he asked me why I didn't stay home and write, but wandered about at night... I think he used the word 'prowling.' So I told him I'd kill him if he didn't stop prying, but he shouldn't think it was personal. A few more threats like that, as well as a realistic appraisal of how likely it was that he could ever expect to be believed, and he calmed down a lot. Now maybe he can reward me for my tolerance of nosey reporters."

So David and Simone, after a great deal of leaping from roof to roof, which was much easier than running along the roads, seeing that people were far less likely to spot them and their ludicrous speed, called at the paper's offices, expecting to be told that Madders was out on a story, and that they would be jumping around half the night.

But he was there, and he came to the reception desk a bare minute after he'd been sent for, a-goggle at Dave and his companion.

"This is my friend, Simone," said Dave. "She is psychic, so don't go thinking any lascivious thoughts."

Madders sniggered mirthlessly, clearly not sure if this was a joke or not.

"I need all the names you've got in the trawler death case. You are covering it, right? You said you were the best..." Dave said.

"Ah... I don't suppose you want to tell me why."

"No, don't suppose I do," was the flippant answer, but Dave's expression was stony.

At Madders's behest they waited in the lobby while he went to collect the information.

Meanwhile, Dave brightened up. He didn't like to stay dour for long, unlike Philippe, who could get both anxious and a bit self-pitying, or Christophe, who had a very serious worldview, all about self control. Of course, everybody, especially vampires, has to have self control but sometimes the reins need to slacken.

"He needs a treat, poor bloke has to chase up all these tragedies, it must get him down." Simone read what was coming next. The Paris vampires would be horrified but they didn't know the meaning of the word 'fun'.

When the reporter returned with the names and addresses they asked him to come outside with them. Then Simone held one hand and Dave the other, then gently adjusted the arrangement till their arms were safely around his. Then they jumped. Up.

At first the man was speechless. But it was a balmy evening. They couldn't have picked a more pleasant night for the trip. Most of the city was pretty low rise but nearer the docks the buildings were much taller. Dave and Simone were pretty good at this by now so there was some swooping and showing off.

At last they landed on one of the Liver building's towers, where they had a terrific view of the river and the city, although Madders could only see the city lights, not possessing vampire vision. He wasn't quite relaxed, and no vampire mind-reading powers were required in order to work out that he was afraid they would drink his blood till he shrivelled like a deflated balloon, or simply let go of him at the wrong moment.

Dave and Simone only had to think something and they knew what the other was contemplating. So they soothed the newspaperman and made their request.

"We will give you a lot of money, you sort these people out, also, you get quite a lot of money for doing it," Simone summed up. "Tell the relatives of the dead one that he was in a pools syndicate with the others. Tell the others to stick to the line. Tell them to remember the widow, or whatever, doesn't know the truth. Tell them they don't know the whole truth, either. Tell them to stick to the story, that he must have slipped overboard while it was noisy."

Dave pulled out a great wad of high denomination notes.

"In case you're wondering, this death was the direct result of actions taken by the enemy during the war, so don't worry, it won't happen again. Trust us, and we'll look after you. Betray us, tell the police, or whatever, and we'll destroy you. To the last drop…"

The reporter contemplated his choices; death at the hands of two bloodsuckers, or instant wealth. He bowed as he took the money, while they reassured him there would be plenty more.

As he headed back to the office Simone was marvelling at how things turned out. Now they could leave the complicated stuff to Madders, while they considered the impact of the arrival of Graves aka Kerr aka Sir William, possibly before their reinforcements got there.

It pays to delegate, thought Dave. Now, let's head back to my place. I don't want anyone getting too interested in my comings and goings, not at the moment.

But when they got back to the house the sensations of anxiety and dread which both vampires had been feeling were proved useful guides to what was going on. The first thing they saw as they touched down on the rooftops of Dave's street was what looked like a staged tableau, lit as it was by the lamp post over the heads of the actors: one was a man, improbably held in the arms of a woman, or at least someone wearing a skirt. This woman was holding the struggling man in a grip he couldn't seem to get out of: Something not right was going on. They weren't having a romantic late-night kiss, for sure.

Simone went straight to the pair but before she could separate them the female vampire, for that's what it was, dropped her victim and turned to Simone with a snarl.

And, as she already knew in her heart of hearts, the female vampire was Doris.

She heard a wail from Dave, an achingly primitive sound that was pure despair. She heard him cry out inside as well: it hurt her head. At last he cried angrily, "You! You have brought death to my door!"

At first Simone thought he meant her, and she cringed at the feelings of nausea at her own guilt, but then she started to tune in to where all this drama was coming from, and turned around to see William standing behind her.

Dave flew at William's throat, but Simone was more careful. She knew William had probably organised an entourage for himself. She knew that doing this could be difficult and could cost him a lot of time, unless he adopted measures like, for example, raiding hospital wards. Sure enough, a handful of people still wearing their pyjamas, one with a wire trailing from his arm, were circling around the scene.

None of them looked the philosophical type. In fact they were all very old, and although their brains must even now be repairing themselves, they looked animal-like, or worse, demonic. There's a difference, Simone had often thought. Humans aren't supposed to be dominated by their animal natures, but to command them. Else they change into a new life form... demon's as good a word as any.

She pulled up a wooden fence post from somebody's back garden and thrust it without hesitation through the heart of the nearest new vampire. The thing screeched, and vanished in a cloud of dust as it hastily returned to the Earth. Simone wouldn't have been able to articulate how she knew that this one would never preserve its humanity, as she herself had done – even after all that time below the sea – once she had hold of herself.

The best she could come up with in the heat of the moment was that Kerr's army reminded her of Edith and her horrid twin servants. You just felt a vacuum where any feeling should be: The voices were inhuman, screeches one could imagine pterodactyls making, more metallic than the cries of gulls. Then there were the eyes, red veined whites and expanded pupils, and the eagerness to feed that manifested itself as, amongst other phenomena, pink drool...

Well, she did that herself when very hungry. Anyway, she was revising her theories on how it was that some retained their humanity, mostly, when changed, and some became nightmares. It was nothing to do with inclinations to philosophy, surely, or any intrinsic virtue. It was just luck. Some – the great majority – were robbed of their souls as well as their lives, and a few weren't.

Were the unlucky ones reunited with their souls at any point? That was a question she hadn't the courage to try to answer, and probably wouldn't have for some time.

Meanwhile she saw David, crimson black tears streaming, hold back a flailing Doris while withdrawing a piece of sharpened wood from inside his jacket. It seemed that he had anticipated that trouble might show up on his doorstep. But he probably hadn't dreamed that it would come to this.

William bellowed 'No' once but then hastened to save Doris, who was yelling too, but wasn't about to stop... unless stopped. She was struggling against David, who seemed to hesitate. No wonder, poor bastard, thought Simone. Then David, still gripping his lover, started yelling, a long high screech of woe that utilised his vampire strength to make a truly ear shattering noise, which Simone noted, while clutching her head, probably had more of an impact on vampires, given their enhanced senses.

William hesitated a little but David had his arm back ready to deal the fatal blow. William threw himself towards Dave, desperate for some reason to preserve Doris, perhaps just because she was still attractive and younger than the people he'd stolen from their deathbeds, and now a vampire. But she would not have been much of a companion for anybody now, not without a soul. Eventually it would have palled...

So it was, ultimately, loneliness that killed the evil vampire, for William did not see the rapid turnaround Dave made, and he did not hear the warning in Dave's thoughts either, for Dave's screech from hell had blotted out everything; speech, thoughts, everything, for just long enough to spin on his heel and drive his stake, not into Doris's heart, but into William's.

The plan had worked, the anguished noise had done its work of hiding Dave's intention. It helped that the anguish had been genuine. As William turned to ancient dust Dave turned back to Doris and with an almost casual air plunged the same stake into her heart. Doris, too, turned to dust. From the dust a little trickle of breath arose and blew the dust upward, like a dancer leaving the stage at the end of the evening.

Dave fell to his knees. Simone despatched the elderly vampires with another piece of fence. She hoped the neighbours had slept through it all, otherwise they'd be demanding replacement garden furniture, which would be a devil of a job to install at night. She hoped that they were all about to die anyway. That would have made it less awful. They did look very ill... she hoped that someone would come up with answers as to where they had all gone; aliens, perhaps...

When she got back to Dave she didn't need to get close to hear his thoughts, which were mainly of the guilty 'I should have taken her somewhere safe. My arrangement for her protection was casual, inadequate, sloppy. I killed her' variety... and then he'd picture a door held wide and a sunny day beyond. She put her arms around him, and after a while, led him into the house.

Then she listened to him, and tried not to say anything stupid, like, well it was going to happen anyway, at least you haven't had a long lead up to a desperate final illness, or anything like that at all. Everything sounded crass, so she just let him cry. His bloody tears soon made his room look like a slaughterhouse.

Eventually she warmed up some more blood from the capacious freezer. David drank it, and then looked bewildered at how healthy his appetite was... if you could truly say that of a vampire. Then he looked shamefaced, as the newly bereaved often do when they realise how hungry they are, so soon after the unthinkable has happened.

She was wondering about William's soul, or the lack thereof, and at one point David ceased his self flagellation and said aloud that he did have a soul... he wouldn't care about companionship or women otherwise.

At last he dozed a little, but Simone, who had her own load of guilt that she didn't want to think about, looked for comfort in the only place she could think of; in the piles of paper in various kinds of disorder which were apparently preliminary notes for Christophe's great philosophical magnum opus. The couple of bits of paper she had read were perched on a spindly coffee table. There were several separate piles at her feet, and in other locations as well. And folders. These had no labels of any kind.

Like life, thought Simone.

And she picked up a folder, opened it up, and stared at a title page that read "Seventy-Two."

She sat down and looked at the last thing she'd read, lying there on the table. Why was he called Set?

Set, she knew, was the evil brother of Osiris, and an entirely mythological figure. Now she read that he was a vampire, and it made some sort of sense. Osiris was born again, resurrected, like Jesus, only from a wooden chest instead of a cross, having been imprisoned by Set.

"Set had seventy-two helpers," she read. "The number is assigned to many phenomena and many fantasies too. Because of its connection with the precession of the equinoxes, whereby the axis of the earth moves one degree in seventy two years, it is connected to life and death. This is not just an almost abstract bit of astronomical observation. The healthy resting heartbeat of a woman is about 72 beats per minute. There are 72 angels going up and down Jacob's ladder. Jesus had 72 apostles outside the inner circle of 12. Inner circle's a good way to describe it.

Here we see clearly the connection between the number and life, and begin to think that it is not just a symbol, but has a deeper, real meaning, because it occurs in nature and is not just an imaginary construct.

The Gnostics regarded life as an unfortunate fate during which one is imprisoned, so in some stories we have seventy two angels, sometimes it is devils, or even houris.

In the last case, the meaning may be that the deserving one has a gift of a new life, with seventy two virgin years unsullied by dark deeds that may have been done. The slate is wiped clean. In any case the reward is for practising jihad, which is civil war within the self, dark against light."

Where is he going with this, wondered Simone. Good or evil... a number can be either. So can a life. At this point, Simone's eyes began to close. She was willing to follow the points Christophe was trying to make up to the bit when he started to use words with which she wasn't familiar. Fair enough, he did explain 'jihad.' He hadn't – at least, not on this piece of paper – added that 72 multiplied by 5 equalled 360, which was a perfect circle. She read a bit more, about Mercury playing chess with the Moon to win 5 extra days, because the year wasn't perfect. 5, apparently was and is the number of Humankind.

It looked like mathematics was in fact the common language in ancient times, and the story of the Tower of Babel, when the civilisations of those times collapsed, probably was really about the sophisticated astronomy and maths before the builders sank back into – might've guessed – seventy two languages. The story of the tower made Simone think of pyramids: Maybe they had to stop building a super big one because they lost the skills.

But a man – a vampire – was going through the trauma of bereavement, somehow almost worse since he thought he had a while before it happened... all that worrying about the time when Doris would grow really old, a total waste: she would never grow old. There might be a secret wrapped in all the stories which included this number. Interesting, but useless, as far as Dave was concerned, no balm for a broken heart.

She slept, the light, dream-filled doze of the vampire. In the dream a man wrote on blackboard. She couldn't read what he had written, as it was all in Greek. Still dreaming, she thought it meant that she needed a teacher.

Then she awoke, and Philippe and Christophe were standing in front of her.

It was so startling that she shouted aloud. Then she stood up, grabbed Christophe's hand and cried 'Seventy-two is the number of Life!'

"It is a number of human life," he answered, with barely a blink. "Whether there are real connections or whether it has intrinsic meaning is something I've not yet established. If there are real links between this number and certain phenomena; that is what I'd like to know. Tentatively, if there were, it may be to do with what ties us into our human body, threads of flesh, nerve, sinew... that are tightened when we are finally born, after being loose... until the soul enters the newborn on the wings of breath."

He strode round the big room, which also had plenty of space for pacing up and down.

Up and down and round and round, and lots of muttering as Christophe sought an answer.

"The 72 years are near to the later 70, which is not the biblical lifespan, but is a later tidying up. Neither 7 nor 70 divide into 12. But 12 is important in astroarchaeology. So is 7, just because it doesn't divide into 12. There are 7 spirits around the Throne of god: That clearly refers to the planets... then there are the 24 elders... my head hurts. Even so I feel as if I am getting somewhere. You won't find it in those papers, though. I have done much work since I made those notes. Which is all they are."

David entered the room. It was fortunate that no one needed to speak. He seemed to have heard Christophe's list of numbers.

He spoke aloud. "What on heaven or earth does all that stuff do but confuse you? Perhaps it's a key to something back in the very dawn of civilisation by the Nile or the Indus. Perhaps it's a key to what we have become, to the existence of vampires. Maybe Set's little helpers get their threads of life strengthened, or something. But even vampires die, eventually, and as for humans, here today, gone tomorrow… hardly worth noticing, let alone caring for."

He doubled up, clutching his midsection as though fainting, or being sick. Then he howled, not loudly, but it was as if he was too weak to be loud. He sounded like a dying animal. Simone took his arm, and lowered him onto the sofa. Then she bit him.

The anaesthetic took hold, and for a blissful while he slept.

Simone straightened up. "Truth is, it won't revive the dead, your study of numbers. It might have loads of meaning, but it can't conquer death. So who cares? No problem solved is worth a damn, because no-one and nothing will save us, one day, from that."

"That might be… not wholly correct," said Christophe, cautiously.

"Right," she said, dismissively. "Then let's talk about the fact that it seems everyone is mistaken, and it is possible to kill the one who changed us, without dying ourselves."

"It must be a lie, put about by Bill Kerr so we wouldn't kill him, not unless…" Philippe hesitated, not wishing to mention Doris.

"It is a lie, then," mused Christophe. "I did wonder. My, er, sire told me not to revenge myself on him, when I realised what he'd done. But he did not have a lengthy existence, even though I believed what he had said. You can see it's a useful lie. Unless someone is beside themselves with rage and doesn't care. To be honest I was never sure if I'd die or not, and there was a time when I didn't care. I thought I was just lucky to get away with it. If you can call it luck."

"And now you're the most powerful vampire on the planet," said Simone.

Christophe just looked embarrassed.

"It's never what I wanted, never what I hoped. My only wish was to find a teacher."

Simone exclaimed, "My dream, you've broken my dream…"

"Sorry," muttered Christophe, who clearly hadn't heard the expression before.

They settled down a bit, and tried to make normal conversation, although since they were vampires, they were limited as to how normal they could be. Also, Dave was fiercely suburban while the others were… you could almost describe them as dilettantes, living in a faded aristocratic milieu. Even Philippe, with his poor peasant background, had a certain air about him, but that probably came with living in Paris. Still, they were a bit more useful during the war than Dave had been, unless he had been doing something that she didn't yet know about.

"I want to walk out of here and throw away the key," said Dave, suddenly. "I feel like a bad person. A good person would want to stay around, keeping memories alive. I don't want to do that. I want to pretend this life never happened, then there will be no pain."

The others nodded, respectful but not really understanding.

"Come back to Paris with us," said Philippe. "It's a different life; not better, but different."

"Do you want me back, as well?" asked Simone, tartly.

"Of course," said Philippe, surprised.

They had to wait through the next day before they could leave, so they guzzled all the blood in the freezer. Dave left a couple 'just in case'. Simone briefly wondered what that could possibly mean: she could imagine no circumstances in which any of them would be stuck and starving in this house, especially as no one was coming back. Still, no one was arguing with Dave at the moment. They would go along with anything that kept him from breaking down and crying.

There was a plane waiting in an airfield not far away that would take them to Paris. The pilot was waiting in a hotel and would be ready after a phone call. It was much easier than travel by boat and train, where a holdup of any kind could seriously endanger a vampire's existence.

As evening fell, they left the house, three of them unencumbered by luggage, while David had a small suitcase with him. The pilot presumably did not know what his passengers were, but in any case he showed no surprise at the quick turnaround or the luggageless travellers. He was very expensive to hire, and very discreet.

Simone was astonished at the number of lights below. The others took it upon themselves to tell her all about the history of the last twenty-two years. It took most of the journey. Christophe went in for complex analyses of historical trends to try and explain events and trends. Philippe, less so, although he was quite excited about cultural phenomena not really known in the 'forties, like pop groups, and the Cold War. Dave was quiet.

That night Simone entered her old home, although she could not comprehend the length of time she'd been away.

"Where is Charles?" she asked the room.

Philippe replied, "He is very old. He is in a home for old, rich people. We thought it would be the best care we could get for him, but he's surrounded by right-wing collaborators who lie about their roles in the war. That's according to him. It keeps him involved in life, anyway, even if he can't move about. He just argues all day long. They know we can't come for visits till evening. We pay a lot, so they don't ask awkward questions."

A man stepped out of the farthest corner, where he'd been lurking, waiting to be introduced.

"This is our housekeeper now; George, he's called. Been with us fifteen years."

George smiled shyly. "Feel free to read me, Simone," he said.

His mind was welcoming and strangely, unafraid. She saw someone from London, and prior to that, from Jamaica, who had come to the city to work, as requested by the British government; someone who didn't tolerate the way he was treated and spoken to, and who eventually snapped. It seemed the government hadn't checked on how welcoming the locals were when they invited help from abroad. Or weren't.

There was daily humiliation. Even the most petty digs, added up and conjoined with more serious threats, got to him till one day he snapped. He was a big chap, and it was lucky that the red mist dissipated before George killed the tormentor. When he realised the trouble he was in, he left for the continent, which was just as bad if not worse, at least, in his experience.

The vampires had stumbled upon George one night, surrounded by people who appeared to want to kill him. In fact it wasn't mere appearance: They could feel the dark intent in the minds of his attackers.

It was almost as if you could unwind the minds that hosted these thoughts, and travel back along the trail of evil to where it began in each of them. But Simone had no wish to visit such depravity. It all began in bitter childhoods, and having understood that, she was confident she didn't need to look further. But she did sometimes pray, that all the children in the world would grow up in loving circumstances. She prayed as Pascal suggested, because she could not lose by wagering that there was a God.

So matters were settled with the would-be attackers, and no one was seriously hurt, except that they had to endure a lecture from Philippe, who never gave up an opportunity to improve people.

Soon after they arrived in Paris, Simone decided to clear up a few things with Christophe.

Ruth Lewarne

Chapter Twenty-One

A man's wisdom maketh his face to shine

(Ecclesiastes)

"So you knew Socrates?" Simone asked Christophe.

"Yes," he answered.

"Would you like to show me?"

There was a slight pause. Then he came and sat next to her and held her hand.

I've never shown Philippe, not once, his thoughts whispered.

"Why not?" she asked aloud.

"Because I don't want to be shaken to my core with emotions that have no outlet for me anymore. I might look young but I'm not. I'm not resilient, emotionally I mean. Not when it comes to that."

Simone considered that Philippe was nothing like pushy enough. He'd known Christophe for a century or two, and hadn't asked? The others had shown her their sorrowful tales, even Christophe had shown her his first encounter with the late Sir William. But Socrates was famous, really, really famous; gosh, Christophe could have written academic studies that turned ancient history upside down. If he didn't want to, maybe she could…

He, meanwhile, was shaking his head, and allowed himself a little smile.

"Show me," said Dave, "before I die."

There were oaths and exclamations from the male vampires. Simone stayed quiet. The others muttered that Dave had outlived his loves before, many times, and that very same end would have befallen Doris too, as is the natural way of things. But it seemed not to make any difference. He would have been ready, he said. It would have been right, after another twenty, thirty years: She would have had her due. But she had fallen in with him, and lost all that life. They could anaesthetise him all they liked, one day he'd wake up, and the sorrow would be there again. There would be no time lapsed for him, no healing would take place. They could not stop him: He'd had enough.

Perhaps a journey into the past might help.

Christophe reached for David's hand, which was covered in blood, as was his face and clothes, since he could not stop crying. The flood of bloody tears would slow at times, but didn't stop. So David looked like a victim of terrible violence, though the violence was emotional, and more terrible for that, especially for a vampire, for whom physical suffering is a very short-lived problem.

Dave and Christophe shut their eyes. Philippe and Simone watched. As they looked on, Dave's face seemed to unknot itself, the frown lines slowly smoothed, and the air somehow felt cleaner, although it was so delicately scented that it could have been either a spring day in a meadow, or nothing, just imagination.

But as he tilted his face as if towards the sun – and it may be the sun he was seeing behind those still closed eyes, or it may have been something else – the bloody tears that crept slowly down his face seemed more of a watery pink, and then flowed more quickly, until not only did they flow as fast as ever but they now flowed transparent, like real tears. A smile even appeared, small and shy upon his lips.

He opened his eyes.

"It's all right," he said, "it's all right."

Christophe was wide-eyed now, as well. His smile was broader, but his eyes were downcast, not in sorrow but in recall.

"You'll discover why, if you still want to look," he said quietly, responding to her thoughts.

"Of course I want to look, especially now," she replied.

"Shut your eyes," he whispered. I'm going to try and get it chronological."

But he failed in that. The first thing and the only thing she saw was Socrates, sitting on a bed, in a white painted room. Even the walls looked dark, though, next to the source of light that was his face. It was the face of an old man, yet still round, with big eyes and that famous snub nose, more broad really, a bit like that of an African; like George's. The Greeks loved high bridges on their favourite noses, she thought later. Perhaps that is why history records Socrates as being 'ugly'. But he had described himself as a citizen of the world, and his face could have come from anywhere. It was a workman's face; a mongrel face, her father would have thought, for he too considered high bridges on noses somehow indicative of noble virtues. To these prejudices Socrates gave the lie, for who could match him in being noble and virtuous?

Afterwards, she would describe it as like looking at herself. There was no resemblance, of course, just a feeling that she had come home. There was no sense of intellectual grandeur, just an expression in those eyes that went beyond kindness and forgiveness, but seemed to say there was no need to be kind and forgive. All such considerations were washed away…

Suddenly she was expelled from the scene and the next thing she knew she was lying on the floor, half on top of Christophe, who was also on the floor. They had both passed out.

It was not the millennia that had passed that made that face the only thing Christophe remembered from the scene. Beside it nothing was memorable. If it had happened yesterday, all he remembered would have been Socrates's face. Simone knew that. It had happened before, to a degree. It was only natural, if that word were to be allowed anywhere near this situation.

Unless they put their minds to it, no one accurately pictured what they saw. The tendency was always to focus on what meant most.

But what was odd was that Socrates was looking at her, which couldn't be true. He must be looking at Christophe, or rather, must have looked at him, back then. The shiver of awe on Simone's part made the hairs on her body stand on end. There were many, not just scholars, who would do anything to experience what she just did. But in reality it was not her encounter.

This first impression faded, a little, but the word 'effulgent' popped into her head; a word that she'd only encountered in hymns, back at school. Full up with light, Simone thought. Or just radiating…

Stop thinking, please, thought Christophe.

Then their eyes were open.

"I never thought one day to be looked at like that by a man long dead," said Simone. "Or by a man looking at someone else… Wasn't he?"

"Who knows? He was no ordinary man. But he was no magician. He seemed prophetic because he saw clearly.

He was as great as Jesus and had the same role. The followers of Jesus had to make up a gruesome execution for their Master because they wanted him to be as popular as Socrates, but no Master of that stature needs to endure such pain, and doesn't need to die at the age of thirty three either. That's not the point, anyway. The point is they're not afraid to die, because they know death does not exist." Christophe paused.

Simone felt a trembling note of longing like the flutter of a butterfly in the cavern of her empty chest, and it got stronger, as if someone played a note, or the wind blew across a stringed instrument, evoking an ache at her core. I have to see him again, she thought. Please, Christophe.

"I knew it. I felt it too. His eyes…wise yet innocent and full of joy, like a baby's. I saw him many times. I was hopelessly in love, seduced by a man of seventy, but not in any way you can imagine. Or perhaps you can, now. Plato saw him the way all of us did, through the prism of his own character and tendencies.

That famous arse, Alcibiades, loved to tell of his own attempt at seduction, back when he was beautiful and our culture was all in favour of the love of young males. No one would have given it much thought, but whether Socrates was truly tempted or safe, because he cared only for women, in that way – well now it's all there in Plato, and we must believe what he says."

Christophe stood up, a man who looked to be in his twenties, handsome and vital.

"Plato was against the indulgence of these desires, or said he was. Beware of him, he makes Socrates sound like an academic, but then, at least he didn't invent his own religion and foist it on the memory of his Master, as happened with Jesus. The minute these human doorways to another world are dead, the religious stuff fills the gap where a real live Messiah has been. The academics grabbed Socrates, via Plato, for their own, but they got it as wrong as Jesus' would-be followers."

"Chris… it would be easiest if I call you that.." he nodded assent... "I can feel anger in you as well as devotion," Simone offered.

"He could have saved me. He must have known, though he said he knew nothing. It was like my wedding night, my wedding to the divine inside me, the fulfilment of my life…"

"I had not thought of Socrates as a holy man," said Simone, "till now. As an argumentative philosopher, maybe."

"People turn to the East, now, for spiritual answers, and some suggest Jesus went there. I don't know about that, but there is a famous story someone wrote down, about an Indian in Athens meeting Socrates and asking him what was the nature of his philosophy. When he answered that it was an investigation into human life, the Indian laughed and said, 'You cannot fix your gaze on human truth without knowledge of the divine.'

Socrates barely left Athens, except to help defend it, so there are no tales of *him* travelling to the East. But it was a tale of his early manhood, and I have always thought that word of this determined seeker of truth must have reached the ears of some saint who sent a messenger to see what kind of man he was, with the command to instruct him in certain meditative practices should he be worthy. There was a lot of commerce between these places, which modern people would probably be surprised by. But our ships did not just sail for warlike purposes.

I'll show you something, then don't ask me anymore."

Christophe took Simone's hand, and they shut their eyes.

It was night-time and they/he were walking on paved streets. There was a near-full moon, and torches burned here and there, but it was much darker than a modern city street at night.

At last they slowed before a modest home, which nevertheless had torches burning at either side of the door. Christophe – telling her silently – had an engagement to meet Socrates here, to receive certain instructions regarding meditation practice, at Chris's request. He had been waiting a long time, listening to Socrates daily, and wanted to commit himself further to the joyful task of living a virtuous life in the service of the knowledge Socrates passed on.

But what the earlier Chris didn't know, the current one did, and Simone shared that knowledge and some of the experience of these moments, but mostly a sense of dread and the realisation that the dread was well-justified. And alongside that, most dreadful of all: both of them still felt the hope of the man whom she knew was going to suffer disappointment that was off the scales, if anyone measured such things. It was not like the first time. She could feel Chris's reluctance. She sensed what was about to happen.

A woman, tiny, and fierce: Xanthippe, Socrates's allegedly shrewish wife, came to the door and told Chris that he was early, and must go away and come back a little later. She addressed Chris familiarly as Critias, and seemed polite and kind, not at all as she'd been described. That was when Simone realised she was understanding the ancient Greek, thanks to the hook-up with Chris's mind. But there were three people involved in this encounter with Xanthippe: Christophe, who was just a memory of a feeling, which didn't quite go away, and the current Christophe, playing host to a visitor, Simone.

The original Chris walked away, his stomach churning with excitement, and of course Simone shared that feeling. Critias, the current Chris informed her, was his uncle for whom he'd been named; an oligarch of whom Socrates had been too tolerant, and who had brought him trouble and enemies.

But he was one who would later try and persuade Socrates to run from Athens to escape the hemlock. It felt odd, being told this in a room in a house in the twentieth century, albeit with eyes closed, while walking through a landscape of Athens in the fifth century BC.

Meanwhile the heart that had been beating, kept them going through the streets, and the breath that he was breathing was a sweet taste of what they'd lost.

Chris's mind was in turmoil. He couldn't change any of this. People didn't understand how awful it was to see again the worst moments in his extremely long life, to walk through them in perfect three dimensional enactment of the original events. As he walked, he realised that the only thing he could control was his mind. But the visit he was about to make to Socrates was supposed to give him the tools to do that. If anyone was not ready to die, it was Critias.

But die he did, that very day, to this ordinary life. And the funny thing was that the initiation into the secret of the Knowledge of Socrates had been described as a death to the world and a rebirth so dramatic it was as if a person brought up in a cave first saw daylight.

That was what had happened to Critias that day, but in a way he did not anticipate.

He was walking by the city walls, unable to keep still, forcing himself to stay away from the house for an hour at least. But time did not go by at its usual steady pace. It seemed like an hour, but it wasn't: Those moments which were most vivid were remembered and it could only have taken minutes before he was greeted by someone he didn't know, someone who smiled, briefly. Then in a matter of seconds he was on the ground, pinned down by arms that seemed ridiculously strong, about to be anaesthetised by long fangs, his heartbeat going like the pounding hooves of a horse pursued by a lion.

But before he fell into the paralysing sleep he yelled 'no!' and the beastly thing did not, at first, bite, but continued to pin him down with that unnatural strength. It laughed in the face of his desperation and Simone looked up into its eyes and thought it looked reptilian, as though evolution had taken some swamp beast as the species chosen to rule the world.

Simone felt the pain as the vampire bit into the neck of Critias, and realised no anaesthetic was used. So she was not surprised that as she felt the heartbeat slow inside his chest the beast withdrew and whispered "Do you want to live?" And she heard the body of Critias cry out "Yes, yes!"

And then it was like the day she died and was reborn a vampire, and alongside Christophe and his ancient self she drank from the proffered arm of the creature.

Then the scene was dreamlike, probably because the memories were not equal. It was the more vivid ones that counted, so it shifted to the house where they had been earlier. Now Critias was about to knock, but stood there, arms dangling at his side, and Simone felt the despair when after a while, he went to peer through a window.

She saw Socrates, through Critias's eyes, look straight at him and hence, her. Once more the glance appeared to include her: it was quick and delicate, rather than probing, but so powerful... as if it had crossed the centuries. Or as if two thousand years meant nothing to a hungry heart.

Socrates spoke. Simone understood his speech. It seemed that she heard two languages at once, but without them both becoming unintelligible.

"What hovers – an insect at my window?"

"It is I, Critias, Master, but I cannot enter!" Simone felt the body's trembling.

"Such a thing as you have become can enter, if invited," replied Socrates.

"Oh Socrates," said Critias, "I cannot." Simone felt the words exit from her mouth. It was a most peculiar sensation, especially as, if she had her way, her lips would form wholly different words. For she had fallen under the man's spell, and in her heart she was begging Critias to plead that he should not be exiled from Socrates's presence, and that although something awful had befallen him, it was not his fault, and they should proceed as planned. And all the while she knew full well that it was impossible to change anything that was past: by definition, it was too late.

But Critias was having none of it, and she began to feel what he was feeling. Any ordinary person – if such a one existed – would either hate or make a decision to ignore Socrates, or love him, for once he was encountered, none could remain indifferent. But it was easy, inevitable in fact, to feel unworthy, like some creeping thing. Alcibiades himself had declared him the most beautiful of human beings, and though Alcibiades was feted for his own beauty he was all too aware of his many faults, and it was Socrates that would not let him escape that awareness, not by nagging or criticism, but just by being. But there were many who could not bear to look into those eyes, afraid as they were of being judged and found wanting.

What had befallen Critias was a terrible descent into degradation, and his anguish was palpable to Simone, especially since she had shared it, when she first became a vampire. What if he, unable to control the vile appetite passed on by his assailant, attacked Socrates? That was an obvious concern, but it masked a deeper fear; that Socrates might look at him with disgust. Better, thought Critias, sharing the thought with Simone whether he willed it or not, to hide away forever in the darkness, bereft both of natural light, and the light-bearer who helped chase the inner dark away.

Socrates spoke again, facing the window.

"It seems you have a twisty fate, Critias, from which even your longing for knowledge cannot completely save you. But the gods have granted me a boon, the licence to save souls, and so I claim yours. Though you cannot consort with me again before I die, your sincere longing must be fulfilled, and therefore you will survive until another Socrates is born and grows up. If you cannot find him, then find the next. Ask for his blessing, and you shall be freed at last from that fate of yours, which is both curse and opportunity, because now you have a kind of immortality."

Socrates lifted the cup beside him, and raised it to Critias, skulking at the window. The scene disappeared.

Back in the twentieth century Christophe sank to his knees, with a sob catching in his throat.

"I heard of many, many who said they were his heir. It was hard to travel, but I travelled as best I could through places where death by sunshine was a constant threat. And then, one day, it wasn't.

I was skulking in Athens, bribing slaves to sell me their blood, the darkness in me always nagging me to just take what I wanted, when I wanted it. A couple of times I walked into sunshine, as I had heard that it would kill me – but it hurt…"

"But…" Simone began.

"I know what you're going to say. Yes, I didn't realise it because no one had properly explained it. I should have combusted in seconds. It was only after I fought my sire, pushing him out into sunlight and then following him that I understood. He was ash… I was merely burned and soon healed. There could only be one explanation; Socrates. His curse, or blessing, meant that I really cannot die until I see him again."

"But, you have avoided the sun all the time I've known you," exclaimed Simone. Philippe nodded to indicate that although he'd been around much longer than her, he didn't know Christophe's secret, either. That explained why he'd never been offered a trip to the ancient world, then.

It also explained the confusion about whether one could kill one's sire without also dying. It didn't actually prove that you could, or couldn't, because it was clear that Christophe was a special case. The fact that David was still alive suggested it was possible, though he was like a sorrowful ghost. Still, that was to do with his loss, rather than his revenge for it.

Christophe continued.

"I heard about Jesus, but it was long after he died. Anyway, he could have been another pretender for all I knew. I heard of Mohammed and his dancing sufis but did not find him. Travel has always been difficult, and it's doubly so for a vampire. Even for me: I might not die, but I have often endured great pain. Many times I have wanted to die, but could not…

And then today we have radio and TV. We have a postal service, we have newspapers and still there's a lot we don't hear about. I've always heard stories but sometimes centuries too late. In this twentieth century information is spread about all kinds of nonsense but amongst the dross there are secrets the seeker wants to discover."

Simone was in turmoil, but she didn't speak. There was much she didn't know, and even more that she didn't understand. It was hard to believe that Christophe did not find another like Socrates in two thousand years. Then again, perhaps it wasn't so strange. Perhaps there was one such being in every generation, but you had to be in the right place.

Was there a part of Christophe that didn't want to meet such a great soul again? Because he revered his master so much he didn't want to find another... or because he didn't want to die?

And that raised another question.

She hadn't been trying to conceal her thoughts.

"Yes," said Christophe, sounding weary, though vampires don't get physically tired, not really. Emotional exhaustion is another matter. "My destroyer looked... like his eyes were snake's eyes, almost. They were strange, like those of a different species. Not one with feelings of any sort, or interest in anything but killing. But he died like an ordinary man."

"You saw that when you killed him? None of our eyes are snakelike. Was he a different species?"

"For a long time I thought he must be, or else very, very old. He was dark-skinned, like an Egyptian. Did you see that? I even wondered if he was bred from a human and a crocodile. But now I am very, very old, and my eyes are not reptilian. Mind you I don't look in mirrors much, so do tell me if they are going that way."

"No, they're fine," said Dave, kindly.

"I saw my soul, felt it, while listening to him. He would talk about something and bring it alive. Even Plato's prose became poetry. But my Master was about to give me my own key to the inner kingdom. One more time, Simone?"

She could not say no to his longing, and indeed, felt it too. She took Chris's hand and shut her eyes, and was transported: Sitting behind his eyes was like being in a control tower without control... for a moment the analogy of the top front seat on a double decker bus sprang to mind. They were in a room, people were there,

Ruth Lewarne

Socrates was there, talking. The people looked eager, as if trying to convince the Master that they were utterly sincere, which no doubt they were.

She heard a voice, as if emanating from her own lips, saying 'Speak to us of the soul, O Socrates'. A daft social reflex made her want to cringe at being part of that, as if she were a schoolgirl sucking up to teacher

But Socrates said, "The soul of each is light. If I were to say that it was golden, it would be brighter and more beautiful than gold. If I compared it with the full moon low in the sky, it would be more resplendent. If I said it was like a desert night full of stars, it would be more scintillating. If I said it was like the setting sun, it would be more vivid, and if I compared it to the aurora, it would be more brilliant and more playful. It is more dazzling than lightning, more radiant than the dawn, more incandescent than the sky at noon. Nothing can be compared with its splendour, and all that may be described as beautiful merely borrows from the shadow of its glory.

The soul of the human being is harmony. All sound issues from the silence that is no silence. All created things sing, and the Creator conducts the choir. But the song of the human soul is the most divine of sounds, and it resonates through infinite octaves. It is higher than the fleshly ear can perceive, and lower. It is higher than the song of the stars, and lower. Its music extends through every chord, vertically, and there was never a time that it did not sing, nor will there ever be. It has always sung and will always sing. It is melody, it is rhythm, it is percussion. It is pulsation, it is dancing. Neither the human voice nor any instrument can approach it in power or sweetness. Nothing can be compared with its sublimity, and all that may be described as musical merely borrows from the echo of its glory.

The soul of every one is the breath of life. The breath is the spirit, and on its thermals the awakening consciousness glides, ever upwards, into the high airs where it soars on an ascending updraught of joy. The breath is the food of the soul, and the drink. It is flight without wings. It is the intoxicant that brings health. It is the elixir of life. The soul sips the breath, and is inebriated. It plays among the stars, and inhales their fragrance, It breathes out its waves like the ocean and life floods forth to cover the earth with abundance. It is play, and it is interplay. It exhales creation, then inhales all the perfumes it has distilled from heaven. It is joy, joy, joy. Nothing can be compared with with this ecstasy, and all that may be described as delightful merely borrows from the ripples of its glory.

The soul of each human being is love. And love is the only truth, and everything that is not love will perish. Love is immortal and all that is not love will fade and be forgotten. Love is life and all that is not love is death and illusion. Love is generous and love is kind. Love is God and Love established creation so that there might be a love affair. There is the One and there is duality. The soul of each is a mirror that reflects the face of God. The lover and the beloved live in the soul. That there are two is an illusion, but it is the illusion that begins the drama of love.

The one who cleaves to the soul knows the bliss of union, and in the bliss of love suffering dissolves. When this bliss reigns in the heart there will be no more sorrow, for the soul of us is rapture, the soul of us is gladness, and compassion is the very stuff of the soul of us. The kiss of God is bestowed upon the true lover, then the darkness is swept away and all is soul. And the mortal who scuttles over the face of the earth, whose days are numbered and full of trouble, whose desires are endless and insatiable, whose flesh is destined to decay into the dirt, is utterly changed, and walks upon the earth filled with generous love, free of pride, and eager that all the sleepers might awaken. For nothing compares to this ravishment, and all that may be described as kindness merely borrows from the memory of its glory."

In a moment they were back, as Christophe opened his eyes and Simone had to do so too.

He sobbed. "I am lost and lovesick. I'll never recover. To have come so close. You forced me to remember. You've awakened a longing that is hopeless. I'd say it would be better if you killed me, but I can't even die. It would have been kinder if I had been killed long ago. The wound I've been dealt bleeds not blood but longing. Who will bind it? Who will mend this broken heart?" His tears left dark streaks down his cheeks.

So powerful was the influence of one man that his memory rendered a vampire 24 centuries old, the world's strongest – man, sort of – crying like a baby.

"Don't despair," said Simone. She felt a little awkward, but heaven's above, she had been inside his head, after all, so she slipped an arm through Christophe's looking at the others while she did so, hoping to include them all, somehow, in her gesture.

"There is pain and there is also love," she said. "Even vampires cannot see what is going on, but like every thinking being, we see a part of the picture. Maybe we have to die before we see the whole, but perhaps we'll get a chance before that time comes. I'll search for truth with you, Chris, but you'll have to go into the sunshine alone: Socrates hasn't blessed me, nor cursed me. I'm subject to the same rules as other vampires, and cannot survive the daylight."

"Don't be so sure," said Philippe. "You saw the man as well, perhaps…"

"But I wasn't a thwarted devotee, on the brink of revelation. Just someone along for the ride," she replied.

As she spoke she was aware that Philippe and David were also affected by the encounter she and Chris had just had. Dave had stopped crying: he had hope now. Philippe was a little less gloomy. Indeed, she could almost feel his speculations wind themselves up…

"So," he said, "Socrates explicitly believes in reincarnation, the evidence being his promise to Christophe that he would not die until they met again."

"But," said Dave, happily joining in," It might only exist for people of that stature, not for sinners like us, or any other human either."

"Perhaps a kind of crown, invisible to us, lands on the heads of those who follow the line of spiritual kings," suggested Christophe, "and when they die, the crown lives on."

But Philippe didn't like this talk of crowns.

"We are all princes, sons of God, or none is," he said, sternly.

Simone could out-stern him. "And princesses!" she supplied.

"Anyway, we'll search for wisdom and its heralds together, won't we?" Christophe was looking at Simone but they all knew he meant the four of them, and probably George too, if he wanted.

"In the mystical verse of the Sufis there is much reference to the Friend, or the Beloved" said Philippe. "With capital letters. While we're waiting to meet him – or her – we can comfort ourselves with the companionship of …lower case friends."

He looked pleased with himself after that little witticism, then debate began about the Friend supposedly within oneself as compared with the prophets and gurus who introduced one to that inner Friend… who was friendliest? But

Simone had enough at that point, and besides she had a feeling that arguments took one so far but no farther.

What did the old fellow say? "The Grape that can with Logic absolute, the Two and Seventy jarring Sects confute..." She wondered what wine would taste like, now.

"It's spiritual ecstasy, not drunkenness... meant to be a state beyond the possibility of argument," Christophe said, and then concluded with the famous quatrain: "The subtle Alchemist that in a trice, Life's leaden metal into gold transmute..."

Now she was moved as never before, and she didn't want to dwell on whether she'd feel like that again... or not... though her chances of doing so were greater if she hung around Christophe, had to be... He had been singled out and told that he would meet Socrates again one day... and Love would walk the earth again in human form.

And when it happens, she thought, careless for a moment of who might be listening in, I'll be there.

THE END

(Blank)

(Blank)

(Blank)

Writer's CHAMPION

Writer's Champion (CW) is a facility and an imprint of MAPublisher. CW provided supportive facility, service and financial-wise; and works around the writer's circumstance to get the writer self published.

For more information email: mapublisher@yahoo.com

MA Publisher Catalogue

ISBN/Titles /Image/Author	Descriptions
978-1-910499-V6 Book of Lived By Penny Authors	2020 This year many poets from UK have come together during the lockdown to present their life experiences of "Covid 19".
978-1-910499-50-4 V5 Book of Lived By Penny Authors	This issue is truly the vision, new poets and even the cover images is by a local artist. Volume 5 is the 1st that is what the founder's purpose for this anthology was - to give aspiring writers and artist a hand.
978-1-910499-35-1 V4 Book of Lived By Penny Authors	After the third instalment the momentum for the Penny Authors to come together and share their life journey in so that the reader finds that "missing Jigsaw" piece in their life. If this anthology serves one soul then it has served its purpose. The "V4 Book of Lived is now settling in to its positioning in the world of souls.
978-1-910499-29-0 V3 Book of Lived By Penny Authors	V3 Book of Lived". After the experiences gained from the previous two publications, It became clear that these books were more than average poetry books, These were lived moments recorded. This is the first anthology with the new name. It is a wonderful place to expand ones horizon.
978-1-910499-17-7 Anthology Two By Penny Authors	This is the second of the Penny Authors Anthologies. Titled, "Anthology Two". It is filled with so many more different journies. Many are the same journies but experienced by different people of various cultures. It is a wonderful place to expand ones horizon.
978-1-910499-15-3 Anthology One By Penny Authors	This is the first of the Penny Authors Anthologies. Titled, "Anthology One". It is filled with so many different journies.

ISBN/Titles /Image/Author	Descriptions
978-1-910499-02-3 (eBook) & 978-1-910499-00-9 (Paperback) Father to child By Mayar Akash	This EBook version Father to Child is a collection of inspirational poems and musings that follow the author's life from his own childhood up to when he had children of his own, and wishes to pass some of wisdom to them.
978-1-910499-16-0 River of Life By Mayar Akash	This journey in the river of life, a metaphor for living, a contrast between the British life and the Bangladeshi lives' in both parts of the world. Reflect on the integrational change acquired and adopted as a result of living in UK.
978-1-910499-14-6 The Halloweeen Poem By Zainab Khan	This short poetry book written by Zainab who was an 8-year-old. She writes about her experience of Halloween in poetry form, especially as a young Bangladeshi Muslim growing up and integrating into the British society.
978-1-910499-36-8 Delirious By Liam Newton	Music is powerful enough to change people's views on aspects of the society they live in or the world around them. In this book the writer gives the reader snapshot insight of his life in the form of lyrics. Music keeps him going and hope it keeps you going too
978-1-910499-39-9 Eyewithin By Mayar Akash	This is the 3rd book of Mayar Akash. The book catalogues the lost paintings by himself.
978-1-910499-37-5 My Dream World By Rashma Mehta	This is the first of Rashma's book filled with her imaginary world of experiences and perception.

978-1-910499-41-2 When You Look Back By Rashma Mehta	This is Rashma's 2nd book filled with her imaginary world of experiences and perception.
978-1-910499-49-8 Cry For Help By Bhupendra M. Gandhi	This is Bhupendra's 1st poetry book published through the Penny Authors' facilities. His work is truly inspirational and has depth that make to fell human.
978-1-910499-42-9 My Life Book 1 By Mayar Akash	This is Mayar's unabridged collection of classics catalogued. Book 1 of his work to 2016.
978-1-910499-44-3 My Life Book 2 By Mayar Akash	This is Mayar's unabridged collection of classics catalogued. Book 2 of his work to 2016.
978-1-910499-52-8 Lit from Within By Ruth Lewarne	This is Ruth debut poetry book of Sonnets. This keeps the to the traditions of the old Shakespearian rules.
978-1-910499-53-5 Angel Eyez By Rashma Mehta	This is Rashma's next accomplishment over 400 hundred pages of her creative writing following on from her previous two books.

www.ingramcontent.com/pod-product-compliance
Lightning Source LLC
Chambersburg PA
CBHW020417030726

47495CB00006B/1552